BOOKS BY WILLIAM J. CAUNITZ

One Police Plaza
Suspects
Black Sand

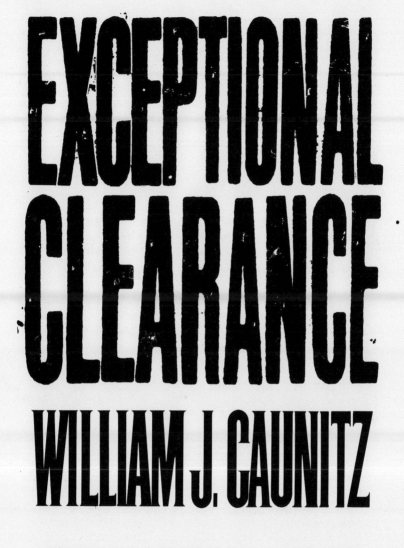

EXCEPTIONAL CLEARANCE

WILLIAM J. CAUNITZ

CROWN PUBLISHERS, INC. • NEW YORK

Published by Crown Publishers, Inc., 201 East 50th Street, New York, New York 10022. Member of the Crown Publishing Group.

CROWN is a trademark of Crown Publishers, Inc.

Manufactured in the United States of America

Library of Congress Cataloging-in-Publication Data

Caunitz, William J.
    Exceptional clearance / by William J. Caunitz.
        p. cm.
      I. Title.
    PS3553.A945E93   1991
    813'.54—dc20   91-12079
                                                                CIP

ISBN 0-517-58485-9

10 9 8 7 6 5 4 3 2 1

First Edition

To Knox and Kitty with gratitude for all that they have done for me, and with love for all that they mean to me.

ACKNOWLEDGMENTS

I would like to thank the following people for their help in the writing of this book: Anthony E. Gragrasso, M.D., Surgeon, Connecticut State Police, Assistant Medical Examiner, for taking the time to tell me about forensic medicine. Garry Goldstein, D.D.S., Chairperson, Department of Prosthodontics, NYU School of Dentistry, for explaining to me how the human mouth works, and for making me such a delightful pair of fangs. Evan Cohen, D.D.S., for allowing me to turn him into such an agreeable vampire. Stephen Burke, M.D., Associate Attending Surgeon, The Hospital for Special Surgery, for taking the time to explain to me how to treat a shattered kneecap. My pal, Barry Zide, M.D., Associate Professor of Surgery, NYU Medical Center, and a great reconstructive plastic surgeon, for spending so many hours with me, showing me how to take apart and reconstruct the human face. Jerome Levin, Ph.D., for his guided tours through the paranoid mind. My buddy Jim Pollack for teaching me about "fast ropes" and plastic explosives, and other very nasty things. Jennifer Weider for the use of her poem "Dinny'O." Knox Burger and Kitty Sprague for their many hours of wise counsel, and for being there whenever I needed them. My friend and editor, James O'Shea Wade, for his many suggestions and his magical pencil.

I would like to thank Chief of the Department Robert J. Johnston, NYPD, for his suggestions and advice. Captain Bob Syndrones, Commanding Officer, Public Information Section, for opening any doors I needed to walk through. Lieutenant Donald O'Donnell for his many kindnesses.

A special thank-you to the Crown Family for again pulling it together and making it all work, and especially Jim Davis and George Wilson for a terrific cover.

Thou know'st that I have dived into hell,
And sought the darkest places of fiends;
That with my magic spells great Belcephon,
Hath left his lodge and kneeled at my cell.

FRANCIS BACON

O N E

THE NIGHT WAS COLD; NOVEMBER'S SNOW BANKED deep along the curb. A young black woman climbed up out of the subway at Bergen Street, a shopping bag filled with gaily wrapped presents clutched in her right hand, and her pocketbook wedged tightly against her body. Waiting for the light to change, she gazed across Flatbush Avenue at the limestone fortress that was Brooklyn's 78th Precinct station house. A policeman was in front of the station house, fitting tire chains around the wheel of a patrol car. She looked to her left and saw the sign in the window of Pintchik's Decorating Center proclaiming a mammoth pre-Christmas paint and wallpaper sale. The clock in the window read a little past seven o'clock. The light changed. The woman looked in both directions before stepping off the curb and starting across the wide avenue. A car sped by, its tires churning up a wave of slush that she barely avoided. A blast of frigid air made her tuck her head deeper into her coat's upturned collar.

Stepping onto the curb on the other side of the avenue, she spotted two crack dealers loitering on the corner of St. Marks Avenue, a block away. Her pace quickened as she neared the sullen men. She turned into St. Marks Avenue, hurrying for the safety and warmth of her home in the middle of the block. She sucked in a mouthful of air, savoring the clean sense of life that it gave her, increasing her feeling of accomplishment and worth.

Thelma Johnston had been free of drugs for five years, and off the welfare rolls for two. Life was looking good to her again, real good. Instead of going home after work tonight, Thelma had decided to do most of her Christmas shopping for her two fatherless children. She was determined to make this holiday the best one yet for her kids. There were still thirty-two days remaining before the big day. Thelma wanted to get the shopping behind her so that she would be free to put in as much overtime as possible during the holiday rush at her job as cashier in Jerry and Ben's clothing store on Court Street.

She looked up at the moon; dark patterns etched its barren landscape. Hurrying along the deserted, windswept street, she became aware of the muffled clop of her own booted feet, and quickened her pace. She heard a movement off to her right and had started to turn to look when something cold and horrible shot out of the darkness and clamped over her mouth. Her eyes widened in terror as she was hoisted up off her feet, her legs and arms flailing in the night. Her children's presents tumbled over the snow.

"Dear Jesus protect me," she prayed, as she was bodily lifted into the dark on the side of the brownstone's stoop. Something was pressing in on her. Her terrified eyes stared up at her attacker. She felt his warm breath on her throat; her body shook with fear, and she begged God's protection for herself and her children. Suddenly she felt a pinching sensation in her throat, quickly followed by an overwhelming feeling of suffocation. And then, as abruptly as the nightmare had begun, it was over. She was free, floating along in a crimson abyss, with the inaudible words, "Help me, help me," forming on her lips.

T W O

THE POLICEMAN ASSIGNED TO THE SECURITY booth saluted as the black sedan rolled onto the ramp leading down into the headquarters garage of One Police Plaza.

Chief of Detectives Sam Leventhal relaxed in the back of the department auto, reading the recommendations of the Mayor's Committee on the Consolidation of the Transit Police and the NYPD. The members had concluded that both departments should remain separate entities. I could have told them that and saved the taxpayers a lot of money, Leventhal thought, gathering up the papers scattered over the dark blue velour-covered seat.

The police driver drove the car off the ramp, and steered it into the C-of-D's parking space alongside the cinderblock wall of the dispatcher's cage. Leventhal got out and walked over to the executive elevator set into the alcove behind the cage. He inserted his key into the lock, and when the door opened he stepped inside.

Leventhal was a tall man with wavy hair that he dyed black. At forty-six years of age he was the youngest, and vainest, chief of detectives in the department's history, a man who would never dream of appearing in public without giving meticulous attention to every aspect of his clothing and grooming. His lordly way of dressing had earned him the nickname "Sam Staypress."

Studying his reflection in the elevator door, he adjusted his tie and brushed down the sides of his hair with his palms. He bared his teeth, making sure that no trace of his morning bran muffin remained. His trim body was complemented by a brown tweed suit set off by a white shirt and paisley tie. A camel's-hair coat was draped rakishly over his shoulders.

He strode into the chief of detectives' suite of offices on the thirteenth floor, and was greeted by a babble of "Good morning, Chief," from his clerical staff. "Good morning," he replied, walking for his office, noticing Sergeant Jack Reilly, his lead clerical, anxiously waiting for him. A bad omen to begin the day.

"We gotta talk, Chief," Reilly said, following the C-of-D inside his corner office.

Leventhal slid off his coat and hung it up inside his closet. "What's up?"

"A homicide went down in the Seven-eight last night. Same MO as the Lucas homicide in the Eight-eight last week."

"Shit!" Leventhal snatched the case folder from his lead clerical and, walking to his desk, began reading the official reports.

Reilly left the office and returned shortly with a mug of black coffee, which he put down on the desk.

Leventhal opened the envelope inside the folder and took out the crime-scene photos that showed Thelma Johnston lying face-up in a pool of blood. He dropped the hastily dried color prints and picked up his mug of coffee. He sipped thoughtfully and then said, "The Seven-eight and the Eight-eight adjoin each other."

"Yeah, at Atlantic and Flatbush avenues. Could be the doer is a local guy."

Leventhal's mind worked at high speed. This could be big trouble. Who could he trust to handle it and contain it? He glanced at a picture in an old silver frame on his desk. The photograph showed two young policemen standing in front of a radio motor patrol car, with their arms around each other. They were uniformed in the outmoded dark blues of long ago. One of them was sticking his tongue out at the unseen photographer. Leventhal smiled in fond remembrance and asked himself where all those years had gone. He looked at the desk clock, saw it was 8:40 A.M., and asked, "Is the PC in the building?"

"The balloon went up at oh-seven-fifty."

"Get me copies of the Sixty-one on the Mary Lucas homicide," Leventhal said, dialing the police commissioner's phone number.

The Honorable James P. Coverton, the police commissioner of the City of New York, had come up through the ranks. A handsome man of fifty-eight years with a head of thick silver gray hair and a heavy jaw, he had been closeted inside his fourteenth-floor office for forty minutes with the commanding officer of the Office of Management and Analysis, going over the final details of the department's new closed-circuit arraignment procedure that was about to go into operation in Brooklyn and Queens. When the PC's lead clerical interrupted the conference to announce that the chief of detectives was on his way to see him, the PC let his pencil fall from his hand and sighed. Sam Staypress never ventured onto the fourteenth floor unless it was important. The PC turned to his C.O./O.M.A. and said, "We'll continue this later, Chief."

Three minutes passed before Leventhal was ushered in by the Commissioner's clerical. The PC beckoned his chief of detectives into the chair at the side of his desk. "What's up, Sam?"

Leventhal handed him the two homicide case folders. Coverton took his time digesting the Sixty-ones (U.F. 61 Complaint Reports) and DD 14s (Résumés of Homicide Cases). When he finished reading, he looked at his meticulously dressed C-of-D and asked, "What are we doing about it?"

"As you can see, both victims were black, and both had their throats sliced open in exactly the same way, which would indicate the same killer. Until last night there was no indication we were dealing with serial killings. I think we had better give some thought to forming a task force."

Coverton leaned back, stroking his jaw. "I don't like task forces, Sam. Experience has taught me they usually get sucked in by the media. And we end up with a bunch of television stars instead of detectives. Has the press gotten wind of this yet?"

"Black homicides generally aren't big news for the papers or TV. So far we've been able to keep it in-house."

"Any hue and cry coming from the black community?"

"Not yet."

"I want you to reach out to some responsible community leaders in Park Slope. Let them know about the two homicides, and tell them we're on top of the situation."

"We could take a few of our best people and assign them to the case. Keep it compartmentalized within the detective division, use only solid guys who can keep their mouths shut."

"Has the National Crime Information Center been checked?"

"This morning. NCIC has no record of a similar MO. Looks like this guy is just getting started."

"The prick *would* have to pick New York for his playpen. I'm going to have to brief the Mayor on this one." Coverton toyed with a crystal ashtray on his desk. "Sam, the job does not function well under the glare of publicity. We have two black women with their throats ripped out. This could be racial. This is just the kind of case that can slide downhill fast, pulling us all into the shitter. Solve it, and solve it fast. Have you given any thought to a Whip to head up the investigation?"

"No, but he'd better be the best we got."

"Pick your Whip, Sam, and make sure he's camera-shy and has congenital lockjaw."

Five minutes later, Chief of Detectives Leventhal was looking out his office window at the people scurrying along Pearl Street. The door opened and Inspector Paul Acevedo, the detective division's executive officer, entered carrying several folders tucked under his arms. Acevedo's portly frame always bulged out in his badly fitted suits. "You wanted to see me, Chief?"

Not turning from the window, Leventhal said, "We need a Whip for a homicide investigation."

"A sergeant or a lieutenant?"

"A lieutenant."

"There's Kelly in Midtown North, and Howard in One-fourteen, and Greenberg in Safe and Loft."

"Where is he, Paul?"

"Who, Chief?"

"You know who."

The detective guide stated that the duties of the Missing Persons Squad were to locate missing persons, investigate and establish the identities of persons and dead human bodies, and cooperate with other members of the department in cases of missing and unidentified persons or dead human bodies. One of this squad's many unofficial duties was to provide a parking place for flopped detectives until such time as the celestial powers on the thirteenth and fourteenth floors of the Big Building considered them rehabilitated.

Lieutenant John Vinda was one such fallen angel. He had been dumped into Missing Persons when the stakeout unit he commanded was disbanded. His current make-work duties included verifying the accuracy of the DD 8 (Index of Missing Persons) and the DD 13 (Missing-Unidentified Persons Report). He was a tall, handsome, well-built man with a slight olive cast to his skin and the sharply defined features characteristic of his

Portuguese ancestors. He wore his long black hair brushed straight back without a part to where it formed a turned-up tuft in the back. His intelligent black eyes glared out from under his heavy brow, and his jaw tapered to a diamond-shaped dimple in his chin.

Sitting at his desk inside the glass cubicle that he had been assigned on the eleventh floor of One Police Plaza, he looked warily at the telephone when it started to ring, wondering who it was this early in the morning. "Lieutenant Vinda, file clerk, how may I help you?"

There was an almost deliberate pause before a very familiar voice came over the line. "Lou, this is Inspector Acevedo," the detective division XO said, addressing Vinda with the diminutive for *lieutenant* that was routinely used in the Job.

"Morning, Inspector, how's everything on the thirteenth floor?"

"Leventhal wants to see you, forthwith."

Vinda slowly put down the receiver and got up. Walking over to the coatrack, he took his blue blazer off the hook, wondering why he had been summoned into the chief of detectives' august presence. Maybe I've been using too many paper clips, he thought, going over to check himself out in the locker's mirror. Dark gray slacks, yellow tie with blue dots, and a sky blue shirt with a white collar. He occasionally sneered at himself for having acquired that Palace Guard look.

"Sit down, John," Leventhal said, beckoning him to the chair at the side of his desk.

Vinda thought that the C-of-D looked unusually worried. Brushing an imaginary speck of dirt off his trousers, Vinda asked, "How have you been, Sam?"

"Pretty good, John."

Then there was a moment of awkward silence while each man looked appraisingly at the other.

Vinda tried to ease the strain. "How's your mother?"

A genuine, unforced smile broke across Leventhal's face. "You wouldn't know her. She moved into one of those swinging retirement communities in Daytona Beach after Dad died. Dyed her hair blond and changed her name from Gussy to Ginger."

Vinda laughed. "Hope springs eternal."

Leventhal looked over his nails, his expression somber. "How have you been getting along since . . ."

" 'Bout the same. Like they say, time heals all wounds." He picked up the picture frame from the desk. "We sure were young."

"A couple of white knights going forth to free the city of crime."

Vinda's eyes narrowed, forming tiny furrows around the edges. "I never thought my lance would get stuck in a pile of political bullshit."

Leventhal leaned forward, saying, "I did everything I could to protect you and your men."

Vinda set the frame back down. "Protect me? From what, Sam? I did nothing wrong."

"Your unit blew away forty-three people in twenty-six months. The press branded you the leader of the department's 'death squad.' "

"The scum we blew away were all killed while exercising their First Amendment right of free expression to rob and kill the victims of their choice."

"Spare me your sarcasm, please."

"Every one of those scumballs was taken down during the commission of an armed robbery. You personally formed the stakeout unit because the robbery and homicide rate had climbed into the ionosphere, and you made me the Whip because you knew I'd do a job for you. The rate took a nosedive after word got around that we were in operation. We saved lives, Sam—decent, working people's lives."

"But did you have to waste so many?"

His voice brimming with anger, Vinda answered, "Yes, damn-

it. In each and every case we identified ourselves and ordered
the perp to drop his weapon—and in each and every case the
mutt opened fire first, or made a threatening motion to do so.
And in each and every case the grand jury and the Firearm
Discharge Review Board found our use of deadly force justified
under the Penal Law and department guidelines."

Leventhal absentmindedly ran his index finger over a large
brown mole on his right cheek, the one blemish on his otherwise
perfect features.

"You seem to be unable to appreciate the pressure I was under
to disband that unit." Leventhal looked the lieutenant in the
eyes. "Not one of your people got hurt. Each one of them was
eased into less . . . stressful assignments."

"Like filling out requisitions in the Quartermaster, or outfit-
ting rookies in the Equipment Bureau. You cut the legs out from
under some fine people who were out there doing a dirty job for
you."

"What did you expect me to do?"

"Go to the wall for them!"

Leventhal's shoulders slumped; he said, softly, "Those days
are long gone, John."

Vinda noticed the deep lines around his friend's mouth and
eyes. The loving energy of life seemed to have been drained
from him, replaced by a kind of resignation. He made a small
shrug of his shoulders that clearly meant *The hell with it*, and said,
"I ran into Izzy Cohen the other day. He now calls himself
Inspector I. Jacob Cowan."

Leventhal laughed. "I hear he got married again."

"That guy gets married every time he goes out for cigarettes."

Leventhal looked down at the two case folders on his desk.
He picked them up and handed them to the lieutenant. "Take
a look at these."

Vinda sat back and read the reports. Then he took the crime-
scene photos out of the second folder. Both victims, their limbs
contorted in the strange dance of death, lay in great pools of

blood. Terror was forever frozen on their faces, and there were gaping wounds in both their throats. "I've never seen wounds like these," Vinda said, turning the photographs around to look at them from different angles. He slid the photos back into their folder, placed the case folders on the desk, and said, "You got a problem. The same person probably whacked both those women."

"You're sure?"

"C'mon, Sam. Both victims black, both with hideous wounds in the exact same place. It's the same doer, okay."

"We think he's just getting started." Leventhal's eyes looked down at the top of his desk. "Do you want the case?"

"Why me?" the man asked.

"Because you're good, because you still care."

Vinda sighed. "I don't care as much as I used to, Sam."

Leventhal refused to let his friend's discouraged tone deflect him from his plea, for it was that. He knew that in spite of his right to command his subordinates, this was a case where you *asked*.

"You just might be able to save another woman's life."

Vinda looked around the office's paneled walls covered with commemorative tablets and police memorabilia. He thought of his years on the Job, and recalled the anguish and shame he'd felt when they hung him out to dry. He knew that he could walk away from this. But he thought of the two murdered women with their throats torn out, and he knew that he needed to take on this case to regain his own self-respect.

"I'll need help."

"I'll send down a telephone message transferring you into the Major Case Squad. If you need exotic equipment or experienced detectives fast, they're there. You can reach out and bring in two of your own people. But I want a compartmentalized unit, free of any leaks."

"We'll need wheels."

"I'll notify the motor pool downstairs." Readying his pencil over a pad, Leventhal asked, "Who are you picking up?"

Vinda leaned back in his chair, toying with the hair at the back of his head that formed into a duck's tail. "Moose Ryan and Tony Marsella."

Leventhal grinned. "You seem to like working with fallen angels."

"We try harder, Sam," Vinda responded. "It's our ticket back to the real world."

THREE

THE SPECIAL INVESTIGATION DIVISION WAS THE umbrella command for the Major Case Squad as well as the Special Fraud Squad, the Joint Robbery Task Force, the Safe, Loft, and Truck Squad, and the Missing Persons Squad. The division occupied the eleventh floor of police headquarters at One Police Plaza, close to City Hall and Wall Street. The various units were separated from one another by portable partitions covered with wanted posters, department orders, and retirement party announcements.

After leaving the chief of detectives, Vinda returned to his tiny, cramped office and gathered up the missing person index and the rest of his busywork. Stepping outside, he plopped the stack of official documents down on the clerical sergeant's desk. "I've just been rehabilitated, Sarge."

The sergeant, a gaunt man with forty years in the Job, looked up at Vinda. "You're going back out into the street, Lou?"

"Yes."

Scratching his jaw thoughtfully, the sergeant said, "Some guys just don't ever learn."

A long aisle ran the length of the eleventh floor, connecting the various SID units. Vinda made his way down the corridor into the Major Case Squad. It occupied the entire north corner of the floor, and had ranks of glass-fronted offices with outside windows along the east and west sides of the floor. These offices served as private work spaces for the bosses. As soon as Vinda stepped into the Major Case area he felt as though he was back in the real war. Every typewriter was being used, detectives moved about, consulting each other on active cases, and a radio muttered police calls over the special detective band.

Vinda reported to the CO of Major Case, who told him that the chief of detectives had personally telephoned and directed him to be on the lookout for Vinda. After leaving the commanding officer's office, Vinda was escorted by a sergeant to his new glass cubbyhole with a corner view of Police Plaza and the Municipal Building.

Vinda sat down at the standard green metal desk and reread the homicide reports. Studying the crime-scene photos, he was again struck by the ferocity of the wounds. What *kind* of an instrument makes a hole like that while slicing into the body?

Reaching down into the desk's form drawer, he took out two DD 5s (Supplementary Complaint Reports), forms that were used to report on all phases of an investigation, and rolled one of them into the typewriter, thought a few seconds, and typed out the DD 5 transferring the Mary Lucas homicide from the precinct detective squad to the Special Investigation Division.

Good move, he told himself, knowing that when the press got wind of the case, he and his men would be buried deep enough to buy some moving-around time. On the bottom of the report, he typed, BY DIRECTION OF THE CHIEF OF DETECTIVES.

Pondering what name to use in the signature box at the bottom, he took out the official roster and began flipping pages. The corners of his mouth spread in a gleeful smile when he saw the

name of the commanding officer, Criminal Assessment and Profiling Unit. He typed in the name I. Jacob Cowan, and forged a
signature to the report, hoping that his old friend still had his
Bronx sense of humor.

He typed another Five transferring the Thelma Johnston homicide to his unit, and tossed both reports into the department
mail basket. Next to it was another wire basket, full of incoming
mail. On top was a brightly colored brochure, a mailing from the
Lieutenants Benevolent Association offering package tours. He
was about to throw it away as he was clearing out the remaining
mail for forwarding to the office's previous occupant when he
noticed that a nine-day package to Portugal was featured on the
front cover. Vinda couldn't resist looking quickly at the pictures
inside, of the beloved land where he had spent so many childhood vacations.

Then his mind was filled with powerful memories of that
spring day eleven years ago when he was the Second Whip of
the Two-oh Squad. His official day had started with his checking the details of investigation reports to "insure that they fell
within the parameters of detective division guidelines"—which
meant that all asses were covered, especially his own. It was a
perfect and warm early-May morning. He had gone out into
the squadroom to read the latest batch of department orders
when he spotted her being interviewed by one of the detectives.

He thought she was the most beautiful woman he'd ever seen.
Her lips were exquisite, and her perfectly oval face had dimples
in the corners of her mouth. Her auburn hair touched her shoulders; it seemed to glow in the rush of sunlight flooding into the
squadroom. He saw the excitement dancing around inside her
green eyes. Her light blue spring dress softly molded the con-
tours of her shapely body.

Pretending to read a Personnel Order, he looked out of the
side of one eye and was consumed by an urgent need to meet
her. She glanced his way; their eyes met and held. He smiled;

her lips smiled back. He returned the clipboard holding the orders to the wall hook and walked back to his office. Sitting on the edge of his desk, he counted to twenty, snapped up the telephone, and dialed the extension number of the desk where she was being interviewed.

"Detective Kooperman, Two-oh Squad."

"Is she married?"

"Negative."

"What kind of case?"

"Ten-twenty-one," Kooperman said, using the radio code for a past burglary.

"Do the right thing."

"You got it."

Vinda hung up and rushed over to his locker and checked himself out in the mirror. He smoothed down his hair, straightened his tie, grabbed down some after-shave, and rubbed a few drops onto his face. He was at his desk, taking copious notes on absolutely nothing, when Kooperman led the complainant into his office.

"Sarge, this is Jean Wilson. Her apartment was burglarized last night." Offering her a chair, Kooperman explained, "Sergeant Vinda supervises our burglary investigations."

"Really?" she said, looking at Vinda, who was still occupied with his notes. When Kooperman left the room, Vinda picked up the Complaint Report that the detective had put on his desk, and began reading the details. "How long have you resided at your current address, Miss Wilson?"

"Twenty-four years. I was born there, Sergeant."

"Do you live alone?"

"Yes, I do. I used to live with my parents, but they're both dead."

"Has anyone dusted your apartment for fingerprints?"

"Not yet," she said with a knowing smile, "but I suspect you are going to volunteer to do the job yourself."

"What's so funny?" he asked indignantly.

"When I was a teenager, my uncle always made me laugh with his stories about the Job . . ."

Her use of the word made his stomach plummet.

". . . especially when he talked of the tricks detectives used to meet women. Perhaps you've heard of my uncle? Assistant Chief Dan Wilson, CO of Brooklyn North Detectives?"

"Oh?" he said, his hand groping the air in front of him, searching for an escape hatch to crawl into. "I know the Chief."

They drifted into silence. He decided that honesty was the best policy. "Looks like I'm going to have to cop a plea. I just had to meet you, you're beautiful."

Her appraising eyes looked straight at him. She got up and announced, "I don't date married men."

"Not married, never have been," he said, standing up, afraid that he'd blown it.

She opened the door and looked over her shoulder. "My phone number is on the Sixty-one," she smiled. " 'Bye."

On their first date, a week later, they ate in a trendy SoHo restaurant and afterward they strolled the busy streets of China-town, making their way across Canal Street into Little Italy, trying to decipher some of the graffiti scrawled on the sides of buildings. She wore a yellow dress, and her legs were bare. They ambled into Carmine's on Mulberry Street and squeezed into a curbside table, blissfully ignoring the crowd flowing along the narrow, brightly lit street. They drank cappuccinos and shared a dish of zabaglione and raspberries, while they took turns talking about their lives.

She was a special-ed teacher who worked with brain-damaged and retarded children at Humanities High School. A lover of animals, opera, dance, and movies, Jean particularly loved the "two hankie" romantic movies of the late thirties and forties.

He told her about his childhood summers visiting his grand-parents in Silves, Portugal, and of how he and his friends used to play, despite strict injunctions not to, on the battlements of the

tenth-century castle that the Visigoths had built on the hill overlooking the ancient city. Portugal represented the side of his life
and identity that he never talked about on the Job.

It was two in the morning when a waiter's diplomatic cough
made them aware of all the empty tables around them. "Let's
walk," she said, putting her arm around him and pressing close.

It took them almost another two hours to stroll uptown to her
rent-controlled apartment in a massive old building on the east
side of West End Avenue at Eighty-second Street. The sun was
up and the birds were singing as they ambled arm-in-arm into
the marble lobby with its high Doric columns.

He rode up with her to the seventh floor and left her unkissed
at her apartment door, secure in the knowledge that he had met
the woman he was going to marry.

They married that August, and honeymooned in Portugal.
She met all his aunts and uncles and cousins, savored the rich
Portuguese sauces at family meals, enjoyed the biting taste of
freshly caught fried sardines, and posed happily for family photographs under the castle's portcullis.

The newlyweds set up house in her three-bedroom apartment
on West End Avenue, and several blissful years faded into happy
memories. To their mutual disappointment, Jean did not con-
ceive. There were tests and more tests, and always the doctors
gave the same report: there was nothing wrong with either of
them. Rx: Relax.

One day three years ago, soon after he had been dumped
into Missing Persons and the stakeout unit disbanded, he arrived home after doing a day duty to find Jean in the bathroom, running the fingers of her hand over the right side of her
neck. Watching her watch herself in the mirror, he saw her
frightened eyes lock on his reflection and heard her say, "It's
swollen."

The next day a surgeon did a needle biopsy that revealed a
line of swollen lymph nodes. Further tests revealed the primary
source to be a mole concealed in her hairline. The final answer

came a week later, exploding from the doctor's mouth in an
irreversible sentence of death: Melanoma.

Vinda tossed the brochure into the wastebasket and swung
around to face the window, preventing anyone outside his office
from looking in and seeing his tears. He pulled his handkerchief
out, wiped his eyes dry, and shoved the cloth back into his
trouser pocket. He spun back around, picked up a yellow legal
pad, and began outlining the case. First he listed the times and
dates of occurrence, the names of the victims, and their pedigrees. The more he examined the crime-scene photos and studied the similarity of the wounds, the more convinced he was that
the killer was someone who needed to kill.

He went over to the portable blackboard pushed flush against
the wall. Checking the notes he had made on the tablet, he
wrote out the key elements of the crime on the board. He took
a few of the crime-scene photos and thumbtacked them to the
board's wooden edges. Then he stepped back, examining his
work.

He knew that he needed the Job more than ever now. His
Jean had died four months ago. The void left by her death was
filled now only with loneliness and regret. It was good to be
back. It was all he had to hold on to, all that he had to give his
shattered life any meaning.

The slam of the door to his office made him look up and see
Tony Marsella and William "Moose" Ryan standing in front of
his desk, silly grins plastered on their faces.

"Good to see you guys," Vinda greeted them.

"When that telephone message came down from the C-of-D
transferring us to SID, we ran out to our cars and drove like hell
to get here," Moose said, looking around the office. "We both
felt our former leader's devious hand lurking somewhere in the
background."

"They had me and Moose invoicing auto wrecks at the White-
stone Pound," Marsella said. "It was getting time for us to aban-

don ship anyway. So? What kind of a dirty job they got for us this time?"

"A couple of homicides," Vinda said, picking up the case folders and handing them to the detectives.

"Will the illustrious Sam Staypress fuck us over again if the media screams for fresh meat?" Moose asked.

"No one ever promised you any tomorrows in this job," Vinda said, watching them read the reports.

The detectives exchanged folders. Moose asked, "You're the Whip?"

"Yeah," Vinda answered.

"That's good enough for me," Moose Ryan said. "I'm tired of all that pencil-pushin' bullshit. I wanna get back out in the street. I miss all that blood and carnage and down-to-earth, do-me-dirty shit."

Watching them digest the reports, Vinda thought how much alike the two detectives were, yet how different. Both were street-smart cops who believed in the rights of crime victims, both were married and had children, and, like most of their contemporaries in the Job, both were deeply in debt to the Municipal Credit Union.

Moose Ryan was a big man with a fat neck that bulged out over his shirt collar. His tiny brown eyes were partially hidden under his heavy, overhanging brow. Moose was, in short, a liberal's nightmare of what cops should look like. And he could indeed be a hard-ass when he had to be. But buried inside of him was an amazing degree of sensitivity. Only his wife, children, and a very few other cops knew that. He and his wife were animal-rights activists, and Moose was forever wearing an assortment of animal-rights buttons pinned to his lapels. People often did a double-take when they saw these unexpected decorations on him.

Marsella, in contrast, was a handsome man with a swarthy complexion and a trimmed mustache that gave him the look of a Latin gigolo. He was an elegant, thin man who favored

European-cut clothes and double-breasted sport jackets, while his partner consistently dressed in an unmatching rainbow of polyester.

"Whaddaya think, Lou?" Moose Ryan asked, looking up from his folder.

"I think we're dealing with a major wackadoo."

"Similar MO," Marsella observed. "According to the ME's report, there was no rape. Underclothes undisturbed. No sperm in any of the orifices, or on the clothes. None of these reports mentioned if any money was taken."

"Neither of the ladies lived in a high-rent district," Moose said.

"Where do we start?" Marsella asked.

"I want you two to go to Central Records and duplicate all the paper. Then go to the precincts of occurrence and interview the detectives who caught the cases. See if they have any information scratched on the back of a matchbook that they didn't put on the Fives," Vinda said.

Holding a pack of cigarettes in front of his mouth, Marsella took one between his lips and asked, "And if they want to know why the case was transferred?"

"Tell them the Bias Unit Investigation Section is interested in a possible racial motive," Vinda said, adding, "That'll make them happy to be rid of the case."

Moose Ryan said, "This could be a racial case. Both victims are black."

"That's something we're going to have to take a look at," Vinda said. "I want you to recanvass the scenes, interview friends and relatives. According to the Fives on the Mary Lucas homicide, the victim's mother was too distraught to be interviewed when detectives went to her home. She has to be interviewed." Vinda handed them index cards. "Give me phone numbers where you can be reached."

Marsella wrote down an extra number. He didn't bother to tell the Whip that it was his girlfriend's.

"What about wheels and communications?" Moose Ryan asked.

"Two cars have been assigned to us," Vinda said. "I've arranged for Radio Operator Forty-seven on the City-Wide band to be our communication link." He picked up a large manila envelope and shook out three beepers. Handing one to each detective, he said, "If these things go off, get on land line to Operator Forty-seven."

The detectives clipped the instruments to their belts.

"Let's get back to work," Moose Ryan said, making for the door. He paused with his hand on the doorknob, and said quietly, "You know, Boss, I've got my twenty years in, come April. I don't wanna get jammed up on this one."

Marsella edged the department auto between two snowbanks to park across the street from the Seven-eight Precinct. The detectives got out and hurried through the blustery wind into the station house. Walking across the muster room toward the staircase, Ryan held up his shield to the desk officer and announced, "We're going up to the Squad, Lou."

The desk lieutenant nodded and continued making his blotter entry. The second-floor squadroom was a collection of old desks and old typewriters scattered around a spacious room with a detention cage cut into the east wall. The three detectives who were typing reports ignored the man standing by himself in the middle of the room. He was dressed in a white running suit, and wore white sneakers and white cotton gloves, and was spraying himself with something that smelled like disinfectant.

Reaching over the wooden gate to release the latch, Moose Ryan said, "Joe McMahon?"

A heavyset detective looked up from his typewriter. "I'm McMahon."

"I'm Tony Marsella, and this here is Moose Ryan. We're the guys who inherited the Thelma Johnston homicide."

"You are, hmm?" McMahon said, going back to his report. "I'll be with you in a second. I wanna finish off this Five."

Ryan looked over his shoulder at the man with the spray can. "Who's your friend?"

"The Lysol Man," McMahon said, as he typed. "He lives on Pacific Street and comes in here every morning and evening to disinfect himself." He pulled the report out of the typewriter, signed it, and tossed it into the opened case folder on his desk. "Another crime brilliantly solved." He looked at Moose. "You guys from SID?"

"Yeah," Moose said.

McMahon sat back, lacing his hands across his rather ample stomach. "Why the hell is the Special Investigation Division interested in a homicide in my backyard? We're the raggedy-ass part of Park Slope."

Marsella improvised quickly. "Word is that someone on the Fourteenth Floor got it into his head that the killing might be racially motivated and wants the investigation run out of the Big Building."

"Bullshit. There was nothing racial about that homicide. She was probably whacked by some crackhead looking for buy money."

"We still gotta go through the motions," Marsella said, watching the Lysol Man spray his crotch.

"Any physical evidence to indicate an attempted robbery?" Moose asked.

"Nothing. People around here don't carry much money with them." McMahon's attention was momentarily diverted by a 10:10 Shots-Fired alarm coming over the radio. "Like I told you, some crackhead tried to take her off, she resisted, and he Roto-Rootered her neck with some instrument."

"Anything on the murder weapon?" Marsella asked the squad detective.

"Nothing. Emergency Service searched the entire area, sewers, under cars, garbage cans, they even sifted the snow, and came up dry." McMahon went into the details of the preliminary investigation conducted at the scene.

The Lysol Man sauntered out of the squadroom, spraying the air in front of him.

"Our canvass failed to come up with any witnesses," McMahon said, getting up out of his seat and going over to the window. He shoved it open from the bottom; a blast of cold air swept across the squadroom. "We psychoed that guy a dozen times, but the shrinks always release him the same day. Now we let him do his number and he leaves."

"Did you form any impressions at the scene?" Marsella asked.

McMahon walked over to the five-drawer file cabinet and opened the middle one. He flipped through several folders and yanked one out. Opening it, he took out the crime-scene photos on the Thelma Johnston homicide, and studied them for several minutes. Then he closed the folder, dropped it back into the drawer, and walked back to his desk.

He sat, leaning forward, intense, and said in a quiet voice, "I've never seen a wound like that. And there were a couple of other things about the scene that bothered me. It had stopped snowing, and we were able to track her footprints to the spot where she was grabbed. Her left foot was clearly visible in the snow, and then nothing. She must have been hauled up off her feet in midstride. She weighed a hundred and thirty pounds and had several layers of clothing on. The doer hadda be one strong bastard. I figure he was hiding in the shadows on the side of the stoop. The brownstone's owner had just shoveled that area, so there weren't any footprints there."

"Did the people inside the brownstone see or hear anything?" Moose Ryan asked.

"Nothing. They're in their sixties, and have lived there for over forty years. The husband had all he could do to shovel that little area around the stoop." McMahon looked Marsella in the eye. "We don't have a clear picture of where this guy got to after he killed the woman."

"Maybe he fled into the building," Moose Ryan said.

"We checked that out," McMahon said. "The couple have turned that brownstone into a fortress. All the windows are barred, and the doors bolted from inside. Nobody got into that place uninvited."

"Could the perp have climbed up and over the stoops and gotten away?" Moose Ryan asked.

"Possibility," McMahon said, "but the really odd thing is that Forensic couldn't find any trace of blood leading away from the scene. Now you tell me how someone does a number like that, and doesn't get himself soaked in blood?"

Kings County Hospital occupies twenty-eight acres of land along Brooklyn's Clarkson Avenue. Tall, tediously uniform buildings, looking more like stark monoliths than places for the care and treatment of the sick, stand like resolute sentinels over some of the inner city's worst blight.

Vinda drove the maroon department car along New York Avenue, and made a right-hand turn into Clarkson. The car's wipers thudded against the accumulating snow. A woman hurried along the street, lugging a bundled-up child into the emergency room.

Vinda drove into the morgue's entrance and stopped in the driveway to identify himself to the security guard. "Park in visitors' parking, Lou," the retired cop told him. Vinda steered the car into the courtyard between the C and D buildings and parked. Foreboding gray afternoon clouds cast gloomy shadows over the snowy landscape. He got out of the car and, with his gloved hand, scooped snow off the windshield.

A brick building resembling a school stood between the C and D towers. It was the medical examiner's Brooklyn morgue. Several hearses idled by the loading bay.

Snow crunched beneath Vinda's feet as he made his way toward death's warehouse. He had gone a short distance when a woman's voice called out his name. Detective Adriene Agueda was walking down C Building's ramp, waving to him. With her was another woman.

"Hi," Vinda said, watching them coming over to him.

"Lou, this is Detective Joan Hagstrom, the newest member of Brooklyn South's Sex Crimes Unit," Agueda said.

"Hello," Vinda said to the detective.

"I've been trying for years to get the good lieutenant here to join the Hispanic Society, but he refuses to go for the twenty-buck initiation fee," Agueda told Hagstrom.

"First of all, Detective Agueda, I'm Portuguese, not Spanish," he said in an exaggerated accent, "and second, I happen to believe that there are too many religious, fraternal, and ethnic organizations in the Job; and third, when I was a kid, I always got 'F' in 'Plays and Gets Along Well with Others.' "

"A likely story," Agueda said, brushing her thick black forelock from her forehead, and smiling at him. "What brings you out of the Big Building on such a cold day?"

"Following up on a missing-person case," he lied. "What about you?"

"We got some scuzzball operating in the borough who gets off on sodomizing women over seventy," Hagstrom said.

Vinda winced. "Why, Detective Hagstrom, don't you realize that the poor man is probably acting out some horrible psychological trauma of his childhood, and shouldn't be held responsible for his acts?"

"Really?" Agueda said. "Well, Lou, when we catch up with him, we're going to cut off his trauma and end all his problems."

"Right on, Detective Agueda," Vinda said, and turned to leave.

Adriene Agueda hurriedly said, "I was sorry to hear about Jean."

"Thank you," he said, and walked away. He knew that she was sorry for his loss, but that there was much more that she wanted to say to him. At this point in his life, he couldn't deal with it. Knowing that he couldn't postpone a conversation with

Agueda forever, he pushed aside the two swinging doors that led into the pathology suite.

Dr. Patricia Marcal, an assistant medical examiner, was a handsome woman of considerable girth. Dressed in a lab coat, with her pince-nez dangling from a long silver chain around her neck, she was perched atop a stool, peering into a microscope, when Vinda knocked and walked into the room. "Hi, beautiful."

She spun around. "When did they let you back out in the street?" She slid off her perch and hugged him. "It's good to see you, John."

Leaning back so that he might better see her face, he said, "You're as lovely as ever." He kissed her cheek.

"Don't you try that olive-oil charm of yours on me, John Vinda. I'm a happily married lady." She released her grip on him, a sad cast coming over her cheerful face. "How are you managing?"

"I guess okay. I take it a day at a time. I'm glad her suffering is over, but I miss her very much."

"I know. Anyway, what brings you here?"

"Mary Lucas and Thelma Johnston."

Concern furrowed her brow. She had seen many good cops shoved down the drain of obscurity because they stumbled into homicides that turned out to be racial or political or both. "Pass on them, John. My guts tell me they're the kind of cases that could end careers."

"I can't. They're my ticket out of purgatory."

She sighed and affectionately patted his cheek. "I can't tell you what killed them, but I can tell you how they were killed. Come on, I'll show you."

Thelma Johnston lay atop a stainless-steel table with draining canals around the sides and top. Her sternum had been sliced and pried open, and her cranial vault sawed off and her brain removed, leaving in its place a bleached white bowl. Stacked body organs were on a tray next to the table. "I did the post on both victims," she said, turning the corpse's head so he might better examine the wound.

Bending at the knees, he closely studied the gaping hole in the dead woman's throat.

"The common carotid artery, the jugular vein, and the superior thyroid artery of both victims had been severed," Marcal explained. "It's almost as though some sharp instrument slashed around inside their throats. And, John, there are no entrance marks, no puncture wounds. But look here, to the right and a little below the wound."

Vinda saw what appeared to be two bruises about two inches apart. He ran his finger over them. "They appear to be puncture wounds that didn't break the skin."

"That's right. Both victims had the exact same marks in exactly the same spot."

"Could an animal have done this?"

"No way. Animals rip and tear at the flesh, leaving teeth marks on their prey. There were no dental impressions on either victim." She pulled a pair of plastic gloves out of a nearby box, stretched them over her hands, set her pince-nez on her nose, and stuck her thumb and forefinger into the lesion, groping for parts. Stretching out a severed vein and artery, she said, "Look at these. They've been surgically severed."

Vinda took the body parts in his hands; blood oozed out of the artery. "What could have done this?"

"An instrument that makes a massive puncture wound going in and slices coming out."

"Was any trace evidence found?"

"The clothing of both victims was vacuumed, and we found nothing that could be of value for microscopic or instrumental analysis."

"We're batting zero."

"I did standard hematocrit tests on both victims to measure the amount of blood in the body. Both tests were inconclusive."

"Why?"

"As soon as an artery is severed, there is a forceful rush of blood that continues until the heart stops pumping. The body contains about eleven and a half pints of blood. We sopped up as much as we could at both crime scenes; we still can't be sure how much blood is unaccounted for—if any."

Vinda frowned and said in a puzzled tone, "I examined all the crime-scene photos, and couldn't find any trace of blood leading *away* from the area."

The pathologist looked at the policeman, shrugged, and said, "Maybe this guy can fly."

F O U R

THE UNMARKED POLICE CAR SLID ALONG THE CURB and parked in front of Thelma Johnston's house on St. Marks Avenue. It was six-thirty in the evening, and winter's darkness had cast its cheerless hue over the city.

Moose Ryan and Marsella remained inside the car, staring out at the row of gracious brownstones carefully maintained by the residents of this middle-class enclave. Neither man paid much attention to the police calls coming over the radio. They had just come from interviewing Mary Lucas's family, and their thoughts were full of the despair and grief they had just left. Mary Lucas's mother, her face blank with shock and disbelief, sat in a wicker rocking chair, clutching a photograph of her murdered daughter to her chest, staring vacantly ahead, her lips mumbling a prayer. The dead woman's children, and her sister, moved about like dazed sleepwalkers, afraid to wake to the horrors of real life. The mother could not be brought back to reality long enough to be interviewed, which meant that the detectives would have to return at some later date to speak to her.

Marsella reached into the bag on his lap, took out a container, and handed it to Moose. "Let some air in here," Moose said, prying off the plastic lid.

Marsella pressed the door button, and the window slid down a few inches. Frigid air swept through the car. "Lucas's family were genuinely nice people," Marsella said, setting his container down on the lid of the glove compartment.

"Yeah." Moose sipped coffee, then put his container on the dashboard. Steam vapored the windshield. "Being off the street for a while almost makes you forget the shit that goes on there, like what heartbreak looks like."

Marsella closed his eyes and leaned his head back. After a while he said, "My dad did almost thirty years in the Job, and when I came on, he told me to keep my fly closed and my eyes open. But when I saw my first DOA child, a six-year-old crushed under the wheels of an oil truck, I knew that a cop hadda get some kind of a crutch to help him forget all the shit he sees."

Moose glanced at his partner. "So you forget by running around with your fly at half-mast?"

"Friend, when you find something better than pussy, call me." He picked up the container and, holding it in front of his mouth, said, "I wonder how I'd react to losing one of my children like that. Having some nut job rip out their throats." He drank, pulled a sour face. Cracking the door, he dumped out the coffee. "Why do cops drink so much of this crap, anyway? I don't even like the stuff."

"Me either," Ryan said, and emptied his out the window. "Ya know, it's one thing to lose a child to disease, but to have some scumbucket kill them?"

"I really wanna get this guy, Moose."

"Me too," Ryan said, and shoved open the door.

The name on the doorbell was Johnston. Marsella pressed the

button. They waited inside the vestibule, looking beyond the curtains at the mahogany staircase. A lanky man with steel-gray hair walked out of a side room. The man's black tie was askew, his shirt collar open. Walking to the door, he assessed the two white men waiting on the other side, and smiled faintly as he opened the door. "How ya doin'? I'm Ken Hayes. I'm with the Housing Police."

The instant rapport of cops took hold as the three policemen shook hands and the two NYPD detectives introduced themselves. Hayes told them he was Thelma Johnston's brother-in-law, and watched as the detectives struggled out of their rubber overshoes and placed them on a sheet of newspaper next to the radiator. Hayes led them into a parlor with high ceilings and elaborate nineteenth-century molding. A frail old woman, her dazed face lined with grief, sat on a brocaded sofa, cradling two scared children and singsonging a Baptist prayer.

"That's Thelma's mother and children, Dwuana and James," Hayes said.

The other people in the parlor continued their hushed conversations as Hayes led the detectives into the dining room, where a woman sat at a butcher-block table, dabbing her eyes with a lace handkerchief.

"This is Thelma's sister, my wife, Sirlena," Hayes said, sliding a consoling arm around her shoulder. He introduced the detectives to his wife, telling her that they were assigned to Thelma's case. Her tear-swollen eyes moved up to meet theirs. "It's not fair, it's just not fair," she lamented. "Thelma worked so darn hard to make a home for her children. So hard. And then to have this happen." She slammed her fist down on top of the table and cried.

Moose Ryan bit down on his lip. "We're doing everything possible to catch the person responsible."

"I know that," she sobbed. "We come from a police family. My dad, my husband, my brothers."

"Are your brothers here?" Marsella asked.

"They're making the arrangements for Thelma," she said.

"Can you think of anyone who might have wanted to hurt your sister?" Moose asked gently.

"No," she said, shaking her head and blowing her nose.

"What about someone from her past, when she was into the drug scene?" Marsella asked.

Outraged by his question, she glared up at the detective and said, "My sister walked away from that sleaze and never looked back. She started a new life for herself and her family."

Marsella nodded and asked, "Where is her husband?"

"He was a no-good drunk who used to beat up on Thelma. The drink finally killed him," she said.

Stealing a look at the grandmother and children in the next room, Moose asked, "What's going to happen to them?"

"Sirlena and I are going to raise them. Thelma wanted it that way. We have two of our own, but we'll manage," Hayes said.

"Was there any insurance?" Moose asked.

A sarcastic grin twisted the housing cop's mouth. "There ain't no insurance, and there ain't no estate."

Marsella gestured to his partner that it was time to leave, then looked at the housing cop and said, "We'll keep you informed."

Watching Marsella leaning up against the hallway wall, stretching his overshoes back on, Moose asked, "How much bread you got?"

"About forty bucks."

"Lemme have a quarter."

Marsella snapped on his left overshoe, counted out twenty-five dollars, and handed it to his partner. Taking the money and going back into the dining room, Ryan removed a similar amount from his wallet, placed the fifty dollars on the table, and said, "Buy Thelma's kids a Christmas present from us."

Sirlena looked up at the detectives, tears brimming in her eyes, took hold of his retreating hand, and said, "God bless you."

•   •   •

Elegibos, on Hudson Street, just off the corner of King Street, was a restaurant that specialized in Caribbean food and samba-reggae music. Brazilian bands sang in Portuguese and Yoruban, decrying broken promises and telling of love and hope. It was almost eleven o'clock that night when Vinda parked the department car on Hudson Street. Since Jean had died he had been unable to go directly home from the Job. His apartment was too full of memories that would not go away, each shadow a photo-play from the past. He would frequently go to Elegibos, where he would lose himself on the dance floor, dancing alone or with groups of gyrating strangers until he was exhausted and covered in sweat. Only then would he drive home, undress, toss himself into his lonely bed, and fall asleep.

Margareth Loopo, a tall, dark Brazilian beauty with long, twisted braids, owned Elegibos. She stood at the door each night collecting the entrance fee, in cash. When she saw her old friend walk in, she left the woman she had been talking to, and went and threw her arms around Vinda, saying in Portuguese, "It's good to see you, handsome. Are you okay?"

"I'm trying."

"Well, if you ever need a warm body to help ease your way back into the world, you can have mine." Leaning forward, she kissed him, ever so gently piercing his closed lips with her tongue.

"Thanks, Margareth, I needed that," he said, reaching into his pocket for money.

She grabbed his elbow, stopping him. "Your money is no good here."

"Thank you," he said, and walked into the restaurant.

The dance floor was packed with a mosaic of the city's Third World people: the band was playing *"Tudo A Toa,"* a samba-funk song whose lyrics expressed disgust with the living condi-tions in Brazil's urban slums.

Vinda moved out onto the dance floor, standing there, allow-ing the music to take control of his body. He closed his eyes and purged his thoughts of homicides, and the Job, and Jean. Slowly his hips began to sway to the beat, and his shoulders rocked in the space around him, his head rolling, his hands shaking above his head, as the lyrics burst from his mouth, *"Tudo A Toa."*

All to you, he thought. All to *who?*

F I V E

NEEDLES OF FROST GLISTENED OFF THE CANOPIES of buildings on Sutton Place. The CBS Sunday-night news magazine "60 Minutes" had just finished its time slot. People relaxed inside their luxurious co-op apartments snugly protected from the howling winds sweeping in off the East River.

Inside the glass penthouse atop 47 Sutton Place South, Adelaide Webster slammed the telephone down on her now ex-boyfriend and cursed, "You lying son of a bitch."

Uncoiling herself up from her sofa, she ran into the bedroom, grabbed the photograph of a man in tennis whites off the chest of drawers, and hurled it across the room, defiantly watching as it smashed into the wall, shattering glass over the rug. Rushing over, she fell to her knees, scooped the picture up from among the shards, and tore it into pieces.

"You bastard!"

Getting up, she threw herself across the bed, took the portable phone off the night table, and dialed her girlfriend Beth. For
the next ninety minutes, Adelaide tearfully confided how she
had caught her boyfriend with another woman. The women
commiserated over the immaturity of men, swore they wanted
nothing more to do with them, agreed that life must be easier for
gay women, and made plans to meet for lunch the next day at
the Pierre.

Adelaide put the phone down and remained on the bed, petting her pet black mongrel, Boo. She was never going to trust
another man, never, she swore. She pushed herself up and went
to look at herself in the mirrored wall. She was wearing a black
pleated skirt and a four-ply white cashmere sweater. Running
her hands through her long blond hair, she studied her side
view. Twenty-two, with a master's from Penn, a great body, and
I still can't find a man to love me, she lamented. God damn it!
She turned abruptly and went into the kitchen, where she took
a quart of ice cream out of the freezer. Then she walked back
into the living room, spooning peanut-butter crunch into her
mouth. She opened the terrace door and stepped out onto the
wraparound balcony. Ignoring the battering wind, she ate more
ice cream as she stood on the terrace, gazing across the street
into other apartments. The man she had named the War Hero
was walking around naked in his duplex. Why don't men know
how silly they look with their balls and their things flopping all
about? she asked herself, moving around to the river side, looking down into the white billows swirling over the black water.
The ring of the telephone brought her back inside, lunging for
the instrument. "Hello?"

Beth was calling back to make sure she was okay. Gulping
disappointment, she said she was just fine, and they talked for
another twenty minutes. Hanging up, she saw Boo sitting by his
leash. "Boo, I forgot all about you, honey." The dog's tail
wagged. She went and opened the closet and took out one of her
mink coats. Removing a silk Hermès scarf from the pocket, she

slid it around her neck, slipped into the coat, and unwound the leash from the knob.

The sundial at the entrance to Sutton Place Park sat on a tilted pedestal set in cobblestones. The vest-pocket commons was nestled against Adelaide Webster's cooperative apartment house on the north, and by Fifty-third Street on the south. The park's eastern wall overlooked the FDR Drive and the East River. Sutton Place South bounded it on the west. Stone planters brimming with carefully trimmed evergreens decorated the park's entrance, and three stone steps led down to a plot of asphalt bordered by green benches. Pachysandra and rhododendron, green against the black and white of winter, were thickly planted across the front of the park.

A man crouched under the overhanging green umbrella, his back against the wrought-iron fence overlooking the FDR Drive. His hands locked his knees to his chest as his cold eyes studied the whirlpool of debris dancing over the park. An automobile sped down Sutton Place, barely slowing for the stop sign, and turned west into Fifty-third Street. The man's eyes searched the apartment terraces above him, watching people inside moving about. Doormen in livery waited inside the vast lobbies of the surrounding apartment buildings. The man in the bushes groaned from his hunger and despair. He remained motionless, a watcher in the night.

Voices. Movements. His ears pricked up. A doorman across Sutton Place was holding a door open for an elderly, mink-clad woman and her poodle. He listened to them exchange banalities about the weather, and watched the dog strain at its leash. The woman's mink hood hid her age. His eyes followed as she left the building and walked carefully and slowly out of the curving driveway to the street. She stopped under a street lamp, and watched as her dog squatted. The pool of light bathed her lined face; he became acutely aware of the pain knotting his stomach.

Then he heard another voice, closer. A young voice, the one

he wanted to hear. "Boo, stay in the park." Her dog bounded down the steps and into the park. A young woman walked past the sundial, making for the steps. His eyes locked on her face and his heart surged. His muscles coiled, ready to strike. He looked across the street and saw the old lady and her poodle hurrying back into the lobby.

The young one stood in front of him, the back of her fur coat shining faintly in the streetlights. A leash dangled in her right hand as she watched her pet run free in the park. The dog came over to where the man was hiding in the bushes and stopped, its snout sniffing out the scent. Its tail fell between its hindquarters and it ran off whimpering. "Boo, what's the matter?"

He struck, springing up and clamping his hand over her mouth, muffling her terrified cries. Hoisting her struggling body aloft, he bent her body to him, and kissed her throat. Pulling back, he looked into her horror-stricken eyes, smiled, and lunged his face forward, biting deep, allowing blood to gush from her throat.

Police floodlights illuminated the crime scene.

Vinda, Ryan, Marsella, and the chief of detectives huddled inside the park, watching the lone photographer move about the frozen zone, taking pictures of Adelaide Webster's body. She lay in the bushes, her legs and arms unnaturally bent, her torso splayed across her mink bier, her features twisted as though revolted by the dreadfulness of death.

"This one ain't racial," Marsella said, gaping down at the body. "She's white, and rich."

Vinda nodded silent agreement. He had been on the edge of sleep when Operator 47 telephoned.

Vinda looked across the street. The temporary headquarters trailer and the crime-scene station wagon, along with a phalanx of other police cars, were parked in the cooperative's curving driveway. Bundled-up people stood on terraces, looking down at the controlled chaos of police work. The people looking down reminded Vinda of Eskimos squatting patiently over a seal's breathing hole in the ice.

Technicians loitered around the headquarters trailer awaiting their summons into the "frozen zone," the crime-scene area marked off by orange tape.

Vinda looked at Moose and Marsella. "Whadda we got?"

Consulting his notes, Moose Ryan said, "Female, white, twenty-two, resides alone at Forty-seven Sutton Place South. According to the doorman, she takes her dog for a walk around twenty-two hundred. Forty minutes later she hasn't returned, which, according to the doorman, is unusual. So the doorman puts on his coat and goes searching for her. He finds her DOA, with her dog crying over her body. He snatches up the dog, runs back into the lobby, and, using the house phone, dials nine-one-one."

Vinda bent down and examined the spattering of bloodstains circled in yellow chalk on the black asphalt.

"I want you and your people to catch this case, too, John," Sam Staypress said. "The precinct squad will assist on the preliminary."

Vinda asked the chief of detectives, "We got help coming?"

"I directed Manhattan North and South to fly in thirty detectives to assist with the initial canvass. I also got the ME out of bed and asked him to assign Dr. Marcal to do the post. This way we'll have medical continuity in the chain of evidence," Leventhal said, looking down at the body.

"I don't see any press," Vinda observed.

"We got lucky," Moose said. "There were no radio calls for them to pick up on. All notifications went out over land line. And the guys in the first car on the scene were smart enough to use the lobby phone to notify the desk officer."

"That'll buy us some time before the circus starts," Vinda said. "This is no ghetto. The media will be all over us like flies on shit once they find out a homicide went down on Sutton Place."

Detectives from outside commands were arriving and reporting in at the temporary headquarters trailer, where their names, shield numbers, commands, and times of arrival were recorded in the headquarters log.

Vinda noticed that there was another entrance to the park on Fifty-third Street. He told Moose he wanted barriers thrown up along the entire front of the park, and at both entrances.

"I'll telephone the Wagon Board and have them send a truck-load," Marsella said, hurrying off.

Vinda walked out of the park, crossed the street, and climbed inside the temporary headquarters trailer. Shouldering his way past the crowd into the clerical compartment in the rear, he asked in a loud voice, "Who's from the local squad?" Looking over the crowd of detective sergeants packed into the small and stifling space, and realizing from the cautious way their eyes met his that they recognized him too, he waited for the local Whip to announce himself.

A tall, wiry man with bulging eyes raised his hand. "Tommy Bowden, Seventeenth Squad, Lou."

"I want one of your people to maintain the Assignment Log, Tommy."

"Done." Bowden slid a stack of department forms from the pigeonhole above the small metal desk and said, "Here are the Thirties." He was referring to the U.F. 30 Detail Rosters that listed the official "pedigrees" of members flown in to assist.

Vinda looked at the forms. "I want a tight span on this one, one sergeant for every five detectives. And I want every apartment facing . . ." He picked up on Bowden's indulgent grin, made a slightly embarrassed gesture with his shoulders, and said, "Do what has to be done, Sarge." He left the trailer and returned to the park.

The photographer had finished his task. Marsella started to wave another technician into the frozen zone, but Vinda told him to wait. The Whip circled the body, careful not to step into

the globs of blood. He bent down and examined the gaping
wound in her neck. Carefully he ran his hand below and to the
right of the hole, and felt two indentations. They were covered
in her blood, but they were right there, in the same place as on
the other victims. "Light," he demanded. Marsella handed him
a penlight. He directed the beam into the wound and cursed to
himself. He moved the beam up to her face, taking in her grotesque death mask: mouth agape, with teeth half-hidden behind
lips purple in the glaring lights, tongue half out of the mouth;
eyes wide and blank; pasty skin drained of blood. Adelaide Webster's legs were spread apart, her skirt up around her stomach,
white silk panties showing through the top of black panty hose.
He pulled her skirt down and whispered, "Rest in peace, little
girl." He nodded to Marsella; the detective motioned the next
technician into the frozen zone.

The technical moved under the orange crime-scene tape and
put his kit down. He took out plastic bags and covered the
corpse's hands with them. Using a small clean spoon, he carefully scooped up blood from around the body, and the blood that
had splashed on the mink coat. He carefully spooned the blood
into test tubes coated inside with a saline solution.

Several minutes later the barrier truck rolled up on the scene;
Moose Ryan and Marsella helped the two policemen from the
Barrier Section set up the wooden sawhorses.

Leventhal came over to Vinda and said, "John, it's a little
after one and I've got an eight A.M. conference with the PC, so
I'm going to take off."

"I'll keep you informed," Vinda said, noticing Bowden coming into the park. The chief of detectives and the detective
sergeant nodded as they passed each other.

"The assignments have been made and recorded, Lou," Bowden said, coming over to the Whip.

"What about notification of next of kin?" Vinda asked.

"I've got two men inside her apartment now, going through
her telephone book. They'll come up with someone," Bowden

said. "The doorman told one of my guys that her father is a big deal on Wall Street."

When the lab man finished his work, Vinda told Bowden to send in the sketch man. Vinda had long ago learned that detailed descriptions and accurate measurements were the only safe way to record a crime scene. A camera's lens cannot capture the exact locations of objects, or their relationship to other objects. A sketch prepared by an expert can.

"What kinda sketch you want, Lou?" asked Bowden.

Vinda surveyed the entire crime scene and said, "Triangulation, using both park entrances as poles, with the triangle's apex fixed on the body."

The desk officer's telephone rang. "Lieutenant Gebheart, Seventeenth Precinct."

"Lou, this is David Pollack from the *Post*. I just got a rumble that a truckload of barriers were sent into your precinct. Anything doing?"

"Naw, nothing. A chunk of sidewalk caved in on East Fifty-seven. No injuries, no big deal."

"Thanks, Lou."

A self-satisfied smile spread across the lieutenant's ruddy face as he put the phone down. He got up out of his well-worn swivel chair and walked out from behind his desk. He crossed the muster room and brought his hulk into the sitting room, where two policemen sat at a long table, devouring an anchovy pizza. "Finish eating later," he ordered, scraping a strand of cheese from the box and swallowing it in one gulp. "I want you to take a ride over to the Sutton Place crime scene and tell the detective Whip that the press has got the scent."

David Pollack laced his thin fingers behind his head and leaned back in his chair, slowly looking around the empty press room on the mezzanine floor of police headquarters. In the old days, he reflected sadly, there would have been half a dozen cop junkies doing the late tour with him. They'd get through the night drinking booze-laced coffee and regaling each other with ancient cop sagas. Pollack was the last of the old breed still working the cop beat; police reporting no longer fit into the higher priorities of today's Fortune 500 newspapers.

A gaunt man with an oversized Adam's apple, he still wore a pearl gray Stetson with its crown creased lengthwise and its brim bowed jauntily on the sides and front. He loved to wear gaudy, oversized bow ties. When he'd started on the police beat over thirty-two years ago, only first-grade detectives and police reporters sported a Stetson; it was a status symbol recognized throughout the Job. You seldom see a cop in a hat today; the new breed wear "gimme caps" that advertise motor oil and soft drinks. So be it, he sighed, looking up at the list of important telephone numbers taped to the wall. "I might be old, but I can still hear the swish of that blue curtain falling over a case," he said to the empty room. Pollack picked up his Stetson from the desk, set it rakishly on his head, and dialed. A crafty smile pressed his lips together. This was the part of his job he loved best: the cat-and-mouse intrigue of digging out a story. When he finished dialing the night emergency number of the Department of Highways, he drummed his fingers on the desk while he waited for someone to answer. A husky voice finally came on the line: "Highways."

"You guys got anything on a cave-in on East Fifty-seventh?"

"News to me, pal."

Pollack pressed down the plastic button and dialed the operations desk at Detective Borough Command Manhattan South, and said to the sergeant who answered, "How ya doin', Sarge? This is David Pollack from the *Post*. It's quiet tonight and I'm scratching around for a story. You guys in the South got any newsworthy capers going down?"

"It's as quiet as a whore saying her rosary. Only thing we got is a felonious assault in the Two-four. Some guy slipped into his Jekyll-Hyde mode and sent his wife to the hospital with multiple skull fractures. Word is she might be going out of the picture."

"What's the time of occurrence?"

"About oh-two-hundred. You interested in the gory details?"

"Naw," Pollack said, playing with the typewriter's platen knob, "I'm looking for something more glitzy. Thanks anyway, Sarge." He disconnected and dialed the Crime Scene Unit's dispatcher. "This is Pellegrino in the Two-four Squad," he lied in his best thoroughly annoyed tone. "I called over two hours ago, and I'm still on the scene waiting for one of your units to respond. I got a fe-lo-ney baloney where the victim's going to buy the farm, and I need your lab boys to go over the scene."

"Lemme check the run sheet. What time did you phone in the job?"

"About oh-two-ten."

"That job was logged out to unit six. They shudda been there hours ago."

"Well, they ain't. What's going on with you guys tonight, you got a party going?"

"We're behind on our jobs because of that Sutton Place homicide. Sam Staypress is on the scene, and he's got his tight pants on. He's flying in detectives from all over the North and South."

"I know. We sent two of our night watch. Who got killed, anyway?"

The serology detective wore a down coat and had a long, multicolored scarf coiled around her neck. Her jeans were tucked into fur-lined boots. She and Vinda were kneeling, examining bloodstains. "What can you tell me?"

"I can tell you that you're lucky they shoveled the park, because if they hadn't, you would have no bloodstains." She shivered and pulled the knitted cap down over her ears. "Blood has different appearances depending on the height from which it falls. A short distance, round drops. The greater the height, the more jagged the edges, and when you get beyond six feet, the drops break up and sprinkle into many small drops."

They stood. "But what I just got done telling you only holds true if the bleeder is stationary. When he's in motion and the first part of the drop hits the ground, the remaining portion is still moving in a horizontal direction and splatters over the first part, forming a drop that resembles an exclamation point with the tail and dot pointing in the direction the bleeder was moving. The faster he's moving, the longer and narrower the exclamation point."

They followed the blood trail. It led to a crimson pool surrounding the body. Vinda looked at the detective, noticed her wispy curls sticking out from under her cap, and asked, "What does it all add up to?"

"As I read the signs, Lou, the victim comes into the park and stops about here." She pointed. "The perp is hiding there. He snatches her here, and sweeps her up off her feet, whirling her toward the bushes. While they're in motion, he punctures her throat with something. Notice these exclamation drops." She pointed. "The dots are pointing at the bushes, and that long, thick blood trail leading up to the body is from an artery."

"Let's try an experiment," he said. Using both his hands, he swooped her up off her feet. "He grabbed her, and is hustling her into the bushes when he does his number on her throat." He thrust the detective into the bushes and stopped. "You're not struggling, but we have to assume she did. The doer had to use both his hands to carry and control her. So, with his arms full, how did he employ the murder weapon?"

"Maybe he held it in his mouth," she said.

"Maybe." He noticed the imposing hulk of Dr. Marcal standing on the steps watching him. He set the detective down and called to the doctor, "A little experiment."

"So I see," the ME said, moving down the steps, surprisingly light on her feet.

The detective picked up her kit and left.

Vinda watched the ME examining the wound. "Could a man do that with his teeth?"

"No way. The human mouth isn't constructed for predation.

The human grip isn't powerful enough, and the incisors and canines aren't long enough or strong enough to make a wound like this." She removed a penlight from her medical bag and directed the beam into the wound. "It's similar to the others, and appears to have been made by some sort of cleaving device. See how the skin has been shredded." She moved her fingers to the right and a little below the wound, felt the two indentations looked up at him, and said, "Same marks, in the same place."

"I know. Any sign of rape?"

She opened the victim's mouth and directed the beam inside. "No sign of semen or pubic hair." She felt the breasts. "Her bra is intact." She lifted the dead woman's skirt and passed the beam over her. "Underclothes are intact. A superficial exam doesn't indicate sexual molestation. But I'll have to wait until I get her on the table and do some lab tests to be sure."

Vinda sighed. "At least it doesn't appear that our doer is into sex—or if he is, it's one of the perverted kinds. I've encountered plenty of that over the years."

The doctor got up and walked out into the pathway. She moved over to the railing and looked out over the river. A Blue Circle cement barge was being pushed upriver by a tug. Across the river in Queens, the sun's first rays glowed on the distant horizon, giving the blue-green pyramid of Citicorp Center a golden aureole. Vinda came over and stood beside her, his eyes fixed on the collapsed roof and crumbling façade of the abandoned Civil War–era hospital on Welfare Island. "Hell of a way to make a living," he said.

"I guess it could be sexual," she said, almost to herself. "Some sick minds associate blood with sexual arousal. The object of some sexual murders is shedding blood, not to cause death. Cases like that almost always produce wounds to the neck."

Vinda stared down into the water. A frightening question formed in his mind. "How many more before we stop this guy?"

SIX

THE SQUALL BLEW ACROSS THE COLOMBIAN BASIN, churning up whitecaps and then disappearing into the west, leaving in its wake a boundless vista of cobalt-blue water.

The *Adelaide*, a 150-foot yacht powered by twin GM .16 V-140 diesels, sliced through the sea, its tethered Bell Jet Ranger helicopter casting a shimmering outline upon the water.

Belowdecks in the fantail area, Malcolm Webster stretched his big frame over a brown calfskin-covered lounging chair and talked into the telephone: "There is to be no Thirteen-D filed with the SEC. If I wanted to show my hand, I would have told you." He placed his hand over the mouthpiece and said to a crewman standing nearby, "Bring me a bottle of Badoit."

The young sailor went to the bar and returned with a bottle of mineral water, which he put on the low mahogany table next to

Webster. Then he filled a glass with ice. Webster nodded his thanks.

"Never mind telling me that, I know the rules too," he said, sipping at the glass. "And just in case you've forgotten, it was me who dreamed this one up, not your corporate finance department."

Webster twirled his glass as he listened in exasperation to the voice from Wall Street. "Harry. Don't try to con me about legitimizing the deal by raising your corporate finance fee. You know the people to call. Tell them if they don't play on this one, I won't be there when it's my turn to make their deals go." He sipped his drink. Tinkling ice, he looked across the saloon at the crewman and said into the phone, "We should earn ourselves sixty million, less interest, on this one."

He stretched his neck to get a better look at the woman who was walking up the grand staircase that led up to the sundeck lounge above. Great ass, he thought, suddenly irritated by the voice from New York. "Screw the unfunded pension liability in the unprofitable subs. Once we've taken it private and gotten rid of management, we'll shove them into receivership. Let the unions collect from the trustee. Call me when you have the list together." He hung up, and took another sip from his glass. He picked up a pair of binoculars from the table, adjusted the focus, and scanned the rolling, verdant hills of Barranquilla, off in the distance. Then he put down the glasses and left the saloon for the deck above.

Malcolm Webster was a lean, bony man with a still-youthful though somewhat acne-scarred face and abundant energy that belied his sixty-two years. Dressed only in white shorts and Topsiders, he had that rich, glowing tan that only a lot of money could buy. As a dirt-poor kid working in the Texas oilfields in the forties, he'd sworn he would be rich one day. He'd made his first million when he was thirty-five and never stopped to count the rest. He owned vast amounts of real estate, shopping centers, and oilfields, and had one of the world's largest collections

of primitive art. During his lifetime, Webster had collected three
ex-wives, a dozen or so mistresses, including two movie stars,
and several champion horses, but the only thing that really mat-
tered to him was his only child, Adelaide.

Webster reached the sundeck in time to see the woman peeling out of her bikini bottom. "Having a good time?" he asked,
gliding his hand over her soft skin.

"I love it when you touch me, Malcolm." He slid his hand
over her voluptuous body and between her legs. She moaned
softly.

"Let's go below."

The master suite was done in rosewood and marble. Webster
threw himself across the bed. The woman fell over him, pulling
down his shorts and kissing him, screwing her tongue deep into
his mouth. The bedside phone rang. "Damn," he said, reaching
out and bringing the instrument down to his ear. "Yes," he
snapped. Seconds later he shoved the woman off him and shot
upright.

"What?" he screamed into the mouthpiece. His lips went
tight as his jaw muscles began to twitch. The color drained from
his face, leaving behind a twisted mask of grief and rage. He tore
the receiver away from the phone on the wall and threw it across
the stateroom. His companion, who had been pushed off the
bed, was on all fours on the thickly carpeted deck of the huge
cabin. In terror, she crawled away from the man on the bed; her
lover had suddenly been transformed into a wounded and dangerous animal.

S E V E N

THE SUN ROSE, SLOWLY CASTING POCKETS OF
fleeting warmth over the Sutton Place crime
scene.

Residents had begun leaving their apart-
ments for work around 6:00 A.M., only to be questioned inside
their lobbies by teams of waiting detectives; other teams were
still busy making their way down from top floors, knocking on
doors, rousting some people from sleep, asking the same question over and over: Had they seen or heard anything?

Outside, an Emergency Service Division loudspeaker van
drove through the area, blaring out an appeal for witnesses to
come forward.

Inside the blue police department temporary headquarters
van, courier detectives brought hastily filled-out Fives from the
teams working the apartments, tossed them into baskets, and
left. Clerical cops would type up the Supplementary Complaint

Reports from the handwritten ones. Later in the tour the issuing detectives would come into the van to read and sign their canvass reports.

On East Fifty-third Street, outside the entrance of the Midtown Garage, a flag with the word POLICE emblazoned across a field of green fluttered in the wind. The flagpole was secured inside a cement-filled Civil Defense water can.

It had been a little after 4:00 A.M. when the first television crew rolled onto the scene. More media quickly followed.

John Vinda, though secretly dismayed that the press had caught on so soon, immediately ordered a restricted zone established around the Sutton Place area from Fifty-third Street to Fifty-fifth Street, blocking all access to Sutton Place from First Avenue. To placate the media, he directed that the garage be commandeered and used as a press center. The parking garage's sloping driveway led under a twenty-story co-op; expensive automobiles were crammed together over a vast field of battleship-gray paint. Sergeant Bill Brady, Public Information Section, stood on the down ramp, briefing about forty men and women from the television stations and the newspapers. "Hold it! Hold it! One at a time!" he shouted, brushing aside the sea of black-sheathed microphones thrust in his face, acutely aware of the gasoline fumes that tinged the air.

"Who found her?"

"What was the cause of death?"

Brady gritted his teeth and once again went over the few facts about the murder. He tried to avoid giving away the grimmest details.

"What was her name, Sarge?" a woman demanded.

"C'mon, you know no names until next of kin is notified," Brady replied.

David Pollack had been leaning against the brick wall, listening to the sergeant trying to cope with too few answers for too many questions. He stepped out into the street and walked west, hurrying to First Avenue, where he turned north and

walked to Fifty-sixth Street. Turning east, he saw the line of barriers strung across the southern terminus of the street, effectively
blocking pedestrian and vehicular traffic from Sutton Place.
Keeping close to the building to avoid the full force of the wind,
he made his way to the corner, heard the police plea for witnesses
coming from the sound truck, and thought about how rarely he
had seen such a police turnout in all his years on the beat.

Several police officers stood behind the sawhorses. Approaching the barrier, Pollack saw teams of detectives gathered in the
roadway comparing notes.

"You can't pass unless you live on the block," one of the cops
shouted to him.

This guy looks like a junior high school hallway monitor, Pollack thought, putting on his wide-eyed get-'em-off-guard look
and asking, "What's going on, Officer?"

Mustering as much authority as his baby face allowed, the
policeman barked, "A homicide."

"Really?" exclaimed Pollack, leaning into the sawhorse.
"Anyone famous?" he asked, as his eyes came to rest on a cluster
of detectives huddled at the north entrance of Sutton Place Park.

"Some rich lady got her throat slashed," said the policeman.

"How awful," Pollack said, looking past the cop at the solitary
figure of John Vinda.

"So far we've come up with four witnesses who all basically tell
the same story," Marsella said, consulting his steno pad. "They
all live in apartments that face the river, they were all looking
out their windows at the time of occurrence, they all claim to
have seen a white male of medium height, wearing jeans and a
hooded mackinaw, with a red knapsack strapped to his back,
walk out of the park and hurry north on Sutton. One of the
women said she didn't get a look at his face, but was sure that
she saw him stuffing a towel into the knapsack."

Looking across the river at the old hospital, Vinda asked,
"None of them got a good look at his face?"

Moose, hitching his trousers up and thoughtfully scratching his crotch, nodded. "Affirmative. His hood was up, concealing his face from the sides."

Vinda asked, "Did they all see the towel?"

"Affirmative," Moose said dryly.

Vinda had started to ask another question when Sergeant Bowden rushed up to announce, "We've located another witness."

Mrs. Gail Phillips, female, white, middle forties, sat in the living room of her tastefully decorated third-floor duplex, nervously playing with the belt of her silk kimono.

Walking into the room, Vinda was immediately aware of her nervousness and whispered to Bowden, "Ten-eighty-five a female officer." Going over to the witness, Vinda gestured the two Manhattan South detectives away, and said to her, "You have a lovely apartment."

She looked up at the Whip and smiled. "Thank you."

"May I sit down?" Vinda asked, aware of Bowden's soft voice speaking into the walkie-talkie. Smiling at the witness, he remembered a cardinal rule taught in detective training courses: Never, if possible, question a female without the presence of a female member of the force. "How long have you lived here?"

"Twenty years," she said, looking at the other detectives. Vinda decided to stall for time until the female MOF arrived, so he talked about the last snowstorm and how cold it had been lately. A few minutes went by, and a uniformed female police officer slipped into the apartment. The newcomer smiled at the witness. Obviously relieved at the presence of another woman, the witness smiled back.

"Do you mind answering a few questions?" Vinda asked her.

The witness looked across the room at the other woman and said, "I'd be happy to."

"Please tell us what you saw," Vinda asked, pulling out an RN 89 miniature tape recorder and setting it down on his lap.

"As I told the other detectives," she began, "my husband is away on business, and whenever he's gone, I have trouble sleeping." She went on to tell them how, unable to fall asleep, she had gotten up and gone over to the bedroom window to watch the river's soothing flow. "I saw this man come out of the park, wiping his face with what looked like a bath towel. Then he reached behind and stuffed it into one of those red nylon knapsacks all the young people seem to be wearing."

"Did he appear to be cleaning his face?"

"Yes, come to think of it, he did."

"What color was the towel?"

"I really can't be sure. I think it was white, but it looked dirty."

"You said he stuffed it into his knapsack. When he did this, were you able to get a look at his face?"

"No. He turned his face to his right, so I could not see it."

"Please show me where you were standing."

She got up and led him into the bedroom. The large window looked out over the river and the park. He studied the scene below. A mass of shrubbery had concealed the killer as he went about his grisly task, Vinda concluded, as he walked back into the living room with his witness. He questioned her closely for another ten minutes, thanked her for her cooperation, and left with the others.

They rode the elevator in silence down to the first floor, and stepped out into a black marble lobby adorned with large Chinese vases filled with fresh-cut flowers. The uniformed woman officer strode outside into the cold; the detectives formed a circle inside the warm lobby. Vinda said to Moose Ryan, "I want you and Tony to see that there is no mention of the towel in any of the reports."

A shadow fell across Marsella's face. "Do you think maybe this looney-tune believes he's Dracula?"

"You've been around long enough to know blood's an emetic," Vinda replied, looking directly at Marsella, "and I don't recall any vomit at any of the scenes."

Bowden rejoined, "Seven, eight years ago, a cuckoo bird

named Kinahan Goodman thought he was a vampire and used a straight razor to slice Bowery bums' throats."

"I remember that case," Vinda said. "The jury didn't believe he was crazy, and he was convicted of murder two. He's sitting on a quarter to life in Green Haven."

"I'll check, make sure he's still inside," Marsella said, making a note.

A far-off look came over Vinda as his thoughts drifted away. Finally he muttered, "I'm going to see a friend."

"And if we need you in a hurry?" Moose asked.

"I'll be in Corregidor."

Manhattan's midday parade sloshed along as Vinda parked the unmarked department auto in the No Standing zone on the east side of Broadway, parallel to City Hall Park. A dusting of snow swept the streets. Rippling his fingers on the steering wheel, Vinda watched hunched-over people scurrying for the warmth of comfortable office buildings. A ragged group of them crossing Broadway dodged ahead of a bus. Vinda thought of Jean, and his hands tightened around the wheel as he lowered his forehead on top of it and closed his eyes. He remembered how she used to call him in the office and use buzzwords to tell him how much she loved him. She'd feign a drawl and say, "Why, Colonel, sir, you give me the vapors." But all that was over from the day her illness was diagnosed.

He wished that it were possible for him to run home, grab Jean, and hold her in his arms forever. Even as she was dying, they would watch videos of old movies until two or three in the morning, holding on to each other the way they did when they were first married. How wonderful it could have been.

Vinda lifted his head up off the wheel and saw an RMP, a radio motor patrol car, cruise past. The cruelty of his reality overwhelmed him: his Jean was dead, and he was a lonely cop trying to stop a killer from murdering again. In an attempt to revitalize his tired body, he sat up tall, gripping the wheel and stretching his arms so that his back pressed into the seat. He breathed in deeply several times, tossed the vehicle identification plate on the dashboard, and got out of the car.

Standing on the curb waiting for the light to change, he looked across Broadway at the intricate architectural details of Manhattan's Cathedral of Commerce, the Woolworth Building.

Pushing his way through the gilded revolving doors, Vinda entered the Woolworth lobby and cast an appreciative eye up at the sparkling mosaics of the vaulted ceiling. He walked past the building's directory and glanced over the list of police line organizations that had offices in it: CEA, Captains Endowment Association; LBA, Lieutenants Benevolent Association; SBA, Sergeants Benevolent Association; SOC, Superior Officers Council. He checked the time; Corregidor's tunnels would be filling up.

Walking behind the majestic marble staircase, he reached the down staircase that emptied into a subterranean tunnel leading to Harry's Restaurant. On both sides of the rathskeller's double doors were lithographs of Lower Broadway and Bowling Green dated 1826.

Vinda pushed through the doors and entered the restaurant, the favorite watering hole of the Palace Guard. Entirely underground, Harry's had long ago been called Corregidor because it evoked, for some cops who could remember, the fortress made up of tunnels carved out of the rock of that Philippine island. He moved across the wide entrance foyer to the U-shaped mahogany bar. Familiar faces abounded: the assistant director of the FBI's field office was deep in conversation with Jimmy Tower, the LBA president; the Queens PBA trustee was huddled with the boss of DEA's undercovers.

For the first time, Vinda noticed how virtually everyone spoke in low tones, even whispers. Corregidor: it certainly suggested the Job's siege mentality, but did the name also mean they were losing the war?

A tunnel led from the foyer into the main dining room, where more tunnels branched off into other dining areas, all of them with barrel-vaulted ceilings. The bar was to the right of the dining room. Vinda headed straight for it.

The bartender came over; Vinda ordered an orange juice. The lunchtime crowd trickled into the restaurant; a host and hostess greeted the patrons.

Jerry Goldstein, the Whip of Safe and Loft, walked in with a brunette clinging to his arm. Spotting Vinda at the bar, he disengaged himself from the woman and came over. Placing his back against the bar, facing the wall, Goldstein grinned wickedly and said quietly, "Hear you've been rehabilitated."

"Word travels fast." Vinda realized he was almost whispering too.

"Big building, small job."

Vinda looked at the waiting woman. "Who's your friend?"

"A horny detective from Pickpocket and Confidence. What a great job this is. See ya 'round." Goldstein went back to his friend.

Vinda watched the hostess greet a group of newcomers. He made eye contact with the man he'd come to see. He quickly moved into an alcove near the bar and sat at one of the two tables inside. Rows of wine bottles filled the wall behind him.

Special Agent Gus White, the man Vinda needed to see, had been the FBI's liaison with the NYPD for twenty years. That long in *that* job meant that White had done very well indeed; he had earned the trust of the NYPD brass, who had little love otherwise for the Bureau. Completely bald, with sky blue eyes and a Texas twang, he had an affinity for boldly striped shirts and Gibsons.

White passed under the alcove's arched entranceway and pushed out a chair. Lowering himself next to Vinda, he quietly asked, "What's up?" He betrayed no surprise at seeing Vinda rescued from obscurity.

"I'm looking for a guy who gets off on killing women by ripping out their throats with some kind of slicing tool."

"Did you check with NCIC?"

"They have nothing that matches up with the MO."

"John, if the guy you're looking for is not in the files of the National Crime Information Center, how can the Bureau get hold of it for you?" White whispered, his eyes roaming the bar crowd.

"Gus? Don't pull my chain, okay? Your people have a line into every department in the country," Vinda said, taking in the gathering of police elite, and thinking, We're meshuga, the system has turned us into a bunch of whispering schizoids.

"This wouldn't have anything to do with the Sutton Place homicide, would it?"

Vinda's eyes flashed to the FBI man. White grinned and explained, "It went down last night and you're wearing that scraggly late-tour complexion."

"What you don't know is that Adelaide Webster was his third victim."

The restaurant door opened and a tall, distinguished-looking man wearing a black overcoat came in, surrounded by laughing mid-level PD brass.

"Your brand-new deputy commissioner of community relations just made his grand entrance," White said. "I've not yet had the pleasure, what's the word on him?"

Vinda pondered the question a second or two, and answered, "He ain't gonna win the jackpot on 'Jeopardy.' "

White scoffed, "Another political deadhead." His eyes came back to Vinda. "You want us to check out every damn department in the U.S.?"

"As we say in the trade, you got it."

White dropped his hands on the table and made a move to get up and leave. Vinda pushed his shoulder down, and said, "One good turn deserves another," and added softly, "Your photo blind across from the Iranian Mission has been blown."

"Oh?"

" 'Fraid so."

"Are you sure?"

Vinda steepled fingers in front of his mouth to explain. "Last week an RMP responded to a ten-fifty-two noise complaint in the building where you have your surveillance equipment set up. The cops discovered the apartment door unlocked, so they picked their way inside only to discover one male and one female agent screwing each other on a Bureau-issued sofa."

"Assholes," White hissed, then got up and angrily stalked into the dining room.

Vinda remained seated, watching the horse-trading going on around him. More police business was conducted in Corregidor than in the Big Building, he thought. A waiter came into the alcove and placed a tub of cheese and crackers on the table. Reaching for the knife sticking out of the tub, he spotted David Pollack standing by the entrance, and Vinda's eyes widened. The people around the bar also spotted the reporter, and a hostile silence fell over the bar. Several people called for the tab.

Coming over to the table, Pollack tossed his Stetson on one of the empty chairs and said, "Hello, John." He sat.

Vinda gave him a welcoming smile. "Ever notice how a bar empties when you enter?"

"That's because they're insecure. You're not like that," Pollack said, breaking a cracker in half and tossing it into his mouth. "I saw you engaged in some heavy-duty conversation with Mr. FBI. Got anything to do with Adelaide Webster?"

Vinda looked expressionlessly at the reporter. "Can I buy you a drink?"

"I gave up the firewater. Got tired of sitting on the bathroom floor night after night, hugging the porcelain altar. Anyway, I spotted you at the crime scene and figured you'd end up here, passing out some markers. The scenario I come up with is Sam Leventhal brought you back from the land of the flopped to work on the serial killer who is just starting up in our city. Since some people think you're the best we've got, Sam Staypress hopes you'll be able to clear the case before it turns into another Green River caper."

"The homicides in Seattle?"

"The same. Almost four dozen women in five years, and the police haven't a clue as to who the guy is. A nightmare for a police administrator."

"I have no personal knowledge of any serial killings in New York," Vinda said, taking the knife and digging out a chunk of cheese.

"May I remind you that I was the only game in town to stand behind you when the Big Building's bureaucracy of self-preservation whined, 'It's not our fault Vinda and his assassins killed so many feral youths.' "

"I remember."

"After I spotted you and your guys this morning, I nosed around and discovered that an ME from Kings County had been assigned to do the Webster post. Knowing that Brooklyn MEs do not do Manhattan autopsies, I inquired further and found out that Dr. Marcal had recently done the posts on two black women who were the subjects of homicides with similar MOs, to wit: the perp tore out their mother-lovin' throats."

Vinda gazed out at what remained of law enforcement's ruling class. Timothy W. Eberhart, the chief of patrol, whose wild temper tantrums and unkempt red hair had earned him the nickname within the Job of Agent Orange, was holding court at the other end. As he talked to Gillis of Secret Service, Agent Orange's eyes slowly inventoried the crowd; when they fell on Vinda and his guest, they turned cold.

Vinda had long ago been painted with Sam Staypress's brush, and the C-of-D and the C-of-P hated each other. Thus Vinda was also the C-of-P's enemy. Vinda returned the hostile stare. Agent Orange nervously shifted around, presenting his back to Vinda. Reinstated, but not yet permitted to walk among the living, Vinda thought.

"John, I've been in this business over thirty years and I make

a lousy forty-two K while those capped-teeth humps on television make millions. And with few exceptions, none of them
could find an elephant in a snowstorm. Hell, most of them can't
read English. I need this case, John. If it is as big as I think it is,
if I get ahead of the pack, I got the biggest story of my life here."

"You'd have made a good detective, David."

"Hell, I *am* a good detective."

EIGHT

LINDA CAMATRO NODDED HER THANKS TO THE
doorman in the brown and gold pillbox hat and
walked inside Rue St. Jacques, a momentarily
fashionable and ferociously expensive fashion
mecca on East Fifty-seventh Street. Unaccustomed to shopping
there, she was relieved to find a sign that told her the swimsuit
collection was on the mezzanine floor. As she walked toward the
stairs, she paused to admire the silk scarves and the jewelry
display.

Linda was a twenty-one-year-old legal secretary with Abatch
& Williams, a firm specializing in real-estate law. A tall, attractive woman with penetrating black eyes, Linda had been saving
for, and looking forward an entire year to, a winter vacation in
Mexico, fantasizing daily about how she and her boyfriend were
going to spend ten carefree days strolling crescent beaches,
swimming in the Pacific Ocean, and sipping margaritas under
thatch-roofed palapas.

She had decided some time ago to leave shopping for a new swimsuit until the last possible moment. That time had now arrived; they were leaving Friday, four days away. Knowing how depressed she got whenever she had to go through the dreadful ordeal of trying on swimwear, she had taken today off from work to go to Rue St. Jacques, reasoning that if there was a really knockout suit anywhere in New York, it would be there.

The mezzanine projected out over the ground floor. It was aglow in a rainbow of bright colors: yellows and oranges and shiny blacks; greens, whites, and cinnabar; copper and peach and pebble. Artfully arranged displays of the latest swim fashions lined the floor.

Browsing and trying to summon her nerve to start looking in earnest, she suddenly plucked a one-piece black suit with large yellow circles off the rack and held it up in front of her. Definitely one-piece, she thought, maybe one with horizontal stripes to hide my tummy. She selected a black one with white horizontals, and held it up in front of her. Twenty minutes later, with six suits over her arms, she went over to a saleswoman and asked her where the dressing rooms were. "They're upstairs," the saleswoman said, lifting her chin at the white spiral steps set into the middle of the far wall.

The staircase led up half a flight to the second floor, where intimidatingly well dressed women walked down the carpeted aisles, stopping to look at and handle spring dresses of lace and floral prints, dresses Linda knew would cost more than she made in months. Off of it ran a corridor lined with dressing rooms. Wide archways at both ends of the corridor led back into the dress department on the second floor.

Entering the corridor, Linda became aware of the unnatural quiet surrounding her. There were no people; there was no hum of conversation. She walked over to the archway, looked inside, and saw the reason. Jessica Merrill, the actress, was holding a designer dress up in front of her while two saleswomen waited nearby. The other people scattered about the department were all silently gravitating toward the movie star, all of them trying their best to act nonchalant.

Jessica Merrill was one of Linda's favorite movie actresses; the legal secretary from Morningside Heights could not resist the temptation to get a closer look at her.

Coming near, she saw that the actress was taller in person than she seemed on the screen, and that her flowing blond hair reached below her shoulders. When she heard the star's throaty voice discussing the dress, Linda felt a strong urge to ask for her autograph. Suddenly a man thrust himself in front of the actress, waving a pen and paper in Merrill's face. Linda watched Jessica Merrill's initial annoyance turn into a patient smile as she took the pen and paper and gave the man her autograph. Linda chided herself for even thinking of invading the star's privacy; she turned and left.

Walking back into the corridor, Linda opened a dressing-room door and stepped inside. A large window with a sheer white curtain looked out over the jagged Manhattan skyline. A beige carpet covered the floor, and a white glass table stretched the length of the right wall; opposite, on the other wall, was a large mirror with winged movable side panels. A Queen Anne–style chair stood in the corner.

Linda put the swimsuits on the table and undressed down to her underpants. She hung her coat on one of the hooks, and neatly folded her clothes on the chair.

She put on the black suit with the horizontal stripes, and sucked in her stomach, and cried inwardly as she looked in the mirror, I can't hide my tummy, and I can't fill out the top. She looked down at the other suits and decided to try on the one with the yellow circles. She stepped out of the one she had on, and picked up the new one. She was balancing herself on one leg, trying to thrust the other one through the leg opening, when the door flew open and, before she could regain her balance, a hand was locked over her mouth, silencing the terrified screams gathering in her throat. Propelled forward, her head rammed one of the mirror's side panels, spiderwebbing the glass. Pinned by powerful arms, she fought against her attacker, kicking him. She bit the hand over her mouth, but it wasn't human skin, it was some kind of monster skin. She struggled to see its face, and when she did, her eyes grew enormous with terror. "How lovely you are," he whispered, and jerked her head to one side, exposing her throat.

Carrying two dresses into the fitting-room area, Jessica Merrill paused, deciding which room to use. She noticed a thick ribbon of liquid suddenly seep under one of the doors. Puzzled by it, she looked questioningly at the growing red stain and knocked on the door. There was no answer. She knocked again; there was no reply. Her first thought was to call for a salesperson, but instead she pushed the door open. Her hands flew up to her face, blocking out the gruesome sight. A dry retching sound came from her throat and grew in intensity until a scream exploded from her famous mouth. The two dresses lay forgotten on the floor.

N I N E

LINDA CAMATRO'S BODY WAS PROPPED ON ITS knees, wedged into the space between the mirror and the upturned Queen Anne chair; except for her underpants and the tangled swimsuit around her leg, she was nude.

Standing outside the fitting room, straddling the pool of blood, a crime-scene photographer aimed his camera in at the body. Detectives and Emergency Service search teams prowled the five floors of Rue St. Jacques in search of her killer.

On the second floor, inside the designer dress department, John Vinda, his face reflecting his depression and fatigue, conferred with the chief of detectives, Marsella, and Moose Ryan. "How the hell is it possible for a woman to be murdered in a crowded store, and no one sees or hears anything?" Leventhal said, clenching his fists until the knuckles turned white.

"According to the witnesses, Jessica Merrill was swanning

around and everyone else was too busy gaping at her to see anything," Vinda explained.

"And where is this movie star?" Leventhal asked, adjusting his tie.

"Over there, near the stockroom," Marsella said. Vinda glanced over at her. She was standing between two racks of clothes, talking to a detective. Her face was animated, her hands constantly in motion. Five other witnesses were also being interviewed, including two saleswomen.

"Who's the guy?" Vinda asked Moose, looking at a vaguely familiar face.

Moose, following the Whip's line of sight, answered, "Michael Worthington, another actor. He was with Merrill."

Vinda asked Marsella, "Where's the store manager?"

"Downstairs, trying to calm down some of his customers," the detective answered.

"Go and tell him that I want all of today's sales slips," Vinda said.

"Done," Marsella answered, and walked off.

Vinda went and stood inside the corridor of dressing rooms. Once again, no bloodstains led away from the scene. Leventhal came over to him and, as though reading the lieutenant's mind, said, "Maybe he uses a towel to clean up before making his exit?"

Vinda shook his head. "There's too much blood; it'd take much too much time." Looking in at the body, Vinda wondered what dreams Linda Camatro had for her own. He looked over at Moose. "Mosey around and see if there are any men with briefcases or knapsacks. Our doer must be carrying some kind of container around with him, using something to sop up that much blood."

Moose nodded and walked off.

"Have you figured out the time sequence yet?" Leventhal asked in a quiet voice.

"Merrill went into the fitting room at about twelve-thirty. She discovered the body and screamed. Salespeople ran over, security was called, all the doors and fire exits guarded, and nine-one-one called. The first RMP arrived on the scene at twelve-thirty-one."

"Could the perp have exited by one of the fire doors before security put men on them?" Leventhal wanted to know.

"Don't think so. All of the fire doors are alarmed, and none of the alarms went off and none were tampered with."

"Then he might still be inside the store," Sam Staypress said.

"That's the reason for the interior search," Vinda said.

A nervous twitch made the C-of-D's left eyelid flutter. "All the others were done in the streets."

"I believe Camatro was a target of opportunity. He must have seen a chance to kill and went for it. We're dealing with somebody who thinks he can get away with anything."

"Which means . . ."

". . . he's always ready to kill," Vinda supplied. He asked Leventhal bluntly, "This case is now totally public. You still want me to run with it?"

Leventhal's face smoothed into the noncommittal mask of the Palace Guard when he said, "For better or worse, it's your baby. Besides, nobody but us knows about the two Brooklyn homicides."

Vinda decided not to tell the chief of detectives about David Pollack. Moose returned, slightly out of breath from his climb up the stairs. "No knapsacks, but a few of the men on the first floor have attaché cases, and one of them is holding on to a stained flight bag as though it contained the family jewels."

"Stained with what?" asked the C-of-D.

"Dunno," Moose said. "Could be blood."

"Could be halvah, too," Vinda rejoined.

Moose bellied up to the Whip, his beady eyes tightening as the shadow passed over his face. "Want me to give those bags a toss?"

Vinda brushed a hand through his thick black hair, fingering the duck's tail in the rear, as he tried to remember the fine print of department Legal Bureau bulletins dealing with warrantless searches. The store entrance and fire exits were now guarded by policemen, effectively preventing the perp from escaping; there were no existent circumstances that demanded an immediate search in order to save a life or prevent the destruction of evidence. Since the perp was unable to escape, Vinda had ample time to apply to a court of competent jurisdiction for a warrant to search those attaché cases and that flight bag. The problem was he could not show reasonable cause to believe the murder weapon or evidence of crime was concealed inside any of them. He knew from long, bitter experience that courts did not issue warrants to conduct speculative random searches. He also knew that the fruits of a warrantless search would be inadmissible in court and the suspect set free. If he did order a search, and the doer was identified, he would be able to get him off the street for a while, perhaps save lives. And while the killer was in jail he could try to dig up admissible evidence to use against him. He looked first into Leventhal's impassive face, and then at Moose. "Try to obtain their consent to search."

"Lou," Moose pleaded, "none of those guys looks like a dummy; no way they're gonna give me consent to search their property."

A sly glimmer sparkled in Vinda's dark eyes. He looked at Moose and said, "Then you know what to do."

Moose winked at the Whip and walked over to the telephone on the floor supervisor's desk. He dialed 911. When the emergency operator answered, he adopted a rough Hispanic accent and reported that a bomb had been secreted inside a man's attaché case—and that this man was at that very moment inside the Rue St. Jacques on East Fifty-seventh Street. He gave a vague description of the anonymous man, and added that the bomb was set to go off in eleven minutes. He hung up and turned up the volume of the miniaturized walkie-talkie clipped to his belt. When he heard the transmission, 10:33—Report of Explosive Device—he lowered the volume and made for the staircase.

Jessica Merrill had emerald green eyes. As Vinda listened to her tell how she had discovered the body, he realized that this woman had a powerful erotic presence. Her stance, her head tilted to one side and her leg thrust jauntily out in front of her; her closely fitted suit unbuttoned to the cleavage, just enough to give a tantalizing peek at her breasts; her thick, round lips glowing deep cinnamon to complement her dark skin tone. Even the way she had casually tossed her sable coat over the dress rack reminded him of a reckless sexuality. But he also thought he detected an occasional tremor of insecurity in her voice.

Looking at one of the search teams, and then to Vinda, she blurted, "It's just like the movies, isn't it?"

Vinda brushed a hand across her sable coat. "Not really; this body is a real one."

"Yes, I know. I've never seen anything so horrible. Who could do such a thing?"

"A lot of people could do such a thing," Vinda said, unsure of the sincerity of her revulsion. Her tone was right, and her face still retained a shadow of real fear, but there was something off-key about her. He could not help wondering to what degree she was playing a part now. "Did you see anyone acting suspiciously?"

A bitter smile turned up the corners of her mouth. "Lieutenant, whenever I'm in public, people act funny. It's a price you pay in a society that is hooked on celebrity." She glanced at the chief of detectives, who had been staring at her in a totally unprofessional fashion.

"When you were making your way to the dressing room, did you notice anyone leaving or standing nearby?" Leventhal asked, smiling at her.

"No I didn't," she said flatly.

Leventhal seemed to be aware that she was more comfortable talking to Vinda so he kept his mouth shut.

Vinda questioned her for another twenty minutes or so. He thanked her for her help, and then he and the C-of-D walked off to interview the actor, Michael Worthington. As they were making their way between the racks of clothes, Leventhal leaned close to Vinda and said, "Did you catch that long blond hair? It almost reaches her ass." He glanced furtively about and added, "I wonder if her sleeves match her cuffs?"

"I suspect that's something you'll never know, boss," Vinda said as they walked over to the actor.

Michael Worthington had long ago become used to people looking at him with a puzzled "I know I've seen that guy somewhere" expression on their faces. Only in his last few films had he graduated from supporting to leading roles. He had a face that just missed being handsome, but its features were defined strongly enough to make him stand out a bit from the crowd. Piercing blue eyes, which seemed to glow from some inner light, often surprised people when he looked at them directly, as he did now at Vinda. Close up, the detective and his chief could see the network of fine lines in the corners of his eyes that, along with the silver-streaked black hair carefully swept back over his ears, hinted at his fifty-nine years. Vinda started to remember some of the films he had been in, always playing a supporting role with superb professionalism. In fact, Jean had particularly liked one of his earliest films, in which he had played a village priest in a rough frontier town.

Worthington was standing in the tiny aisle between racks of clothes, his Burberry casually draped over his left shoulder.

Vinda made the introductions.

"What an awful thing to have happen," Worthington said. "That poor woman and her family."

"Just a few questions," Vinda said, admiring the actor's brown turtleneck sweater and Harris tweed sport jacket, as well as noting his physical fitness and almost aristocratic bearing. "I understand from Jessica Merrill that you two were on your way to lunch when Miss Merrill decided to do some shopping."

Worthington smiled and admitted, "Jessica considers it a sin to pass a place like this without at least taking a peek inside."

"Where were you while she was looking at dresses?" Vinda asked.

"Standing right here," Worthington said, "being as patient as

I always am when she cons me into shopping with her. It bores me to tears—but it makes her happy for some reason when I tag along. I generally stay in the background, amusing myself by watching people watching her."

"Did you notice anyone loitering in the fitting-room area?" Vinda asked.

"Yes, I did," Worthington answered.

Vinda and Leventhal exchanged hopeful looks. "Tell me," Vinda said.

"A man was hanging around the dressing rooms. He wasn't doing anything, or paying attention to what was going on inside the salon. He appeared to be waiting for someone to come out of one of the rooms."

"Describe him," Vinda said.

"A tall white man, middle to late fifties. Distinguished look-ing, with thinning gray hair. Well built. Green eyes. He was wearing a camel's-hair sport coat, gray slacks, brown tassel loaf-ers, and a light blue button-down shirt. I'm not certain, but I think he had a light brown overcoat over his right arm."

"You're very observant," Vinda said, looking at the actor with respect.

"Lieutenant, an actor is a lot like a cop when it comes to seeing, really noticing people. We learn to study them, to use them as raw material for creating a part."

"Did you notice anything out of the ordinary about this guy?" Vinda asked.

Worthington put his coat on the top of a nearby dress rack. He folded his arms across his chest, his sober expression a reflection of his deep thought as he tried to remember more.

While he waited, Vinda looked over at Jessica Merrill, who was halfheartedly examining a blue spangled dress. She finally dropped it on a chair and gazed sadly in the direction of the dressing room.

"Yes," Worthington said suddenly, as if agreeing with his own thoughts. "I remember thinking that was odd." He looked at

Vinda. "Here was this well-dressed man, and he was toting a dirty red knapsack around with him. It just did not go with the way he was dressed, it was . . . out of place."

A surge of excitement raced through Vinda. Mrs. Gail Phillips, one of the Sutton Place witnesses, had seen a man leaving the park stuffing a towel into a red knapsack. "I need you to work with one of my detectives to prepare a composite sketch of the man you saw."

"I don't have much time. My wife is waiting for me at home."

"It won't take much time," Vinda said, motioning one of the detectives over, and telling him to get hold of an artist from the Crime Scene Unit and tell him to bring his composite sketchbook with him.

"I'll do whatever I can to help, but I must call my wife. She'll get nervous if I'm not home on time."

"Of course," Vinda said, pointing to the telephone on the sales supervisor's desk.

While Worthington was talking on the phone, Jessica Merrill came over to Vinda and said, "Lieutenant, I'd appreciate it if you could manage to keep our names out of this tragedy. Neither of us wants this type of publicity. And, frankly, I'm scared. It's dangerous enough being a public figure—but it really worries me that whoever did this might just have been looking for me."

Vinda tried to reassure her. "That's not too likely. You came in here on impulse. Nobody knew you'd be here, so I can't see you being the target. This thing was random, crazy. But don't worry. We'll do everything we can to keep your names out of it. We don't want the press to know about you, any more than you do. Movie stars involved in a case generate a huge amount of publicity, and that is one thing we don't need."

The police artist from the Crime Scene Unit showed up and reported to Vinda, who explained to Worthington that the artist was going to work with him on making the composite sketch. "Go someplace where it's quiet," he told them. Looking around, he suggested, "The stockroom should be okay."

"I'll go too," Jessica said. "I'd like to see how this is done."

"We don't need you, Jessica. You go home. You've had the most awful experience. You must rest," Worthington said firmly.

"But I'd like to see how it's done," she insisted.

Worthington looked directly at her and said in a stern tone, "Jessica, this is one set you're not needed on. Go home!"

She snapped her coat off the top of the rack, slid into it, picked up her two shopping bags, and demanded, "How do I get out of here without the press seeing me?"

The chief of detectives stepped up to her and said, "Come with me. I'll show you."

Watching them stroll off toward the service elevator, Vinda absently picked up the sleeve of a dress, and thought, How does Worthington get away with talking to her like that? Are they an item? He glanced down at the pricetag on the sleeve and dropped it as if it were electrified. *Fifty-five hundred dollars?* he screamed inwardly, and picked up another, thirty-six hundred dollars, speculating about the women who bought them, and the men who paid for them. They certainly weren't cops.

Ten minutes later he wandered into the stockroom and watched Worthington work with the Crime Scene Unit artist. They were standing over a small desk, and Worthington was selecting plastic overlays of eyes, mouths, hairlines, noses, chins, ears, and foreheads to be put onto a blank face, forming a composite sketch of the man Worthington had seen near the dressing rooms at the time of the murder. Perhaps the killer, perhaps just a man with a red knapsack who was waiting for his wife. Whatever he was, the composite sketch of his face was about to be sent to every patrol precinct and detective squad in the city.

Marsella poked his head inside and gestured for the Whip to come out. "I've got all the sales slips."

"I want every one of those people interviewed," Vinda said.

"Right," Marsella acknowledged, adding, "David Pollack's on the phone. He wants to talk to you."

Vinda went over to the floor supervisor's desk and picked up the telephone. "Yes, David?"

"The AP received an anonymous call stating that Jessica Merrill was almost murdered today in Rue St. Jacques."

"Shit!" Vinda hissed. "Any chance of squashing the story?"

"Are you for real? It's already been the subject of news bulletins on all the majors."

"Now the fun begins. With Jessica Merrill involved, we're really going to be feeling the heat."

Pollack responded with sympathy. "Yeah. I know. But it gets worse. The AP also got a tip linking the Webster homicide to two other unspecified cases."

Vinda felt the first stab of a blinding headache as he put the receiver back.

T E N

A BURLY DETECTIVE SAT AT HIS DESK STUDYING
the case folder. The travel clock next to his
dictionary said 7:26; it was only hours after
Camatro and Webster had been murdered.
The eleventh-floor squadroom of the Major Case Squad was
empty except for the five detectives doing the night duty. Most
of the overhead fluorescents had been switched off, bathing the
room in a strange ballet of dancing shadows. The vertical blinds
were open, revealing the incandescent sprawl of the city. A base
radio that could communicate with detective units in the field
was on top of a desk in the corner, while in another corner a
television screen showed a local news anchorman's trademark
hair and gloriously capped teeth. He was telling the world about
Jessica Merrill's harrowing escape from death at the hands of the
depraved killer who was terrorizing the city. "Fear is abroad in
New York City tonight," the anchorman said, as the composite

W I L L I A M   J .   C A U N I T Z

sketch of the killer came onto the screen. Below the face, confidential police telephone numbers appeared, and the anchorman asked viewers to call if they recognized the man in the sketch. The next segment played up the announcement that department stores throughout the city were going to put on added security.

The detective's ears pricked as he looked up from the open folder and glared his displeasure at the face on the screen. "Another asshole," he growled, heaving himself up out of his seat and going over to the set and snapping it off. Striding back to his desk, he looked down the floor's connecting aisle and saw that Missing Persons and Safe and Loft were busy. He also noticed the lights were on inside the glass-fronted office that had been commandeered by the task force working on the burgeoning murder investigation.

He saw John Vinda pacing inside and recalled working with him in the Two-oh Squad. Jules Kooperman thrust his hands deep into the pockets of his sagging trousers, remembering that May morning when Jean Vinda had come into the squad to report the burglary of her apartment, and how he had ushered her into the Second Whip's office. It seemed like a lifetime ago. His attention was suddenly snagged by the sight of the chief of patrol storming down the warren of cubicles toward the task force office. Chief Eberhart's ruddy face was pumped up with anger, and his rust-colored hair tossed wildly about. Kooperman watched Agent Orange plunge into the task force office and thought, There goes one power-grabbing, erratic son of a bitch.

As Agent Orange burst into the room, he immediately engaged the C-of-D in a heated argument over this month's telephone bill for the detective division, which included two thousand dollars to dial-a-porn numbers. "Watsamatter, Sam, you got a bunch of preverts you can't control?"

Chief of Detectives Leventhal glared at the C-of-P and said, "Fuck off, Timothy."

Vinda looked down at the pile of copies of the composite

sketch on his desk. The Distributing Room had already sent out
thousands to every field unit of the department and every law-
enforcement agency within the metropolitan area. Every newspaper and television station had also received copies. He looked
up from the sketches and saw Moose and Marsella typing the
names and addresses of witnesses who were inside the boutique
and still had to be interviewed.

He listened to Leventhal and Agent Orange going at it. The
two of them had hated each other since their Academy days.
Some ancient slight had developed into a lifetime dislike that
increased with their rise to stardom within the Job.

Moving over to the window, Vinda banished them all from his
mind and looked out at the darkness over the city.

A crescent moon was high in the sky. Gazing at it, he thought,
How beautiful and peaceful it is, so far out there, safely away
from the cruelty of man. He thought of the telephone calls he
used to receive from Mr. Snow, and tension rekindled in his
stomach. Mr. Snow was the pseudonym used by the Universal
Collection Agency. Back then he had been behind two months
on the loan he had taken out to pay off Jean's medical expenses.
He still felt angry when he recalled Mr. Snow's condescending
voice lecturing him on the importance of maintaining a good
credit rating. Vinda had spent a week at a backgammon club on
Tenth Avenue, playing the game and winning the money to pay
off his medical bills.

He felt hungry, tired, and dirty. Detective crud. It had been
almost twenty-four hours since Operator 47 notified him that a
homicide had gone down on Sutton Place. A hot bath was the
best way of getting rid of the creeping crud of a long tour. The
superchiefs were still locked in argument; the detectives ignored
them, going about their business.

Vinda recalled those two anonymous phone calls to the AP.
Did it mean that the killer wanted publicity? Was he the kind of
guy who got off on playing the puppeteer, remaining hidden but
pulling the strings from the darkness, with the department dan-

gling in the wind? He turned away from the window and walked past the chiefs, leaving the office.

David Pollack was hunched over his desk inside the press room, devouring a meatball-and-sausage hero. His oversized Adam's apple bobbed in time with his hasty masticating. When he saw Vinda, he reached down into his drawer and took out his backgammon set. "Wanna play a fast game?" he asked, taking another bite of his sandwich.

Vinda's grandfather had taught him the game when he was a child, and he had learned well. Pollack had been trying to beat him at it for years, and up to now had never been successful. "Don't you ever get tired of me beating you at this game?" Vinda asked, opening the board and setting up the stones.

Pollack rolled the first die for the privilege of going first; he rolled a three. Vinda cast a six, and won the first roll. He put the pair of dice into the cup and cast two sixes. "A double," he said, with a grin.

Pollack sighed.

Moving his stones, Vinda said, "Those calls to the AP, you happen to know who received them?"

"I'm way ahead of you," Pollack said, rattling the dice and casting them on the board. "I've spoken to both of them. It would appear that the doer has a hard-on for the Job. He told both reporters that he intended to destroy the department."

Casting dice, Vinda asked, "And exactly when did you plan on telling me all this?"

Pollack took a bite of his sandwich and said, "As soon as I finished eating."

Vinda walked into his apartment and felt the loneliness pressing in on him. He went into the bedroom and stared at the stack of cassettes on top of the VCR. They were all of Jean's favorite movies. He pulled out *Waterloo Bridge*, turned on the set, slid the cassette into the slot, and sat down on the bed. Watching the opening credits roll across the screen, he recalled his life with

Jean. It had been wonderful. Even as she lay dying, she had thought of him. "When I'm gone, don't live in the past. Live in the present," she would beg, over and over. Watching Robert Taylor toss his cigarette into the River Thames and walk off toward the waiting staff car, he recalled the last time he had watched this movie with Jean. As "The End" had rolled across the screen, he had switched off the set and turned, taking her sunken body into his arms, and slowly rocked her like a child until she drifted off to sleep.

With tears seeping from the corners of his eyes, he said to the darkness, "I can't get on with my life, Jean. I just can't."

I have to get out of here, he thought. Getting up, he changed into jeans and a light shirt, and left.

Elegibos was crowded. Margareth was at the door; when she saw him walk in, she gave him a loud greeting in Portuguese, threw her arms around him, and kissed him. "Will you dance with me later?" she asked.

"I'll dance with you anytime," he said in Portuguese, taking out money to pay the entrance fee.

"Put your damn money away; it's no good here. You should know that by now. Why do you want to insult Margareth?"

"Because I'm afraid one day you may want my body as payment for all the times you let me in here for nothing."

She moved very close to him and rubbed her body up against him. "That would not be so terrible, would it?"

"No, it wouldn't," he said, lifting up her chin and kissing her nose.

E L E V E N

ARLY WEDNESDAY MORNING A RUPTURED WATER main on East Fourteenth Street sent thousands of gallons of water cascading onto the tracks of the Lexington Avenue subway, bringing service to a stop. At eight o'clock the same morning a steel girder atop the Manhattan Bridge surrendered to years of neglect and broke away, crashing through the windshield of a car, decapitating its driver. At nine-fifteen, as workers streamed into police headquarters, fifty pickets for a group called Women Against Female Genocide appeared and attempted to storm the lobby. Out went an urgent transmission of code signal 10:46, Rapid Mobilization: one lieutenant, eight sergeants, and forty police officers responded forthwith with hats and bats to One Police Plaza.

Within minutes, RMPs squealed to a stop inside the plaza, disgorging policemen wearing riot helmets and swinging night-

sticks. Within a short time the demonstrators were corralled behind hastily erected barricades. Two attorneys from the Legal
Bureau raced down from the tenth floor to advise the police
commander on the scene of the constitutional rights of the demonstrators.

The raucous protesters circled behind the barricades chanting
slogans and hoisting placards at the television cameras: MALE
DOMINATED POLICE PERMIT CRIMES AGAINST WOMEN; STOP FEMALE
GENOCIDE.

On the fourteenth floor of the Big Building, the police commissioner glowered at the chiefs of detectives and patrol. "Why
didn't Intelligence have advance word on this?"

"Commissioner, they're not a mainstream organization," the
C-of-P explained. "They're an ad hoc group from The Women's
Register."

The superchiefs were sitting directly in front of the PC's antique desk.

Leventhal lifted his gray trouser leg and stretched the recal-
citrant sock back up over his calf. "It's only the beginning.
Every TV station in the city is devoting large blocks of time to
the story. Panic is next. And Merrill's involvement has stoked
the political coals. Every feminist organization in town is going
to try to get in on the free publicity that this case is generating."

Agent Orange nervously ran his fingers through his tousled
hair. "Perhaps Lieutenant Vinda's personal distractions have
caused him to conduct a less-than-zealous investigation. We
might want to consider replacing him with someone without his
personal problems."

Leventhal withered the C-of-P with a scornful glance. "Replace him with who, one of your cronies from the Patrol Bureau?"

"I was only—"

"You were only trying to piss on the detective division," Leventhal snapped. "In case you've forgotten, homicide investigations are the purview of the detective division, not Patrol."

The PC leaned forward, hands clasped, and responded coldly, "True, Sam, but as you are well aware, tables of organization are fluid things. We could always, if things didn't go the way they should, move the detective division under Patrol's umbrella."

Agent Orange smiled smugly.

"But then, Commissioner," Leventhal said, his voice heavy with derision, "you would also have to replace the current chief of patrol because as everyone in the Job knows, he's incapable of commanding a rowboat."

"I resent that," the C-of-P shouted.

"Resent it all you want," Leventhal shot back, his eyes cold and hard. "The fact is that every command you've ever been given has had to be run for you by your XO."

The PC was more than a little aware of the political constituencies of both superchiefs. They represented large ethnic voting blocs necessary for the Mayor's reelection. The PC had been told to put these two men in these jobs, and he did not want to get rid of either of them, just yet. He smiled. "Calm down, both of you. Sam, are you satisfied with Vinda?" he asked the C-of-D.

"Yes, I am," Leventhal answered firmly.

"Then he stays on the case," said the PC. Then he scowled unhappily and added, "The Mayor telephoned me at home this morning. It seems Jessica Merrill's manager thinks his meal ticket might be in danger and wants us to provide round-the-clock police protection."

"We don't bodyguard civilians unless they're material witnesses or there is a pressing necessity," Leventhal said.

"The pressing necessity, Sam, is that the Mayor wants us to do it. Besides, we simply can't afford to have anything happen to her."

Vinda roosted on the edge of a stone bench in Police Plaza, holding a container of steaming coffee and idly watching the circling demonstrators. They were a mixed bag: straights and gays, well-dressed and slovenly, old and young, some of them familiar faces from bygone protests, gentle faces, dedicated to the cause of equality.

The barricades had been set up on the east side of the plaza in front of the wide staircase leading down into the Equipment Bureau. He studied the protesters, trying to pick out the organizers. As his eyes went from face to face, he zeroed in on a tall, attractive woman with short gray hair who was wearing a long cloth coat and a knitted gray cap pulled down over her high brow. The woman was standing off by herself, outside of the barricade, shouting instructions to the marchers. He smiled, took a final sip of coffee, tossed the container into a nearby stone garbage receptacle, and strode purposefully across the plaza.

May Gold had been a cop in the Two-oh when Vinda worked there. She'd worked steady late tours so that she could go to Brooklyn Law School during the day. She had also helped Vinda prep for the lieutenant's examination. When she was admitted to the bar, she had resigned from the Job and opened her own law practice. Now, seven years later, she had a flourishing practice overwhelmingly devoted to matrimonial matters, a large part of which entailed getting cops divorces.

Vinda drifted up behind the lawyer and whispered, "Out soliciting, May?"

She whirled around and threw herself into his arms. "John," she said, kissing him.

"This your parade?" he asked.

"Guess I'll have to cop a plea on that one," she said, giving him another hug.

"Why are you doing this, May? What the hell do you care about some bimbo movie star? And you're an ex-cop. Why are you looking to embarrass the Job?"

"This has nothing to do with Jessica Merrill. It has to do with preventing another woman from being murdered. I happen to know that there have been four homicides, all by the same perp. The Job is sitting on two of them in an attempt to conceal the fact that there is a serial killer out there doing a number on women."

"C'mon, what makes you say that?"

"The perp told me."

Vinda's mouth fell open and his eyes widened with surprise. "What?"

"Your perp telephoned The Women's Register yesterday. I happened to be the one who answered the phone."

He raised an inquiring chin. "What did he have to say?"

"Only that he had done four homicides, two of them black women, and that the media and the police were in collusion to suppress the facts." Looking him straight in the eye, she asked, "Is it true?"

"There is no collusion, May. The media hasn't picked up on the other two homicides yet. And we don't volunteer information. We don't want unnecessary outside pressure forcing us to get careless."

She brushed a snowflake off his shoulder. "Are you the Whip?"

He shrugged, grimaced haplessness. "Yes. Why do you suppose he telephoned you?"

"The Register has been getting a lot of publicity lately with our pro-choice rallies. I guess he trusted us to get his message out."

"What did this guy sound like?"

"Like the real thing. I was on the Job long enough to hear the difference between a guy who is for real and a guy who's faking it. The man I spoke to was serious, deadly serious."

Looking at the chanting demonstrators inside the barricade, Vinda asked, "What else did he have to say?"

"That he was going to kill again and again, and that the police were powerless to stop him. He also said that the police were only good for destroying lives—that he was going to destroy the department."

"And why didn't you report this conversation to anyone on the Job?"

"I did," she snapped. "I telephoned the information into the

First Squad and spoke to a Detective Gotlieb. He treated me like just another stupid civilian."

"May? You should know that the Job has its share of idiots. Don't blame the department because of one guy."

"John. I checked. This idiot did not bother to report my call. He didn't make out a Complaint Report or a Five. He canned it. So I decided to organize this little party, knowing that someone inside the Big Building would wake up." Her voice dropped and became soft. "I was sorry to hear about Jean."

"Thank you." He gazed across the Plaza at a woman with spiked orange hair who was petting a police horse. "What time did he telephone?"

"About eleven A.M. I'd just gotten back from court."

He telephoned before the Camatro homicide, Vinda thought. "Did you give any of this to the press?"

"Once a cop, always a cop."

"Good. As a favor to me, please keep it to yourself. And pack up your troops and head for home."

She faced him, rested her hands on his shoulders, and said, "I can keep his call to myself, but I can't afford to close up shop without getting some little goody in return. The Register is a political organization; I'm the president." Her eyes drifted around the Plaza. "Bringing a case like this one to a successful conclusion usually means grade money for the detectives who worked on it. Tell me, John, how many women are assigned to the investigation?"

Vinda's lips pursed with understanding. "I'll see if I can transfer two women into the unit."

"Four," she countered.

"Two is the best I can do."

"And Gotlieb?"

"I'll take care of him."

She looked at him thoughtfully for a moment or two before conceding, "You have a deal."

.   .   .

"What kind of a guy is Gotlieb?" Vinda asked the Whip of the First Squad. He was sitting at his desk with his hands coiled around the mouthpiece, and his back to his detectives.

"Guy acts like he's retired on full pay," the annoyed First Squad Whip said. "He was flopped out of the Fifth because he pissed off his boss."

Vinda related Gotlieb's failure to take proper police action on the information furnished by May Gold. An angry silence came back over the line. "I'll take care of it," the Whip from the First said, and hung up.

At 11:27 that morning a message was sent from the chief of detectives' office transferring Detectives Adriene Agueda and Joan Hagstrom from Brooklyn South Sex Crimes to Special Investigations on a thirty-day temporary assignment.

Vinda looked up from the Lucas-Johnston case folders, and studied the crime-scene photos pinned to the blackboard's border. The composite sketch of the killer along with some more crime-scene shots were also pinned on it. Unconsciously he spoke his thoughts out loud. "So far the media hasn't connected the two black women and the Webster and Camatro homicides. Two whites and two blacks."

Moose and Marsella looked up from their typewriters. "Think the racial mix is significant?" Moose asked.

"I just don't know," Vinda said, reaching for a yellow pad. "Let's see what we know about our perp." He discussed the details of each homicide, and spoke at length about the killer's telephone calls to the media and May Gold. "This guy appears to be going after the Job," he said, "which means he has a real or imagined grievance against the department or some cop." He looked at his men. "I think until we come up with something else on this guy, we're going to have to start checking out records. Cover all the bases—the Civilian Complaint Review Board, Corporation Counsel, federal and state courts for lawsuits against the department and any of its members."

"How many years you want to go back?" Moose asked.

"Twenty," Vinda said.

Sighs of exasperation issued from the detectives. "That's a lotta records," Moose groused.

"When we find his grievance, we'll find *him*," Vinda said.

"Lou, hundreds of complaints are filed each year against cops, alleging everything from false arrest to abuse of authority," Marsella moaned.

Vinda held up a protesting palm. "We're looking for something out of the ordinary. Something that could flip a guy out, make him need to kill."

He dialed David Pollack's centrex number. When the reporter answered, he told him what they were doing and asked him to check out the newspaper morgue, going back twenty years.

"There are only about a thousand stories a year relating to police screw-ups," the reporter shouted into the mouthpiece.

"Aren't you the one who bragged what a good detective he was?" Vinda said, and hung up. His next telephone call was to the "Honorary Desk" at the Health Service Bureau. Honorary Police Surgeons were medical professionals who rendered gratis health care to members of the service out of a sense of public service and because they liked cops. He told the sergeant manning the desk what he needed, and was given two names along with addresses and telephone numbers.

Dr. Terry Young's specialty was prosthodontics, the replacement of missing teeth with bridges and dentures. His suite of offices was on the twenty-second floor of a glass tower on the northwest corner of Lexington Avenue and Fifty-fourth Street.

Vinda entered the office. The receptionist looked up from behind her glass cage. "Mr. Vinda?"

"Yes."

"Doctor Young will see you right away."

Late thirties, short, rotund, with a chin and stomach padded with layers of fat. Here is a man who likes to eat, Vinda thought.

Motioning Vinda toward a small sofa inside his private office,

Young said, "Health Services telephoned and said you'd be right over. Now, what can I do for you, Lieutenant?"

Vinda put the morgue photos of the four homicide victims on the desk in front of the dentist and proceeded to tell him about the case. He told Young they were stymied, trying to figure out how the killer was able to control his victims and inflict such wounds at the same time, and that he'd thought the killer might have held the murder weapon in his mouth somehow, but that that surmise had been shattered by an assistant medical examiner named Patricia Marcal, who had told him it was impossible. "I needed to check her conclusions with a dentist specializing in prosthodontics," he finished.

Dr. Young studied the photos of each victim. He took his time reading the autopsy protocols.

Vinda stared at the pastel wallpaper and tried to contain his impatience, waiting for him to finish.

Young looked up from the reports and said, "What you are talking about, Lieutenant, is a prosthesis capable of invading the throat and severing the common carotid artery and the internal jugular vein without causing physical injury to the wearer of the device. In other words, a pair of fangs."

Vinda was surprised. "I suppose you're right. I never thought of the murder weapon in those terms."

"Well, no matter. I'm sorry to have to tell you that your medical examiner was correct. The force needed for such an invasive act could not be generated by a prosthesis attached to the teeth of a human mouth." He picked up a plaster cast of the mouth, and proceeded to give the policeman a lesson on prosthodontics. "The type of device you are looking for would have to protrude from the mouth so that the wearer would not cut off his own tongue when he used it." Darting his pencil over the cast, measuring different parts of the mouth, he added, "The incisors would have to be razor sharp." His face twisted into a thoughtful expression; he looked Vinda in the eyes. "I'm sorry. What you are looking for simply does not exist. The mouth's configuration makes it impossible."

"Can you think of any device that could be attached to the mouth and cause such wounds?"

Young picked up the photos, looked them over again, and said, "No, thank God!"

"Sister? Sister Mary Margaret?" Vinda called, poking his head into the second-floor office at the Manhattan campus of Fordham University.

"Over here," a pleasant voice called out from behind a desk buried deep in academic disarray.

Two large windows faced Lincoln Center and an assortment of indoor plants cluttered the sills. A photograph of Freud hung on one wall next to a wooden crucifix; on another were a peace symbol and several framed diplomas.

Entering the office, Vinda edged his way around the stacks of journals and term papers cluttering the floor, heading for the desk. A head popped up from behind the uneven ridgeline of books.

Sister Mary Margaret Fenner appeared to be in her late forties; she was a short woman with a gentle face, a glowing smile, and amber eyes. She wore a black skirt and a yellow sweater with a brown vest, and sneakers with blue horizontal stripes on the sides. Only her black veil showed she had taken vows.

"I'm John Vinda, Sister," he said, picking his way to the desk. "It's good of you to see me on such short notice."

"When Health Services telephoned and told me your problem, I was fascinated, so I rearranged my schedule so that I could see you today. Now. Sit here and tell me everything," she said, scooping up an armful of books and papers off the chair. She slipped her hand under a stack on her desk and came out with a pack of cigarettes. She shook one out, offered him one, which he declined, and lit her own. "My brother is a state trooper in Kentucky. He's always boasting about how discreet policemen are. Is that true?"

"It certainly is, Sister," Vinda answered with a grin.

"Then you won't tell anyone about my little vice, will you?"

she said, taking a drag and quickly waving the smoke away. "Now tell me all."

Vinda looked up at the portrait of Freud and the crucifix, unsure how to begin. He had homicides being committed with some impossible instrument. The medical people told him there was no such instrument. So if he couldn't identify the weapon, maybe he could start to understand the mind of the person who used it. "I understand you're a psychiatrist, Sister."

"No, I'm a clinical psychologist. I also have a doctorate in theology. I teach graduate classes at the university. And, as a staff member of the Society for the Propagation of the Faith, I am charged with the responsibility of investigating, along with others, all kinds of supposedly supernatural phenomena. Despite what our many critics say, the Church is scrupulously scientific when it comes to investigations of supernatural events and incidents." She smiled. "Do I fit the bill, Lieutenant?"

"Yes, Sister, you do." He took out the morgue photos and passed them to her. She studied them without displaying any emotional reaction while he explained the details of the investigation. "Is it possible for a person to drink human blood, Sister Mary Margaret?"

"Sick minds have a strange way of overcoming the body's intrinsic revulsion to certain acts. For instance, some people are able to ingest human feces. What I see in these dreadful photographs is anger—Eros denied. The Marquis de Sade is a classic example."

Vinda nodded and said, "We have reason to believe that his anger is directed at the police department."

A doubtful expression came over her face. "It's not that simple. If your killer was seeking revenge against your department, he'd vent his rage at the police or police facilities, but he's not. He's killing women. So I suggest to you that his illness is not subject to simplistic diagnosis."

"I suppose people with mental problems believe all sorts of strange things," he said, hedging.

"Sick minds, Lieutenant, are capable of all sorts of aberrations."

"You must deal with a lot of weird people, Sister."

She smiled. "Neurotics build dream castles, psychotics live in them, and psychiatrists collect the rent."

"What type of dream castle does my killer live in?"

"From what you have told me, I would guess that you're dealing with a paranoid whose delusions and obsessions have emotional and symbolic meaning to him. Such people are known as classical paranoids. They function well in most areas, but have a fixed delusional system woven into their lives. A capsulated psychosis that springs out whenever the right button is pushed."

"Could such a person believe he was a vampire?"

Her eyes widened in surprise, and she paused before she said, in a low voice, "Yes."

"Would such a person be knowledgeable about vampire lore?"

"Yes. It would possibly fuel the delusional system."

Vinda leaned forward, a vague uneasiness stirring inside him. "Have *you* ever dealt with people who believed they were vampires?"

"Yes, I have. I've investigated eight so-called vampiric incidents over the years. Every one of them involved pathology, not vampires. And I can tell you that in each case the person who believed he—or in one case, she—was a vampire ended up in a mental hospital." She flicked ash into a partly open drawer of her desk and inhaled deeply on her cigarette. "From what you have told me so far, I see no reason to believe you are dealing with a vampire psychosis. What facts do you have to substantiate such a theory?"

"It's not a theory, Sister, it's a suspicion, one of several that this investigation has engendered, which I have to look at and examine."

"Okay. Tell me what has led you to this, er, suspicion."

"The similarity of the wounds on all victims, the fact that the ME is not sure if any blood was missing, the fact that we cannot find any blood leading away from any of the crime scenes."

She got up out of her seat and went over to the windows. She opened one; a blast of cold air gushed across the room. She tossed out the cigarette, closed the window, and hurried back to her seat. Leveling a cold, almost unfriendly gaze on him, she said, "Most of what you've told me can be explained away, Lieutenant. For instance, arterial evulsion—gushing blood—makes it almost impossible to account for all the blood loss. Perhaps your killer is wearing some sort of blood-absorbing suit. You're not dealing with a vampire, Lieutenant, real or imagined."

He couldn't keep the shock out of his voice. "*Real* vampires?"

"The earliest references to vampires are in Chaldean and Assyrian tablets. Ancient Greek and Roman lore contain many references to incidents of vampire attacks," she said, obviously trying to sidestep the question.

Vinda was hooked. He forced the issue and asked bluntly, "Sister, do they or don't they exist?"

Sister Mary Margaret did not respond for several long moments. She seemed to be struggling to make a decision of some sort. Finally she sighed and said, "I guess that all depends on your perception of God and life."

"I might be looking up the wrong tree, Sister, but it's a tree I have to look up. And you can help, maybe save a woman's life."

She nodded slowly in agreement and went on: "The first thing you must do in order to understand the phenomenon of the vampire is to separate the ones of Hollywood and fiction writers from the body of scientific knowledge on the subject. A true vampire, Lieutenant, is someone neither dead nor alive, but living in death. A corporeal being with its own body, one that requires blood to prevent decomposition."

He looked at her in disbelief. "How can you believe that stuff?"

"You asked me, I told you. Both the Old and New Testaments cite many examples of the dead being brought back to life."

"That's the Bible. I can't use that on a witness stand. We're talking about four homicides in 1991 A.D."

"Do you know what November second is?"

"No."

"It's the Feast of All Souls. When many still celebrate the annual return of the dead to this world. In 1991 A.D.! Many people still believe that the dead retain a certain material form, that they even have hunger and thirst. The custom of bringing food to the grave and eating it there has survived from the very distant past because people still believe the dead will be strengthened and comforted by the sight of living people eating, Lieutenant."

Looking at her in bewilderment, he leaned up out of his seat and asked, "What does that have to do with this case?"

"The significance of this custom," she continued, ignoring his question, "implies that the feeding of the dead is done so that their hunger will be sated, so they won't come back from the grave and attack the living."

Vinda sat back in the chair. He had stumbled into strange territory that belonged to philosophers and theologians, not cops. Stick to the Patrol Guide, he admonished himself. Don't get tangled up in this religious gobbledygook. He looked at her and asked, "According to the lore, how does a person become a vampire?"

Nervously toying with her pack of cigarettes, she answered, "By being a victim of a vampire, by committing suicide, by having been excommunicated, or by being the illegitimate son of an illegitimate son."

Recalling Linda Camatro's brazen daylight murder, he asked, "Is it true that vampires can only come out at night?"

"That is a Hollywood idea. According to tradition, they can function any time, day or night, and they appear normal in all respects. The only restriction on their movements is that they may not leave their burial place on a Saturday."

"Why is that, Sister?"

"Because Saturday is sacred to the Mother of God. Saint Bernard tells us that the day after the death of her son, Mary remained constant in her faith."

Vinda looked at her with open skepticism. "The entire subject of vampires is steeped in religious mysticism."

"Yes, I suppose it is. C. S. Lewis wrote that all important truth comes to us through myth, not necessarily through scientific formulae and laws."

"I always thought God created us in His image and likeness."

"He did. He created the angelic and man, both good. They did evil because God gave them free will. Lucifer was an angel whose great crime was his desire to equal God. Perhaps your killer thinks he is like Lucifer?"

Vinda felt a mounting sense of frustration. He tried to get things back on the rails. "You said before that they appear normal in every respect. Is there any way to spot them?"

The nun said, with some reluctance, "The ancient Church believed they could be detected by their foul and fetid odor. But I'm not too sure about the probability of that."

Grasping at straws, Vinda asked, "Anything else?"

"Paranoids are extremely adept at drawing people into their delusional belief systems. They're the perfect confidence men; they fabricate a life in their own minds and can even make you a part of it. That's something you might look out for."

"Can you think of any reason why he would kill only young women?"

"According to the tradition—the myth, if you will—their blood is pure and strong, and it is the blood that sustains and nourishes the vampire, prolonging its existence of life-in-death."

Vinda slid a brown department envelope out of the inside breast pocket of his sport jacket, removed several small photographs, and handed them to her. "These are enlargements of the wounds on each of the victims. Look carefully at the marks to the right and a little below each wound."

He watched her scrutinize the first one. Her mouth fell open in shock; she looked up at the crucifix, and her lips moved in silent prayer. She stared at the cross for a long time, not saying anything.

"Those marks, what are they?"

She replied softly, "The impulse to bite under stress of strong sexual desire is a common act. With some vampires, the taking of prey is a sexual act. They kiss the throat first, as if engaging in foreplay, and then bite deep. Those marks are known as the vampire's kiss. I've never seen them, only read about them." She looked at two more of the photographs and shuddered.

Vinda was suddenly aware of the weight of the revolver on his hip and asked, "How is a vampire destroyed—according to the myth?"

She quickly took out and lit another cigarette. "Why do you want to know?"

"I have to know everything there is to know about this guy if I'm to stop him from killing again."

She took a deep breath, and said, "There are several ways. Cutting off its head, driving a stake through its breast, burning it and scattering its ashes to the wind, or transfixing its heart. But you must be careful to transfix it with a single blow, because two or more would restore it to life. Or so tradition says."

Vinda got up out of his chair and smiled at her. "Thank you. You've been a great help."

She walked with him to the door. "If you need me again, don't hesitate to come back and see me." She took hold of his wrist, stopping him. "You should know that as time passes he will become more audacious and bloodthirsty. I'll pray for you and your men. The importance of the myth is that the killer believes it. It's real for him—and he's making it real for the rest of the world."

T W E L V E

A WRAP PARTY FOR THE CAST AND CREW OF *LOVERS and Friends* was being held in Paula's, a Third Avenue restaurant favored by high rollers and showbiz types. Replica Tiffany lamps filled the ceiling in a rainbow of shimmering color that ran the length of the art deco bar and continued back into the restaurant, where a five-piece jazz band belted out "The Sugarman Blues."

A mixture of sawdust and mica flakes covered the bleached wooden floors; waiters pushed through the crowd, offering silver trays filled with assorted canapés. Three bartenders worked the bar.

Michael Worthington, who played a supporting role in the movie, was sitting comfortably on one of the banquettes in the bar, joking with the costume designer and the sound mixer. He looked at his watch: 9:26 P.M. The party had started at eight. The potbellied sound mixer looked at Worthington and asked, "Where the hell is Jessica?"

Worthington smoothed down his tie and smiled. "Jessica is being fashionably late, as usual."

The costume designer, a heavily made-up woman on the late side of forty, wearing a black jumpsuit with large silk lapels and opera-length pearls, sipped her drink and said, "The way the media is playing up her involvement in that dreadful murder, I wouldn't be a bit surprised if it didn't turn into a box-office bonanza for us."

Worthington turned, fixed the costume designer with his powerful stare, and said, "That's not very likely. We've just finished shooting. The movie won't be released for almost a year or more. The police will have solved it by then."

Sipping bourbon from a shot glass, the sound mixer said, "I wonder who dear Jessica is sleeping with these days?"

"I wouldn't know," Worthington said, selecting a stuffed shrimp from the tray presented by a waiter.

The costume designer lowered her gaze into her glass and said in an undertone, "I hear she's into girls, these days."

The sound mixer leaned closer to Worthington. "Did you see the body?"

Worthington was about to reply when he saw Jessica Merrill gliding into the crowd like royalty on a goodwill visit. She was wearing a floor-length sable coat over a stunningly simple white silk dress.

Worthington watched expressionlessly as she pulled off gauntlet gloves, slipped out of her coat, and dropped both casually on a banquette.

Worthington smiled and waved. He didn't bother to get up and offer her a kiss.

"Who are the grim types with her?" asked the costume designer in a whisper.

Worthington answered her in a normal tone of voice. "Detectives. The police department does not want anything to happen to our leading lady."

"Well, that makes good sense. I mean, just look at all the

publicity," the sound mixer said. "The script girl isn't here because she's afraid to leave her hotel room."

Merrill's arrival was the signal for the party to move into high gear.

Worthington moved gracefully through the densely crowded rooms, carefully taking time to talk, if only briefly, with everybody from the key grip to the gaffers. People in the business liked him because he didn't ignore the foot soldiers and just hang out with the brass. When he reached the end of the bar he walked over to Jessica and, caressing her face, whispered, "I'm glad you took my advice and got some rest. You look ten years younger than you did this afternoon." He walked off, leaving her smiling happily.

He had made his way into the restaurant when a slender hand clutched his shoulder, and a young woman kissed him on the cheek. "You were wonderful in the dailies, Michael."

Laura Steward was a bit player who was in only a few scenes and had precious few lines. Staring thirty in the face, tall, quite beautiful, and a skilled manipulator since childhood, she was the unlikely protégée of Jessica Merrill.

He had noticed her earlier, networking the crowd, attempting to turn acquaintances she had made during the filming into real friendships. "Hi," he said. "I saw all of the dailies, and I can tell you that the camera likes you. But *you're* afraid of it. You've got to learn to make love to it and ignore it at the same time."

"Any advice?" she asked respectfully.

Worthington gestured her to come close and whispered, "Try learning how to become another person. That's what acting comes down to."

Shortly before ten, one of the regulars came into an all-night delicatessen on Second Avenue. The counterman greeted him, "You're late tonight. How ya doing?"

"Good, Morris. And how are you?"

"How should I be? The lousy landlord just raised our rent. We need that like a *lokh in kup*. And how's the missus?"

"She's wonderful," he said, adding, "Tonight we'll have—"

"I know, I know," Morris Goldberg interrupted, waving his hands and smiling broadly. "You want the usual—two corned beefs on rye, one very, very lean, and two cream sodas, to go."

Morris's customer lived in a two-bedroom apartment on the seventh floor of his Tudor City co-op, an enclave of Tudor-style buildings hidden on an expensive promontory between First and Second avenues, overlooking the United Nations.

Going into the kitchen, he opened the refrigerator door and the light came on to reveal shelves filled with rows of brown bags identical to the one he was holding. Reaching inside, he pulled out the bag on the extreme right of the first rank, and carefully rearranged the other ranks until all the bags were in new positions. Stretching his arm inside, to the back of the first shelf, he inserted the new bag containing two corned beefs on rye and two cream sodas into its proper place in the last rank.

Pushing the door closed, he dropped the grease-stained bag containing two stale corned beefs on rye and two cream sodas into the plastic garbage can under the sink, and walked into his bedroom, where he undressed and meticulously put his clothes away.

Naked, he padded into the bathroom, where he showered and shaved. After toweling himself dry, he slathered on a heavy dose of after-shave and walked back into his bedroom, where he picked up the TV remote from the night table. He went to the window, and from there he flicked on the television. Looking out, he saw a reflection of the TV screen in the glass. The composite sketch was being shown on the news, while a voice-over told the viewers to call the confidential police telephone number at the bottom of the screen if they recognized the killer. He laughed and tossed the remote on his bed as he left the room.

He walked through the living room and entered a room done in pastel colors with a soft pink rug, Roman shades, and a double-wedding-ring quilt on the bed. In the middle of the room was a prie-dieu. Kneeling on it was a five-foot inflated doll dressed in a nun's habit. New York City has something for everyone, for every taste and the most desperate needs.

T H I R T E E N

THURSDAY DID NOT BEGIN WELL FOR VINDA. HE had been jolted awake during the night after dreaming of a coffin draped in a blanket of lilies—and Adriene Agueda, dressed in skimpy underwear, standing over the coffin, reading a eulogy. Why did I bring her into the case? he asked himself in his dream.

He tried to get back to sleep, but couldn't. When the alarm went off at eight, he slid out of bed, showered, and dressed.

Going into the kitchen to make himself a cup of instant coffee, he opened the refrigerator and saw the stack of throwaway aluminum containers stacked in the back of the box. They held food left over from Jean's mourning feast. Stuff must be really ripe by now, he thought. He cleaned all of the stuff out of the refrigerator and took it outside to the hallway incinerator, where he tossed all of it into the garbage chute in a plastic bag. Another gesture of letting go.

. . .

Arriving at the squad shortly before nine, he found Adriene Agueda and Joan Hagstrom sitting together behind one of the two desks that had been hastily ordered from the quartermaster. They were going through the case folder. Agueda looked up, smiled, and said, "Good morning, Lou."

"Welcome aboard," he said, going behind his desk and picking up the latest department orders. Vinda gave a smile of satisfaction when he read that Detective Stanley Gotlieb had been transferred from Manhattan's First Detective Squad to Brooklyn's Six-seven Detective Squad, otherwise known as the Land of Oz, Rastafarians, and homicides. Department justice, he mused, sure, swift, and arbitrary. The next time Gotlieb receives a tip on a homicide, he'll pass it up the chain of command. He had just finished reading the orders when Marsella and Moose arrived, carrying containers of coffee in soggy bags.

Marsella looked at the women and said, "Good morning, ladies." He slid out of his coat, tossed it on the rack, squeezed in behind the desk next to Hagstrom, and said, "Cramped quarters, hmm?" Resting his leg against hers, he asked, "Have you read the Fives?"

"Most of them," Hagstrom said, picking up her tea and discreetly eyeing her new partner over the rim of the container. Vinda made the introductions and picked up his copy of the case folder. He would let them discuss the case among themselves, allow the natural bonding process to work. He went down the list of names of the men who had been inside Rue St. Jacques when the first RMP arrived. A jackhammer digging up the street broke his concentration; he looked out the window at the upthrust skeleton of a building rising out of Park Row. It hadn't been there two days ago. He looked back at his team. Marsella was giving Hagstrom his undivided attention. She was just his type, too. Tall, with lustrous brown hair, eyebrows that formed perfect arches, and a great body. Sultry black eyes lurked inside a beautiful face.

Stepping over to Agueda, Vinda handed her a list of names and ordered her, "Do a background check on these men. After you do that, scoot over to CCRB and start checking out civilian complaints against cops." She took the list from him, and their eyes met briefly.

Vinda thought about Sister Mary Margaret's point about vampires not killing on Saturdays. The first homicide went down on a Monday, the second on a Tuesday, the third on a Sunday, and the fourth on Monday afternoon. He's skipped Saturday, Wednesday, Thursday, and Friday. So what did that mean? He threw his hands up in frustration. "I want you and Tony to start with the Department of Mental Health."

"What about checking out the Corporation Counsel for lawsuits against cops?" Moose asked, tugging his tie loose.

"Later, if we have to. When plaintiffs bring an action against the Job they almost always file a civilian complaint against the cops involved as a matter of course. Things might go faster if we start with CCRB and Mental Health," Vinda said.

"Makes sense," Marsella said, smiling at Hagstrom.

Vinda asked the two male detectives, "Have either of you gone back to interview our first victim's mother?"

"Haven't had time, Lou," Marsella replied.

"I'm going to Brooklyn to check out the two crime scenes," Vinda said. "I'll stop by her house and speak to her."

It was almost ten when the four detectives got up to leave the office. Agueda stopped at the door, looked back at the Whip, and asked, "Did you get the application I sent you in the department mail?"

"I keep telling you, I'm Portuguese, not Spanish."

She gave him a small smile but closed the door with a bit more force than was required. Watching her through the glass wall as she walked down the hall, he remembered how easily her body once moved under a clinging dress, and saw that she had put on a little weight since the old days. But it somehow looked good on her.

A few minutes later, Special Investigation's lead clerical walked in and tossed a report on Vinda's desk, saying, "Hot off the press, Lou. A new procedure for clearances."

Vinda picked up the report and saw that it was an amendment to the Administrative Guide adding another method of closing cases. The new subdivision, titled Exceptional Clearance, stated that a case might be closed when the identity and exact location of the offender were known, and there was enough information to support an arrest and prosecution, but for some reason beyond police control, the offender could not be arrested.

Vinda tossed the blue pages into the file basket, thinking of *his* killer, wondering when he would kill again.

Winds howled out of the north down Madison Avenue's canyons, sweeping up trash and whirling it along streets and gutters. A stylish older woman wearing a mink jacket had her skirt lifted up by a sharp, sudden gust. A taxi driver saw and shouted, "Yo, babe, great bod."

Vinda waited on the northwest corner of Madison and Fifty-third. His breath frosted the air as he stamped his feet against the biting cold and complained to himself, Another of the Job's paranoid orders: go, and do, and then forget what you didn't do. A hunched-over wagonmaster pushing his caravan of eight shopping carts caught his attention. Each of the carts was bound to the other by S-links, and each one brimmed with the homeless man's worldly possessions: scavenged deposit bottles, tattered clothes overflowing from tall bags, an aluminum folding chair, slabs of cardboard tied together. A rug rested across the tops of four carts, secured through the push-handles. Vinda glanced around him at the ski-slope sides of the Continental Illinois Center, intrigued at how the pleated glass sloped inward to form a rectangular prism. He looked back just in time to see the wagonmaster maneuvering his column of baskets into Fifty-fourth Street, and thought, The land of good and plenty—for some.

Vinda's eyes were heavy from lack of sleep, and as he watched the parade of beautiful women along Madison Avenue, he kept asking himself, Why Jean? Why? He checked the time: 11:37. His gaze moved across the street to the blue and white façade of the savings bank's twenty-four-hour banking center, and he thought, Here I am, wasting valuable time, digging through piles of horseshit looking for a horse.

A Rolls-Royce with darkened windows drew up in front of him, and a muscular bodyguard type emerged from the passenger seat. Mr. Biceps, who looked as though he existed on a diet of steroids, looked uncertainly at the Whip and asked, "Mr. Vinda?"

"Yes."

Biceps pulled open the back door, inviting him to enter. Vinda peered into the luxurious interior and saw a man sitting in the corner, staring out the window. He was dressed in an immaculately tailored gray suit, soft white shirt, and black tie. Deep acne scars blemished his face, and black half-moons accented his deepset eyes. He had thinning brown hair streaked with gray, and his high forehead had a bandage on it, glaring white against his tanned skin.

Vinda got in, and the door closed behind him with a thud. He found himself inside the surprisingly quiet interior, staring at the stranger huddled in the corner, ignoring him.

"You have a name, pal?" Vinda asked impatiently.

The stranger turned, scowling at Vinda. "Malcolm Webster is my name, Lieutenant."

Vinda's voice softened. "My condolences."

"Adelaide was my only child." He made a sigh that sounded more like a groan, and said, "I've been informed that you are in charge of the investigation."

"Yes," Vinda answered cautiously, wanting to hear what was coming next, watching the car slowly pull out into the traffic headed uptown.

Webster looked back out the window. "Do you know who murdered my daughter?"

"Not yet."

"Why was my daughter killed, Lieutenant?"

Leventhal had set up this meeting, so Vinda reckoned that whatever Leventhal knew, Webster now knew too. The best way to handle this uncomfortable situation was to placate and stall until this guy got to the bottom line, Vinda thought. He said, "We believe your daughter was the random victim of a serial killer."

Webster said nothing; he kept staring out the window, his face deliberately turned away.

Vinda had the strange sensation of riding through Manhattan's harsh, discordant noises in a soundproof compartment, and he thought of the homeless man struggling with his train of shopping carts through the heavy, dirty traffic toward his next oasis of garbage cans, where he would scavenge for his daily bread.

Webster turned to look at Vinda. "As soon as you know his name, I want you to tell me. And I want this done before any arrest is made."

"Knowing who it is and proving it are two different things, Mr. Webster."

"Proving? You don't have to prove anything, Lieutenant. The man who murdered my daughter is not going to get off with any insanity plea."

You get enough money and power, Vinda thought, and you think you're God. "I have to operate within the framework of the law, Mr. Webster. It's not a cop's function to determine guilt, innocence, or degree of culpability."

Webster gave him a hard look. "*I'll* determine culpability and degree of diminished capacity; you just provide me with his name."

"Can't do that."

Webster's eyes widened in anger. "Can't?"

"You got that right."

"Do you know what it took for me to get you here this morning?"

"Probably a telephone call."

"And what does that tell you?"

"That you know what buttons to push."

Webster relaxed back against the soft leather seat, his eyes fixed upward. "I won't bore you with threats about what I could or could not do to affect your career . . ."

Vinda thrust out a silencing palm. "I've been dealing with men like you ever since I came on the Job. You believe you're a law unto yourself, but I'm here to tell you, you're not. I know from bitter experience that when the brown stuff hits the fan, your kind runs for the foxholes, leaving the guys on the bottom of the heap to take the fall."

"Your cynicism is refreshing, Lieutenant. But I wonder how *you* would feel if it was your Jean who was murdered in Sutton Place Park instead of my daughter?"

Vinda tried to keep the surprise from showing on his face. "I'd probably feel the same way you do," he answered, wondering what else Webster knew about his private life.

"I'm sure you would." A consoling tone crept into his voice when he added, "I'm sorry about your wife."

Vinda nodded in acknowledgment and rapped on the partition between the front and back seats, motioning the chauffeur to pull over to the curb. The bodyguard looked up into the rearview mirror, trying to catch Webster's eye. Webster nodded his assent, the bodyguard said something to the driver, and the limousine glided to the curb. Vinda pushed open the door; city sounds and cold rushed into the warmth.

Webster's voice halted Vinda. "During your time in the department, haven't you ever bent rules?"

Vinda smiled. "Good-bye, Mr. Webster."

Sunbeams speared through the clerestory windows, illuminating the central portion of Saint George's Church with bright sunlight. Inside the church, a scattering of people praying and meditating knelt in the pews, their eyes fixed on the altar's golden tabernacle.

A passerby, his tan cashmere overcoat draped over his shoulders, stood at the bottom of the wide steps, looking up at the church's spires towering over the new nineplex movie theater at First Avenue and Thirty-second Street. His gaze fell to the massive bronze doors that depicted Christ in His Majesty and Abraham leaving the sepulcher. He put his foot up on the first step and then withdrew it. Clutching both lapels, he debated with himself whether or not to enter the Eternal One's house. Perhaps He would give him a sign, perhaps He would listen to his pleas. He sucked in a mouthful of air and went quickly up the steps.

Entering the marble vestibule, he looked down at the bénitier and, without realizing what he was doing, plunged his hand into the holy water. A soothing sensation flowed into his fingers and up his arms, engulfing his body in a sea of tranquillity. Pulling his hand out of the sacramental liquid, he held his dripping fingers up and shook drops of water off of them. Going inside, he slid into the last pew without genuflecting. The bench extended under one of the ambulatory's arches, and was bathed in shadows. Sitting alone in the darkness, he sat perfectly still, hidden from the world and filled with rage at the injustices he had suffered. Why have You forsaken me? I've done everything You have told me to do. What more do You want of me? Tell me. I beg You, don't allow them to take Valarie away from me. Please, not again.

He sat for a long time staring out at the altar, aware of the pain gnawing at his stomach. An aching cold had invaded his body, numbing his bones; he pulled his coat tight across his chest. Give me some sign, he prayed, close to despair.

Movement off to his right made him turn. Three Sisters of Saint Joseph were walking down the aisle. The one in front was young and very beautiful. The watcher's mouth fell open, and his eyes grew wide in astonished recognition. It was his Valarie. Rising up out of his seat, he watched as she genuflected at the foot of the altar, pushed open the brass gate, and walked up the carpeted steps toward the altar. The Eternal One had sent him His message. He had commanded him to send Him more nuns to replace Valarie. Not one at a time, but several at once. That way their Trinity would grow strong, bonding the three of them together, forever.

Morty Hymowitz, professionally known as Marshall Hawthorn, for some curious reason liked his friends to call him Vinny. He favored beautifully cut Italian clothes and Gucci accessories. He stood a bit over six feet, loved to dance, and had sharp features that many women called handsome. A slight feral aspect to his face had been remarked on by those who disliked him.

Vinny was a theatrical agent who relished being seen at his favorite table in the Four Seasons Grill Room, sipping white wine. He enjoyed watching all the important people making their lunchtime deals. Being there, he felt that he was a player, the head gonif in the Land of Gonifs, and not that poor lanky kid from Eastern Parkway who the big kids used to call the skinny asshole.

Vinny was toying with his wineglass, waiting for his guest to arrive. He usually enjoyed this lunchtime game-playing, but not today. Today he had to deal with his most pain-in-the-ass client, Michael Worthington. Whenever Vinny would suggest that this or that was the way to go on a deal, Worthington would balk, and want to do the opposite. Vinny could never figure out whether he did it because he got off on being a contrary son of a bitch or because he was one of those guys walking around with a constant committee meeting going on in his head.

Then he saw Worthington coming over to the table with a very unpleasant expression on his face. Glancing disdainfully around the room as he sat down, Worthington said, "You know I don't do lunch, so why the it's-important-we-meet phone call?"

"Two days ago I expressed you the screenplay of *Reckless Disregard*. Did you read it?"

"Yes. It's violent, moronic junk."

Vinny hid his dismay and anger behind a false smile. Ignoring his client's reply, he continued as if he hadn't heard Worthington. "Paul Hiller called me from the Coast this morning. He's packaging the movie, and he wants you for the male lead."

"I just got done telling you, the screenplay is crap."

"Michael, I've spoken to at least a dozen other people who've read it, and you're the only one who doesn't think it's great."

"So sue me."

"This movie could make the difference to your career. It's the lead, Michael. Jeff Wilder is directing, Lawrence Hill did the screenplay, and your friend Jessica Merrill has already agreed to do the female lead. These are all top people. I'm telling you, Michael, this project has real money written all over it."

"I'm not interested. And stop bullshitting me. Jessica told me she gave you a 'maybe' on this one, not a 'yes.' "

The bastard's tormenting me on purpose, Vinny thought. He mustered every ounce of courage he could, and said, "I've worked hard for you, Michael. When you first came to me years ago, you were broke, and didn't have a decent screen credit to your name. I've developed you into one of the industry's leading supporting actors." Vinny leaned across the table; his patience had run out. "Christsake, we're talking about the lead opposite Jessica Merrill. A chance like this comes along but once, if you're lucky."

Worthington let his wrist hang limp over the edge of the table. "Where is it going to be filmed?"

"Here in Manhattan."

Vinny noted, with dawning hope, that Worthington suddenly seemed less negative.

"What kind of a deal did Hiller offer?"

Vinny brightened. "Five hundred thousand, five hundred per diem, and, more important, equal billing."

"What about a piece?"

"Negotiable. I can probably get you two points of the net."

Worthington picked up his butter knife and began restlessly scraping the blade over the tablecloth. "I'm surprised Jessica has agreed to do another film so soon after the last one."

"Jessica wants to stay on top, and she knows the best way to do that is to continue to make good movies."

Worthington scanned the elegantly spacious dining room, enjoying Vinny's discomfort. Finally, without looking at his agent, he said, "I'll think about it."

Vinny's shoulders gave a slight sag of relief. "What about you and your wife having dinner with me and my lady friend one night this week? I've never met her."

"I've told you many times, I keep my family life and my professional life separate. I don't want my wife getting involved in this lunatic business. We keep our social life private." He picked up a menu and began to study it.

You scumbag, Vinny thought. So I'm not good enough for you socially. I just keep the money rolling in. Well, pal, what you don't know is that I'm going to make more money out of *Reckless Disregard* than you are. And it *is* a piece of shit!

On Forty-seventh Street, just west of First Avenue, there is a warren of small street-level stores that are difficult to rent because of their size. Three years ago, Worthington had rented one to use as his own personal exercise room and rehearsal hall. All the walls were mirrored, and the floor shone with polyurethane varnish. Banks of white fluorescent light fixtures hung down from the ceiling. The only furniture in the store was a complete set of home Nautilus exercise machines, a bridge table with a television on top of it, and a folding chair in front of the television.

Worthington had completed most of the Nautilus circuit and was working on the abdominal machine. He was wearing only shorts, and his body glistened with sweat. His flat stomach showed the strain of the workout. While he went on with his exercise program, he grinned at the irony of his agent's desperation. Taking the role in *Reckless Disregard* would suit him perfectly. It *was* junk, but it would keep him in New York, freeing him to implement a plan that, had Vinny known about it, would have turned Vinny's delicious lunch into ashes in his mouth.

F O U R T E E N

THE OBELISK-SHAPED CLOCK TOWER OF THE
Williamsburg Savings Bank had long been a
Brooklyn landmark, its towering dome, holding the tallest four-faced clock in the world, a
beacon of a glorious past.

Vinda parked the department car on Hanson Place. It was
bitterly cold outside; the car was filled with warmth and the
windows fogged over. He got out and looked across the street at
the Long Island Railroad's Atlantic Avenue station. Walking to
the corner, he saw that Bickford's Restaurant and the adjoining
Oyster Bar had been turned into cinderblock tombs. He grimaced in sadness and walked away from the corner, heading for
the first homicide victim's residence on South Elliott Place. He
had just come from visiting the Lucas and Johnston crime scenes;
both victims had been murdered near their homes. He wondered if the place of occurrence was significant. It was a little

before four o'clock, and a sullen winter twilight was gathering on the horizon. He ruminated about his earlier meeting with Malcolm Webster; since that morning he had been suppressing the urge to telephone Sam Staypress and voice his indignation over being set up. He knew better than to do that; the chief of detectives would deny ever having heard of Webster. Vinda would only get angrier and angrier, and might say something stupid to his boss. Hurrying along, he saw that the wholesale meat market on Sixth Avenue was closed for the day. The butchers began their day at two in the morning and ended it around 9:00 A.M. Empty trucks were parked parallel to the curb, and most of the premises were shuttered behind steel accordion doors. Scurrying cats scavenged scraps of offal. Other creatures lurked inside of doorways, behind trucks—two-legged creatures prepared to rob, mug, and rape. As Vinda neared South Elliott Place, his cop instincts alerted him to danger. He reached inside his coat, slid out his .38 Colt detective special revolver, and thrust it into his overcoat pocket.

"Yo, mah man," someone called out to him.

Vinda continued walking fast, his hand tightening around the checkered grips of his gun. He heard movement behind him and spun around. There were two of them, one tall and white, the other short and black, both wearing the junkie's uniform of the day: dirty, torn jeans, old worn sneakers, T-shirt under olive-drab field jacket. The taller one had on a Yankee baseball cap, its bill turned sideways. Their faces had long ago become masks of despair, with glazed, sunken eyes. The white guy was twitching and shivering, holding a filthy rag to his running nose. Vinda thought wearily, Here come the fun-time twins, Lamont Scumbag and Danny Dickbrain.

"Yo, mah man, got a match?" the taller one called.

"Yo, Lamont, you got any hope of recovering from your wounds?" Vinda shot back.

The shorter of the two began shuffling and twisting in a dance of arrogance. "You t'ink you bees a bad motherfucker. Bro, I ain't ehfreid of jou."

"Wha' motherfuckin' wounds?" the taller one asked, approaching warily.

"The ones I be puttin' in you with this," Vinda announced, aiming his revolver at the tall one's face.

" 'eeeeeeet, man, we only be wantin' a match," the taller one said, turning and swaggering off. His partner glared at Vinda, spat on the ground, and then followed him.

Vinda watched their backs until they disappeared around a corner.

South Elliott Place was a block of row houses waging a winning war against the pestilence of decay and drugs. The Lucas home was halfway down the street and had small planters of hardy ivy decorating both sides of the steps. Two signs were attached to a pole sunk into the well-tended plot of yellowish green grass. One said KEEP OUR COMMUNITY CLEAN, the other, JUNKIES NEED NOT APPLY.

A tall, attractive black woman in her mid-thirties peered out from behind the door curtains. Her pleated white skirt and tan sweater were set off by a long strand of black pearls. "Lieutenant Vinda?"

"Yes," he said, producing his shield.

She opened the door and stepped aside. "I'm Vanessa Brown, Mary Lucas's sister."

He took off his coat and placed it in her waiting hand. She hung it on the wall rack just inside the vestibule and said, "Lieutenant, my mother is not well. My sister's death has devastated her. I really don't see why it is necessary for you to interview her."

"Mrs. Brown, your mother might possess some scrap of information that could set us on the right course. It's important, or I wouldn't be here."

She sighed in mild annoyance and led him through a large living room with chintz-covered furniture and a floral carpet, and into the side parlor that served as a den and television room. An old woman dressed in mourning black sat slumped in a heavy armchair with doilies on both the arms. Her deeply wrinkled face still bore traces of her youthful beauty. Vanessa Brown introduced the policeman to her mother and went and stood behind her, protective hands planted firmly on her mother's shoulders. The old lady sat staring off into her own sorrowful void, her fingers moving rapidly over a rosary. Her dazed eyes looked up at the policeman and she said in a quavering voice, "Mary was a good girl."

"Yes, I know," he answered in a sympathetic voice.

"Mary was a good girl," she repeated. "Everyone liked my Mary." Her fingers gripped the beads. "My Mary was a good girl."

"Is this really necessary?" Vanessa Brown pleaded.

He looked at the grief-stricken women and thought, Enough is enough! "Thank you," he said softly, and walked out of the room.

Back in the living room, he noticed the pictures on the baby grand piano next to the window. One of them drew him over. "Our family," Vanessa said, coming over and standing next to him.

One of the pictures in front was of a policeman standing beside an old-style RMP sedan. The green-and-blues had been off patrol since the seventies, and the green metal box visible under the rear window, which contained the RMP's rifles, had been taken out of radio cars in the early fifties. The husky patrolman wore the old-type cartridge bandolier around his gunbelt. "Our dad," she said. "He was the first black policeman ever assigned to the Sixty-first Precinct."

"I didn't know your dad was on the Job," he said, giving the photograph his full attention while he recalled the old-style sedans with the radios that never seemed to be able to receive ungarbled transmissions. The department had come a long way since the first radio-equipped car cruised the city in 1917. "What year was this taken?"

"I'm not sure. Dad was appointed in 1946, and put in thirty-five years before he retired. We lost him five years ago in a freak accident." She looked at him with new intensity. "The media is full of Jessica Merrill, and the murders on Sutton Place and in Rue St. Jacques, but not one mention is made of my sister. Don't black women count, Lieutenant?"

People moved back and forth in Corregidor's tunnels; middle-aged men gathered around the bar, talking in muted tones while their suspicious eyes watched the crowd. A cloud of cigarette smoke hung over the bar, its plumes separating and floating upward, disappearing into vents in the carved hardwood canopy.

Marsella and Moose Ryan had arrived a little before six, and had appropriated one of the scarce alcove tables. They were going over their notes, sipping drinks, and digging chunks of cheddar from the tub, when the rest of the team arrived. Getting halfway up from his seat, Marsella waved to them. Vinda nodded. Moving toward the alcove, Vinda scanned the bar and spotted Agent Orange and his coterie huddled at the end. Vinda and the chief of patrol exchanged blank stares.

"Anything?" Vinda asked, walking into the alcove and pulling a chair back from the table.

"Lou, we spent the day at the Department of Mental Health. The sick ones are in hospitals, and the ones that aren't so sick are in group houses or some sort of work program," Marsella said.

"We spoke with one of the shrinks, and he told us that there is no real way of telling which sicko is our sicko," Moose said, pulling a folded page from his jacket. "Here are forty possibilities who might fit the bill. You can see from their diagnoses that they all have direct lines to J.C."

Vinda unfolded the sheet and studied the list. "Lou, checking out all those names is gonna mean that we need more people to help us. The four of us can't do it all," Marsella said.

"Remember the pipe bomber? It took almost fifteen years to nail him by checking records," Agueda chimed in.

"We'll do what we have to do, but we're going to get this guy," Vinda said. "So we just keep punching."

Marsella signaled the waiter for a round of drinks. A flurry of

activity made them look toward the entrance, where they saw
the chief of detectives arriving with his retinue. Leventhal
peeled away from the others and came over to Vinda. "May I see
you a minute, John?"

Vinda got up and walked outside the alcove. The C-of-D
assumed the position, hand partly across his mouth, and confided, "Pollack and his editor know about the similarities of the
wounds in the Webster and Camatro homicides."

"How?"

"It doesn't matter how. The point is that they know. The up
side is that David Pollack has convinced his editor that revealing
that information could jeopardize our investigation, and his editor agreed to sit on it for a while."

"Looks like I owe David one."

"Perhaps you should let him win at backgammon once."

"There are limits, Chief."

"I find it strange that they didn't connect the Lucas and
Johnston homicides," Leventhal said thoughtfully.

Vinda looked down the bar and directed a nasty look at Agent
Orange. "Their stool didn't know about the other two."

Leventhal gave Vinda a cynical smile. "That prick." He carefully adjusted his tie, tugged down his suit jacket, and said,
"I've got an appointment." He moved off into the tunnel that
fed into the main dining room. Vinda watched him heading
toward the detectives waiting for him, and then noticed an attractive female detective standing in the middle of the group.
She was giving the chief of detectives a warm smile.

While Vinda was outside the alcove, Marsella leaned close to
Hagstrom and whispered, "How'd you like to have dinner
later?"

Brushing her hair off her shoulders, she lowered her eyes and
whispered, "Why, sir, you're a married man."

"I don't park my car in that garage anymore."

"Where have I ever heard that song before?"

"Are we having fun yet?" a familiar voice asked Vinda from
behind.

Vinda turned and was taken aback by the blazing chartreuse in Pollack's oversized bow tie. "David? Where do you get the nerve to wear those ties?"

"When you're secure with yourself, my policeman friend, you can wear whatever you're comfortable with."

Brushing an imaginary hair off the reporter's blue pea coat, Vinda said, "I owe you one."

The reporter shrugged indifference and, jerking a thumb at the bar, asked, "Listen, and tell me what you hear."

Vinda's ears pricked. Ice tinkled above the swirl of hushed conversations. "Ice."

"Ice," Pollack echoed. "Do you realize that this is the only bar in town where the ice cubes make more noise than the customers? And do you further realize that any one of those whispering paranoids at the bar could be your killer?"

"Cops are xenophobic, David, they're not killers."

A waiter darted past them, balancing a tray of empty glasses. "Have you come up with anything in your newspaper's files?"

"Not yet. I've gone back four years and come up dry. I'll keep trying."

"Thanks," Vinda said, and walked off into the bathroom. Standing at the urinal, he became aware of a hurried movement beside him, and looked to see the chief of patrol staring down into the urinal.

"I hear there has been a leak to the press," the C-of-P muttered.

Stiffly courteous, Vinda zippered up and said, " 'At's funny, I haven't heard a thing." He turned and left the room.

Returning to the alcove, Vinda found the team exchanging ideas about the case. He noticed that someone had placed a glass on top of the page containing the list of forty names. He removed it, noticing the brown ring the glass had made on the paper. Absentmindedly he took out his pen and wrote on the fold, "Blood and murder weapon?"

Moose looked at the writing and asked, "You think that's the way we should go, Lou?"

"I think we have to figure out how this guy does his number without leaving a blood trail. There is just no way he can kill like that and not be steeped in blood," Vinda said.

The detectives retreated into their own thoughts.

"A condom," Agueda offered.

"A what?" Marsella asked.

"You know," Hagstrom said, "one of those rubbery things that men slide on their thing before they do it. But a big one—a body condom. He puts it on before he does his thing, and takes it off when he's finished."

"And what about in a public place like Rue St. Jacques?" Moose asked.

Digging a chunk of cheese out of the tub, Vinda said, "He ducks in someplace, slips it on, does his number, takes it off, and stashes it in a bag or briefcase."

"Sort of a wetsuit," Marsella said, rubbing his chin. "I got a detective friend of mine in Hawaii who could solve this caper for us."

"Yeah, I know," Vinda said. "He wears a white hat and has a thin, drooping mustache, and his name is Charlie."

"Charlie Chan, how'd you know that?" Marsella said.

"I'm the Whip, I'm supposed to know those things," Vinda said, getting up. "It's late. I'll see you in the ayem."

Twenty-three minutes after Vinda had left Corregidor, a bedroom telephone rang inside a brick ranch-type home in Plainview, New York. Wendy Marsella's bare arm stretched across the bed, and pulled the receiver to her ear.

"Hi, honey, how are you and the kids?" Tony Marsella asked his wife.

She sat up in bed, keeping the phone close to her mouth. "Where are you, Tony, at the station?"

"I'm still at work, honey. How's everything?"

"Fine. The children are both at sleep-overs."

"During the week? What about school and homework?"

"They're doing their homework at their friends'."

"Honey, Frank, my fireman friend, is having a poker game at his house tonight. Would you mind if I sat in for a few hands?"

"Of course not, honey, you need a little relaxation."

"If it gets too late, I might sack out in the office."

"Just let me know either way so I don't worry."

"I will. Love you."

"Me too."

As she slipped the phone into its cradle, a hand came out from under the blanket and caressed her naked back. "What did he say?"

"He's playing cards at your house."

F I F T E E N

N HER RENT-CONTROLLED APARTMENT ON BE-
thune Street in Greenwich Village, Adriene
Agueda lay in bed dressed in underpants and a
white terrycloth robe. She was half-watching a
late-night movie, half-listening to the Cajun music filtering down
from the apartment upstairs, snacking on the contents of a box of
puffed rice, and going over the details of the case. The more she
thought about it, the more convinced she was that the perp was
wearing some kind of a body condom in order not to leave a
blood trail when he fled the scenes.

She propped her head higher on the pillow and looked over at
the photograph of Vinda atop the oak dresser. He was dressed in
faded jeans and a yellow shirt; his black forelock hung carelessly
over his forehead, and he was sporting that devilish grin that had
made her fall in love with him long ago. She had taken the
picture during one of their many Central Park picnics. She be-

came increasingly conscious of her body, and pressed her legs together and sighed, remembering the incredible sensations she had experienced every time they made love. She rubbed her eyes hard, as if trying to blot out the painful memory of him telling her it was over. "Adriene, I've met someone," he had begun, avoiding her eyes. Just like him to be painfully honest. Why couldn't he have lied? Why couldn't he have loved me as much as I loved him? I'm tired of listening to myself list all the "why couldn'ts," she thought, and smiled sadly.

She got out of bed and snapped off the television, then slipped off her robe, tossed it across the bed, and crawled under the blanket, accompanied by the jamboree music of "Tipitina." She raised her head up off the pillow for one last look at him, switched off the light, and went to sleep, trying hard not to think about Vinda.

The distinctive silhouette of the United Nations Secretariat Building stood out against the night sky.

Worthington was standing in his bedroom, looking out across the river at the lights of Queens. He was barefoot, dressed in a long black silk robe that had scrolled piping on the cuffs. I need inspiration, he thought, watching the blinking running lights of a helicopter over the river. Walking away from the window, he went to the living room, where he took Valarie's dry cleaning off a chair, scooped up the bag of personal hygiene articles he had purchased in the supermarket, and walked into his wife's bedroom. He switched on the lights and moved to the wall closet. Sliding one side of the double doors open, he pushed clothes aside and hung up the dry cleaning. He slid that side of the closet closed, and pushed open the other. Seven shelves rose vertically from the carpeted floor, and were crammed with neatly stacked feminine hygiene articles and cosmetics. Taking the new items out of the shopping bag, he put each one on top neatly in the appropriate place.

Sliding the door closed, he turned to see Valarie kneeling on her prie-dieu. He liked how her black habit flowed gently over her body, concealing her from the rest of the world.

As he wandered through the apartment, he was thinking about alternative ways to carry out his mission. This time he was going to send Him a worthy offering.

Walking over to the console table in the foyer, he looked down at the week's worth of unopened mail. Idly going through the pile, he came across an orange flyer bordered in black. He pulled it out and read that The Women's Register was holding a rally next Monday night to protest the discriminatory pricing policies of the pharmaceutical industry. May Gold would be introducing the guest speaker, Dr. Florence Myers, former CEO of Bristol Cosmetics. He reread the flyer, amazed that his prayers had been answered so quickly. But sooner or later, they were always answered.

A little after two that morning, a taxi stopped at Roosevelt Avenue and Sixty-fourth Street in Woodside, Queens. Worthington paid the driver and got out. His greatcoat reached down to his cowboy boots, and his brown corduroy trousers were cuffed. A silk scarf was jauntily wrapped around his neck, and a white Cordoban hat sat on his head. He was carrying a stout oak walking stick.

Strolling toward Sixty-second Street, his nose wrinkled at an appalling stench of urine as he passed a man sleeping inside his cardboard-box hovel in the doorway of a cinderblocked store. Reaching into his pocket, taking out a wad of money, he peeled off a single fifty-dollar bill and tucked it into the sleeping man's hand. "Things'll get better, ol' friend."

Fitzgerald's, a dingy and cheerless bar, was on the west side of Sixty-second, about forty feet in from Roosevelt Avenue. As you entered, the bar was on the right, running about twenty feet toward double doors that led into a kitchen. To the left was an elevated area with tables and chairs. In the rear, two doors opened into filthy toilets. Five men and one woman sat at the bar, most drinking shots and beers, the way serious career drinkers take their booze.

Worthington threw open the door and walked inside like he owned the place. What little conversation there had been stopped as he came in. He gallantly tipped his hat to a woman half-falling off her barstool. Reaching the end of the bar, he smashed his stick across it and roared, "Innkeeper, drinks for my friends."

Stonefaced, the bartender, a wiry little man with a great mole on the side of his nose, came over and said coldly, "They only drink with friends." His brogue had all the warmth and welcome of Catholic Belfast for English troops.

"Aye, if assholes could fly, this place would surely be an airport," the actor lamented, smiling and quickly adding in a light brogue, "They're me misguided friends. Give 'em all a drink on Dinny'O." Leaning over the bar, he pointed his walking stick at another man behind the bar who was bending over, scooping up garbage, and dumping it into a can. "And give himself a drink, too," Worthington ordered.

The other man had massive shoulders and iron gray hair cut close to his scalp. His dungarees had slipped down, revealing the elastic band of his grimy underwear and the upper crack of his ass.

"Hello, Otto," Worthington called to him. He strolled over to the elevated part of the bar, where he removed his coat and hat, carefully put them across a table, and sat down.

Ignoring the newcomer, the man called Otto pushed the garbage can up against the wall. Then he crossed to the upraised area, pulled back a chair, and sat facing Worthington.

A somber expression came over Worthington's face as he looked at Otto and said, "Aye, 'tis a sad day when the likes of you is relegated to sweeping floors."

The bartender came over. Worthington ordered: "A bottle of Dom Perignon '85."

Otto said flatly, "Two beers."

As the barman walked off, Otto looked expressionlessly at the newcomer. "Who the fuck are you?"

"It saddens me to think that you don't remember your old boyhood friend from the Cincinnati School, the same feller who used to stunt with you in the movies."

Slowly, Otto's expression showed some faint cheerfulness. He asked in an unsure tone, "Is it really you?"

"Aye, Otto, it's really me."

"But your face, it's all changed. You look completely different. But not your voice. It's the same."

"We can talk about that later. Tell me, ol' friend, you still in the same business?"

The barman came over, set down two beers, and left. Otto picked up his mug, drank, wiped froth from his lips with the back of his hand, and said, "I might be. Why?"

"Friends in Miami sent me a shopping list."

"What are they looking for?"

"Something that will convey a proper message."

Otto drank. "A proper message, is it? And to whom are these friends of yours planning on sending these tidings?"

"I don't think you want to know that, my friend."

"I suppose you're right," Otto said, drinking more beer and adding, "I can let you have some M-545s, fragmentation and frag-incendiaries. I also have two hundred and seventeen impact frags with time-delay fuses."

"Nothing more . . . imaginative?"

"Ednons with electronic delay fuses."

"Claymores?" Worthington asked, as he raised his mug to his mouth.

"Maybe. But they're very hard to get."

"Plastique?"

"Semtex in bars."

Worthington said, "Dinny'O has a long shopping list for his old comrade."

.   .   .

Vinda walked along Centre Street, past the old headquarters building, looking up with fond remembrance at the Romanesque dome, and shaking his head with dismay when he saw the LUX-URY CONDOMINIUMS FOR SALE sign attached to the façade. Walking on, he glanced in at a store's display windows, noticing the new lathes and drill presses that were sold in this part of town.

Morning traffic had gridlocked Spring Street, resulting in the strident blasts of clamorous horns.

Nearing Kenmare Street, he ducked into a doorway and climbed the rickety staircase to the first floor, where the peeling inscription on the door read, SOL WEINTRAUB, INDUSTRIAL CLOTH-ING.

A waist-high counter ran from wall to wall, and beyond, rows of metal racks containing bins filled with plastic-wrapped uniforms covered the worn wooden floors. To the right, past the counter, was a rolltop desk, its pigeonholes stuffed with invoices. Sitting there with his feet up on the pull-out board was a man of sixty or so with a mane of white hair, tapping a pencil as he diligently went about digesting the daily *Racing Form*.

Sol Weintraub was a retired bookmaker who had gotten himself swept up in the Knapp Commission investigation into police corruption in the early seventies and had done a year inside for contempt of court for refusing to testify against accused policemen. Upon his release from prison, he'd gone into the industrial uniform business. Because of his deep blue eyes, Sol had long ago been dubbed Solly Blue Eyes.

"Morning, Solly," Vinda said, lifting up the counter and walking inside.

A grin of recognition spread across Solly Blue Eyes' face when he swung his feet to the floor and saw Vinda. "Long time no see, John. I heard they banished you to no-cop land."

"I got time off for good behavior," Vinda said, nodding at the *Racing Form* and adding, "I see you're still at it."

"Yeah," he said sheepishly, "I'm still looking for that one big score that's gonna make me even. You always figure the next

race, but it never comes." He shrugged, asked, "What brings
you here?"

"Industrial uniforms. Is there such a thing as a body condom?
Something strong and pliable that can be gotten on and off fast
and folded so that it would fit inside a briefcase or a knapsack?"

"What you're looking for is called a 'clean suit.' It's made of
Saronex and is so tightly woven that it's impervious to dust and
solvents. They're used in sterile work environments. Pharmaceutical houses, microchip manufacturers."

"Would they be waterproof?"

"Of course, nothing can penetrate them. Water would just roll
off."

So would blood, Vinda thought, asking, "Do you sell them?"

Solly Blue Eyes went off down the aisle and reached up into
a bin. He pulled down a wrapped clean suit, came over to Vinda,
and tossed it to him.

Vinda pulled it out of its plastic, and shook it out of its folds.
There was a white overjacket and pants, and also a hood with a
glass face plate and a white cape that went over the shoulders.
The glass face plate had breathing holes. There were also orange
neoprene gloves that taped at the wrist with silver duct tape, and
overboots of the same material that sealed at the knees with duct
tape.

Vinda put the suit on over his clothes. Walking about, swinging his arms and kicking out his legs, he tested the suit's pli-
ability. He had the sensation of being inside a space suit. The
perp wouldn't have to wear the entire suit, he reasoned; all he
would need was a covering to take that first gush of blood. He
could then turn his victim away so that the spurting blood would
not get all over him. Working his way over to Solly Blue Eyes,
Vinda asked, "Do they come with mouth openings?"

"That would defeat their purpose. You'd have snot, spit, nose
hair, saliva, and all sorts of germs falling all over the place, and
that'd be the end of your sterile environment."

Vinda undid the suit and stepped out of it. Holding it up by
its shoulders, he examined it thoroughly.

"Whaddaya looking for?"

"I'm looking to see if you could make a mouth cutout in the face plate."

"Of course you could. But you can remove the glass entirely."

Vinda brought the suit over to the counter and spread it out. He began refolding it along its crease lines. It folded into a box configuration about fifteen inches by seven inches. He pressed down on it, forcing out the air and flattening the suit. The perp could wear the top part of this outfit to keep the blood off himself, he thought, and it would be a simple matter to roll it up after he was done and conceal it under a coat or a jacket. But what if it was dripping blood? He certainly wouldn't put it on his own person; he'd stash it someplace quickly, and he wouldn't take time to fold it. The witness to the Sutton Place homicide had stated she'd seen him wearing a knapsack.

"Wanna take it with you?" Solly Blue Eyes asked.

Lost in thought, Vinda did not hear the question. He continued staring down at the suit. Happenstance, he repeated over and over to himself. A vague uneasiness began to mount inside his stomach, and he thought, Catching this guy is going to be like grabbing smoke.

"You hearing me, John? You want the suit or not?"

Vinda schooled a smile onto his face and said, "Yeah, Solly, I want the suit."

Vinda's mind had been racing down new paths as he headed downtown. He stopped for the traffic tie-up at Bowery and Grand and casually looked up into the rearview mirror at the traffic jumble behind him. He didn't spot them at first, but when he saw the familiar face scrunching down in the passenger seat of the black Camaro, he tensed. Keeping his eyes on the car, he slid out his revolver and put it on the seat next to him.

The driver of the Camaro was a pug-nosed man somewhere in his late forties. Vinda didn't recognize him. But the man sinking down in the passenger seat was definitely Mr. Biceps, Malcolm Webster's bodyguard. Why are they on me? he asked himself, immediately thinking up applicable violations of law to use against them, starting with harassment as a misdemeanor and inflating it up to felonious assholery.

The bottleneck broke; traffic spewed out. The Camaro stayed behind him. He made a right turn into Canal Street, and found himself fighting the traffic creeping into the Holland Tunnel. If Mr. Biceps was part of Webster's security staff, he'd more than likely be armed, ditto Pug-nose. An idea brought a flush of excitement to his face. So they wanna play, do they? he thought, snatching the handset from under the dashboard. Holding it chest-high so they could not see what he was doing, he pressed the transmit button and radioed, "Special One to Central, K."

"Go SP-One."

"This unit has uninvited guest, K."

"Your location, SP-One?"

"Heading west on Canal toward the tunnel, just passing Sullivan Street."

"Can you ID guests, SP-One?"

Vinda gave descriptions of his shadows and their car, advising Central of the identity of Mr. Biceps.

"Do you want backup, SP-One?"

"Negative that, Central. Notify New Jersey state police to Eighty-five this unit the other side of tunnel."

"Ten-four, SP-One."

A crescent of sunlight signaled the end of the underwater highway. As he came out of the tunnel, he noticed the revolving turret lights of two New Jersey state police cars flashing yellowish beacons over the highway. The cars were parked alongside a green garbage dumpster.

Vinda reached under his seat and took out the portable turret light. Opening the window, he slapped it onto the roof, and waved to the two state troopers waiting inside their patrol cars.

The Camaro drove out of the tunnel. Vinda stuck his hand out of the car window and pointed to it, at the same time nodding to the two troopers.

The troopers acknowledged, and wedged their cars into the traffic flow, intercepting the Camaro, boxing it front and back. The loudspeaker of one of the police vehicles blared, "Keep your windows closed and follow us."

The Camaro was convoyed through the traffic over to the dumpster. The troopers got out of their vehicles. Both young, well-built men, they took their time strutting over to the Camaro.

This was going to be their show, so Vinda got out of his car and walked slowly over to the dumpster to watch.

"Turn off the ignition and get out," the taller trooper ordered. Pug-nose, who had the battered features of a losing middleweight contender, demanded, "Why'd ya pull us over?"

The shorter of the two officers came up to Pug-nose and barked in his face, "Assume the position."

Biceps glared at Vinda, who smiled and shrugged innocence.

Biceps and Pug-nose turned and spread-eagled against the dumpster. The shorter trooper began frisking Pug-nose. "My, my, what have we here?" the trooper said, yanking a nine-millimeter S&W automatic from a hip holster.

"I got a carry permit," Pug-nose announced smugly.

"Really?" the taller trooper said in mock surprise. The shorter trooper shoved the automatic into his Sam Browne belt and proceeded to frisk Biceps.

"I got a carry permit too," Biceps said, when the trooper patted his holstered .38 Colt.

After sticking the Colt in his belt, the shorter trooper said, "Let's see those permits."

They took out their wallets, removed their permits, and handed them to the trooper. Scrutinizing the official documents, a scowl of disappointment glided across the trooper's face. Without comment, he passed the permits to Vinda, who looked at them and said to Biceps, "You don't have anything to say, and I strongly advise you not to."

"Whaddaya mean?" Biceps growled, thick cords taut against his neck.

"The lieutenant means," the taller trooper said, "that your permits license you to carry concealed weapons in New York State, not in the State of New Jersey. You're both under arrest."

"You Mickey Mouse cops can't arrest us," Biceps shouted into the trooper's face.

"I bet when the weather gets real hot your IQ can get as high as fifteen," Vinda snarled at him.

"Fuck you!" Biceps shouted back.

The troopers separated, slowly backpedaling, their hands drifting toward their holsters. The taller one reached across his chest, plucked the nine-millimeter from his belt, and tossed it in front of the prisoner's feet. A nervous twitch started up in Pug-nose's right eye and cheek. "It's a setup! They're gonna whack us."

Vinda rushed them, shoving them up against the dumpster. "You scumbags got a choice, you can go quietly now, or in the morning, with the garbage."

"I hate lawyers," Malcolm Webster bellowed across the expanse of his twenty-fifth-floor lower Broadway office. "And you're forcing me to spend good money on them to defend my people on your trumped-up charges."

"We all have bad days, Malcolm," Vinda said, standing before the plate-glass wall, soaking up the spectacular view. The ferry was making its run to Staten Island, sunlight gleaming off her wheelhouse as her prow bit into the incandescent water. "You know what we call it when we find a dozen lawyers floating facedown in the East River?"

"What?" Webster snapped.

"Urban renewal."

Despite himself, Webster laughed. He had installed himself behind a large redwood desk that appeared to stretch halfway across the room and was bare except for two telephone consoles on the right side.

Vinda turned away from the wall to ask, "Why?"

Webster turned and gazed out at the scudding clouds. "I want the man who murdered my daughter. And I want him punished. I thought by having you followed . . ." He pulled an ironed handkerchief from the inside pocket of his suit jacket and, without unfolding it, brushed it across his eyes.

Vinda came over and sat on the edge of the desk and said, "Even God can't change the past, Malcolm. I want to catch this guy too. And you have to be made to understand that by hindering me, you are helping him. Time, that thing that keeps everything from happening at once, is on his side, not ours."

Webster's shoulders sagged. "Assign more detectives. I'll pay for them."

"We've assigned all the resources we can. The NYPD has caught over twenty-nine hundred homicides so far this year, and we're still counting. We're stretched thin, very thin."

"How do you know you'll catch him?"

Vinda evaded the question, saying, "If you get in the way you can screw it up—and then we won't nail him."

Webster took in a deep breath, and said, "I won't interfere again."

"Now I can get back to work," Vinda said, picking up his coat from the leather-covered couch against the wall.

Watching the detective, a forlorn expression on his face, Webster said, "Isn't there something I can do to help?"

Slipping his arm into one sleeve of his coat, Vinda said, "Maybe." Every cop in the Job quickly learns: You do what you gotta do. And every cop was also aware that the Disciplinary Orders were filled with Charges and Specifications against cops who did what they had to do—and got caught. The thinking of the Palace Guard had not changed since that first watchman patrolled his New Amsterdam beat back in the seventeenth century: Do it! Don't let me know you're doing it. And if you get caught, you're it.

Walking back to the desk, Vinda placed his palms on the edge and, leaning forward, explained, "If you should aid this investigation, it would have to be done confidentially. No one, and I mean no one, could know." As he leaned across the desk, he could smell the faint scent of Webster's after-shave. "If what you did should become public knowledge, any fruits of your help would very likely be inadmissible in court, and could result in the perp walking. A man like you has a lot of connections; you can get into places that I can't, and you're in a position to grease palms, which I can't do." He fixed his eyes on the face of the dead girl's father. "Still want to help?"

"Yes," Webster replied in a subdued tone. "I'll do anything I can."

Vinda jammed his hands in the pockets of his overcoat and chose his words carefully. The instinctive distrust that cops have for all civilians was overcome only with difficulty. "I've got a psychological profile on this monster from one expert. What she told me would get me thrown off the case if I put it in a report." Looking away from Webster, he said thoughtfully, "I want you to reach out and find some other top experts—you know, shrinks who make sense, people that courts will listen to. I'll give you copies of some of my notes. Find people who can tell me more about this guy."

He started to leave, and had a last-minute thought. "I'll need a very secure phone number, a direct line I can reach you on, day or night."

SIXTEEN

ACACOPHONY OF TRAFFIC BLENDED WITH THE RE-frain of Christmas carols as streams of people poured into subway stations. It was Monday evening, and the Empire State Building's spire stabbed the low clouds against the black of the sky. The usual pre-holiday revelry had been subdued by the horrible murders that dominated the headlines and filled the television screens. White-collar bars emptied quickly as darkness fell, and men walked their female co-workers to catch their buses and subways.

Around the corner from the famous landmark, on Thirty-third Street a little west of Fifth Avenue, most of the furniture showrooms had closed for the day. On the south side of the street, six buildings in from Sixth Avenue, a steel gate was locked across the front of an empty store with a large FOR RENT sign in the window. Five of the six lofts above the store were in darkness;

the one on the first floor was dimly lit by a bare bulb hanging down from a tin-covered ceiling. Inside this loft a woman in her twenties stood on a folding ladder, tacking feminist posters to the wall. A lectern stood in front of ranks of folding chairs that stretched back across a wooden floor. On the speaker's platform stood a boom-box playing a tape cassette of Haydn's *The Creation*.

Kate Coswell's long, bulky sweater came down over her jeans to mid-thigh. Kate had always been a believer in women's rights, but had not become active in the movement until one night last year when she had taken a shower in her boyfriend's apartment. She had planned on spending the night there, so she had brought along her personal articles and a change of clothes. While in the shower, rubbing a fragrant skin conditioner over her stomach, she noticed a tube of the same product standing upright in the shower caddy. Curious, she picked it up and saw that it was the same size as hers, manufactured by the same company, had exactly the same ingredients, and cost two dollars less than the ladies' body scrub. It was labeled FOR MEN. She had squeezed a glob of the green paste into her hand and lathered it under her breasts, finding that it felt and smelled exactly the same as the stuff in her tube. Her girlfriends were right: if men menstruated, Tampax would be free. It was at that moment that Kate Coswell decided to become active in the movement.

Climbing down, she carried the ladder to the other side of the room, and put up more posters.

Outside in the street, Michael Worthington loomed back in a doorway, staring up at the first-floor loft with the big sign in the window announcing tonight's meeting of The Women's Register. Lost in the gloom of a winter's night, Worthington clutched a shopping bag crammed with the supplies he had so carefully packed. Stepping out of the doorway, he looked up and down the street and then quickly crossed to the other side, slipping into the vestibule of the building.

The narrow lobby had a cracked tile floor and an elevator with ancient sliding doors with gilded scrollwork. The staircase was to the left. He took the steps swiftly and silently, aware that he did not have much time. Reaching the first level, he put his ear to the door and heard, *"Wir preisen dich in Ewigkeit!"* We praise Thee in eternity, he translated, thinking, Someone has the good taste to be listening to Haydn. He carefully turned the doorknob, opened the door a crack, and peered inside. A woman was standing on the top step of a ladder, tacking posters to the wall. He looked around and, seeing no one else, concentrated his attention on her. Her hands were young, and her long hair flowed down her back. His mouth went dry, and flashes of warmth surged across his stomach.

Opening the door wide, he slipped inside and stood with his back against the wall, watching her, unable to suppress his budding desire. Looking about, he spotted a door a few feet to his right, and inched his way over to it. He slipped inside and found himself in a cleaning-supply room filled with the pungent smells of solvents and cleaners. He switched on the light and saw the large cardboard drum standing against the wall. He removed the metal lid, and saw that it was one-quarter filled with some kind of granulated cleaning compound. He turned off the light, went to the door, and cracked it. When he saw her again he was convinced that the Eternal One had sent her to him—it was His will. Suddenly he realized that he had not brought his vestments with him, and he admonished himself. That was dumb, dumb. But he did have his sacred instrument. He quietly undressed and folded his clothes, putting them up on one of the shelves. Naked, he inserted his gleaming implement and padded over to the door. *"Dem Schopfer haben wir gedankt."*

Kate walked to the back to admire her work. She was standing with her hands on her hips a few feet in front of the supply room, with her back to the door. He plunged out, grabbing her, cupping his hand over her mouth, sweeping the terrified woman up into his arms, and hauled her back into the cleaning-supply room.

The Creation drowned out the sounds of her muffled screams.

Her nails clawed at his back in her desperate struggle for life.

"How sweet you are," he said, arching her thrashing body up to his mouth so that he could reach her young, vulnerable throat. His heightened excitement made him oblivious of the bloody gouges she was digging across his shoulders. He ran his tongue over her throat and gave her a vampire kiss. He jerked his head back, saw the stark terror in her eyes, and then struck, slashing as he withdrew. He snapped her body away from his, so that her blood would gush into the cardboard drum.

The tape deck abruptly stopped; the loft was quiet.

Worthington cleaned himself off with a roll of cheesecloth he found on one of the shelves. He dressed now, acutely aware of the searing pain in his shoulders. Back in the main room, he spent several minutes studying its layout and noting the ventilation grilles in the walls. He smiled and muttered, "Piece of cake for ol' Dinny'O," easily slipping back into character.

He carried the ladder over to the grille behind the lectern and climbed up. He took a Swiss Army knife out of the shopping bag, pulled out the screwdriver blade, and unscrewed the grille, carefully placing each of the six screws in his shirt pocket. Reaching back into the bag, he took out a bar of plastique and placed it down on top of the ladder. Pulling out the larger knife blade, he cut off a quarter of the bar, picked up the grille, and molded the explosive over the back. Going back into the bag, he fished out a three-inch tube that resembled a meat thermometer with an electrical wire running out of one end and leading into a digital timer with a watch-sized face. He inserted the detonator into the plastique. After checking the time, he set the timer for an hour and a half. He proceeded to check the bomb to make sure he had set it up properly. The detonator was inserted firmly into the explosive. When the minute hand of the timer struck the appointed time, the alarm would go off, closing the circuit, sending a current of electricity into the plastique and exploding it.

How excellent and fitting a sacrifice, he thought. And, for a moment, it was as if two men stood there in the room, each a stranger to the other.

S E V E N T E E N

A TEMPORARY MORGUE HAD BEEN ESTABLISHED IN the Bagel Joint, a luncheonette five doors east of the disaster scene. A row of blistered, oozing, unrecognizable hulks were lying on plastic ground sheets on the floor in front of the lunch counter.

The building where The Women's Register had held its meeting no longer existed; in its place was only a huge mound of smoking rubble, protruding beams, and jagged slabs of masonry.

Emergency Service Division police officers and Fire Rescue Teams gingerly picked their way over the rubble, probing it for survivors, while heavy-duty cranes stood ready to lift debris off any that were discovered.

C-of-D Leventhal stood outside the temporary headquarters trailer with other police brass. An Emergency Service sergeant, his uniform caked with plaster, came over to them and announced softly, "Definitely an explosive device. So far we've come up with eight bodies, and we're still looking." The grim-faced officials looked at each other. The sergeant drew the C-of-D aside by the arm and confided, "Chief, we've found something you should see."

Thirty minutes later, Vinda stumbled his way over the rubble to the knot of detectives huddled around the entrance to an underground chamber that had been formed out of tumbling I-beams and debris. Floodlights illuminated the cavern; a parachute harness had been set up to lower and raise people from the chamber.

Vinda strapped himself into the harness and was lowered into the cavity. The air inside was filled with a fine mist of dust particles, and smelled of coal and cornstarch. Unstrapping himself, Vinda looked into the chief of detectives' worried face, and asked, "Why the 'forthwith'?"

"A bomb did this. It was planted in the first-floor loft where The Women's Register was holding a meeting."

Vinda's thoughts leaped to May Gold, the former cop turned lawyer. Then he focused on the crumpled cardboard drum wedged between beams and timbers, and asked in a puzzled tone, "What has this got to do with my caper?"

"The victims were all women." Leventhal pointed at the drum, adding, "Take a look."

Vinda made his way around and between the I-beams and timbers into the space where the drum stood in an upright position. Looking inside, his face contorted in an ugly expression of disgust. A woman's body had been wedged into it; the lower torso was mired in ruby-colored mud. He reached down into the drum, tilted the head, and examined the enormous, ghastly wound in her throat. Looking up at Leventhal, he called, "Have someone give my team a 'forthwith.' "

Standing under the opening, Leventhal shouted out orders.

Measuring the wound, Vinda brushed his fingers over the marks of the vampire kiss, knowing his killer had struck again.

A multiple homicide this time. He wondered what had caused him to make such a radical departure in his MO. Probing the wound with two fingers, he pulled out severed arteries that had the same clean cuts as the others. He cleaned his hands on Kate Coswell's bulky sweater. Hearing a commotion behind him, he turned to see Dr. Patricia Marcal being lowered in the harness, holding her medical kit against her chest.

Leventhal rushed to unstrap the doctor.

"Over here," Vinda called.

The assistant medical examiner passed her medical kit through to Vinda and, stretching her leg over the first beam, climbed into the chamber. Hunching over, she made her way over to the drum. "Take a look," Vinda said.

After a brief examination, she looked up at Vinda and announced, "It's him again." She plunged her hand into the awful mass in the drum and pulled out the dead woman's slim hand. With her own hand she carefully wiped off some of the fingers and said, "Get the Baggies out of my bag. Looks like she scratched him. Those skin balls under her nails will give us his genetic fingerprints."

Twenty-two minutes later, Vinda, Leventhal, and Dr. Marcal watched the drum being hoisted up and out in the parachute harness. "It's a miracle that it survived the explosion," Leventhal said to Vinda.

"I've seen things like that before," Vinda answered. "A building explodes and things like the stained-glass windows survive intact. The girders protected it when the rest of the building came down."

The detective whom Leventhal had dispatched to notify Vinda's team returned from temporary headquarters to report that Moose, Agueda, and Hagstrom had all been notified. Detective Marsella's wife stated that her husband was not at home; he was playing cards with a friend in the city.

Vinda walked into the temporary morgue. Missing Persons Squad morticians were kneeling on the floor, trying to make identifications. A woman detective moved along the file of bodies, attempting to match up a severed leg with one of the blackened hulks.

Lowering himself onto one of the aquamarine plastic–covered counter stools, Vinda said to the C-of-D, "It's getting worse instead of better. Now he's blowing up buildings."

A badly shaken chief of detectives moved his head in agreement. "Something must have set him off." Leventhal looked at Vinda and said in a frightened voice, "Jesus, we gotta find this guy now, John. He's going to shut this city down."

A few minutes later the team arrived. Vinda motioned them outside. They gathered around the Whip. "The few survivors have been rushed to Bellevue. Hagstrom and Agueda, get over there and try to interview them. Tony, I want you and Moose to hit the bars and restaurants. It's Christmas-party time, and someone might have seen our boy."

"Right, Lou," Marsella said, avoiding the Whip's eyes.

Vinda walked over to the Bomb Squad station wagon, noting the array of tools aligned on the sidewalk: wheelbarrows, power saws, cutting torches, metal detectors, screens for sifting debris. He went up to the sergeant who was standing by the opened rear door, and identified himself.

"I'm Sergeant O'Boyle, Lou," the sergeant told him.

"Have your people come up with anything yet?"

"Yeah, a few things. First off, whoever did this is a pro. He planted the stuff in the vicinity of the load-bearing walls. When those support walls blew, the entire structure came tumbling down." The sergeant arched his back and stretched. "Most people say the dead don't talk. That's not true in a bomb case. All sorts of shit ends up embedded in victims. My guys went over the bodies and dug out the plastic end cap from a block of plastique. We also found pieces of a detonator in the same body."

"Plastique," Vinda said, a desperate edge to his voice.

"When that crap blows, it hurls debris at the rate of twenty-six thousand four hundred feet per second," O'Boyle said.

"Is it easy to come by?"

"Not really. The military and a few police departments use it to take out steel doors, and a few demolition companies around the country. It's a tightly controlled substance. Here, lemme show you something." Vinda moved up to the station wagon's lowered rear door. A black box with an eyepiece sat on the door. "Take a look, Lou."

Vinda peered into the eyepiece; a slate blue pebble shone against a black backdrop.

"You're looking at a chunk of Semtex we scraped off a twisted grille. Semtex is a Czech-manufactured plastique, a favorite of terrorists."

"How can you tell it's Czech?"

"By the color."

"And where would a guy get his hands on this Semtex?" Vinda asked, again thinking of May Gold, and hoping she had not attended tonight's meeting.

Corregidor's tunnels were almost empty.

Vinda walked into the bar and saw the barkeep playing chess with one of the five night owls. A starry-eyed couple held hands across one of the alcove cocktail tables.

Vinda waited for the bartender to work out his next move: Bishop to Knight six, Check. The barman looked up at Vinda. "It's kinda late for you, isn't it, John?"

"Soothsayer around?"

"In the back," the bald man said, going back to his endgame.

The tables were set for the next day, gleaming white tablecloths, sparkling place settings. As he entered the largest of the dining rooms, he saw the man he sought, sitting at a corner table partially hidden in shadows. Another man was with him, leaning across the table, whispering.

Vinda stood by the entrance, waiting his turn to see Soothsayer. This man's epic spanned forty years; some was legend, some myth, but most of it true. Not many people in the Job remembered his real name. They knew he was a retired first-grade detective who had spent his entire career in the Job's various intelligence units; they also knew that he had body-guarded some of the most powerful and influential men in the country, men who considered Soothsayer a friend and confidant. It had even been whispered in the corridors of the Big Building that Soothsayer had been the head Watergate bagman. Yet his name was never mentioned in any court papers, nor did it appear in any newspaper. Nowadays he could be found in one of Cor-regidor's tunnels after 4:00 P.M. Monday through Friday, bring-ing people together, making deals, dispensing favors, calling in markers.

The man at the table got up and left, passing Vinda without acknowledging he was there.

Soothsayer's wrinkled, age-spotted hand came out of the shad-ows, beckoning him. Vinda crossed the room, pulled out a chair, and sat. Soothsayer was a dark, undefined shape in the shadows. Only his right hand, resting on the table and toying with an eighteen-karat gold ring shaped into a replica of a detective shield, was in the light cast by the nearest overhead lamp.

"Nice ring," Vinda said admiringly.

"Nelson gave it to me when he came back from Washington." His face came forward into the light. Deepset eyes like those of an ancient sea turtle dominated his face with its pale wrinkled skin and thick, cracked lips. His hair was cropped short, in military fashion. "I hear you caught a real bitch of a case, Lou. Anything I can do to help?"

Folding his arms across his chest, Vinda went over the details of the bombing. "The Bomb Squad boys told me Semtex is difficult to get hold of." He let the unasked question hang.

Soothsayer's thumb toyed with the ring. "All you have to do, Lou, is know where to go, who to see, and what to say." He picked up a bottle of Delamain and poured cognac into a snifter. He held the glass under his nose, inhaling the aroma, then set it down firmly. "Would you like a drink?"

Vinda shook his head no.

"You know, Lou, years ago we could take a handshake on a homicide." He cradled the snifter in his hands, gently swirling the cognac. "The perp would tell you he had something important to do over the weekend, and that he'd surrender himself first thing Monday morning, and like clockwork, Monday morning he would show up. He'd show his appreciation, of course, and everything would be cool." He sipped cognac. "That's all changed now. You got yourself a high-tech, remote-control killer. Who also happens to be as crazy as a bedbug. He's clever, resourceful—and he isn't going to turn up in any of the usual data banks."

Soothsayer shook his head slowly and muttered, "This one was a sleeper. My guess is he's been a walking bomb for years. He'd be a loner, keeping the wild side secret, waiting for the right moment. Hell, I don't think even he knew when it would be."

Vinda frowned in perplexity. "So how do I get a line on this phantom?"

Soothsayer smiled. "He's done you a favor. Using the Semtex—that is going to leave a trail. And knowing how to use it—that means he got demo training somewhere. Most likely the military. So you gotta start looking for him in his past—not his present." He looked at Vinda and something resembling a smile drew back his lips. "Tell me what little you know about this perp of yours."

"Male, white, doesn't like women or the Job."

"A hard-on for the Job?"

"Yes."

"Hispanic?"

"Don't think so."

"That probably eliminates the narco crowd. They don't much trust gringos."

Vinda watched him sip cognac and waited for more.

"There aren't too many local hardware guys who deal that type of explosives. The Feds keep a tight lock on it because of the terrorism business. Your best bet is one of the bomb free-lance dealers, not any one of the true believers like the IRA. There are only four or five of them in this area who deal plastique. Now, I can tell you who some of them are and where you're likely to find them, and I can also tell you they don't deal with strangers. Either they know you, or someone vouches for you. Take out a pen, Lou. Hope your insurance is paid up."

After leaving Corregidor, Vinda drove to the Photo Unit to try to match up the names Soothsayer had given him with mug shots and yellow sheets.

When he arrived back at the disaster scene fifty minutes later, the fire department was still hosing down the debris.

Climbing into the temporary headquarters trailer, Vinda saw the police commissioner angrily chewing on a cigar. A cloud of smoke hung in the air. "Are you sure it was him?" the PC demanded of Leventhal.

"Yes," the chief of detectives said.

The PC slumped down on the counter of the communication console. "Exxon and Met Life have just announced that they're leaving the city for Connecticut, citing crime as one of the main reasons for the move. Our department stores are half empty because women are afraid to leave their homes." He glared at the detectives. "If we keep losing business, it won't be long before we lose our tax base, and Fifth Avenue looks like a ghost town." He glared at Leventhal. "Am I getting through, Chief?"

"Loud and clear," Leventhal said.

The PC turned his attention to Vinda. "What have you come up with so far?"

"We have a list of forty names from CCRB, mental patients who might fit, but we haven't had time to check them out."

The PC looked at Leventhal and ordered, "Assign more men. I want every one of those people checked out by seventeen hundred tomorrow. And I want Vinda and his people out in the street pushing for real leads, not sitting around doing record checks."

The police commissioner left the van. Leventhal held a brief conference with Vinda, and then he left. Vinda went over to Hagstrom, who was leaning against a file cabinet checking her notes. "Anything from any of the witnesses?"

"Negative. There were only seven survivors, and they were all being worked on when we got to the hospital," she said, looking into the Whip's eyes and adding sadly, "May Gold's body has been identified."

Vinda winced with pain at the memory of her intelligence and spirit. He let down a folding seat from the wall of the trailer and slowly lowered himself to it, staring down at the floor. For a time he sat in silence, grieving for the families of the dead, wondering how parents were able to survive such heartbreak. And he thought of his Jean, and all the suffering she had to endure, and he grieved for all the anonymous crime victims whose sufferings went unnoticed, and he wondered what kind of world it was that created monsters who killed and maimed. Finally he muttered to himself, "You do what ya gotta do," thrust himself up off the tiny seat, and hurried outside.

The Emergency Service truck was parked behind the headquarters van. A sergeant knelt on a tarpaulin, oiling a hydraulic jack. "Hi, Sarge," Vinda said, walking over.

"Some mess, hmm, Lou?"

"Yeah." Vinda needed to make an instant friend, so he asked offhandedly, "How's things in Emergency Service?"

The sergeant rolled his eyes. "The Palace Guard just sent us a new CO, an empty suit who spent the last twenty years in the Big Building pushing paper. They sent him to us for field experience, so they can justify this rocket's next promotion. Deputy Inspector Irwin J. Sheaffers, know him?"

"Yeah, I know him. The hump wouldn't piss up your ass if your guts were on fire."

"That's the one, Lou," the sergeant said to his new best friend in the Job.

Vinda spent the next five minutes commiserating with him

over the sad state of the Job. "Look at what's happenin', Lou, we got dwarfs on patrol."

"Yeah," Vinda agreed sadly, "they lowered the height requirement in order to bring in women and Hispanics, and all they ended up with was a lot of short Italians." Squatting on his haunches with an expression signifying deep thought, Vinda confided, "I'm about to throw a surprise party for a couple of scumbags, and was wondering if you might help me select a present or two for them?"

The sergeant looked at him suspiciously for a moment and then grinned. "Why not, Lou. What's your pleasure?"

Fifteen minutes later, holding a canvas sack in his hand, Vinda stuck his head inside temporary headquarters and shouted, "Agueda, grab your pocketbook, we're going for a ride."

They rode in silence over the Queensboro Bridge. Agueda was driving, the Whip relaxing in the passenger seat, staring past her at the tram sliding below the bridge on its descent into Roosevelt Island.

Passing headlights illuminated her olive-hued skin, throwing the lines of her face sharply in relief against the darkness. She felt his eyes on her and smiled. "This is the first time we've been alone in a long time, John." Her voice was filled with an easy intimacy that took Vinda back in time.

"I know," he said, reaching out and touching her face, gliding fingertips over her cheek and across her chin. "Has life been what you wanted it to be?"

She didn't answer him, just reached over and gave his hand a brief squeeze.

A sudden spark of excitement ignited inside of him; he remembered the passionate moments they had shared, Adriene's magnificent body moving easily under him, then thrashing with abandon. She would press her face into his shoulder to muffle her shout when she climaxed. Equally vivid in his memory was the expression on her face when he told her it was over, that he had met Jean and had fallen in love with her. He looked at her and said softly, "Adriene, I'm sorry for the pain I caused you."

A flicker of anger crossed her face. "I'm tired of listening to men's 'I'm sorry's.' "

As she drove off the bridge into the Queens Boulevard lane, she asked, "Did Jean know about us?"

"Yes. There were no secrets between us," he said, looking out at the hookers cruising for tricks on Bridge Plaza South. "Why haven't you married?"

She winced at the clumsiness of his question, forced a smile to her face, and said, "I've never met anyone who could speak Portuguese."

A metallic squeal resonated off tenement walls as the F train navigated the winding curves at Thirty-second Avenue. Overhead tracks cast down slatted shadows on the roadway, while the sidewalk was aglow with the blaze of gaudy lights from Hispanic clubs and restaurants. El Capital, Los Borrachos, Los Cuatros Papagayos.

As the unmarked car moved along Roosevelt Avenue, Vinda reflected on how this once working-class Irish neighborhood had, in a few short years, been transformed into a miniature Sodom where every form of sin was for sale—and where most of the clubs and restaurants served as consular offices for the Medellín and Cali cartels.

Agueda drove into Sixty-second Street and parked near the corner, facing Fitzgerald's bar. She switched off the headlights, noticed the Motor Transport's warning sticker pasted to the dashboard—Carbon Monoxide Kills—and cracked the window a few inches at the top. Cold air swept into the warm car, bringing with it the sounds of reggae.

Vinda pulled a multi-use department envelope from his inside pocket, took out a mug shot and yellow sheet, and handed them to her, saying, "Otto Holman." Pointing to Fitzgerald's, he added, "That's his place of business."

She unfolded the criminal record sheet, read it, and then looked at the mug shot. "Sweet-looking guy. Love his skinhead cut. I see most of his collars have been federal, mostly by agents of the Bureau of Alcohol, Tobacco and Firearms."

"Holman's in the bomb-selling business. Soothsayer gave me four names. Holman's was at the top of the list."

They watched a man walking his dog.

"I want you to do a stroll-by, see if he's inside the bar."

"Right, Lou," she said. As she got out, Agueda looked back at him as if she were about to say something. Apparently changing her mind, she reached inside her coat, lifted her sweater and released her two-inch Cobra from her in-skirt holster, and stuck it into her coat pocket.

Strolling past the bar, she glanced inside and continued on for a short distance before slipping into a shoemaker's doorway. Peering out, she gave him the high sign that Holman was inside. Vinda came over to her.

"He's alone at the end of the bar," she said, as he joined her inside the doorway. "I didn't see anyone else except the bartender."

Vinda checked the time: 12:15 A.M. "When we hit the door, I want you to secure the bartender."

"How are we going to play this drama out?"

"Like Frank and Jesse James."

The smell of spilled beer was rank in the air when Vinda threw open the door. They stepped inside, saying nothing, their grim faces giving nothing away.

Holman's hands were curled around a mug of dark ale; the bartender was counting the day's receipts.

Glaring at the strangers, Holman's hands slipped away from the mug and fell to his sides.

Agueda slid out her revolver, locked the door, and closed the venetian blinds across the front window of the bar.

"What the fuck do you think you're doin'?" the saloonkeeper asked.

Agueda leveled her weapon at the barman. He raised his hands. Agueda motioned him out from behind the bar.

Vinda walked over to Holman, carefully rested the canvas sack on the bar, and said, "I want to see those hands of yours, Holman, and when you bring them up, make sure they're empty."

"Who are you?" Holman whispered, putting his hands flat on the bar.

Vinda did not answer; he yanked back a barstool and sat facing the bomb dealer.

The barman broke the moment by lifting the bar cutout and stepping out from behind the bar. Agueda pushed him through the double doors into the kitchen. She switched on the lights. Cockroaches scurried into crevices. She ordered the barman to sit on the floor in front of the cold, unused restaurant oven. Reaching into her coat, she withdrew two pairs of throwaway handcuffs, Spanish-manufactured and without traceable serial numbers, that the Whip had given her. She shackled the saloon-keeper's left hand to the oven's handle. With the other pair she cuffed his right hand to his left ankle. Looking down at the hog-tied man, she decided not to waste time frisking him, that he couldn't reach for any weapon in that state, so she switched off the light and left.

An elevated subway train rumbled in the distance.

Agueda waved Holman off his stool and over to the raised area of the bar that held some battered tables and chairs. Vinda picked up the canvas sack and followed, then grabbed a chair and slammed it down in front of the steam pipes running down the wall. "Sit!" he ordered Holman.

The bomb dealer's cold gray eyes fixed on Vinda. Lowering himself onto the chair, Holman fixed his eyes on Agueda's revolver. "Big, isn't it?" she said.

Holman licked his lips. Vinda reached into the sack and pulled out a pair of latex gloves. Snapping them on his hands, he saw Holman's puzzled expression, and grinned to himself. *He figures we can't be cops, and he's trying to make out who we are,* he thought. Vinda took out three sets of cuffs and a length of nylon cord. He handcuffed Holman's wrists through the back slats of the chair, and then cuffed his ankles to the chair's legs. Unfurling the rope, he passed it around Holman's chest and hog-tied him to the pipes.

Turning his back on Holman, he moved slightly to his right so the man could see him remove what looked like the ingredients for a bomb: a glob that resembled bluish mashed potatoes, electrical wire, AA batteries, a travel clock, a screw, a screwdriver, and a slender silver tube. He placed them on the table and turned to see the terror in Holman's eyes.

"Who are you?" Holman demanded again, vainly struggling against his bonds.

Now placing himself so that Holman couldn't see what he was doing, Vinda called out, "Time?"

"Oh-oh-forty-six hours," she answered.

"We'll set it for oh-one hundred," Vinda said, tightening a screw in the face of the travel clock.

Holman struggled against his bonds.

Vinda moved so that the bomb man could see the assembled device. He placed it carefully inside the sack and carried it over to Holman and placed it on the floor under the chair.

Forcing a steely calm into his voice, Holman asked, "What do you want?"

Stepping back, Vinda said, "Only a name."

"Who?"

"The man you sold the Semtex to."

"Eleven minutes," Agueda called out.

Holman's breathing had become irregular, causing his chest to heave erratically. "I don't know what you're talking about."

Vinda turned to Agueda. "Get the door."

She rushed to the entrance, snapped open the lock. "What about the barman?"

"What about him?" Vinda asked. Looking at Holman, he said, "Send me a postcard from hell."

He rushed for the entrance.

"Wait!"

Vinda stopped, swallowed a smile, turned slowly. "What?"

"I don't know his name."

Vinda walked back. "Tell me what you do know."

Holman hesitated, bit his lips, and finally said, "In '62 the Agency hired me on as a contract employee and shipped my ass to Saigon, where they billeted me in an apartment near the Embassy. My job was to customize explosive charges for South Vietnamese Special Forces. The Agency would give me the order and I'd fill in at Long Ton, a CIA base thirty-five miles out of Saigon."

"Why did they hire a civilian?"

"We were just getting started over there. I wasn't Army or Agency, therefore I was deniable if I got myself killed or captured. They needed me because the South Vietnamese could never get it into their heads that you needed different-shaped charges to take out different kinds of targets."

"Five minutes," Agueda called out.

"Skip the preliminaries, and get to my man," Vinda ordered.

"There weren't many of us over there then. The watering hole was the Blue Bird on Tu Do Street. A slimy stripper joint where you could get a beer and a blow job for ten bucks. Anyway, everyone'd be in civvies, and the unspoken rule was, you didn't ask the next guy what he did, or who he did it for. The guy you're looking for was in the Blue Bird almost every night, singing Irish ballads and carrying on like the rest of us, only he never went with any of the ladies. 'Call me Dinny'O,' he used to tell us. Never knew his real name, or who he worked for. Now for God's sake let me go!"

"Describe him," Vinda said.

"About five-eight or -nine. Heavyset, yet not fat, you know what I mean. Thick brown hair and brown eyes. You know, just a regular-looking guy, nothing out of the ordinary, no distinguishing marks or anything. Wait, the ears, yeah, his ears stuck out from his head."

Vinda sensed that the man in the chair was playing games with him. Before leaving the scene of the explosion, Vinda had cut off the identifying edges from a copy of the composite sketch that contained the NYPD's logo and serial number, so that only the sketch of the perp showed. He took it out and held it up to Holman. "Is this your friend Dinny'O?"

Holman studied the sketch. "I'm not sure. It could be him. Only my guy's face is chubbier now, and his eyes are closer together. But I guess it could be him. I'm not sure."

"Did you stay in touch with him after you came home?"

"Naw. Ten, twelve years go by, and one day I'm sitting at the bar of the Ambassador in L.A. and this guy plops down on the next stool and says, 'Don't you recognize your ol' buddy from the Blue Bird?' I look at the guy and can't make him. Then he says, 'It's Dinny'O.' After all those years it was him. We bull-shitted for a while, and I gave him Fitzgerald's address and phone number."

"Did you ever do business with him?"

"Five years ago he stopped by. I sold him Semtex and delay detonators." He squirmed against his restraints.

"When did you sell him the Semtex this time?"

"Yesterday."

Vinda again showed him the composite, demanding, "Is this the guy you sold the Semtex?"

"He looks different in the drawing, but I guess it could be him."

"What else did you sell him?"

"Claymores and fragmentation grenades."

"Where did you deliver them?"

"I didn't. He picked them up here in a rented truck."

"Where do you store the stuff?"

"One minute," Agueda called.

"In the kitchen freezer and the basement," Holman blurted. "Cut me loose."

"Cut yourself loose," Vinda said, rushing for the entrance.

•   •   •

Four minutes later, as the unmarked car drove into Roosevelt Avenue, Agueda looked at the Whip and said, "I bet that was the longest minute our Mr. Holman ever spent."

"He's still sitting there sweating out the big bang. I bet when he does get free, the first thing he'll do is change his Jockey shorts."

Agueda gave him a rueful glance and said, "By selling that plastique to him, Holman became a principal to a multiple homicide. We should have arrested him."

"He would have walked at his arraignment. We just got done violating a dozen laws and civil-rights statutes, not to mention department regulations. Skinhead wouldn't have been so concerned if he thought we were on the Job. There are other ways of taking that guy out," he said, fishing around in his pocket for quarters. He told her to stop at the next public telephone booth.

She saw one a few blocks away and drove up to it. He pushed open the door and started to get out. She reached out and drew him back by the arm.

"What?" he asked, looking at her.

"Nothing, John. I was just wondering if you needed change."

He looked at her with mingled sadness and tenderness. "What I need is to get back the last ten years of my life."

EIGHTEEN

VINDA'S FACE SAGGED WITH FATIGUE, AND HIS late-tour mouth had the consistency of cotton balls doused with rancid butter. Six o'clock in the morning, and he, Agueda, and Marsella were installed in a window booth inside the Road Show Diner at Tenth Avenue and Fifteenth Street. Steaming coffee, crisp bagels, and eggs over easy helped assuage the foul tastes in their mouths.

Agueda watched with mild amazement as Marsella smothered his eggs in ketchup.

After returning to temporary headquarters at the scene of last night's explosion, Vinda dispatched Moose and Hagstrom to the hospital to interview a witness who had regained consciousness. He wanted to talk to Marsella for a few minutes, so he asked him and Agueda if they'd like to have breakfast.

The waitress came over and refilled their cups. Agueda took

her pocketbook and slipped out of the booth. "I'm going to powder my nose."

The lunch counter was shoulder-to-shoulder with truckers. Waitresses rushed around taking orders, pouring coffee, slapping roving hands.

Vinda pulled a napkin from the holder and placed it in his saucer to soak up the coffee that had spilled from his cup. He looked at Marsella. "You still dancing with Hagstrom?"

"Not to worry, Lou. I get off on living on the edge. I'll dance around with her for a while and then dump her."

"The lady carries a gun; suppose she doesn't want to be dumped?"

Sopping up egg yolk and ketchup with a chunk of bagel, Marsella answered, "I've been playing these games for a lotta years, Lou. I'm a pro at it. Won't be any problems with Joan. One of these days I'll give it all up, and play house with the wife."

"No, you won't, game players always play games," Vinda said, piercing an egg yolk with his fork.

Agueda returned. The men stopped talking. Sliding into the booth, she asked, "Did I interrupt boy talk?"

"Naw," Marsella said, tossing a chunk of bagel into his mouth.

"Negative results," Agent Gus White said quietly, squeezing into the booth fifteen minutes later. "Where is the rest of the team?"

"You just missed them," Vinda said. "They've gone home for a shower and a change of clothes. We're meeting at the office at oh-nine hundred. Now, what did you mean by negative results?"

"I ran a check through VICAP, our Violent Criminal Apprehension Program, and our psychological profiling file of criminal personalities, and our MO files, and I've contacted every field office in the U.S., and have come up with a big zero. There is nothing, official or unofficial, on anyone like this guy."

The gum-chewing waitress came over. "What'll it be, sport?"

"Poached two on blueberry muffin," White said.

"You got it, sport," the waitress said, pouring coffee into the FBI man's cup.

Dumping sugar into his cup, White said, "After you got me up at that ungodly hour this morning, I went directly into the office and checked the hot sheet. Your little explosion was number one on the list." Taking his time stirring, he looked across the table at Vinda and said, "The ATF boys made a big bust in Queens last night. A big haul of explosives."

"Really?" Vinda said, drinking coffee.

Continuing to stir his coffee, White said, without looking up, "The official version is that acting on a tip from a reliable CI, they hit this dump where a hump named Holman attacked one of the agents, necessitating the lawful use of force, et cetera, et cetera, et cetera. You know the rest of the fairy tale." Raising his cup to his mouth, he added slyly, "I'm happy to see you didn't leave your balls in purgatory."

Vinda smiled. "Will Holman do time?"

"Long and hard."

Clasping his hands together in front of his mouth, Vinda leaned forward. White put his cup down and did likewise. "My vampire has changed his MO," Vinda whispered.

"Oh, shit," White said, making the connection. "The explosion was *your* guy?"

"Yeah. Holman was his supplier. According to Holman, my guy was in Saigon in '62, went by the name Dinny'O, and hung out in a slime pool called the Blue Bird on Tu Do Street. Holman didn't know if this Dinny'O character was military or Agency. Can you check back? See if you can come up with a name, maybe a photo."

"That's a lot of years ago. There were a lot of spooks over there then. And it doesn't sound like you got the guy's work-name."

"Someone alive hadda know this guy, and somewhere there is

a pedigree on file for him. You're my only hope. If I don't get a line on this guy's past, I got no hope of putting a finger on him."

"Hey, John," White burst out. "How come you keep saying it's a guy? Could be a woman."

"No way, Gus. Women don't kill this way."

NINETEEN

THE POLICE COMMISSIONER GLARED AT THE FIVE superchiefs sitting around the oval table in response to his calling an 1100 conference. The sleepy and worried brass, all of whom had been at the explosion scene, squirmed impatiently in their seats, waiting for the detective from the Intelligence Division to complete his daily electronic sweep of the room.

"Are you going to take forever?" snapped the PC.

"Just a few more minutes, Commissioner," the detective said, passing the wand of his electronic bug detector over the molding. Several long minutes passed before the detective pronounced the room clean, hurriedly gathered up his equipment, and left.

The PC stiffened. Clasping his hands on the table in front of him, he began talking in a low, deceptively calm voice. "Gentlemen, the hotel association has informed me that as of oh-nine hundred this morning, every major hotel in this town has a sixty-percent cancellation rate, which they directly attribute to our incompetence."

His nostrils flared, and his fingers tapped the table impatiently. "I can also tell you that our retail stores are really hurting. And as I am sure you are all aware, the media is full of nothing else but Jessica Merrill and her alleged brush with death. Now they've got this 'mad bomber' stuff. Also, for those of you who are brain-dead, let me advise you that almost every feminist group in town is screaming for our heads."

The chief of patrol lifted his hand in protest. "Commissioner, I think—"

"I don't want to hear it," the PC said, "I want results. I want an arrest." His eyes bored in on Leventhal. "Talk to me, Sam."

Leventhal leaned forward in his chair. "Every television station and newspaper has agreed to run the composite. I've assigned my XO and twenty detectives to run down every name that Vinda and his people come up with."

"What else?" asked the PC impatiently.

"Vinda has come up with some promising leads," said the C-of-D. He looked directly at the chief of patrol and added, "If the media ever found out about what we got . . ." He let his implied warning hang in the charged air.

The PC picked up the gauntlet and hurled it at Agent Orange. "If anything discussed in this room leaks, I will know the culprit, and will forthwith reduce him to his highest civil-service rank and ship his ass to Brooklyn North, where he'll be the permanent late-tour duty captain."

The chief of patrol looked down at the blank pad of paper in front of him as if some priceless truth were inscribed on it.

"Continue," the PC ordered Leventhal.

"Vinda has come up with a name: Dinny'O. Our perp might have been in Saigon in '62. The FBI is checking that out. Vinda has also come up with skin scrapings from under Kate Coswell's nails, and he's identified the high-order explosive used—

Semtex." The chief of detectives went on to brief them on all aspects of the investigation. When he finished, he leaned back and asked, "Any questions?"

The chief of Organized Crime, a burly Italian who packed his gun in an ankle holster, and who, for years, had coveted the C-of-D job, looked at Leventhal and asked, "In your opinion, Sam, has *your* boy Vinda covered all the bases?"

You guinea scumbag, Leventhal thought, smiling at Organized Crime and saying, "Yes, he has. Every crime scene has been canvassed and recanvassed, they've been measured, photographed, vacuumed for trace evidence, and grid-searched. Every piece of forensic and physical evidence has been meticulously invoiced, and letters of transmittal attached to preserve the chain of evidence."

Organized Crime's expression showed that he remained unconvinced. "We should consider designating a captain or above to head up this investigation, in view of all the publicity the case has generated."

A tense silence filled the room.

Sam Staypress's eyes roamed over the rows of photographs of former police commissioners, then settled on the twenty-sixth President of the United States. "I want to stay with Lieutenant Vinda."

The PC stared straight ahead, his face betraying nothing of his feelings.

"With the movie star getting so much publicity, it might be wise to put more weight at the top," Agent Orange said to the PC.

When I was studying for sergeant, I never dreamed that one day I'd be dealing with such backstabbing cunts at the top, Leventhal thought, breaking in to head off the stampede. "If we assign more weight at the top, and the case is not closed satisfactorily, then the 'captain or above' who we assigned would see his career flushed down the toilet."

The PC looked at Leventhal. "The detective division is your shop, Sam. Go with whoever you want."

"Vinda," Leventhal declared firmly. But he knew that John Vinda had very little time left to accomplish what seemed impossible. So he would be the first one who would have to be thrown to the wolves.

"Bitch," Worthington cursed, standing naked before the medicine cabinet, his head turned so that he could examine, in the mirror, the bloody furrows gouged into his back. Stretching his left hand around his shoulder, he bathed the wounds with a gauze pad soaked in hydrogen peroxide. Stinging froth bubbled in the wounds. "Bitch."

Carefully placing fresh gauze pads over the injured area, he fastened them in place with strips of adhesive tape. Straightening up, with his arms at his sides, he relaxed his body. Staring trancelike into the mirror, he tried to make contact with the Eternal One. He closed his eyes and saw ill-defined shapes, glowing white in the darkness. He strained, trying to make out what they were. Then he could see featureless faces framed in veils of pure black. The Eternal One was thanking him for sending Him more brides of Christ.

He opened his eyes; overcome by dizziness, he balanced himself by grabbing the sink and resting his head against the coolness of the mirror. Tasting a lingering coppery flavor of blood, he savored the delicious mixture that bonded him and Valarie to the Eternal One, thus ensuring their protection. Their Trinity, their three-way bond. Now no one will ever be able to take her from me again, he exulted inwardly. He swallowed, and the warm wetness slid down his throat. His heart beat faster; blood flooded his penis. "Valarie," he moaned, stroking his erection.

Fifteen minutes later, his head resting on a pillow and his well-muscled, aging body stretched across the bed, a sheen of sweat covering his heaving chest, Worthington lazily moved his hand up to hold hers. Sunlight filtered through the blinds, reflecting on the ceiling. His eyes followed the golden movements of dust particles in the heavy, still air of the overly heated room.

The beams of light creeping across the ceiling seemed to form constantly changing, suggestive shapes. "I wish I could cross over, without pain, from life to death and sleep." He sat up, resting his cheek in his palm, and looked into her large, black, dead eyes. "The police are after us again, Val. But the Eternal One will protect us; He has shown me how to destroy them."

Vinda parked the department auto on Fifty-seventh Street, east of Fifth Avenue, and got out. It was not yet noon, and one of the city's main shopping areas was almost deserted. He crossed west on Fifth Avenue and walked to the main entrance of Rue St. Jacques.

The doorman saw Vinda coming, and left his door to greet him. "How ya doin', Lieutenant?"

"Good. How's business?"

"Between you and I, it stinks. My tips are way off. You'd better hurry and get this guy."

"I have to go upstairs," Vinda said, walking away into the store. Salespeople stood idle behind uncrowded counters. He went up the staircase to the mezzanine, entering the rainbow-colored world of swimwear, and thought again about the vacation that Linda Camatro never had. He walked along the aisle to the stairs leading up to the designer dress department.

A single well-tanned woman browsed in the racks of expensive dresses.

One of the saleswomen recognized him and rushed over. "Hello again."

"Hi. Mind if I look around?" he asked. Not waiting for an answer, he walked down the aisle toward the dressing room where the homicide had occurred.

The bloodstain in the carpet outside the room had been cut out, and a matching patch inserted. A smell of paint was still in the air. He opened the door and saw all signs of the carnage had been removed. The Queen Anne chair was upright; the shattered glass of the winged mirror had been removed and a new panel substituted. The blood-spattered curtains were gone.

Stepping inside, he closed the door behind him and took out the composite. He hung his overcoat on a hook, pulled the fragile chair away from the wall, and sat. Leaning forward with his forearms on his knees, he held the composite in his hands, studying it, attempting to force himself into the killer's psyche.

"You saw her come in and needed to touch her, to run your hand between her warm legs." He stopped. "Naw. That's not your bag. You're not into ordinary sex. You're into sucking on blood, you have to feel their struggle for life, to see the sheer terror in their eyes. But that's only the foreplay, isn't it? You really get off on taking their lives."

He felt his anger growing. "You're crazy, yet you take precautions not to get their blood on you, not to be seen. Yeah, you're sane enough to do that. But why do you have a hard-on for the Job? And why did you telephone the press? I know why. You wanted to raise the ante, didn't you? See if you could get me mad at you."

He thought about the swimsuit tangled around Camatro's ankle. "Why didn't anyone see you bust into the dressing room? You had to be suited up *before* you broke in, because you knew you'd need both hands to control her. Yet no one saw you. No, Worthington saw you, but he said you didn't have your clean suit on." He repeated, "You didn't have your clean suit on."

He sat in the room for another half hour, thinking, hoping for an epiphany.

Inspector Paul Acevedo was standing next to a file cabinet inside the Safe, Loft, and Truck Squad, digesting the list of names that detectives Agueda and Hagstrom had just handed him.

Walking up to the detective division's executive officer, Vinda smiled at the two women. "How's it going, Inspector?"

"We're about organized at this end," Acevedo said, adding, "Unfortunately I had to waste half the morning playing grab-ass with squad commanders. I send down telephone messages transferring detectives here on a thirty-day steal . . ."

". . . and they sent you the names of detectives on vacation or terminal leave," Vinda interrupted.

Acevedo nodded annoyance. "You got that right. The Two-four Whip had the balls to send me the name of a detective on extended sick for a year and a half."

Vinda grinned knowingly and commiserated. "Squad bosses hate to lose people to temporary assignments. The work keeps piling up."

"Know what I did?" Acevedo said, looking over at the two female detectives. "I sent down another telephone message transferring two of his best detectives by name." He pointed. "That's them sulking in the corner. That'll teach 'em to play grab-ass with the king of grab-ass."

"Your people checking out the names of all those mental cases?"

"We're on it. Anything jumps out, I'll give a holler." Acevedo walked away, heading for the two unhappy-looking detectives.

Vinda looked at Agueda and Hagstrom and said, "Continue with the CCRB records—and while you're at it, check to see if any of our victims ever made a civilian complaint."

A press information officer was holding a media briefing on the mezzanine of One Police Plaza. Vinda edged his way around the crowd, and went inside the press room.

David Pollack's bow tie was undone, the collar of his salmon-and-gray shirt was open, and his pea coat was thrown hastily over a nearby typewriter. Its rumpled form reminded Vinda for some reason of one of the corpses he'd seen at the makeshift morgue.

Pollack sat in front of a computer screen, inputting his follow-up story on last night's explosion. Three stained Styrofoam cups stood beside the keyboard. Lowering himself onto the edge of the table, Vinda looked down at the grimy butts floating in the cups, and asked, "How come you're not outside with the rest of the assholes?"

"Because I don't waste time listening to that 'arrest is imminent' bullshit. Most of those assholes out there are *television* assholes, and therefore too dumb to realize your press guy is pulling their chain."

"And I thought you aspired to be an anchor on the seven-o'clock news."

"I do." He turned and looked at Vinda. "I paid my dues, John, and I'm tired of living like a peon."

"So am I. Why don't we both try a new line of work?"

"Have you come up with any new leads?" asked Pollack.

"I'd say that the solvability factors definitely do not justify the allocation of additional manpower."

"What you're telling me is that the Job has decided to use the media to generate external pressure in order to justify assigning a lot of troops."

"That's the way it works when the bosses are really worried. It's known as the boomerang effect." Vinda looked around the room. "What can you tell me about Jessica Merrill?"

"American Academy of Dramatic Arts in New York. Went out to L.A., where she broke into small parts, playing sultry ladies in nothing movies. Her break came in *Mora Flats*. Why do you ask?"

Vinda shrugged. "Don't really know. She's getting a lot of free publicity on the backs of my homicide victims."

"You can't seriously think she's involved in any way?"

"No, I don't," Vinda said, sighing wearily. "I just like to know all the players. I never bought her as a target—but I just know she's a factor in this somehow."

"Want me to check her out with our Arts and Theater guy?"

"I'd appreciate that, David. And while you're at it, check out Worthington, the other actor, her friend."

"Consider it done."

"Find anything in your newspaper morgue?"

"Not yet." Pollack turned around and took the backgammon board and dice cup out of his center desk drawer. "Got time for a quick game?"

Vinda smiled and shook his head with regret. "David, I got no time at all."

Riding back upstairs at One Police Plaza, jammed into the corner of the crowded elevator and worrying that he had overlooked something, Vinda overheard a cop announce to a friend, "I've got five years on the Job today."

Five years, Vinda thought, snatching the vaguely familiar words and running them past his mind's eye. Where had he heard those words recently? Where? he pondered. Oh, yes, Otto Holman had told them he had sold Semtex to Dinny'O five years ago. Five years? There was somebody else connected with the case who had recently mentioned something that happened five years ago. Who? He tried to remember.

Getting off on the eleventh floor, Vinda hurried into his office, lifted his desk blotter, and slid out his "squeal envelope," a white department form containing his cryptic inadmissible and illegal notes on the Holman interrogation. Detectives used to keep their personal notes inside the case folder until a recent court decision made all notes made by an investigating officer subject to defense subpoena. Now detectives squirreled their coded jottings in nonexistent squeal envelopes that never saw the inside of a case folder or a court.

Vinda slid out a sheet of paper containing his notes made just after the interrogation that never was: "H 5x Semtex = D/O," he read. Scratching his chin, he wondered what Dinny'O had blown up five years ago. Who the hell else had said something about five years ago to him? He flipped open the case folder, trying to retrieve the vague memory.

Windowboxes for flowers gave hope of an urban renaissance in spring. Vinda pressed the doorbell and stepped back from the heavy wooden door. A black woman's polished nails pushed aside the vestibule's lace curtains, and Vanessa Brown peered out. He had not telephoned ahead; she looked surprised and not particularly happy to see him. She opened the door. Her hair was in long braids. A black wool dress draped her attractive body; she was wearing dark hose but no shoes.

She led the policeman into the parlor, and turned to face him, her expression asking the question, Now what?

"Last time we talked, you told me your father was killed in a freak accident five years ago."

"What has that to do with my sister's murder?"

"What happened to your father?"

"The gas tank of his car exploded while he was driving on the Brooklyn-Queens Expressway."

"Do you remember the date?"

"Wednesday, February nineteenth, 1986, at two-sixteen in the afternoon."

Vinda jotted down the information on a scrap of paper. "What was your dad's full name?"

"James Ellis Lucas. What has this all to do with Mary's death?"

"Perhaps nothing. What was your dad's shield number?"

"I don't know that." She walked over and picked up the photograph of her father on the piano. She held it out in front of her, attempting to see the number of the young patrolman's shield. "I can't make it out." She handed Vinda the frame. He strained to see the number but couldn't, so he put the picture back. "That's okay. I can get the number from the Personnel Bureau."

She folded her arms across her chest. "Is it really important?"

"It might be, yes."

"Wait here," she ordered, and walked out of the room. While he waited, Vinda admired the carefully restored, elaborate ornamentation of the molding. He looked out to the porch and the wicker rocking chair standing empty and somehow forlorn on it. The bookcase under the windows was crammed with books. On the first shelf was a photograph of a little girl and her mother. Both were dressed in their Sunday best. Mary Lucas's face was glowing with the undiluted happiness of childhood. How different from her last photos, he thought. Hearing movement behind him, Vinda turned.

"I remembered this was down in the basement," she said, handing him a dusty plaque.

The redwood had a gold plate with Lucas's name, dates of service, commands, and a replica of his shield. Below the shield were two rows of decoration bars that he had earned while a member of the NYPD. A medal was fastened below the bars. Vinda stared at the Maltese cross with the medallion in the center bearing the seal of the City of New York and surrounded by a circular inscription: FOR VALOR POLICE DEPARTMENT. The cross was piped with black enamel surrounding a green enamel field and suspended by a ring from a green watered-silk ribbon. He read the inscription on the reverse side: NEW YORK CITY POLICE. PATROLMAN JAMES ELLIS LUCAS. FOR VALOR, 1979.

Vinda looked at the daughter. "Do you know the circumstances surrounding your father's being awarded the Combat Cross?"

She shook her head. "Dad never talked about his work, never."

"Is your mother home?"

"Upstairs. I must insist you not bother her unless it is absolutely necessary."

He looked down at the medal. "I guess I can get whatever I need from department records." He thought of the many retirement parties he had attended over the years, recalling the glow of pride on the retirees' faces as they rushed up out of the audience to accept their plaques. "I won't miss the Job, but I'll miss the guys," was the usual opening to the tearful acceptance speeches. He could not help wondering how many other discarded medals lay forgotten in damp basements.

T W E N T Y

A DUSTING OF SNOW COATED THE STREETS AS Vinda drove down police headquarters' curving driveway. He parked in his allotted space, got out, and walked through the sounds of squealing tires to the door that opened into the cinderblock elevator bank, where he joined other waiting policemen. He was anxious to get upstairs and find out everything he could about the fatal accident involving his first victim's father. Before leaving the Brown house on South Elliott Place, he had telephoned ahead and told Agueda to check out the CCRB files for any civilian complaints lodged against retired patrolman James Ellis Lucas. He also told Moose to go into the Personnel Data Unit and pull the retired cop's folder.

Where was the damn elevator? He checked the time. Five after five. Which meant the evening rush to go home, which meant having to wait longer than usual for the perpetually slow elevators. One by one, cursing policemen peeled away, heading for the door with the illuminated Exit sign.

Deciding he could use the exercise anyway, Vinda took off his coat, tossed it across his arm, and walked over to the "Wishing Well," a hollowed-out space partially filled with a winding metal staircase, a place where policemen who were about to sit for promotional exams tossed coins, wishing for luck.

Going up, Vinda became conscious of the clanging treads ahead of him, and the echoing sounds of indistinct conversations. Exiting on the eleventh floor, fighting to catch his breath, he propped his back up against the brick wall and thought, I'm not as young as I used to be. He grinned sheepishly and realized that clichés are clichés because they're true.

Marsella and Moose were going over some folders when the Whip walked in. "Better have a look-see," Moose said to Vinda.

Aware of his smelly armpits and sweaty body, Vinda resolved never to walk up eleven flights again. He hung his coat on the rack, went over to his desk, opened the side drawer, and took out a spray can of deodorant. Opening the buttons on his shirt and pulling his tie aside, he directed the spray under his arms. That done, he buttoned up, looked into his detectives' worried faces, and said, "That bad?"

"Yeah, that bad," Marsella confirmed.

Retired patrolman James Ellis Lucas's folder was spread open. The duplicate Force Record Card, Personnel Data Card, and the rest of the obligatory forms mandated by the Administrative Guide were stacked on the left flap of the eleven-by-fourteen manila file.

The other side contained letters of commendation and arrest reports. The communication on top was the Unusual Occurrence Report on the incident that had earned Patrolman James Ellis Lucas his Combat Cross. Vinda noticed another personnel file under Lucas's. He looked at the name on the flap, and his chest muscles tightened. "Oh, no," he moaned.

It was all there, on a report called "The Unusual," otherwise officially known as the Unusual Occurrence Report, the contents of which were all too often all too usual.

The first paragraph detailed how on Monday, June 18, 1979, at about 1130 hours, Patrolman James Lucas, shield 5593, and Patrolman Willy Johnston, shield 14062, assigned to the Ninth Precinct, performing an 0800-to-1600 tour in RMP 2143, sector Adam, responded to a 10:30—Armed Robbery in Progress—at 927 First Avenue.

Arriving at the scene, the officers confronted four armed white males fleeing a payroll robbery of the Hollaway Electronic Corporation. Alighting from their patrol car, the officers ordered the four suspects to drop their weapons, whereupon the suspects whirled on the officers and opened fire. Taking cover behind their RMP, the officers returned fire. During the course of the next six minutes, forty-two rounds were exchanged, resulting in the deaths of the four perpetrators—and one civilian bystander. Investigation revealed that the civilian, identified as Mrs. Valarie Griffin, FW, 27, was leaving Saint Rose of Lima Church at 894 First Avenue at the time of occurrence, and was caught in the crossfire.

The Unusual went on to identify the holdup men by the B numbers of their yellow sheets, and listed their criminal records. They were alumni of the state's finest reformatories and correctional institutions.

The fifteen-page report contained the names and addresses of ten witnesses. Their statements were attached in Appendix B. There was a detailed map of the crime scene, and a cross-projection showing the impact points of each spent round. Photographs of the scene were attached. The ballistic protocol stated that Mrs. Valarie Griffin expired as the result of being struck by one .38 bullet discharged from Patrolman Lucas's service revolver. The medical examiner's protocol detailed the grisly damage done by the bullet.

Vinda looked up at the detectives, a shadow passing across his tense face. "Our first two homicide victims were the daughters of these two cops?"

"Afraid so, boss," Marsella said gravely.

"No mistake?" Vinda asked, glancing at the folders.

Rubbing his Save the Florida Panther button, Moose said, "We checked and double-checked. Mary Lucas and Thelma Johnston were indeed their daughters."

Lighting a cigarette, Marsella added, "Our doer could be the dead broad's husband."

You're only good for serving summonses and destroying lives, the perp had told the AP.

Vinda got up and walked over to the blackboard. Studying the crime-scene photos, he realized that the thrust of his investigation had been all wrong. They'd been looking for a major wackadoo who killed randomly, but it now appeared that the Lucas and Johnston homicides might have been carefully premeditated.

But what about the other homicides? What about the victims of the bombing? There was just too much forensic evidence tying the same perp to them all. Suddenly Frank Griffin, husband of Valarie, had become a man Vinda wanted to talk to. But if Griffin was the doer, where had he been hanging out for the past twelve years? And why the vampire stuff?

Vinda picked up the telephone and dialed the FBI. When Gus White came on the line, Vinda asked him to check out the name Frank Griffin as a possible Dinny'O. "I'll get right on it," White said. "But you owe me big."

The Accident Investigation Unit's report on the explosion of retired patrolman James E. Lucas's car made no mention of an explosive device. Flat police language claimed that Lucas's car had inexplicably and suddenly exploded in flames. Identification had been made through dental records. The AIU investigator who caught the case reported that the deceased had used his credit card to purchase gasoline fifteen minutes before the accident. The vendor's copy of a credit-card sales slip revealed the purchase and that it had been made at a gas station at Flatbush Avenue and Tillary Street in Brooklyn. The absence of skid marks attested to the suddenness of the explosion. Conclusion: deceased neglected to secure gas cap properly after purchase of gas, resulting in overspill that was accidentally ignited by a discarded cigarette.

Vinda leaned back, thinking fast. The AIU cop who conducted the investigation had no reason to suspect an explosive device, so he didn't bother to summon the Bomb Squad to the scene to look for a killer's signature in the debris. It would have been a simple matter for someone to slap a device on Lucas's car in that gas station. Closing the AIU file, Vinda asked, "What do we know about Frank Griffin?"

"Nothing. Zilch," Marsella replied. "The Unusual gave his name and address. I checked with Telephone Security and Con Edison. No Griffin listed at that address."

"I took a ride over there," Moose said. "A new high-rise went up on the site last year. No Griffin."

"The wife's family?"

The detectives shrugged; they had hit a dead end again.

Marsella came over and perched on the edge of the Whip's desk. "The plot thickens, Lou. After we read the files on the two cops, we contacted Corporation Counsel. Are you ready? No—I repeat, *no*—lawsuits were filed on behalf of Valarie Griffin against the city, the Job, or the two cops."

"What?" Vinda said, unable to hide his surprise.

Moose bellied up to the desk and added, "Agueda telephoned just before you got back. No CCRB complaints were lodged against Lucas and Johnston as the result of Valarie Griffin's death."

Agueda and Hagstrom walked into the office. "You sure about Valarie Griffin and the CCRB?" Vinda asked the women.

"Absolutely," Hagstrom said.

Agueda confirmed that they had checked the records three years before and three years after the date of occurrence, and had come up with negative results.

Vinda looked at the detectives. "Any of you have anything personal to do this evening, shove off. The rest of us are going to tear apart these reports. They're bullshit, but there might be a pony in there somewhere."

Nobody got up to leave.

After a few minutes, Marsella sneaked a look at Hagstrom and walked out of the office. Going into the Major Case area, he picked up a phone and dialed home. He told his wife that he'd probably be stuck late and would, if it got too late, sack out in the office.

"That's okay, honey," said his wife, flipping her address and telephone book open to her list of baby-sitters.

When Marsella walked back into the office, Agueda asked him, "Chinese okay, Tony?"

"Good," Marsella answered, sneaking a wink at Hagstrom. Agueda took their orders and phoned them in to the local Szechuan restaurant.

Fifteen minutes later, spooning noodles into his mouth, Vinda flipped through the pages of the Unusual. He found it hard to believe that in this litigious city not one of Valarie Griffin's family had filed a lawsuit alleging her wrongful death.

Marsella was apparently also puzzled. He slumped into a chair, shook a cigarette out of the pack, lit it, and said, "Ya know, Lou, Valarie Griffin's death was a lawyer's wet dream." Waving his hand confidently, he added, "I mean, the city would have automatically settled out of court for some big numbers on a case like this. There's gotta be some reason no suit was filed."

"Maybe the husband dropped dead or something," Moose said.

Vinda's expression showed his doubt; he picked up the Supplementary Report on the original Unusual. His attention was drawn to the duty captain's indemnification endorsement at the end of the last paragraph: "From my investigation it appears that at the time of occurrence Patrolmen Lucas and Johnston were acting in the proper discharge of department duty and were guilty of no misconduct, and no charges have been or are likely to be preferred against them by reason thereof. Request that the Corporation Counsel be assigned to defend them in any future action."

The Supplementary was dated the day after the shooting. Bending over and pulling out the bottom drawer, Vinda leaned back in his chair, planted his feet on the top edge of the drawer, and looked thoughtfully out at the glass towers in the distance. That duty captain must have been damn sure there'd be no kickback, or else he would never have inserted the indemnification paragraph so soon after the incident. Normally, captains who investigate cop shootouts wait until the dust has cleared before sending in the indemnification endorsement. They want to make very sure that there is no relationship between any of the dead civilian types and the members of the force involved. Many a duty captain's career came to an abrupt end because of a premature hold-harmless endorsement. A bird must have sung a little song into the duty captain's ear.

Captain Cormick McGovern had conducted both the preliminary and supplementary investigations. Vinda dialed the centrex number of the Locator Wheel, and asked the police administrative aide who answered for the current assignment of Captain Cormick McGovern. He was told that the captain died while in service in August of '81.

He put the receiver down just as the door slammed open and David Pollack stormed in, waving a handful of clippings. "Here are the morgue files on the shooting."

Vinda had telephoned Pollack a short time ago, giving him the date of occurrence and asking him to look up the shooting in his paper's files.

The newspaper had carried the story on the front page. Photographs of the scene showed the four perps splayed over the roadway and sidewalk. Valarie Griffin's body lay on the church steps, covered by a gray blanket. There were more photographs and a diagram showing the unfolding of the battle. The article alongside the pictures told how Valarie's husband, Frank Griffin, had collapsed and been hospitalized upon being notified of her death.

Vinda handed the clippings to Marsella.

Pollack, his Stetson pushed back on his head, waited until the detectives had read the article before asking, "Any of you supersleuths notice anything strange about the story?"

"There's no follow-up," Vinda said firmly.

"Give the lieutenant a cigar," Pollack said, sweeping off his hat and bringing it across his chest in a ceremonial bow. "A story like this should have run for at least three tear-jerking days."

"So what happened?" Hagstrom asked.

"Someone outside the paper told someone inside the paper to forget about Valarie Griffin," Vinda said.

"I think the Whip's on the money again," Pollack said.

Moose asked, "Can you maybe nose around, find out who, what, when, where, how, and why?"

"If I stuck my nose somewhere it didn't belong, someone upstairs would cut it off," Pollack responded.

Vinda picked up the Unusual and the Supplementary, holding them side by side, comparing the headings on both reports, aware of something odd, and feeling a growing excitement.

Seeing the Whip's new intensity, Marsella asked, "What is it, Lou?"

"Something's wrong here," Vinda said, scrutinizing the two reports.

They gathered around the Whip. Vinda became conscious of Agueda's scent, and of her presence behind him. "Lou, look at the list of overhead commands that received copies," Agueda said, leaning over him, her breasts touching his shoulder. Feeling his face flush, he leaned forward to separate himself from the disturbing softness of her touch.

Unusual Occurrence Reports are forwarded by subordinate commands up the chain to overhead units with a need to know. Department regulations on Records and Correspondence require that the abbreviated designations of commands receiving copies be typed in the upper right-hand corner of the first page of the Unusual. The last set of initials in the right-hand column glared up from the page at Vinda: BOSS—Bureau of Special Services, the NYPD's defunct intelligence units that had been used to do black-bag jobs for the FBI and CIA, the grandfather of the Job's current Intelligence Division.

"Why the hell would BOSS have received a copy?" Moose asked the crew.

No one could answer him.

Vinda was about to say something when Gus White telephoned to tell him that a few fast phone calls to some of his friends in the world of mirrors revealed no Frank Griffin aka Dinny'O in 'Nam during that time frame. Vinda thanked him and hung up.

"Holman conned us," Agueda said contemptuously, after the Whip told her what the FBI man had said.

"Probably," Vinda agreed. "But Holman is a pro, and I'm sure he mixed up a bit of the truth in with the lie." Looking at Marsella, he asked, "Where is Holman now?"

"Out on half a mil bail," Marsella said. "He's probably holding court in the dive in Queens."

"Want us to scoop 'im up, Lou?" Marsella asked.

"We can't go near that guy," Vinda said, stretching and yawning. "My brain's on overload. Let's call it a day."

Looking into the mirror in the eleventh-floor ladies' room, Hagstrom puckered her lips and applied lipstick. "Do you think this Holman guy really knows a Dinny'O, and who he is?"

"Yes," Agueda called from inside a stall.

"What kind of guy is Holman?"

"A grade-A scumbag who thinks he's Rambo."

After pressing her lips together, Hagstrom said bitterly, "I've known a few of them in my time. How far away is Holman's hangout?"

"No traffic, twenty minutes."

The toilet flushed. Agueda walked out of the stall, straightening her skirt. Going over to the sink, she washed her hands.

Hagstrom dumped her lipstick into her pocketbook, took out her hairbrush, and began brushing her hair. "Do you think a couple of frail female members of the force could induce ol' Otto to tell them all about his friend Dinny'O?"

"Some people just might call that a harebrained scheme, Detective Hagstrom."

"I wouldn't," she said, staring at herself in the mirror. "Female detectives have certain unmentionable advantages that our male counterparts do not have."

"Getting Holman to be cooperative could be really gross."

"You do what you gotta do. Besides, I like the Lou."

"Me too."

"I know."

The jack of diamonds hit the bottle of Delamain and fell faceup on the table. The dealer, a burly man with aging muscles, thinning gray hair, and thick-soled shoes, picked up the card and buried it on the bottom of the deck. He tossed out another card.

Soothsayer picked it up and stuck it into his gin rummy hand. The players were sitting at a secluded table in a niche far back in the empty dining room.

Vinda walked in and put his overcoat over the back of a nearby chair, waiting for his presence to be acknowledged. From somewhere deep within Corregidor's bowels, the din of a retirement party penetrated the silence.

The other player with Soothsayer had a familiar and distinctive shape to his head. Soothsayer tossed in his hand, leaned across the table, and said something to his friend. The other man turned his head to give Vinda a long, careful stare. He was Captain Matt Hanratty, the CO of the Intelligence Division's Public Security Section. Watching him push back from the table, get up, and walk past him without so much as a glimmer of recognition, Vinda thought how the names changed but the players lingered on.

Soothsayer waved him over. "What can I do for you, Lou?" he asked, cradling his glass of cognac with both hands.

Vinda slid copies of the Unusual and Supplementary across the table. Soothsayer looked down at them. " 'Seventy-nine. A long time ago."

"Look at the overhead commands that received copies."

"So?"

"Why would an Unusual involving two uniformed cops be flagged to BOSS? And, more important, why would a contract go out killing the story in the press?"

Soothsayer raised the snifter to his nose, slowly savoring the fumes, his eyes watching Vinda over the rim. He put the glass down, picked up the deck of cards, and began dealing himself a game of solitaire.

Vinda watched, his patience ebbing. "You were assigned to BOSS at the time. Do you remember the case?"

Soothsayer placed the queen of spades on the first file, the seven of clubs went on the second. Soothsayer ignored his question. "Why this sudden interest in ancient history?"

Tapping the Unusual with his forefinger, Vinda announced, "This piece of ancient history popped up during the course of my homicide investigation." A note of anger came into his voice. "Do you remember the case?"

"I remember it. I had just deposited Nelson in one of his pieds-à-terre and went into the office to catch up on what was happening in the Job. I was in the boss's office when the contract came in. The call came from City Hall." He picked up the snifter, breathed deeply of the fumes. "Fuckin' doctor told me I can't drink anymore, but he didn't say anything about smellin' it." He looked across the table at Vinda and said, "Valarie Griffin had been a nun. She hadn't taken her final vows, so when she petitioned for release from her vows to marry, it was granted. Only months after hanging up her habit she married this guy Griffin. And then two weeks later she gets herself blown away leaving church."

Vinda brushed his hand across his jaw and, in a flat, emotionless voice, asked, "Who put the kibosh on the story?"

An impish smile turned down Soothsayer's lower lip, revealing crooked yellow teeth. He reached out and slid the ace of spades from the first file, took out his pen, and wrote a name across the card. He slid the card across to Vinda. "Small world, isn't it, Lou?"

TWENTY-ONE

SALSA MUSIC COULD BE HEARD COMING FROM IN-side the restaurant on the first floor of a tene-ment; a sputtering neon sign identified it as La Capital. The greenish purple neon letters threw light on a filthy, melting bank of snow by the curb.

Detective Adriene Agueda parked her six-year-old Volvo on Roosevelt Avenue, and watched as Detective Joan Hagstrom got out of her ten-year-old Honda across the street from Fitzgerald's, Otto Holman's place of business.

Hagstrom slid out of her car and walked to the corner. Watching her approach, Agueda rolled down her window. Hagstrom reached into her pocketbook and took out her police credentials and passed them through the window to Agueda.

"You sure you want to go through with this, Joan?"

"I'm sure," Hagstrom said, unclipping her in-skirt holster and handing it to Agueda. Then, keeping her hands out of sight, she slipped a compact, heavy object into the pocket of her coat.

"What if Holman's not inside?" Agueda said, taking the holstered weapon and putting it under the seat.

"Then we'll come back. See ya," Hagstrom said, walking off.

Two drunks sat on stools next to each other while the bartender leaned on the bar, paging through a skin magazine.

A gust of wind heralded Hagstrom's entrance. Her black wool coat flared out at the hem, and her spiked heels made her appear taller than she actually was. Her gray skirt was split to the knees, and her white silk blouse gave ample proof of a curvaceous body. She wore black panty hose with a silky sheen. She managed to look both classy and sexy, a novel combination for this neighborhood.

Moving up to the bar, she took a fast look around and spotted a man with closely cropped gray hair over in the raised area. Putting just the right note of distress in her voice, she thrust a dollar bill at the bartender and blurted, "My car broke down on me. I need change to call Triple-A."

"Sure, honey," the bartender said, taking the money.

She unbuttoned her coat and let it fall open. One of the drunks looked up at her in befuddled amazement and announced to the bartender in a hoarse voice, "Charlie, you've got the carriage trade up here tonight."

She smiled at him, took the change, and walked over to the pay telephone. She carefully wiped the receiver with a handkerchief, and then gingerly picked it up. Looking down at her membership card, she dialed emergency road service and read off her identification number to the operator. Looking at the bartender, she asked, "What's the address here?"

The bartender told her; she repeated it to the person at the other end. She casually put one foot on the bar rail, her long leg peeking out from her skirt, her breasts full against the silk of her blouse, the nipples showing darkly through its sheerness.

Holman, sipping malt whiskey, watched her from the shadows. He was immediately turned on by her legs, and began to imagine what it would be like to slide his hand up their smooth, rounded warmth until he reached her pussy. This one was totally unlike the neighborhood bimbos he occasionally waltzed into the storage room, bent over a case of beer, and fucked. This one had real class. He fixed his lustful eyes on her breasts and called, "Hello."

Joan turned her head slowly in the direction of the new voice.

"Over here," he called.

The bartender went back to his magazine, and the two drunks stared morosely ahead. One abruptly rested his face down on the bar, his cheek bathing in a pool of spilled booze.

"Where are you?" she asked, moving tentatively toward the man with the closely cropped hair.

"Here," he said, standing up so the light revealed his features. She recognized him from his latest federal mug shot. Keeping her distance, she regarded him suspiciously.

"Your car broke down?"

"Yes. I've got help coming."

He sipped his malt whiskey, put down the glass, looked up at her, and announced, "If road service doesn't show in a little while, I'll take a look at your car. I know a lot about fixing automobiles."

"That's very kind of you, but I'm sure it won't be necessary." She pointedly turned her back, knowing that her cold-shouldering him would be a sufficient challenge for his over-blown ego. Several long moments elapsed in the silent bar before he slipped into position next to her.

"I'm Otto Holman, and I'd like to buy you a drink."

"No, thanks, I'm driving," she responded coldly. She looked around as if she regretted having come in to get help.

Holman, wearing camouflage fatigues and a green T-shirt, saw her anxiety and attempted to reassure her. "Not to worry, you're safe here with me. I own this joint. Nobody's going to get out of line while I'm around."

"I don't doubt it, but . . ."

"What'll it be?"

She smiled uncertainly and then slipped off her coat, holding it over her arm as if she were ready to leave at any moment. In a tentative voice she ordered, "Dewars and soda, little ice."

Watching him undress her with his mean gray eyes, she thought that Adriene was right on the money; this animal was most definitely a grade-A scumbag type. But she followed him over to his table.

When he handed her drink to her, Hagstrom looked at his wrinkled fatigues and asked, "You in the Army or something?"

"Once upon a time, yeah. Special Forces, 'Nam."

She looked at him with an expression of sudden respect, her breasts moving slightly under her blouse.

"What's the matter?"

"Nothing." She took a big swallow of her drink. "Well, I lost somebody over there."

"Jeeze, I'm sorry. Somebody real close?"

"My big brother. I was only ten when he was killed. He was Army too. Oh, sorry—my name's Joan."

She had set it up perfectly. Holman's guard was down; all he was thinking about was how to get over with her. He didn't pause to wonder why Santa had dropped this present in his lap. Hagstrom slowly drew him out. It was easy to get him to start telling stories, tales she knew were pure fantasy.

Three drinks later he leaned forward and confided, "When I was in 'Nam I did things . . . well, things I'm not too proud of now."

"Did you ever kill anyone up close?"

He drank some whiskey before whispering, "Yeah."

"Did it . . . ?"

"What?"

"Excite you?"

"I never told anyone this before, but, yeah, it did. A few times I even got off on it."

She lowered her eyes. "I think I understand."

"Why? Does violence turn you on?"

She turned away and said shyly, "Sometimes."

"Do you get off on bondage?"

She looked defiantly at him and announced, "Yes." Then, as if appalled at her own words, she blurted out, "I have to go."

"Joan, wait. Please." He tugged her gently back into her chair. "Joan, once, maybe twice during my lifetime I've met a woman who I found exciting, someone I wanted to know better, someone I wanted to get it on with. But? I never had the courage to take command of the moment. And then?" He shrugged, let his shoulders sag. "She was gone, and out of my life for good, and I ended up always regretting not having been able to express my true feelings at that moment." He began caressing her wrist. "You're a very exciting woman, and I don't want to lose this moment with you."

When she said nothing, but remained sitting, Holman gave the bartender a signal. In a few minutes she and Holman were alone in the dimly lit bar. The two drunks had been shoved out the door by the grinning bartender, who then discreetly vanished into the back room.

Holman's fingers made tiny circles on her wrist and then suddenly gripped it hard. He gradually increased the pressure. "Am I making you wet?"

She moaned, "Yes," thinking, What an utter asshole.

"Let's get it on right here and now. The two of us."

She looked at him boldly, her eyes falling to his fingers holding her wrist in an iron grip. "You might not enjoy the same things that I do."

"I bet I will," he assured her.

"I'm into submission."

"So am I." He leaned up out of his chair and kissed her, his disgusting tongue probing deep inside her mouth.

She nudged him back into his seat. "I need you to be *my* slave."

Leaning back in her seat, she brought up her legs, slid her hands under her skirt, and removed her panty hose. She got up and circled him, dancing the hose over his head and face, at the same time toying with the bristles of his short hair with her free hand. When she was behind him, she stopped and slipped the crotch of the panty hose over his head. "Can you smell me?" she asked, leaning over his shoulder and lifting up his arm.

"Yes, I can smell you and I love it."

Pulling a sour face, she said, "I'm glad," and with one leg of the panty hose she tied his wrist to his neck. She did the same with the other arm. Stepping back, she admired her work. Rambo tethered to panty hose. She wished she had a photo of him for next year's Chippendale's calendar. Lifting up her chair, she set it down so that she would be facing him. She lowered herself down and, lifting her skirt above her knees, arched one leg over his. She moved her hand erotically up her leg, and pretended to be masturbating. "Can you see what I'm doing?"

"Yes," he gasped. "Tell me what it feels like."

"I'm all moist and hot. Ahh! Ahh!" She suddenly slapped him in the face with her free hand.

"Again! Hurt me."

She hit him, a real solid blow on his chest. "Talk to me about dangerous things you've done."

"I assassinated five people in 'Nam."

"Oh, yes. It feels so good. Make me come, Otto. Make me come." She moaned, lolling her head, her face strained by simulated passion. "Slave. Tell me what it feels like to kill." She punched him again. His erection made a disgusting bulge in his trousers.

"I'll tell you," he grunted, "but first I want you to take out my cock and suck on it."

"Later, slave. Later." She punched him again; this time her heart was really in it.

Holman's labored breathing filled the silence in the deserted bar. Hagstrom's head lolled back, and her fingers worked frantically under her skirt.

"Open my fly."

"Later. Tell me what it's like to watch someone die. Quick, before I come." She reached down and dug her nails into his crotch.

He moaned and blurted, "Someone planted a bomb under me."

"A bomb!" She squeezed hard. "Talk to me about it. How did it feel?"

"Scary. Exciting. I almost got off."

She moaned, digging her nails deeper. "Who did it? Why? Tell me!"

"They wanted to know. Why do you care about any of that?"

She felt his erection wilting as Holman tried to free himself from her panty hose.

"You've broken the spell," she said, getting up and grabbing her coat.

"Wait," he said, ripping free of the restraints and pulling her back into her chair.

"I love it when you're violent," she said. She licked her lips slowly, invitingly. "Do you like lap dancing?"

"I've never done it," Holman admitted, his suspicion overcome by renewed hope.

"It's great," she said. Raising her skirt, she straddled his lap with her legs and sat down on top of him. She rubbed her body over him, moving slowly, purposefully, her head arched back, her breathing becoming more and more labored.

"What are you doing to me?" he moaned. "It's wonderful. Are you coming?"

"I don't think I can now."

"I'm sorry, I didn't mean to break the spell for you."

She didn't respond, but continued to glide her body across his, circling, pumping, groaning. She snapped forward, sliding her arms around him, clutching him to her, her head on his shoulder. She bit his neck, then his ear, nibbled on his earlobe.

His moans sounded almost infantile. "Bite me hard," he begged.

Instead of complying, she suddenly stood up and dropped her skirt and panties on the floor. Her eyes blazing, she faced Holman, who had worked one hand free and clumsily tried to grab her with it. Avoiding his hand, she reached into the pocket of her coat lying on the next table and pulled out a 9-mm Beretta automatic. In one move she whirled on Holman, slammed the gun against the side of his face, and then jammed it into his surprised mouth.

"You love pain, don't you?" she whispered, her face mere inches from his terrified eyes that stared through the sheer panty hose she had stretched over the upper part of his face. "Time to play, Otto. Time to die!"

Holman didn't even notice the pool of urine forming on the seat of his chair. He sat perfectly still, afraid that the slightest movement would encourage her to pull the trigger. He could taste the oily metal of the gun, feel the trickle of blood from the cut in his gums made by its barrel.

A small voice somewhere in the back of her mind told Hagstrom that she was not only breaking every rule in the Patrol Guide, but she was also giving an Academy Award–level performance to a captive audience of one. "Tell me about the bomb, Otto."

Involuntarily, Holman's body began to shudder and he tried to push some words out past the barrel of the gun. Easing it out of his mouth, she pointed just to the side of his head and squeezed the trigger slowly, while her free hand worked frantically between her legs. The gun went off with the effect of a crash of thunder in the deserted bar.

Holman screamed in terror, and the bartender flew out of the back room.

Aiming the gun at him, Hagstrom shouted wildly, "Fuck off, asshole, unless you want to play too!"

Charlie held up his hands and hurriedly backed through the swinging door to the kitchen.

"Please, lady," Holman begged, tears running down his

cheeks. "Listen—it's no big deal. This guy I used to know. Calls himself Dinny'O. He came here."

Hagstrom put the muzzle of the gun against the center of Holman's forehead, looked directly into his eyes, and said, "Who? You telling me the truth?"

"Christ, yes. The guy's real name is Frank Griffin. We were stuntmen back in L.A., years ago. I swear to God, I don't know what the fuck he's into, but he's got heavy people after him."

Hagstrom allowed herself a small smile of satisfaction. Keeping the gun trained on Holman, she awkwardly pulled up her skirt and slipped into her coat. She could see from Holman's expression that he was beginning to put it all together. "You better believe it, lover. And I'm one of them."

When she reached her car she was trembling from reaction, shocked at what she had found out she was capable of doing. Part of her had gotten off on it, enjoyed it.

Agueda came over and slipped a comforting arm around her shoulders. "How'd it play?"

Hagstrom, feeling a growing sense of shame, knew that she could never tell her friend what had really happened. She smiled wanly and said, "Maybe it played a little too well."

Surrounded by the deserted financial and governmental heart of New York City, the Big Building was a glowing beehive.

On the eleventh floor, detectives hurried back and forth between units. In the Joint Robbery Task Force area the television was tuned to "Shopping at Home," on which a saleswoman praised the qualities of a Rolex lookalike. Detectives typed reports and conducted telephone interviews. In the Special Fraud Squad area, a known Hispanic confidence man heatedly denied "kiting" a losing Lotto ticket and selling it to a Wall Street lawyer. "I nid my lawyer, man. You guys are a pen eendi ass," the unlucky flimflam artist whined.

Vinda, alone in his office, perched on the edge of his desk, staring at the blackboard. The Lucas-Johnston shootout had turned his investigation topsy-turvy. Now he wasn't sure whether he should be searching for a psycho who killed randomly, or for a killer who operated with malice and forethought. He looked at a note that Moose had left on his desk: *Lou, Malcolm Webster telephoned. Will call back in A.M.*

He checked the time: 0017. Wednesday. A new day had begun, and he was still working. He loved it; he hated it. He looked at the telephone and thought of the last time he had spoken to Jean. He had called her to see how she was feeling. "Pretty good," she had said. "I'm watching *Now, Voyager.*"

"You love that movie, don't you?"

"It's one of my favorites," she had said. "Wait. Here comes the best part. Paul Henreid is lighting their cigarettes. He's handing Bette Davis hers." Jean parroted, " 'Why ask for the moon when we have the stars?' "

He had heard the theme music in the background and visualized the camera panning up to the moon. Jean had died that night.

He looked out at the moon. "I miss you, honey." He slumped wearily into his chair, flipped open the case folder, and saw the crime-scene photo of Valarie Griffin's body splayed under a blanket, and he knew with a cop's instinct that her death was the linchpin of the case.

Veronica Place cut across Erasmus Street and continued past the convent of Holy Cross Church, a house of worship renowned for its flamboyant tracery, stained-glass windows, and wide buttresses sunk deep into the Brooklyn earth.

Two large oaks shaded the convent's façade, their barren branches etching shadows across the nunnery. A footpath ran alongside both sides of the convent and met in the rear where it separated, connecting the priory with the church and the school.

The grounds were dark, deserted; a wind gust sent small eddies of snow whirling over the surrounding blacktop. In the back of the church, the silhouette of a man loomed in the shadows.

Worthington studied the convent, a wide three-story brick

building with rows of five windows on each of the three floors; drainpipes came down at both ends of the gutters. Some of the windows on the second and third floors were slightly open.

Worthington's head was deep within the hood of a black parka, and a black turtleneck was thick around his throat. He darted over to the priory and dropped a knapsack on the ground. He took out a length of rope that he tied in a reef knot around his right ankle, and tied the other end to the knapsack's straps.

Standing on his toes, he stretched his arms up and, placing his hands on the sill, shinnied himself up onto the narrow ledge, balancing himself by digging his fingers into the brickwork. Reaching gingerly into his parka, he pulled out a rubber plunger cup and suctioned it against the glass directly over the inside latch. Then he took out a glass cutter, placed the blade flush with the edge of the suction cup, and cut out a circle of glass, which he removed with the plunger cup and carefully placed on the sill. Inserting three fingers inside the hole, he slid open the hatch. With the heel of his palm he pushed up the window, then climbed inside.

Standing perfectly still, he attuned his senses to the sights and sounds of the nunnery. As he crouched on the floor, somewhere upstairs a toilet was flushed.

He untied the rope around his ankle and hoisted in the knapsack.

A large kitchen was to his right. The parlor was on the left; it had heavy, rather ugly furniture and dark patterned wallpaper. He reached into his backpack and took out a Saronex overjacket and pants. He put them on and slipped on the hood and cape. He picked up his fangs and inserted them into his mouth. Reaching back into his pouch, he lifted out a folded piece of black cloth and unwrapped a gleaming new double-bit axe with a sawed-off handle. He slipped thongs attached to the axe's handle around his right wrist, and walked noiselessly over to the staircase.

The stairs led him up into a carpeted corridor with closed

wooden doors on both sides. A night light glowed from a wall
sconce. He padded over to the first door, unmindful of the axe's
cold blade bobbing against his knee. Quietly working the knob,
he cracked the door and stepped inside a drab little room with a
dresser and a small writing table and chair. A crucifix hung on
the wall above the bed.

A nun, who appeared to be in her late sixties and had short
gray hair, snored peacefully. Looking down at her, his face
puffed out with anger. The blood must be fresh, pure, in order
to strengthen the bond. This one was old, useless. He raised the
axe above his head, and was about to bring it down into her
head, when he stopped. No. I'm not going to sully my offering
by taking worthless blood, he told himself, and lowered the axe.

As he was leaving the room, he heard a door open down the
hall and jumped back. Peeking out, he saw a woman walking
toward a door at the end of the hall. She wore a maroon robe and
had short auburn hair glowing with the luster of youth. This one
was young; his skin tingled.

He watched as she went into the room and closed the door.
He padded after her, placing his back to the wall, his hands
outstretched, waiting. A toilet flushed inside the room. Tap
water ran. The doorknob was turning. His lips stretched around
his fangs.

She stepped out, only to have his clawlike hand slap across her
mouth, shoving her back inside. He kicked the door closed, and
forced her over to the bathtub. Her robe fell open, revealing a
pink cotton nightgown. He thrust the hand holding the axe
under her legs. The free-swinging axe clanged against the tub as
he swept her off the floor and raised her trembling body up into
the air. Tears gathered in her frightened eyes, and her face had
a deathly pallor. He arched her head back to uncover her soft
throat. He brought it to his open mouth, his cold fangs kissed
her, pricking her skin, and then he plunged the razor-sharp
incisors into her throat, slashing them about as he withdrew, and
snapping her head away from him as the scarlet jet rushed forth,

spraying the wall and tub. Forcing the dying woman down on her knees, he held her head in the tub until the forceful stream had become a trickle. Then he dropped her body and stepped back. Looking down at the kneeling corpse, he saw that her robe and nightgown had gathered up around her hips. He stared at the thick curls between her legs, and thought of his Valarie. He hurried over to the door, opened it, and peeked out, thinking, Is this the only young one?

A pack of homeless dogs skulked down Woods Place as the RMP cruised into the street. Holy Cross schoolyard was a gaping enclosed space; it resembled a prison recreation area with its twelve-foot-high fence topped by gleaming razor wire.

The operator of the radio motor patrol car, a man in his early twenties with wavy black hair, parked just beyond the glow of the only working streetlight on the block, shoved the transmission into neutral, and switched off the headlights. His partner, the RMP's recorder, who was charged with the operation of the radio and entering the time and verbatim record of all radio transmissions directed to their car, was a tall woman also in her early twenties. Her long black hair was pulled severely back and tied in a ponytail.

She opened the glove compartment, reached down into the soggy bag between her legs, and pulled up two containers of coffee that she set down on top of the glove compartment door. Both officers took their containers, pried off the lids, notched drinking holes into the rims, and replaced the tops. Wisps of steam flowed out of the holes. Sipping coffee, the recorder asked, "You still seeing the medical student?"

"Yeah."

"Did you ever get around to telling her you're on the Job?"

"You kiddin'? She wouldn't piss on me if she knew I was a cop. I told her I was in law school."

Sipping her coffee, she asked, "What do you think of the new contract?"

"It sucks. The PBA sold us down the river again."

"You're right. The damn dinosaurs who run the union only care about enriching their own pensions, and don't ever think about us having to make a living."

He turned in his seat, measuring her with growing interest. "You know, late tours make me horny."

She shook her head, smiled, and said, "If you want, I'll get out and you can relieve yourself, but please use a handkerchief."

He sat stewing in mixed embarrassment and anger for five minutes. Then he looked straight ahead, scratched his jaw thoughtfully, and pointed to the automobile parked in front of them. "Strange place to park a new car, on a deserted side street like this."

"Lovers?"

"I don't see any movement inside."

She opened the door and slid out of the car, unholstering her revolver as she walked. With her flashlight extended in her left hand, she cautiously approached on the passenger side. The operator got out and approached on the driver's side.

Worthington was disoriented and almost faint when he walked from Erasmus Street into Woods Place and saw the policemen walking away from his rented car. The devils want to destroy us, he seethed, his fingers forming angry claws before he caught himself and composed himself, presenting a smiling, benign persona. "Good evening to ya, Officers."

"Do you live around here?" asked the recorder, directing her beam at the gaunt stranger.

"I do. I'm Father McAndrews. I live in the rectory."

"It's two A.M., Father," said the operator, relaxing his guard. "What are you doing out in this deserted place?"

"That's my car," the priest said, "and I'm on my way to give the sacrament of Extreme Unction to a dying parishioner."

"Extreme Unction?" the recorder echoed, arching a puzzled eyebrow at the bogus priest. "I haven't heard a priest refer to that sacrament by that name in a long time. Usually they say 'last rites.' "

"Really?" the priest said, aware of the potential danger of her words.

"Do you have any identification, Father?" she asked.

Shaking his head at his overzealous partner, the operator rolled his eyes and looked away.

The priest looked at her for a second or two and said, "I do, Officer." He walked over to the RMP and slid his knapsack off his shoulder and onto the hood of the police car.

The police officers gathered on either side of him, the operator on his right, the recorder to his left.

"I suppose you just cannot be too careful these days," the priest said, unstrapping his knapsack, rummaging through the contents, sliding his hand around the axe's handle, gripping it. "Ah. Here's my wallet."

Whipping out the axe, he whirled and savagely smashed the flat side of the heavy blade against the recorder's kneecap, shattering bones and cartilage and sending her reeling backward onto the ground, where she lay writhing in agony.

The operator's face paled at the sight of the steel coming directly at his head. Instinctively he went for his revolver, at the same time twisting his body away from the onrushing blade, and snapping his free hand up to protect his face.

But the young policeman was not fast enough. The blade struck, severing his hand at the wrist, and plunging into his skull with a thudding crack.

Splayed on her back, the recorder saw her partner go down and screamed, "You son of a bitch!" She fired three rounds at the fleeing assailant. The pain blurred her vision. She fired another round. Where did he go? Her back was propped up against the schoolyard wall, her face twisted by pain. "Bastard! Where are you?" She opened the cylinder and saw she had discharged four rounds. Reaching under her duty jacket, she pulled out a speed loader containing six rounds, and placed it on her lap.

Keep calm, she told herself, looking at her partner and knowing with certainty that he was beyond help. Keeping her revolver at the ready, she turned awkwardly onto her side and, reaching into her jacket, extracted her portable radio from its holder. Groaning from the pain in her leg, she bit down on her lip, brought the radio up to her mouth, and transmitted, "Sixty-seven Boy, Ten-thirteen Woods Place and Erasmus. Ten-thirteen. My partner's been killed."

Before Central had a chance to retransmit the Thirteen, the sounds of distant sirens splintered the night.

TWENTY-TWO

VINDA PARKED THE DEPARTMENT CAR ON WOODS Place and rushed over to the chief of detectives, who was leaning up against the schoolyard fence. "What happened?" Vinda demanded.

"He killed a nun and a cop." Leventhal filled in the details. Vinda slumped against the fence. "You told me on the phone that the convent was on Veronica Place."

"Yes. Right around the corner. The Cardinal was on the phone to the Mayor before I got to the scene." He sighed. "The Mayor has asked for and received the PC's resignation."

Vinda looked at his old friend, amazed to see him unshaven and wearing a badly wrinkled suit. He looked like he'd aged ten years overnight. "Has the Mayor named a new PC?"

"Yeah."

"Who?"

"Me."

Vinda eyed his friend with a mixture of concern and sadness. "I don't know if I should offer condolences or congratulations."

"Neither do I. But now that a cop's been added to the list, your head and mine will be the next ones to get chopped."

Looking at his friend, Vinda said, "You need a shave, Sam."

"I know," Sam Staypress responded glumly, rubbing his stubble.

"Who'd you name chief of detectives?"

"Bookbinder, from Manhattan North."

"Good man. And what about Agent Orange?"

"Chief Eberhart has decided to throw in his papers. He's going to retire to Florida and pollute the environment down there for a change."

"What goes around comes around," Vinda said, looking at the new PC. Then he stuck out his hand. Leventhal looked at it in surprise and then shook hands silently with John Vinda.

Police cars and service vehicles had cordoned off Woods Place. The Emergency Service floodlight truck that had illuminated the scene during the early morning still had its lamps on, silver beacons glowing into a gray day. The killer's rented car and the RMP assigned to the dead cop were corralled behind orange tape. A chalk outline of a body showed where the police officer had fallen; drying blood pooled next to the outline of the head. Crime-scene technicians, their tasks done, packed up equipment. Emergency Service teams still scoured the area, attempting to account for the four spent rounds the officer had fired at the perp.

Two detectives from Brooklyn South Homicide Task Force came over to Vinda and the PC. "Commissioner," a thin black detective said. Nodding to Vinda, he looked at his memo book and reported, "No witness 'cept the injured cop, no blood trail leaving the scene, which means she didn't hit 'em. The doer's car was rented to a 'James Turner' with an address that turned out to be a convenience mail drop on Twelfth Street in Manhattan."

The other detective, an overweight white man with a hawk nose and a prominent jaw, said, "We sent a team there. It's a phony, rented by some fuckin' phantom a year ago."

"Prints?" Vinda asked hopefully.

"Plenny. All we gotta do now is match 'em up with some mutt," said the thin detective.

Vinda slowly looked over the crime scene. "Any signs of the murder weapon?"

"*Nada*, among the missing," the black cop said.

"Let me see if I got this right," Vinda said, and proceeded to reenact the crime. "He whacks the cop in the head with his axe. The cop goes down here." Pointing, he added, "His injured partner is on the ground over there; she struggles to get her gun out of her holster and lets four go at the perp." He folded his arms across his chest, adding, "And while she's plugging shots at him, the doer is retrieving his axe from the dead cop's skull."

"That's how it plays," Hawknose said.

"If someone was unloadin' lead at me, I certainly wouldn't waste no time in hauling ass out of there," said the thin detective.

"Neither would I," said the PC.

"Unless you were Mr. Super Cool or a major wackadoo," Vinda said, going over to the rented car and bending under the tape. The doors and windows of the car were smeared with fingerprint powder. Squeezing inside and kneeling on the front seat, Vinda looked into the open glove compartment. The car's documents were inside a plastic packet. The doors on the passenger's and driver's sides had been opened, ventilating the car with cold air. Vinda took a deep breath. Despite the eddy of air, the saccharine smell of some strong perfume, possibly aftershave, still clung tenaciously to the interior. The ancients, the nun-psychologist had said, believed vampires could be identified by their putrid odor. He wondered if a twentieth-century version might try to conceal his imagined stink with some heavy-duty after-shave or cologne.

Vinda backed out of the car. He looked toward Church Avenue. Barriers held back the curious and the media. Going to the corner of Woods Place, he looked up Erasmus Street at the impressive stone buttresses of Erasmus Hall High School. Turning back, he saw the new PC standing alone by the schoolyard fence. He went over to him. The PC nudged him out of earshot of the other detectives, and said, "John, to be appointed PC is every cop's dream."

"Not every cop," Vinda corrected.

"I can do a lot of good for the Job and the people of this city."

"Sam? You have my vote, you don't have to sell me."

"I'm skating on thin ice. If this case isn't broken soon, I'm history."

"We'll get him, Sam."

Leventhal turned to face the fence, slipping his fingers between the links. "Are you familiar with the provision of the Administrative Code that allows the PC to appoint one detective lieutenant to the permanent rank of Inspector of Detectives, without benefit of any civil service test? A three-rank jump."

"That line hasn't been filled in over twenty years."

" 'At's true. But the line is still in the budget. Hizzoner asked me to tell you that the rank is yours as soon as you bring this guy down. And there will be grade money for all your people."

"The bureaucracy of self-preservation, protecting their nest with a bribe," Vinda said. "You're in office only a few hours and you're already wheelin' and dealin'."

"John, it'd be a promotion for a job well done, nothing else."

Vinda looked at him and grinned and said, "I'm not in this for the money, Sam. You got to learn not to worry so much."

Vinda found Moose and Marsella at the top of the staircase in the convent. "Whadda we got?" he asked them.

They waltzed him through a reenactment of the murder.

When they finished, he walked down the hall and entered the bathroom. Blood still disfigured the white-tiled room. "The ME was excited about this one," Marsella told the Whip. "During the course of the struggle, the stopper and a washcloth clogged the drain, catching the blood in the tub. The ME scooped up every drop."

She finally got her blood, Vinda thought, leaving the bathroom. "Where are Agueda and Hagstrom?" he asked Moose.

"Interviewing the nuns," Marsella replied.

Looking down the hallway, Vinda saw Agueda and Hagstrom talking to a huddled group of frightened nuns. Agueda looked his way and gave a small wave of her hand, acknowledging him.

Five minutes later, when they were finished interviewing the nuns, the two detectives came over to Vinda and the others. "Lou, can we speak to you a minute?" Hagstrom said, leading them out of earshot of the other cops on the scene. She threw back her shoulders, filling her blazer with her bosom, smiled, and confided, "Last night I had a tête-à-tête with our friend Otto Holman."

"You did what?" Vinda asked, his eyes narrowing.

"We figured one woman playing a damsel in distress might loosen his macho tongue."

"Some damsel," Marsella muttered.

Vinda looked at Agueda. "Did you go along, too?"

"Yes," Agueda said.

Shaking his head in mild approval, Vinda asked, "Did you find out anything?"

"According to Holman, Dinny'O and Frank Griffin are the same person."

Vinda reeled back against the wall, clasping his hands behind his head and staring off down the corridor at one of the nuns who was weeping and being comforted by another one. "Were the sisters able to tell you anything?"

"No," Agueda said.

Vinda continued to stare down the corridor, a jumble of dif-

ferent thoughts racing through his mind. "We need a photograph of Griffin," he said.

"Holman told me that Griffin used to be a stuntman," Hagstrom said.

"Get over to the Screen Actors Guild," Vinda told Hagstrom.
"See if they have a photograph of Griffin. I'm starting to doubt
the accuracy of that composite."

"But Worthington saw the guy loitering near the dressing
rooms," Moose said.

"Did he?" Vinda said. "And if he did, it doesn't mean that he
was the doer." Vinda wondered how Hagstrom had got Holman
to talk, and was tempted to ask her, but after brief reflection he
decided that he was probably better off not knowing, and did not
ask. He said to Hagstrom, "Holman conned me when I spoke to
him. He might have conned you, too."

"Oh, I really don't think so," she said, her cheeks coloring
and her eyes avoiding his.

The Tudor City supermarket on First Avenue was not crowded
at ten o'clock in the morning. The fruit-and-vegetable man was
busy unpacking produce, taking his time arranging his wares so
that they appealed to the eye. Apples had a high polish; grape-
fruits were pyramided so that bruised skins did not show. All the
leafy vegetables had been wetted down.

The lady behind the appetizer counter wore latex gloves as
she culled overaged fish and cold cuts from the display case.

Packers replenished shelves.

Michael Worthington ambled along the aisle, pushing a shopping cart. He grabbed a box of Tampax down off a shelf and
tossed it into the cart. He threw in Q-tips and cotton balls, and
pushed the cart over to the appetizer counter. "Morning," he
said to the woman working the counter.

"Morning, Mr. Worthington," the woman named Mary said.

Bending to examine the contents of the display case, Worthington said, "Valarie loves belly lox."

"Fresh this morning."

"I'll take a quarter-pound."

Mary picked up a long, thin knife and sliced off slices. Wrapping the fish in white paper, she asked, "Will there be anything else?"

"A chub and a quarter-pound of cream cheese and chives."

Going about filling his order, she asked, "How is your wife?"

"She's good today. In fact, we're going to take a drive out to Jones Beach. Valarie loves to watch the ocean in the winter. She can sit for hours watching the surf."

"I know," she said longingly. "I love it too. It's been a long time since I've visited the ocean. I'm trapped here in the city."

"How's your husband?"

"Captain Marvel is considering prying himself away from his soaps and looking for a job. Humph! I should live so long."

"Things'll get better."

"Only when I muster the courage to make them better," she said, handing him his order.

Worthington went up to the checkout counter and paid his bill. As he was about to leave, he spotted the rack of supermarket tabloids. One of the headlines proclaimed, WEREWOLF MARRIED TO NUN IN RELIGIOUS CEREMONY. He pulled the paper from the rack and paid the cashier, saying, "My wife loves to read this garbage."

The cashier took his money and looked at him inquiringly. "Do you think Elvis might still be alive?"

"Could be," he said, and walked out of the store, going next door to pick up Valarie's dry cleaning.

Upon arriving home, he hung her cleaning in her closet, and stacked her hygiene articles with all the other unopened ones on the top shelf of the closet. Going past his eternally praying wife, he kissed her on the head and said, "I'll make breakfast." In the kitchen he put the food inside the crowded refrigerator, making room by dumping some of the old stuff into a plastic garbage bag.

He put the coffee on and then went into the bathroom, took off his shirt, and examined the scratches Kate Coswell had made on his shoulders and back. He took out a bottle of hydrogen peroxide and swabbed them. "Bitch!"

That done, he patted on more after-shave and went back into the kitchen to prepare breakfast. Ten minutes later he walked into the bedroom carrying a tray. He put it down on the bed and sat.

After spreading cream cheese and chives over half a bagel, he placed a slice of lox on it and took a bite. Glancing over at his wife kneeling on her prayer stool, he smiled and said, "It went well last night, Val. I sent the Eternal One a nun, a real one this time. We'll be safe for a while now."

A mood of desolation suddenly overcame him. "I wonder if He will ever forgive me for taking you away from Him?"

The telephone on the nightstand rang. Leaping off the bed, he snapped the receiver up to his ear.

"Morning, Michael."

"And how is the world's reigning movie queen on this fine morning?"

Jessica Merrill, wearing silk bikini underpants and an over-sized T-shirt bearing a teddy bear logo front and back, coiled in the corner of the bed with a telephone stuck to her ear. "I'm fine, Michael."

"Do you still have your police bodyguards following you around?"

"Yes, damn it. I told my agent to get rid of them. They're parked outside my apartment right now, waiting for me to leave. I had to sneak out by the service entrance last night."

"Where are you now?"

"At a friend's in the East Village. Michael, can we meet for coffee? I need to talk to you."

"Meet me at four o'clock in Tudor City Park." He hung up.

Jessica slammed the phone down.

"Well?" Laura Steward asked. She was wearing a yellow silk

kimono and standing by the window in the tiny apartment's bedroom, staring across Third Street at the men's homeless shelter.

"I'm meeting him late this afternoon."

"Oh, Jessica, you've made me so happy." Laura ran over to her friend and hugged her. "You're very good to me."

Reaching up, Jessica caressed her friend's face. Laura untied her robe and, with a shrug of her shoulders, allowed it to slide from her body. She watched as Jessica's eyes devoured her, and smiled when she saw her gleaming lips part. Jessica reached up and glided her hand through Laura's triangle of tightly knit curls, slipping one finger between her slightly parted legs, ever so gently stroking her. Laura took hold of her friend's hand and brought it up to her mouth, licking her wet finger, and, looking into her eyes, promised, "Now I'm going to be good to you."

"Look at the clowns!" Worthington said contemptuously to Valarie, as he spread cream cheese on the other half of the bagel. The television showed the cameras panning over Veronica Place, while the voice-over gave the grisly details of the murder. A close-up featured the new police commissioner promising an imminent arrest.

Worthington laughed. Then he saw the group of detectives standing behind the commissioner, on top of the convent stoop. They were the ones from Rue St. Jacques: Vinda, Moose, Marsella; they were the ones who wanted to take his Valarie away from him. He got up off the bed and took a Mini Mag-Lite off the night table.

Hurrying out into the foyer, he slammed open the hall closet and pushed aside coats, making a hole. That done, he stepped inside and knelt on the floor. Turning on the Mag-Lite, he directed the beam to the molding. Flush with the wood, two hinges, camouflaged with oyster white paint, attached a fake panel to the wall. Standing up, he directed the light to the top part of the panel, then reached up on the closet shelf and took down a grapefruit knife that he kept there. He inserted the knife into the thin vertical line just below the shelf, and pried off the panel. He leaned it up against the wall.

The secret compartment contained five shelves neatly stacked with an assortment of pyrotechnic devices, Claymore mines, grenades, bars of Semtex, detonators, and two Heckler & Koch machine pistols. One end of the shelves contained stacked boxes of illegal exploding bullets.

Worthington, his hands firmly planted on his hips, surveyed his private armory with satisfaction. "Ol' Dinny'O knows how to deal with the likes of them."

The fourth-floor corridors of the east wing of Kings County Hospital were clogged with beds. Emaciated AIDS patients gazed dully at the people passing by. Stepping out of the oversized elevator, Vinda was struck by the look of utter despair etched on their sunken faces.

At the end of the wing, three semiprivate rooms were kept in reserve for injured police, fire, and correction officers.

Police Officer Lucy Seaver shared her room with a female correction officer who had suffered a compound fracture of the left arm trying to subdue a flipped-out junkie.

As Vinda and the two women detectives made their way down the hallway toward Seaver's room, they spotted the group of off-duties milling about. Police Officer Vinny Cutrone, Brooklyn South's chunky PBA trustee, was busy loudly complaining about the Job. When he saw Vinda and the others, he pushed away from the off-duties and greeted Vinda. "How ya doin', Lou?" Cutrone's hands were constantly in motion when he talked.

"How is she?" Vinda asked.

"In a lotta pain," the trustee said. "And I'm gonna tell ya sump-'en else too, I'm gettin' fuckin' tired of gonna cops' funerals."

"Me too," Vinda said, asking, "What did the doctors say?"

"What did dey say? Dey said what dey always say, dey don't know. She'll be on sick report for at least six months. Dey wired da pieces of her kneecap tagether, and if dat don't work, dey go back in and give 'er a knee replacement. Da kid's only worried she'll be surveyed outta de Job.''

"Who is inside with her?" Agueda asked the trustee.

"Her parents," the chunky man answered, stealing a glance at Agueda's breasts.

Hagstrom glanced at the policemen standing around in little, concerned groups and asked the trustee, "Was her partner married?"

"No," Cutrone answered sadly. "He leaves parents, and a brudder and sister."

Lucy Seaver had three drains in her injured knee. The limb was contained within a continuous-passive-range-of-motion contraption that automatically kept bending and relaxing the leg. She looked heavily sedated. A gray curtain separated the beds. Her distraught parents stood up as Vinda and his team entered the room. Vinda made the introductions and said to them, "It's important that we talk to your daughter."

"The nurse gave her Demerol a while ago. She keeps dozing off," her father said.

Hagstrom spoke words of encouragement to Officer Seaver's silently weeping mother.

Vinda made his way around to the side of the bed, and said softly, "Lucy, this is Lieutenant Vinda, can you hear me?"

The injured officer blinked open her eyes.

"Hi," Vinda said. "Are you up to talking a bit?"

Seaver winced. "I'm sorry I missed him, Lou. I always shoot expert at the range."

"You weren't at the range, Lucy, you were in the street. And suffering excruciating pain. You were lucky to get off four rounds. You probably saved your own life." Watching the leg bending and relaxing, he asked gently, "Are you up to telling us what happened?"

She said she was, and haltingly told her story. "We got careless, Lou. We let him get close to us."

"Don't blame yourself," Agueda said.

Vinda held up the composite sketch of the killer. "Lucy, did you ever see this face before?"

"I've seen it on every television station and front page in this city. But that is not the man who killed my partner."

Agueda and Hagstrom exchanged glances.

Vinda felt a chill of uneasiness grip his stomach. "You're sure this is not the man?" Vinda said.

"No," the cop said firmly.

"Is there *any* similarity?" Agueda asked, her tone almost pleading.

"No." Lucy moaned from the pain. "Mommy, get the nurse."

Her mother rushed outside; her father took his daughter's hand, comforting her. Vinda knew that the mother would return soon with a nurse who would in all probability evict them from the room, so he hurriedly asked, "Lucy, think back. What did you think when you first saw this guy approaching you and your partner?"

Two gurneys and three civilians crowded into the elevator on the way down.

The sky was overcast as the detectives walked out of the building. "What do you think?" Agueda asked the Whip.

"I think we're going to have to pull back all those composites," Vinda said. "I'm going to speak with Worthington. Lucy Seaver's perp sounds like a close match to him. God, what an idiot I've been."

He stopped outside the door that led to the morgue. "I want you to give Moose and Marsella a Ten-one through Operator Forty-seven, and coordinate your efforts in finding Frank Griffin. And get a photo of our wonderful witness to show to Lucy."

"John? What are you doing here?" Dr. Patricia Marcal asked, looking up out of a cadaver's chest cavity.

Running his finger over the stainless-steel table, he said, "I hear you retrieved blood from the bathtub."

She peeled off her gloves and threw them into the wastebasket. "I don't believe he's drinking their blood."

Going over to the body on the table, he said, "The poor nun?"

"Yes."

Examining the wound, he asked, "Why the vampire act, I wonder?"

"I think we have to assume it's a sexual thing with him. But we haven't found semen at any of the scenes."

"Maybe he practices safe sex?"

"John," she chided him, smiling. She went over to the sink and washed her hands. Pulling towels out of the wall dispenser, she turned to face him and said, "If you are correct, and he has the murder weapon in his mouth, then, when he bites down and severs the arteries, blood would swill into his mouth, causing him to retch, perhaps vomit."

"That would not happen if he found some way of keeping the blood out. Like maybe snapping the head away the instant he slices into the artery."

"That would require precise timing on his part."

"Not timing, Doctor. Practice."

T W E N T Y - T H R E E

A BRUISED PURPLE-BLUE SKY PEEPED THROUGH the overcast.

A taxi pulled to a stop in front of the fashionable, unpretentious cooperative apartment building on the southeast corner of Fifth Avenue and Sixty-eighth Street. A well-dressed woman got out and sauntered under the canopy that stretched from shiny black doors to the curb.

Vinda watched her from the department car he had parked on the northeast side of Fifth. A limousine with the vanity license plate MALCOLM had parked a few feet away from the awning. Webster is in residence, Vinda thought, tossing the vehicle identification plate onto the dashboard.

He waited on the corner for the gridlock to break, and when it did, he walked past smoking tailpipes and angry horns to the other side of the street.

Walking up on the driver's side of the limo, he stared through the tinted glass and made out the outline of Mr. Biceps. "Ya-te-hey, scumbag," Vinda called out, knocking on the glass.

The window whispered down; Biceps still looked like he was popping steroids.

"How'd you like New Jersey?"

"You cops all think you're comedians, don't you?"

"Naw. We're just a bunch of working fools tryin'a make it home at the end of the day."

"Sure you are."

"Is your master upstairs?"

"Waitin' on you." The window slid back up.

Vinda stepped off the elevator into the penthouse's foyer. Webster was waiting. He took Vinda's coat and hung it in a closet. The foyer was furnished with an antique walnut chest fitted with arms and a back that served for seating, and two walnut hall chairs.

Webster led him into the living room. The glass walls looked out over Central Park; across the park's bare, snow-dusted trees were the buildings of Central Park West etched in the distance.

A tall, distinguished-looking man rose to greet them. "You asked me to locate the best prosthodontist in the country, and here he is," Webster said to Vinda, introducing him to Sidney Polgreen.

Vinda and the doctor shook hands. "I'm working on a murder case . . ."

"I know," Polgreen said. "Malcolm gave me all the details."

Vinda took morgue photos from his breast pocket and handed them to the doctor. Webster saw what they were and said, obviously disturbed, "I have some work to do," and abruptly left the room.

Watching the dentist examine the photographs, Vinda said, "We assume that he needs his hands to control his victims, so we've concluded that the weapon must be held in his mouth. I've spoken to an ME and a prosthodontist and they've both told me that a prosthesis held in the mouth could not generate enough force to kill, because the human mouth is not made for predation."

"They were both wrong, Lieutenant," Polgreen said.

Vinda's eyebrows drew together as a wave of relief washed over him. Polgreen handed him back the photos and picked up his briefcase. He sat down on the calfskin-covered sofa, gesturing Vinda to the empty space next to him.

Vinda walked over and sat.

The doctor opened his case and took out a pencil. "I'd like you to lay this across the front of your mouth and bite down, generating as much force as you can."

Vinda complied with his request, his neck muscles straining with the effort. Removing the pencil, he looked at the marks he'd made and said, "I couldn't generate much force."

"That was because your front teeth, your incisors, are even and act as a vertical stop. Now take the pencil and lay it across your back teeth."

Vinda did that and produced enough force to bite deep into the wood. Removing the shaft, he examined the marks he had made, and said, "I did some number with the back teeth."

"That's because there is no vertical stop." Pointing to the back of Vinda's jaw, he said, "The masseter muscle is large and powerful. It enables us to raise and lower our jaws; it works in a fashion similar to the torquing force of a lever."

"How would such a prosthesis function?"

Polgreen took a bubble-wrapped package out of his briefcase. He unwrapped a plaster cast of the human mouth fitted with a prosthesis that looked like fangs.

"I made these for the production company of a Dracula film," he said. Using his pencil, he explained, "This prosthesis has only four canines, or fangs, if you will, two on top and two on the bottom. I've replaced the incisors with a flat metal bar that connects the canines. The bar strengthens, and acts as the vertical stop. Notice that the stop is an inch and a half above the point of the canines, allowing the user to bite deep before being stopped by the bar. I've replaced the bicuspids and molars with a flat metal bar, and further strengthened it by using crossbars connected to both sides of the bridge."

Tapping the prosthesis with his fingernail, Vinda asked, "Could this kill a person?"

"This? No. This is made for show. It's porcelain. But one constructed of a chromium-cobalt alloy, with razor-sharp canines—that would be a very deadly weapon."

"Why haven't we found any puncture wounds or entrance marks on any of the victims?"

"That is the clever part. Watch." Polgreen took the cast in his hands and opened the mouth. "When your killer bites down, the points of the canines puncture the skin. Then, as he continues his bite, they would come together, shearing through the skin and slicing deep, but leaving no telltale entrance marks or punctures. And the vertical bar across the front of the mouth is flat and would leave no clear marks."

Vinda took the fangs from Polgreen and practiced opening and closing them. "Why didn't the other prosthodontist I interviewed know this? He told me it was impossible."

"I can only surmise that he didn't bother to think out the problem. He probably dismissed the idea out of hand because of the construction of the human mouth. I do a lot of research on the subject because I probably do more work for the stage, television, and movies than any other dentist in the country. That's how I first met Malcolm."

"He made movies?"

"I used to produce them, years ago." Webster had drifted unnoticed back into the room, and had been sitting silently on a settee in a distant corner.

Vinda glanced back at the onetime movie producer and then asked the doctor, "Who could make these fangs?"

"Ah. Now you come to the hard part," Polgreen said, brushing his finger over the canines. "Any good prosthodontist could make the cast, but getting them made would be difficult."

"Why?" Vinda asked.

"No reputable doctor would order such a dangerous prosthesis without some compelling reason—and if he did order them, no reputable lab would make them."

"Couldn't our guy design them himself?" Vinda asked.

"Yes, he could. But he could not take the mold of his own mouth. That a dentist would have to do for him. And no lab would make them without a prescription listing the dentist's identification number."

"So? Where did he get them?" Vinda asked in frustration.

Polgreen sank back into the soft leather, and, concentrating, said, "I'll have to dwell on that a moment."

Vinda heard the tinkle of ice and turned to see Webster standing by the secretary desk made of burr walnut, pouring Wild Turkey into a rock glass. Webster saw him looking, and held out the bottle to him. Vinda shook his head no.

Ruminating aloud, Polgreen said, "No dentist or lab would make them, so your man would have to go into the underground."

"What underground?" Vinda asked.

Polgreen leaned forward, his hands cupping his knees. "Refugee dentists, mostly from the Soviet Union, who are too deficient in English to sit for the licensing exam, or who feel they're too old to go back to school to take makeup courses. There is a flourishing illegal medical network out there among Soviet emigrés. Mostly in the Brighton Beach section of Brooklyn."

"May I keep these for a while?" Vinda asked, looking at the molds in his hands.

"Of course," Polgreen said, snapping his case closed and getting up.

"Like a drink, Sid?" Malcolm Webster called.

"No, thank you, Malcolm, I'm running behind schedule today."

"My driver is downstairs. He'll take you wherever you want to go," Webster said, putting his glass down on the desk and walking Polgreen out to the elevator.

Vinda got up and went over to the wall, where he gazed out over Central Park. Ice skaters whizzed over the frozen pond while a forest of trees sprouted up through the glistening whiteness, mushrooming upward into a candelabra of barren branches. Off in the distance the soft white glow of the thousands of lights that festooned the Tavern on the Green lit up the gray day.

Vinda was suddenly struck by the fact that this would be his first Christmas without Jean; an almost paralyzing depression came over him.

Hearing footsteps, he turned and saw Webster walking over to the secretary for a refill. Vinda shook off his mood and said warmly, "Thank you for finding Polgreen."

Webster made a dismissive gesture and continued to plop ice cubes into his glass. "I'll do anything to get the bastard who murdered Adelaide."

Vinda walked over to the secretary and ran his finger over its beautiful carved wood. He looked at Webster and asked, "You ever know a guy named Frank Griffin?"

Webster picked up his glass and, shaking the ice thoughtfully, finally answered, "No."

"You sure?"

"Lieutenant, I've met many people over the course of my life, all of them occupying different levels of intimacy. Please don't expect me to resurrect a forgotten ghost on a minute's notice." He drank bourbon, slammed the glass down on the secretary, and walked over to the glass wall.

"Twelve years ago you squashed this ghost's story in the media. You also reached into the department and ensured that everything was done properly."

Genuine surprise showed on Webster's face. "*That* Frank Griffin," he muttered, staring off in the distance, concentrating on forgotten memories. "I remember now."

"Why did you have the story killed?"

"Griffin had worked on a few of the movies I produced. I only knew him casually from the set. Anyway, after the accident with his wife, he telephoned me, begging me to use my influence to have the story buried. He'd always been a nice guy, and he was in a lot of pain, so I did it. No big deal." He tossed down the remainder of his drink.

"A casual employee of yours telephones, asking you to kill a news story and ensure that the department stonewalls it too, and you do it, just on the basis of his being a nice guy?"

"Yes, just like that. I get off on helping people. It helps me assuage the occasional pangs of guilt I get over some of my less commendable business activities."

"You expect me to believe that?"

Webster banged his glass down, and sat on the sofa. He looked balefully at Vinda and snapped, "Yes, I do expect you to believe me. I told you, I felt sorry for him. Griffin was a loner who carried around a lot of luggage from his past."

"What kind of luggage?"

"Don't know. He was a strange, brooding man who kept to himself. The only time I ever saw him happy was when he told me he was getting married."

"Did Griffin give you a reason for wanting the story killed?"

"He said he didn't want the world to know that God had punished his wife for leaving Him to get married."

"Didn't you suspect that this guy might be a little nuts?"

"The man was distraught, in a lot of pain. I did what I could to ease his suffering."

"I'm beginning to think you are a pussycat, Malcolm."

Webster's tone hardened. "You don't ever want to do business with me."

"What did Griffin do on the movie set?"

"A stunt and squib man."

"What is a squib man?"

"Squibs are small electric or pyrotechnic devices used to ignite a charge. Whenever you're at the movies and you see bullets stitching along a wall or a car, or when you see some part of a body explode from a bullet's impact, those are squibs, little charges concealed in the wall or on the actor's body and set off electrically."

"Then it's safe for me to assume that Griffin was an explosives expert too."

"Absolutely."

"Whatever happened to him?"

"Don't know. He called me up to thank me, and I never heard from him again." Webster's face clouded over as he saw where Vinda was heading. "Is Griffin the man who murdered Adelaide?"

"I don't know, maybe." Vinda felt a stab of panic. Webster was capable of killing anyone he thought might have killed his daughter. He wouldn't wait for proof.

"How can I help you find him?"

"Do you still have access to the records of those production companies of yours, payrolls in particular?"

"Of course."

"Dig me out Griffin's social security number."

"I'll have it for you in the morning."

"Good." Vinda walked out into the foyer. A houseman appeared, holding his coat ready for him. Vinda slid his hands through the arms and shouldered the coat. He looked Webster in the eye and said, "Thanks. Stay in touch. And resist temptation, okay?"

Webster didn't respond, but turned on his heel and walked away.

The late-afternoon wind whipped across Vinda's face, invigorating him. He dashed across Sixty-eighth Street and got into the car. Tossing the vehicle identification plate back behind the visor, he saw Webster rush out of the building and look frantically around. Vinda got out of the car and called to him.

"I'm glad I caught you," Webster said, running over to him. "After you left, I remembered that there was one person on the set whom Griffin was friendly with. They grew up in the same orphanage. His name was Otto Holman, another stunt and squib man."

Vinda clenched his teeth. "Malcolm, were there any big stars in any of your movies?"

"Stars don't play in B-movies. Although Jessica Merrill did have a bit part in *Thin Lies*. She played the other woman."

"I have a strange feeling that she plays that part well."

"Yes, she does."

Vinda rested his hands on Webster's shoulder and, staring him straight in the eye, said, "Malcolm, ol' friend, I'd like you to do a few more things for me."

A tendril of grayish white smoke came up from behind the barricade of books.

Vinda still had trouble reconciling himself to the dichotomy of seeing Freud and a crucifix side by side on the wall of Sister Mary Margaret's office. He grinned as he made his way around the piles of books and journals cluttering the floor.

Peeking over the top of her desk, he said, "Afternoon, Sister."

"How did I know you would be dropping around sometime today?" she said, following his gaze down to the overflowing copper ashtray. She shrugged. "Who am I kidding? God knows I smoke, and He doesn't mind. So why should I be concerned about what anyone else thinks?"

She looked at him with a troubled face. "I heard about the murder at the convent in Brooklyn."

Vinda drew up a chair and sat down, saying, "We now have reason to believe the killer was married to a former nun who received permission to leave in order to marry, and was killed accidentally shortly after her marriage. We think her husband might be the guy we're looking for."

As he talked, Sister Mary Margaret slid open the top drawer and began unconsciously fingering the rosary coiled up in the paper-clip insert.

He continued, "Last time we spoke, you told me that vampires only kill young women because their blood is pure and strong."

"Yes." She had taken the rosary out and now held it in her lap.

"The young nun inside the convent was murdered the same way the other women were. We now know for a certainty that he is not drinking their blood. He kills as though he were a vampire, but he kills to shed blood, not drink it."

She got up and, with her rosary dangling from her hand, went over and stared out the window. She stood there for some minutes before she turned and carefully pushed plants aside and sat on the sill.

Watching her, he thought how un-nunlike she looked in jeans, sneakers, and a sweater. Her black veil cascaded just below her shoulders.

She looked across at the portrait of Freud, and asked, "Do you know why sick people have a need to shed blood?"

"In some of them it represents a sexual act."

"Yes, that's true. But there is another reason. From earliest times human blood has been used to solemnize the pledged word. To create a bond between people. Blood is considered, even today, the most sacred and irrevocable of seals. The Mafia sheds inductees' blood during their initiation ritual, and the new members are then called 'wise guys' or 'made men.' Fraternities and some secret religious societies draw blood at initiation ceremonies to swear loyalty and brotherhood."

"You think our guy is pledging blood to God?"

"We can hypothesize that the killer was a good man when he married. It is entirely possible that his wife's death finally pushed the man over the edge of sanity. In his own mind he might not be able to accept the death of his wife. He could believe that by shedding the blood of young women he is securing God's protection for himself and his wife."

"How could a 'good man' do murders?"

"As I told you, paranoids assume different personas when they do evil. By doing that, they spare themselves the punishment that their acts have earned them."

"Let me run this by you, Sister. Griffin kills randomly to protect his wife and himself, but he also kills selectively anyone who knew about him and his wife, because he does not want anyone living to know that God damned his wife because she had forsaken Him to marry."

She smiled. "Very good. You must have paid attention during Psych 101 and 102."

"It doesn't come from a classroom, Sister. It comes from twenty years on the Job. Not that I ever ran into anything like this. But I'm starting to get a feeling for what this man is like. Being in his mind is like walking through a dangerous neighborhood, one I've never been in before. So I need for you to give me a map."

T W E N T Y - F O U R

STROLLERS MOVED ALONG TUDOR CITY'S PROMON-
tory in the deepening shadows of early twilight. Inside the vest-pocket park a black
squirrel leaped up onto a tree, scampering to
safety, leaving a frustrated dog scratching the trunk.

Jessica Merrill came into the park, her ears buried inside the
collar of her chinchilla coat. She looked around for Worthington;
not seeing him, she pushed back her sleeve to check the time.
Exactly 4:00 P.M. Glancing at the landscape around her, she
moved over to a bench, dusted it clean with her handkerchief,
and sat down.

She leaned back to watch a group of boys throwing snowballs
at three girls. When she was growing up, there was never time
for such frolicking. Most of her childhood had been devoted to
classes in acting and elocution, dancing and singing. Her childhood had been one big damn lesson. Her father, a misogynistic
runt of a man, had worked in his youth in second-rate clubs as a

comedian. He had been full of determination that his pretty daughter was going to be the star he wasn't. A glimmer flickered across her eyes as she recalled her first acting part. It was in Miss James's third-grade class, where she played the lead in *Alice in Wonderland*. She sighed and thought that catching the dream had not turned out to be as much fun as chasing it had been.

"Hello, Jessica."

Worthington's voice startled her. She quickly recovered. "How are you?"

"Wonderful," he said, relaxing on the bench next to her. Half turning and sliding his arm across the back of the bench, he said, "But you look troubled, Jessica."

"I've been contemplating my life and wondering if it's all been worth it."

"Many women throughout the world would be happy to trade places with you."

"Don't you think I'm aware of how incredibly lucky I've been? It's just that I've been thinking lately about my own mortality. Religion and spirituality. I never did understand the difference between them."

"Religion is for people who want to stay out of hell. Spirituality is for people who've *seen* hell."

"Which of the two do you believe in, Michael?"

A thin smile of annoyance crossed his lips. "Why did you want to see me?"

"Do you remember Laura Steward? She had a walk-on in *Lovers and Friends*."

"I remember her. She has a terrific exterior—and very little beyond that."

Merrill ignored the sarcasm and went on bravely.

"I think she would be perfect for the part of the assistant district attorney in *Reckless Disregard*."

"She's too young. And she doesn't look like a woman who's made it in the kind of tough ballgame they play in a criminal court."

"I admit that the casting would be unusual. But the kid has a certain brassiness and boldness about her, and I believe she could pull it off."

He made a dismissive gesture with his hand. "As I recall, her talent is somewhat . . . limited."

Merrill refused to give up. "With hard work and the proper guidance, I'm convinced she would be perfect for the part."

He brushed a forelock from her face. "I'm sure she would, with the proper guidance." Lightly stroking her face with his hand, he said, "I'm mean to you sometimes, aren't I?"

"Sometimes. But I understand. You've bottled up your hurt inside yourself, and sometimes it's just too much hurt to carry, so you lash out."

"What do you want me to do?"

"I want you to suggest her for the part to Paul Hiller."

"Why don't you put her name in nomination to the producer?"

She looked at the shadows slowly advancing across the snow and said softly, "Because I don't want anyone to know that Laura and I are *friends*." She put a deliberate emphasis on the last word, knowing that Worthington had long understood and sympathized with her secret desires. It was a secret they shared.

"I see."

"Michael, everyone in the business believes you're happily married. If you tout Laura to Hiller, he'll think it's strictly business. If I did it, some damn gossip columnist might just make me a headline in all the supermarket trash heaps. I don't want people prying into my private life."

Worthington stared down at his shoes and said, "Hiller will still want her to audition."

"All I want is for her to have a shot at the part. I'll see that she's ready for any audition."

He reached out and took her hand. "I guess I owe you a favor or two."

She smiled demurely. "I guess so."

"Only for you, dear Jessica, would I praise Miss Steward's considerable acting talents to our producer."

Jessica kissed his cheek in gratitude, and was surprised by the flushed warmth of his skin. "Are you all right?"

"I'm fine. It's just that I'm not used to being kissed by other women."

It was 4:18 when Vinda parked the department car on East Forty-third Street and walked up the grade into the quadrangle. Just inside, he stopped when he saw Worthington and Merrill engrossed in their conversation. A sudden surge of cop adrenaline told him that he had just stumbled onto something important. He ducked into a doorway to watch them. Worthington appeared to be giving her instructions, and she sat there shaking her head without saying much. After about eight minutes they got up off the bench and walked out of the park.

Stepping out of the doorway, he waved to them.

Worthington saw him first and quickly said something to her, and they both waved back to him. "Hello," Worthington called out.

"Hi," Vinda said, waiting for them on the curb. He had seen no police bodyguards shepherding Merrill, so he asked, "Where's your protection?"

"I insisted they be removed. I can't live with guards around me day and night."

"That, Miss Merrill, just might prove to have been a mistake."

Worthington nodded in agreement and said, "My sentiments exactly, Lieutenant. But she will not listen to me."

"Oh, hush, Michael," she said softly.

Vinda said, "I'm glad I found you together." Holding up the composite sketch of the killer, he added, "This is not the man we're looking for."

A perplexed Worthington said, "It isn't?"

"No, it isn't," Vinda said dryly.

"But that's impossible," Worthington insisted. "That is the man I saw near those dressing rooms."

"Maybe it is. But he's not the killer I'm looking for," Vinda said.

"How can you be so positive?" Merrill demanded.

"Because the man I want murdered a nun this morning, and during the course of his escape he killed a policeman. The dead cop's partner got a good look at him. She got a *real* good look at him," Vinda said grimly. "When you see your partner killed, you don't forget the face of the person who did it, no matter how much pain you're experiencing." He held the sketch up in front of Worthington. "Are you positive this is the man you saw?"

"Yes. I. Am." Worthington said.

Trying to gauge the sincerity of his words and expression, Vinda looked hard at the actor, then turned his attention to Merrill and said, "I never understood how you didn't see anyone near those dressing rooms."

"Because I didn't," she snapped, asking, "Is this going to take long? It's below zero standing here."

"Why don't we duck inside?" Worthington said, leading them into the apartment building's lobby.

The plaque above the white plaster fireplace bore a blue coat of arms. Logs crackled in the fireplace. "Did you ever consider, Lieutenant, that your killer might wear a disguise?" Merrill asked.

Vinda answered, "We've thought about that possibility." He suppressed a temptation to ask her about her part in the movie *Thin Lies*, and to query her about the two stuntmen in the same movie, Griffin and Holman. He didn't because cops hold their cards close to the vest, real close.

Worthington's attention had drifted to the ribbons of flame lapping upward inside the hearth. His calm exterior hid his inner turmoil: Vinda is their leader, their Lucifer. He wants to destroy our Trinity. Well, my ol' friend Dinny'O knows how to deal with the likes of him.

Agueda and Hagstrom walked out of the beaux arts lobby of 1514 Broadway. They had just come from the offices of SAG—

the Screen Actors Guild—where they had retrieved glossy photographs of Frank Griffin and Otto Holman from the inactive stuntmen's file.

Agueda looked across the street at the short line of people outside the discount theater-ticket booth on Forty-sixth Street. It was six-fifteen on a Wednesday evening, and usually hundreds of people snaked around Duffy Square, waiting their turns to purchase half-price tickets for that evening's performance.

Duffy Square was almost empty. Hagstrom looked back at her partner and asked, "A cup of tea?"

They walked about ten feet to the open-fronted sandwich shop and ordered. The counterman set down steaming cups in front of them, and pushed off to take care of another customer. Dunking her bag into the water, Agueda asked, "What's happening with you and Tony?"

Hagstrom grinned sheepishly. "Tony Marsella is your average married man with a congenital predisposition toward infidelity. I only keep him around to take the edge off until I can meet someone who is available, and mature enough to want a meaningful relationship."

"I never did understand when a relationship becomes meaningful."

"When it becomes uncomfortable."

They laughed.

Agueda moved close to ask confidentially, "Is he good?"

"He's a selfish lover. He doesn't play all the instruments."

Agueda sipped tea, whispered over the rim of her cup, "Perhaps you should teach him how?"

"I stopped playing teacher a long time ago." Hagstrom pulled the bag out of her cup and set it in a dirty ashtray. Looking down into the dark liquid, she asked, "What's going to happen with you and the boss, now that—"

"I don't know," Agueda blurted before Hagstrom could finish her question. She reached into her pocketbook, slapped down a dollar on the counter, and walked off without finishing her tea.

Hagstrom followed her, feeling dumb for having asked a dumb question.

They had gone only a short way down the street when both their beepers went off.

David Pollack pushed his Stetson back and plopped down on a straight-backed chair in Vinda's office. He leaned the seat back on its two rear legs, looked up at Vinda, and said, "I just got done with Ted Benet, our movie reviewer."

He unfolded a sheet of paper and read, "Jessica Merrill, real name Jessica Ramenki, age thirty-four to thirty-six, depending on which bio you believe. Thrice married, currently divorced. Doesn't drink, smoke, or drug. Stage trained. Born in Camden, New Jersey, and knocked around doing the whole nine yards until her break in *Mora Flats*."

"Private life."

"Nobody knows much about her offscreen." He looked at Vinda, adding, "My guy also told me that she and Worthington have the same agent, Marshall Hawthorn, in real life one Morty Hymowitz, a sleazebag originally from Flatbush who gets off on playing the wise guy, and wants everyone to call him Vinny."

"And Worthington?"

"An unusual Hollywood success story. No training, knocked around at odd jobs doing this and that before he landed a small part as a judge in a movie called *Deadly Verdict*. That part mushroomed into a movie career. Worthington is his real name; according to his bio, he's fifty-eight."

Carefully pinching his chin between his thumb and fingers, Vinda said aloud, "I wonder how he landed that part in *Deadly Verdict*."

"Word is that J. B. King, the producer, was searching for some actor to play the part, and someone whispered Worthington's name to him. Worthington was tested for the part, and the rest is history." His voice honeyed, "Would you like to know who his rabbi was?"

"You know damn well I would."

"Jessica Merrill."

Vinda did some fast calculations: Valarie Griffin DOA in '79; Merrill's break in *Mora Flats* in '80; Merrill and Worthington work together in *Deadly Verdict* in '85; Mary Lucas's father gets himself blown up on the parkway in '86; Thelma Johnston and Mary Lucas are homicides in '91. Ninety-one seems to be this guy's out-of-the-closet year.

"What else can you tell me about Worthington?"

"Very professional. Always comes on the set prepared. Never difficult, except when other actors are late or unprepared. He doesn't drink, drug, or smoke, and keeps his schmuck in his pants. Lives in Manhattan with his one and only wife, Valarie."

Again Vinda felt the sudden surge of adrenaline through his body. Valarie Griffin and Valarie Worthington. I wonder, I just wonder, he mused to himself, remembering Sister Mary Margaret telling him how paranoids drew people into their own belief systems. "Will you find out whatever there is to find out about Morty Hymowitz?"

"I know that guy from way back. He used to be in the porn flick business. Word was that the smart guys put up the money and he put up the know-how. He took a fall for kiddy porn, did three and a half to five."

Vinda thanked the newspaperman for his help, again promising Pollack the inside exclusive on the story once the case was broken. Pollack left the office a few minutes before Moose and Marsella returned, responding to his 10:2, Report Back Forthwith.

Agueda and Hagstrom walked in behind Moose and Marsella. "What's up?" Agueda asked the Whip.

"Did you get the photos from SAG?" Vinda asked her.

Handing him the envelope, Agueda said, "Holman and Griffin hadn't paid SAG dues in over five years. We were lucky they still had their photos on file."

Vinda slid out Holman's photograph, and saw that he wore his extreme military haircut even back then. He slid that picture back into the envelope and took out the other one. His eyes widened when he looked at Griffin for the first time and saw how ugly he was.

Griffin's lower jaw was ludicrously counterpoised below a markedly enlarged upper jaw with fiercely bucked teeth. His teeth were not only protrusive, but the jaw itself was enlarged so that he couldn't even close his lower lip over the widely spaced teeth. He had a real horse face.

Vinda turned the photograph around to make sure they had the right guy. The name on the back said FRANK GRIFFIN, STUNTS AND PYROTECHNICS. "This guy doesn't look anything like the face in our composite."

"We know," Hagstrom said.

"I'm beginning to think our victims were not all the subjects of random homicides. Lucas, Johnston, their fathers, and Adelaide Webster are all connected, in some way, to Frank Griffin," Vinda said.

"How is Adelaide Webster connected?" Moose asked.

Vinda said, "Her father produced a movie in which Griffin worked as a stuntman."

" 'At's pretty slim, Lou," Moose said.

"Not so slim," Vinda disagreed. "Merrill also worked in movies produced by Webster, ditto our bomb salesman, Otto Holman."

Looking at Griffin's deformed face, Vinda told Agueda and Hagstrom, "Go back to SAG and get a photo of Worthington—then get it over to Kings County and show it to Lucy Seaver. Then I want you to pair off, boy, girl, boy, girl, and canvass Worthington's neighborhood. Find out if anyone there knows his wife. I want to know if she really exists. And be cool. I don't want him knowing we're checking on him."

Hagstrom good-naturedly took hold of Marsella's arm and said, "Come on, handsome, I'll show you how to be a real detective."

·　　　·　　　·

Corregidor was crowded. A new police commissioner brings new players into the arena, new faces beaming with the joy that comes with newly acquired power.

Agent Orange, his voice booze-sad, stood with his clique at the end of the bar. Most of the ex–C-of-P loyalists would now retire rather than suffer the indignity of being dumped out of the Big Building into the street.

Tim Eberhart was loudly bewailing the demise of the good old days, while those around him vainly hid their gloom behind stoic countenances. The soon-to-be ex-chief spied Vinda entering and gestured in a drunken fashion, "Lou, come over and have one with us."

"Later, Chief," Vinda called back, plunging into the crowd in search of Malcolm Webster, who had telephoned him a short while ago and asked to meet him. Something urgent, he'd told Vinda. He spotted him ensconced behind one of the alcove's cocktail tables, keenly observing the shenanigans out at the bar.

"This place reminds me of the executive dining room at RJR/Nabisco during the leverage takeover war."

Pulling a chair away from the table, Vinda said, "You were part of that bloodbath?"

Webster smiled smugly. "Avarice, Lieutenant, is the American way." Gesturing to Agent Orange and his supporters, he added, "I assume they are the outs."

Vinda made a gesture of indifference and said, "They hitched their wagons to the wrong star."

Webster slid an envelope out of his pocket and carefully placed it on the table in front of him, folding his hands on top of it. "Adelaide's mother died three years ago in France. We'd been divorced many years, but had remained good friends. We loved our daughter very, very much. And now, with our daughter gone, I have no one, not one single person on the face of this planet, who cares for me, the man, the person. I want the son of a bitch who murdered my daughter."

"So do I."

They fell silent, their eyes locked in a moment of intense empathy and shared loss. Webster suddenly looked terribly old to Vinda; the dim light could not hide his utterly forlorn expression. Webster's shoulders sagged; he sighed and pushed the envelope across to Vinda.

A photocopied spreadsheet inside it listed the payroll records for *Thin Lies*. Computerized columns listed salaries, per diem expenses, taxes withheld, social security numbers, and deductions. Looking up for a moment, Vinda saw Gus White, the FBI liaison, sharing a belly laugh with the new chief of detectives at the bar. Scanning the first column of the payroll record, Vinda found the names of Jessica Merrill, Frank Griffin, and Otto Holman. Taking a cocktail napkin from the pile, he wrote down the names alongside their social security numbers and tucked the napkin into his breast pocket. Vinda took out the photograph of Frank Griffin. "Is this the Frank Griffin who worked for you as a stuntman?"

"Ugly, isn't he?"

"I guess handsome is not a requirement for taking dives out of windows and off bridges."

"No, it certainly isn't," Webster said, shaking his glass at the waiter, ordering another. "Want something?"

"No, thank you," Vinda said, holding up Otto Holman's picture.

"Yes, he worked on the movie too. He was the stunt coordinator. He hired all the stuntmen."

"What else do you have for me?" Vinda asked.

"I found something else while I was searching through those old production records. But before I give it to you, I'd like to ask a question."

"Ask."

"Did Griffin or Holman murder my daughter?"

"The best I can give you is a maybe."

"A maybe on who, Griffin or Holman—or both of them?"

Vinda leaned back indolently in his chair, staring at the man across from him, prolonging the awkward silence.

Webster seemed to recover some of his usual forceful presence. "I'm not a man to be fucked with."

"Neither am I." Vinda got up and walked out to the bar. Shouldering his way over to Gus White, he made a nod of respect to the C-of-D and asked, "Mind if I borrow Mr. FBI for a minute, Chief?"

"Don't keep him too long. The next round's his."

"I won't, Chief."

White trailed Vinda out of the crowd. Leaning up against the dark burnished paneling, Vinda looked at White and said, "I see you're hard at work cementing relations with the new C-of-D."

"It's all in the stroking, John. Nice and easy, like sighting in a hair and squeezing one off."

Vinda took the cocktail napkin out of his pocket and tucked it into White's suit pocket, assumed the hand-blocking-lips position, and said, "I need work histories on those social security numbers."

Pretending indignation before himself making the lip-blocking gesture, White protested, "Those records are sacrosanct. Your department and mine have elaborate procedures that must be adhered to in order to obtain those records."

"Gus, stop pulling my chain and give those numbers to one of your sacrosanct agents assigned to social security. And, Gus, I need it fast."

"Bartender," White called as he plunged back into the crowd, "a Gibson, up, cold, dry, and stirred, not shaken."

Turning to walk away, Vinda found Webster blocking his way. The former movie producer was proffering a business form. Vinda looked down at the form and said without even trying to read it, "Your price is too high."

"Take it anyway. We'll negotiate after you catch him." Vinda took it and walked back to the alcove. He unfolded it and saw that it was an insurance policy.

"Production companies take out policies on their crews and equipment in order to protect their investments," Webster said, walking beside the policeman.

Vinda sifted through the policy's legalese until he got down to the primary beneficiary, and asked, "Who is Harrison Bode?"

"Frank Griffin's teacher at the Cincinnati Boys' School in Dayton, Ohio. I had my people check. Bode is retired, and in his seventies. He's living in Woodstock, New York. A bachelor. He's a graduate of the Yale Law School."

"What about this Cincinnati Boys' School?"

"An institution operated by private funds for orphaned and abandoned boys. Griffin was raised there. And it appears that this Harrison Bode befriended him."

Vinda told him that he would need a few more favors, and went on to tell him what he wanted.

Webster told him he'd take care of it, and wrote a name and phone number on the back of a business card. "Call him when you're ready," he said, giving Vinda the card.

TWENTY-FIVE

AT EIGHT O'CLOCK THE NEXT MORNING A BLUE helicopter lifted off the bull's-eye of the landing pad on the roof of police headquarters and flew out over the city.

The pilot, a well-built man in his mid-thirties, with dirty blond hair, wearing yellow tinted aviator glasses and an Emergency Service Aviation Unit patch on the shoulder of his flight jacket, shouted at Vinda over the whine of the engine, "We're on our way, Lou."

Vinda gave a sharp, nervous laugh. "I hope this eggbeater stays up."

Moving the cyclic control stick horizontally, the pilot shouted, "Not to worry, Lu-ten-ent."

Looking down at the streets of the city below, Vinda thought about last night. He had gone back to his apartment directly from Corregidor. He had undressed and showered and, leaving the bathroom with a towel wrapped around his waist, aimlessly paced from room to room in the large, desolately empty apartment. He'd found himself back inside the bedroom.

On an impulse he had opened Jean's dresser and found all her clothes gone; only her scent lingered, and that too would fade with time. He had forgotten that he had asked Jean's cousin, Bernice, to clean out all of her clothing and give it to charity. Vinda had been incapable of dealing with her personal effects. On her dresser sat cosmetics and hairbrushes, gathering dust.

Going over to the window, he looked down in the street and saw that the cold had partly covered the inside of the glass with a wintry tracery. He scratched Jean's name in the frost. Stepping back, he had looked at the name, and angrily erased it. I have to start living, I have to, he thought. Driven by an urge to get out of the place, he had dressed and left.

Elegibos was rocking with a mixture of samba-duro and samba-reggae music. Vinda darted out onto the dance floor and lost himself in the swaying crowd. He felt released from his misery, at least for the moment. The next song was *"Maravilha Morena,"* a romantic ballad. He remained on the dance floor, swaying to the soft beat, his arms loose at his sides, his head tilted. He felt a presence in front of him, opened his eyes, and saw Margareth, gyrating up to him. Their bodies touched and held, moving as one. He felt the rush of warm blood throughout his body.

"This song is about me," she said.

" 'Dark-Skinned Wonder,' " he said, giving the title of the song in English.

"Yes." Her breasts caressed his chest.

He stared at her full, dark red lips and fiery eyes. It's time, damn it, it's time, he thought, as he pulled her closer to him.

"I have a magical body, John," she whispered in Portuguese.

His breath caught. "I believe you."

"Let me invite you to rejoin the world."

He took her hand in his and led her off the dance floor.

.   .   .

The passing landscape of irregular neighborhood grids had melted into great highways snaking through vast stretches of timberland. Automobiles were toy-sized as the helicopter's shadow swept over them. They overflew housing developments and sprawling malls with huge parking fields filled with more toy cars.

They had been in the air for about forty minutes when Vinda looked ahead and was enthralled by the spectacular vista spread out before him. Overlook Mountain and its massive supporting ridges filled the northeast part of the picture, and there were hills and valleys and streams and lakes, and no matter in which direction he looked, dense forest rose up out of a vast, pristine wilderness.

His eyes fell below Overlook Mountain to the smaller mountains that formed the eastern edge of the Allegheny Plateau. Echo Lake was bounded by woodlands, and in the west he saw where the Indian Head Range disappeared behind Alderbark Mountain. And in the southwest, gleaming with icy brilliance in the morning sun, lay the Ashokan Reservoir.

"Some view, huh?" the pilot shouted.

Shaking his head in agreement, Vinda said, "Sure beats the Bronx."

The helicopter overflew the white steeple of Woodstock's Dutch Reformed Church and circled a clearing just outside of the town. A state police cruiser, its turret lights throwing pale colors across the snow-covered field, was parked at the edge of the woods. A trooper, bundled up in the winter gray of the State Police, leaned up against the cruiser's fender, watching the NYPD helicopter touch down in an uneventful landing.

"Here we are, Lou, safe and sound," the pilot said, reaching across the cockpit and pushing open the door. "Watch your step climbing down."

Vinda ducked under the still-turning blade and jogged over to the police cruiser. The trooper, a middle-aged, burly, homespun sort of a guy with a square face, broad shoulders, and a tapered waist, regarded the city cop with a mixture of disapproval and curiosity. He was dressed in a three-quarter wool coat, heavy wool trousers, fur-lined boots, gloves, and a flap-eared wool cap. Vinda's apparel consisted of a tan overcoat, brown suit, white shirt, and paisley tie.

Running toward the trooper, he became aware of the crunching snow, and a sensation that his feet were burning with pain from the intense cold.

He and the trooper shook hands.

"I'm Al Brophy, Lieutenant. I suggest we get started."

Sliding into the passenger seat, glad to be inside the warm car, Vinda asked, "Mohawk Trail Road near here?"

Brophy's lips drew back in a sort of smile. "Not really. And it's not a road exactly. More like a location on a map. Your Mr. Harrison Bode is a mountain man, Lieutenant."

"In New York State?"

"Don't be fooled by Woodstock's trendy weekend people and its artsy-craftsy shops. Plenty of the people around here hate that sort of crap. Some of them up in those hills'd shoot ya just as soon as talk to ya." He looked at Vinda. "Better put your seat belt on."

They drove through Woodstock and continued on Route 212 for about seven miles before they turned right onto a narrow, rutted road lined on both sides by dense timber. Brophy's attention remained fixed on the road ahead of him, guiding the car as if by some sixth sense around potholes camouflaged with snow and fallen leaves. Sometimes his navigation was a mite off, and the tire rim would slam down into a depression, sending Vinda's head crashing up into the roof.

At the bottom of a steep incline that led nowhere, Brophy stopped the car and announced, "Mohawk Trail Road."

"Where?"

Brophy waved his hand across the breadth of the windshield. "Here."

"But there's nothing here but a mountain."

"Yep. Bode's house is up there," he said, pointing up the side of the mountain. Looking down at Vinda's laced shoes inside his half-overshoes, he added, "Snow around here can run four, five feet deep in places."

Vinda gave a self-deprecatory shrug and said, "Looks as though I didn't dress for the occasion."

"Wait here," Brophy said, and opened his door. Getting out, he trudged through deep snow to the back of the car, opened the trunk, and yanked out a duffel bag with the legend N.Y. STATE POLICE stenciled across the side. Tossing it on his shoulder, he slammed the trunk shut and chugged around to the passenger side, where he tossed the bag up on the roof. Using the car door as a ram, the trooper repeatedly slammed back the blocking snow drift.

Sticking his head inside the car, he grinned and said, "Figured you might not wear the proper clothes, so I stopped by the barracks and picked up some gear from our 'city slicker locker.' " Reaching into the bag, he pulled out a pair of thermal overpants and tossed them to him. "Better take off your coat and jacket."

Vinda wrestled out of his outer clothing and tossed it into the backseat. Lying back across the front seat of the car, he plunged his feet into the overpants, and worked them up over his trousers. "How'd you know my size?"

"Telephoned your office. Spoke to a Detective Agueda."

Sitting up with his legs dangling out the side of the car, Vinda pulled up the fur-lined boots that Brophy had given him. Next came the hooded, fur-lined parka and gloves.

"Ever use snowshoes?" Brophy asked, reaching into the backseat and taking two pairs up off the floor and laying them on the snow.

Vinda looked down at the oval wood frames strung with thongs, and answered, "Many years ago."

Watching the city policeman slide into his new footwear, Brophy put on his own set of snowshoes.

"You coming along?"

A beguiling grin lit up the trooper's weathered face. "I think I'd better, don't you?"

"Yes."

They trudged up the side of the mountain, Vinda following in Brophy's trail. Vinda's arms and legs began to ache, and sweat trickled down from his armpits and coursed over his chest. His breathing became labored. He did not see it at first, the narrow, winding ridge terraced in railway ties above a rutted track that in summer probably passed for a road. Glimpses of tar showed through the clinging snow. "You okay?" Brophy called back.

"Fine," he lied, asking, "How does he get his food?"

"Stocks up in the fall. And he hunts."

They had been making their way uphill for about twenty minutes when faint sounds of music drifted through the air. Soon they were plodding past cords of wood that appeared to have been stacked with almost military precision. The music grew louder. They climbed farther, and suddenly a timbered house reared up on the hill, smoke curling up out of its stone chimney.

Brophy stopped, waiting for the puffing city policeman to come up to him. "I'm going to wait outside for you. I suggest you tread softly with Bode. Most of the folks who retreat up to these mountains do so because they've had their fill of civilization and people, mostly people. They got plenty of hurt and anger hidden inside 'em, and it don't take much to set 'em off."

"I'll be careful."

They made their way over to the porch and took off their snowshoes.

Vinda turned and drank in the view that spread out before him. He wished Jean could be there to share it with him. Then he shook himself out of his reverie, turned, and walked up onto the porch. He had barely raised his hand to knock when the heavy, solid wood door was pulled open.

"What do you want?" Bode demanded.

Not tall or short, but medium-sized and wiry, with deep gray

eyes and thin lips, Bode had a good-sized nose streaked with
bluish veins. His face was almost completely covered in unkempt hair, with a beard that stretched down to his chest. His
eyebrows were beyond being bushy; they grew out of control in
every direction, and his overgrown mustache looked like a spur
running off into his matted hair.

Holding out his police credentials, Vinda said, "I need to talk
to you about one of your former students at the Cincinnati
School."

Bode eyed him with distrust. "What student?"

"Frank Griffin."

Color flooded Bode's cheeks; he silently stepped to the side,
allowing Vinda to enter.

"I'll wait outside," Brophy said, as if reaffirming his presence.

A stone fireplace took up most of one wall of the timbered
room. A balcony circled the living area and served as a library.
Stacks of books were everywhere; the hearth crackled with burning logs.

Bode wore thick-soled boots and a checkered shirt tucked
inside his bib overalls. He walked over to the music system and,
after pausing to listen to the end of a movement of a Mozart
piano concerto, lowered the volume. He turned, with weary
distaste in his eyes, to face the policeman.

One look at him and Vinda could tell that this was not going
to be a convivial chat. He needed some way to win Bode's
cooperation.

The mountain man crossed the room and sat on a wood sofa
with orange corduroy cushions. Lowering himself into a pine
chair across from Bode, Vinda looked around the room, and then
looked carefully at the books stacked on the table next to him.
Many of them were in foreign languages. Two of their spines
bore Portuguese titles. A spark of excitement ignited in his chest
when he realized that he might have discovered a way to get
through to the glacially silent man.

One of the books was on the life of Ferdinand Magellan, the

Portuguese explorer and navigator who conducted the first circumnavigation of the globe. He grinned tiredly at Bode, and said in Portuguese, "I see you are reading about our great navigator Magellan."

Bode's face pinched together with surprise, and he began dancing his fingertips together.

Vinda continued talking in his father's tongue. "Family legend has it that my distant cousin was Francisco Serrao, who sailed with Magellan in 1508 from Cochin to Malacca."

Bode responded in halting but clear Portuguese, "Exactly what do you want of me?"

"Frank Griffin needs your help."

Bode, switching back to English, tossed him a look of infinite scorn. "Since when do the police help people?"

"Since always."

"The police killed Frank's wife; they destroyed his life."

"That was an accident." He knew that he needed to come up with something that would draw Bode out of his shell of isolation. "Frank thought a lot of you. Did you know that he made you his beneficiary? Now he needs your help."

Bode gnawed his lower lip. "What kind of trouble is he in?"

"We have reason to believe that his life might be in danger."

"Why?"

"I can't tell you that. You're just going to have to trust me." He reached into his parka and took out the photograph of Griffin that he had taken along with him. "Is this Frank?"

"Yes."

"Will you please help me find him? I promise you, no harm will come to him."

"I don't know where he is. I haven't heard from Frank in years."

"Will you tell me about him, the kind of person he is?"

Bode sat frozen in silence, staring up at the row of crossbeams. He pushed himself up off the sofa and walked over to the serving table on the other side of the room. He stood there for a while looking down at the oak top and then, as though finally deciding on a course of action, opened the side panel and took out a manila folder. Coming back across the room, he handed the folder to Vinda and said, "In order to tell you about Frank Griffin, I must first tell you things about me."

The old newspaper clippings were from the *Southampton News* and told the chilling story of a sexually abused child killing his abuser, his father. Harrison Bode was twelve when his drunken father first crept into his bedroom, and sixteen when he cowered in bed cradling the shotgun he had just removed from the library gun cabinet. Harrison knew that his father had been drinking and that he would be coming to his room, so he waited with the gun for his tormentor. There were photographs of their Southampton estate, and one of the child and his socially prominent mother. The story offered some hints of the torments Bode had suffered.

Vinda heard the squeak of a cork and looked up from the clippings to see Bode opening a bottle of champagne. "I've inherited some of my father's tastes," Bode said.

The incongruous sight of a mountain man standing next to a silver wine bucket opening a bottle of champagne reinforced Vinda's belief that we all live inside the many worlds of our own heads.

Bode popped the cork, and poured the wine into stemmed glasses. He handed one to Vinda. Sipping, Bode said, "After twenty years of visiting a therapist five days a week, I decided to give up the practice of law to devote my life to helping abused and abandoned children. Hence the Cincinnati School." Looking at the stream of bubbles rising up the center of his glass, he added, "I was never going to be able to marry or have children, so I decided to try to help other boys avoid the hell that my life had become. My father's legacy to me, besides his money, was impotence."

"You're a brave man, sir."

Vinda's compassion caught the mountain man off-guard; he

stared at the policeman for a long time. Finally he sucked in a deep breath and began to talk about Frank Griffin.

Griffin had been abandoned by his parents as an infant, and assigned by the courts to the Cincinnati School. His facial deformity caused him early on to bear the brunt of his peers' unrelenting cruelty. He was constantly getting into fights, so much so that his ears became cauliflowered. As the years passed he became more withdrawn and delusional.

"When I arrived at the school he was already well on his way to becoming psychotic. Frank had discovered the Bible when he was twelve and read it over and over attempting to find answers for his misery."

Vinda sipped champagne.

"Religion became his obsession. He was fascinated with matters involving the action and influence of supernatural and supernormal powers. The more he studied, the deeper he delved, and the more withdrawn he became.

"He came to believe that by possessing the secrets of the occult he garnered the strength he needed to cope with his own inner torment. Somewhere along the line he took it into his head that his parents had abandoned him because he was the illegitimate son of an illegitimate son. Do you know the significance of that?"

Vinda put his glass on top of the stack of books on the end table and said, "It's one way to become a vampire." He looked at Bode and asked him, "Why didn't anyone at the school get him help?"

"I did. We put him in psychotherapy. But he only played mind games with the doctor. I tried reaching him on a personal level, and succeeded to a certain degree. I saw in Frank a kindred spirit of mutual suffering. We related to each other on a certain level, but there was nothing I could do or say to change his belief in the powers of the occult."

"Did he make friends at the school?"

"Only Otto Holman, another loner, who latched on to Frank

and became his protector. Holman was very interested in boxing and gymnastics, and he got Frank interested in them too. Frank had a natural ability for that stuff."

He told Vinda that Griffin had left the school when he was eighteen and worked around the country at odd jobs. Some years later he ran into Holman, and his friend from the Cincinnati School got him a job as a stuntman in Hollywood. Religion remained Frank's main interest, so when he came back to New York between jobs he would take courses. He registered at Columbia University for a course in religious philosophy and ethics. And that was where he met Valarie. She was a Sister of Saint Joseph and had registered to take the same course.

Bode went on in a sad tone, "A virginal beauty and a virginal beast meet and fall in love. Their first encounters were casual. They continued running into each other in the library, and they were drawn closer and closer together. Loneliness does that. You desperately grasp at any signs of love or friendship. Valarie was going through a trying period in her life. She'd not taken her final vows and wasn't sure she wanted to. And before either of them realized what was happening, they were in love."

He gulped the rest of the wine in his glass, poured more, and angrily jammed the bottle back into the ice bucket. "Their love ended as all respectable Greek dramas do, in inexorable, gut-wrenching tragedy."

"Did you hear from Frank after his wife died?"

"Nothing for a while. Then, seven months after Valarie's death, he telephoned asking to borrow ten thousand dollars. I lent him the money and he repaid it within eighteen months. I never heard from him again."

"Seven months after her death would make it January of '80, and repayment eighteen months later would make it July '81."

"That sounds about right."

"Did he tell you why he needed the money?"

"No."

"How did you two communicate after he left school?"

"We exchanged letters."

Vinda reached out and picked up his glass. "Do you still have those letters?"

"No. I threw them away."

Vinda knew somehow that Bode was lying. "Why do you think Otto Holman took Frank under his wing?"

"Holman was also an abused child. He was scared and mistrustful, and tried to hide it behind his bravado. People like that only let the less fortunate get close to them. And Frank's ugliness put him on the bottom of the heap."

"Do you think Frank was capable of taking his own life?"

Bode looked at Vinda contemptuously. "We're all capable of taking our own lives, Lieutenant. All that it requires is the right set of circumstances occurring at precisely the right moment. Death for Frank would have meant release from torment, and the beginning of a great adventure."

"Who is Dinny'O?"

Bode sank into a sullen silence and yanked the bottle out of the ice bucket. "Dinny'O was Frank's childish version of a myth out of ancient Irish folklore. A Robin Hood–type hero who came out of the mountains to smite evildoers. Whenever Frank did something reprehensible, he would try to avoid responsibility for his act by slipping into his Dinny'O act."

He shoved the bottle back into the ice, and, holding the glass by its stem, recited:

> *"From thunderous fire Dinny'O did rise*
> *with ancient fury in his eyes.*
> *Through the darkness he did soar*
> *to fight the demons of the moor."*

T W E N T Y - S I X

DURING THE FLIGHT BACK TO MANHATTAN, VINDA reflected on the differences between the homespun wisdom of the rural cop and the wisecracking cynicism of the urban cop, and decided that there wasn't that much difference, for it was, after all, the same Job.

Bode had reminded him of the dreadful child-abuse problem in our society. He felt sorry for the Griffins, Bodes, and Holmans of the world, but he had a job to do and he intended to do it. In the final analysis, he was a cop, the only advocate most murder victims had.

The helicopter reared up and then set down on the pad at the East Side heliport on Sixty-third Street. Vinda reached across the cockpit and shook the pilot's hand. "Thanks for the ride."

"Any time, Lou."

Vinda climbed down and walked toward the trailer that served as the heliport's office, painfully aware of his aching limbs and the grungy feeling of sweaty wool clothes. Trudging around snow-covered mountains had given him the unpleasant opportunity to smell his own stink. He needed to go home for a shower and a change of clothes. He had radioed ahead and told Moose to have one of the team meet him; he had also instructed him to ascertain the whereabouts of the theatrical agent Morty Hymowitz.

Walking up to the office-trailer, he saw Agueda, and waved to her. "How'd it go, Lou?" she asked.

"Okay, any messages?"

"Mr. FBI left this for you," she said, handing him an envelope.

Walking to the department car, he read the social-security employment histories of Merrill, Holman, and Griffin, noting that Griffin's account had been inactive ever since his wife was killed. He put the histories back into the envelope, and slid into the passenger seat. "What happened with those canvasses of Worthington's neighborhood?"

"A big zip, Lou. Nobody knows Mrs. Worthington. He does all the food shopping, even shops for her too. Some of the people we talked to seem to think she's sick at home, others believe she goes to business."

"Either of which could be true." He glanced at her, and for one strange minute experienced the uncomfortable emotion of having been unfaithful. "Have you located Hymowitz?"

"Yes," she said, starting the car. "He's at a meeting on the West Side, but has a one-thirty lunch reservation at the Four Seasons."

Vinda checked the time. "We have an hour to spare. Would you mind driving me home? I need a fast shower and a change of clothes."

She parked near the corner and tossed the vehicle identification plate on the dashboard.

He turned in his seat to look at her, and said, "You can wait here, or, if you like, come upstairs and I'll make you a cup of tea."

She dropped the car keys into her pocketbook and said, "That is the best offer I've had in a long time."

They rode the elevator in silence. He opened the door and let her pass him and walk into his apartment. Going into the kitchen, he put out a plate of cookies, set down two cups with teabags, put a kettle of water on to boil, and said, "I'll be back," and went into the bedroom and closed the door.

Alone, Adriene waited until she heard the shower running and then, overwhelmed with curiosity about how her former lover lived, got up and wandered about the apartment, peeking into closets and drawers. She saw many female touches, nice window treatments, the eclectic way the apartment was furnished; she also saw the accumulating mess of a man living alone.

The shower stopped. She went back into the kitchen and sat. He returned a few minutes later wearing gray trousers and a white shirt outside his pants, no socks or shoes. He turned off the kettle and poured the boiling water into their cups. They sat across from each other, silently dunking their teabags, their thoughts directed at things other than the steeping tea.

She looked up at him and asked, "How have you been managing?"

He sighed. "Okay, I guess. Time is the great healer." He picked up his bag and squeezed it over the cup.

She reached across the table and put her hand on his. "You must get on with your life."

He took hold of her hand, and looked into her eyes; he could remember the smell of her, the silken softness of her thighs, the feeling of her body moving with erotic energy. He felt his skin flush with excitement, and said abruptly, "I have to get dressed."

Watching him walking away, she also felt a rush of warmth surge through her body. Agueda looked down at her tea, took a sip, got up and followed him into the bedroom.

Rummaging through his sock drawer, he glanced up and saw her reflection in the mirror. She was standing in the doorway, her penetrating look fixed on his eyes. His heart raced. He turned to face her, holding two pairs of balled socks.

They stood in place, staring at each other, not saying anything, their faces glowing with shared desire. He watched her breasts rise and fall, and felt the pounding of his own heart inside his chest. As though on cue, they walked toward each other, stopping when they were toe to toe. He felt the wall of heat between them. Leaning forward, he caressed her cheek with his, slowly moving his lips around to meet her open mouth, taking small, gentle bites of her lower lip, as his arms enveloped her, pressing her close.

Their tongues prowled deep into each other's mouths as they tugged and pulled their clothes off and rolled onto the bed, unleashing long-suppressed passions, kissing, groping, probing, and rubbing. He took her breast into his mouth, and she pushed his head away, begging, "Pound me. I want you to pound me." She took hold of his erection and thrust him inside her body, clamping her legs around him. It was as if they had come together for the first time, each exploring the other's body, impatient and tender, one moment urgent, the next languorous, deliberately prolonging the mounting tension until both were carried away by the insistence of passion.

"John!" She thrust her face against his shoulder, muting her scream as orgasm racked her body.

"Adriene! Ahhhhhh." He fell on top of her, panting. "It's been so long."

"I know," she said, putting her hands on his shoulders, and wiggling out from under him, scrambling up to the head of the bed, taking hold of his head and guiding it between her legs. He complied willingly, moving close to her wet body, and was about to take her into his mouth when an anguished thought pierced his mind: This is Jean's bed, in Jean's house.

He pushed himself up into a sitting position. "I can't. I just can't."

"But . . ."

"I'm sorry. This is Jean's bed."

Her eyes welling up with tears, Adriene slid off the bed and began to gather up her clothes.

.   .   .

Morty Hymowitz, otherwise known as Marshall Hawthorn, was
sitting at his favorite table in the Grill Room when Vinda arrived.
Walking through the passageway into the spacious room, approaching the agent, Vinda made a quick evaluation of the man:
manicured nails, monogrammed shirt, heavy gold bracelet. The
street-smart conclusion: a man who was fundamentally insecure
and trying to impress people in a world where he didn't really
fit in.

"Mr. Hawthorn?"

"Yes," he said, motioning the lieutenant into the chair across
the table from him. "What can I do for you? My guest is arriving
any minute, so make it quick."

"As I told you on the telephone, I'm working on the homicide
that occurred in Rue St. Jacques, and would like to discuss a few
things with you. I understand you represent Jessica Merrill and
Michael Worthington."

"So?" Hawthorn asked uneasily.

Go easy with this guy, Vinda told himself, you're talking about
his meal tickets. "I guess it's difficult getting into show business
without an agent."

"Almost impossible. We weed out the talentless and the lazy."

"Worthington was sure lucky to break into the business so late
in life. I understand he had no formal training."

"Michael is very talented, and besides, Jessica pushed him
along. She brought him to me."

"So they were friends before his acting career."

Vinda looked at him with open suspicion. "Why you interested in them?"

"Routine, no big deal. We're supposed to find out all we can
about potential witnesses in a homicide case."

Toying with his glass of white wine, Vinny said bluntly, "Anything you want to know about any of my clients, ask my lawyers."

Vinda looked him straight in the eye. "It's nice to be nice,
especially to the police."

"You know who I am?"

Here comes the tough-guy routine, Vinda told himself, waiting for the performance to begin.

Vinny delicately picked up his glass by the stem and looked over the rim at the detective. "Tony Fortuno is a personal friend."

"I'm impressed, Vinny. 'Tony No Chin' runs one of the largest crews in the city."

"Yes, he does," Vinny said, passing the glass under his nose.

Vinda looked at him in silence for a minute and then said, "I'm going to teach you how to put a little gratitude in your attitude." He got up and hurried down the marble staircase into the foyer, where he asked the attendant in the coatroom where a pay phone was to be found. He dialed the number Malcolm Webster had given him.

"Yeah?" a harsh male voice answered.

"My name is Vinda."

"I've been expecting your call. What can I do for you?"

"I need a creative choreographer."

"Tell me when and where."

"I'll get back to you."

Seventeen minutes later, Vinda made his way along the warren of glass cubicles connecting the various SID units and went directly to the temporary office of Inspector Paul Acevedo.

"I want a shadow on this guy," Vinda said, writing down Morty Hymowitz's pedigree.

"I'll put a couple of Safe and Loft's people on him," Acevedo said. "Anything else?"

"I'm going to need a couple of guys from the Pizza Squad."

Acevedo aimed a mischievous finger at the lieutenant, and said, "You going trick-or-treating again?"

"Inspector, whaddaya tryna do, gimme a bad rep with the ACLU?" Vinda left the office with a smile on his face.

T W E N T Y - S E V E N

FIRE TRUCKS FOUGHT TO GET THROUGH CHAM-
bers Street's choking traffic.

On the eleventh floor of police headquarters, Vinda leaned back in his seat and re-
played this afternoon's bedroom scene with Adriene. On one
level he was glad that it had happened; on another he was overwhelmed with guilt. He did not want to hurt that woman again.
Margareth Loopo had been just a case of horniness on both
sides. Adriene Agueda was quite another matter.

He picked up the pad of Post-its and jotted himself a re-
minder: Contact Webster's "choreographer," get Pizza Squad
detective for Vinny. Lifting up the desk blotter, he attached the
little yellow note on the front of the squeal envelope.

Suddenly Vinda realized that he hadn't eaten since morning.
He telephoned out for a chicken salad on rye, sour pickle, and
skim milk. As he was hanging up, he noticed a manila folder

with a note from David Pollack attached to the flap: "Thought you might need these at some point."

He opened the folder and saw a stack of publicity photos of Jessica Merrill and Michael Worthington. He studied them for a few seconds and put them away. Taking out the social-security work histories that Agueda had given him at the heliport, he saw that Merrill, Griffin, and Holman had worked together on more than one movie.

After he had left Inspector Acevedo's office earlier, he had gone to the criminal records division and gotten a copy of Morty Hymowitz's yellow sheet. The theatrical agent had taken a fall in '78 for violation of Section 263.05 of the Penal Law as a C Felony, Use of a Child in a Sexual Performance, and had pleaded guilty to a reduced charge and done twenty-one months in Green Haven Prison.

Vinda was perplexed by how Hymowitz, even after his transformation into Hawthorn, had managed to become the agent for a major star like Jessica Merrill. It just didn't add up, he was thinking, when the phone rang and the message came that his lunch was waiting downstairs at the security booth.

He retrieved his lunch and started eating, his eyes fixed on the blackboard. On it he had written:

> Valarie Griffin DOA by Lucas and Johnston
> Lucas's daughter Mary—homicide victim
> Johnston's daughter Thelma—homicide victim
> Webster's daughter Adelaide—homicide victim

Below this he wrote:

> Linda Camatro—no known connection?
> Nuns? No connection

He and his team now knew that this was no random series of killings. There was a clear pattern of relationships—except for Camatro, the nun, and the terrible bombing. It all had to connect, but how? He was chewing on a sour pickle when Moose burst into his office.

"Shit's hit the fan, Lou. I went over to see Lucy Seaver yesterday, but she was having more surgery on her knee. She got out of the recovery room just a little while ago. Now, she was still kind of groggy, but she thought there was a strong resemblance."

"What the fuck are you talking about?" Vinda asked in bewilderment.

"Worthington, damnit. You told me to show her Worthington's picture. She thinks *he's* our perp, not the guy in that bullshit composite."

Vinda felt almost sick to his stomach. How could this make any sense? Frank Griffin didn't look anything like Worthington. But Griffin didn't look anything like the composite sketch either.

Now thoroughly confused, Vinda looked back at his chalked notes on the blackboard. "Jesus, yes," he said. "He kills their daughters."

He almost knocked the console off the desk as he lunged for the phone.

The dried stalks of dead plants in the flower beds set against old hedges cast shadows across the path of snow leading up to the backyard's wooden staircase. A large window to the right of the glassed-in porch revealed a woman moving about the kitchen with a telephone glued to her ear.

Worthington climbed over the adjoining yard's fence and squatted beside a large bush. Opening his knapsack, he took out the polystyrene box that contained his fangs. Clamping them over his teeth, he looked out at the woman, trembling with anger. Reaching back into his knapsack, he took out the upper half of his "clean suit," and slipped it over his head. That done, he tugged on his modified hood with the cutout in its face plate. He took a pair of glass cutters from a side compartment of the knapsack and pulled on his gloves.

Still squatting, he carefully reconnoitered the area. The house to the right was in total darkness while the one on the left had some lights on in front. Standing, he moved furtively toward the porch, his booted feet almost noiseless in the snow. Climbing the staircase and finding the door locked, he used his glass cutters to etch a circle alongside the handle. Pulling out the glass cutout, he tossed it into the mound of soft snow on the side of the stairs. Worthington wiggled his fingers inside and slid back the lock button. Opening the door, he quickly stepped inside. Then he crept up to the inside door that led into the house, where he took hold of the knob and began turning.

Suddenly the unnerving sounds of approaching sirens caused him to jerk his hand back. The wailing was coming closer and closer. He heard a squeal of tires, and the screech of brakes, followed closely by the hurried movements of rushing men. He bolted from the porch.

Vanessa Brown had been talking to her husband, discussing the dilemma of what to do with her mother. They had already decided that they would raise Mary's children, but her mother was a different problem. They wanted to sell the house and have her come live with them, but her mother refused to leave her home of thirty years.

Vanessa was about to say something to her husband when the commotion at the front door made her tell her husband to hold on while she went and checked.

Peeking out from behind the vestibule curtains, she saw several uniformed policemen. Opening the door only a crack, she shouted, "What do you want?"

One of them yelled back, "Open up! You're in danger. Lieutenant Vinda sent us."

She took the chain off, and one of the policemen pulled her roughly out onto the stoop while the rest of them barged into the house.

"Where's your mother?" one of them demanded.

"Upstairs," she said in a frightened voice, watching some of them rush up the staircase.

Vinda arrived fifteen minutes later and found Vanessa talking to her husband on the telephone. "I need that," he told her. After she hung up, he dialed Thelma Johnston's home. Ken Hayes, the policeman brother-in-law of the victim, answered. "Is everything all right there?" Vinda asked him.

"Yeah, Lou," Hayes answered. "We got a houseful of cops."

"Good. Any of my people around?"

Marsella's voice came on the line. "Yeah, Lou?"

"Anything?"

"No sign of him, Lou."

"I've made arrangements to have both families guarded around the clock, starting now."

"We shudda figured he'd go for the other daughters too."

Before Vinda could answer him, one of the policemen came in off the back porch and gestured the Whip outside. Stretching the cord over to the doorway, he looked out and saw the cut-out circle of glass in the storm door, as well as the snow tracks leading to and from the porch. He gave a long sigh of released tension. "I'll get back to you," he snapped, and hung up.

Driving along Hanson Place, Worthington glanced into South Elliott Place and saw the flashing turret lights of the police cars. It was time for Dinny'O to destroy Vinda and the rest of his evil disciples. Turning the car onto Flatbush Avenue and the approach to the Manhattan Bridge, he began turning over in his mind various ways to rid himself of his tormentors.

Emergency Service floodlights illuminated the backyard as policemen searched for other signs made by the killer.

Vinda stood by, watching a crime-scene detective make a plaster cast of the killer's footprints. The detective shook a thin coat of talcum powder over the snow print. Using a spray can, he sprayed shellac over the talcum. He added more talcum while the shellac was still wet, and repeated the operation several times until a skinlike layer of talcum and shellac protected the footprint. Reaching into his kit, the detective took out a bag of fine-grade plaster of Paris that he sprinkled over a pint of water. The plaster of Paris spread across the top of the water and sank to the bottom of the cup. When that happened, the detective stirred the mixture and poured it into the snow print. He did not fill the impression, but stopped when it was about one-third full to add small twigs he had gathered for reinforcement. When that was done, he poured in another layer and allowed it to harden.

Watching the detective, Vinda thought that now he had the perp's footprints, but still not a clue to what the bastard looked like.

Walking up to the entrance of police headquarters, Worthington peered inside, saw the two security choke points, and turned away.

Strolling around to the side of the building, he strode down the wide steps to a side entrance, looked inside, saw another security choke point, and continued down the steps to Madison Street. In front of him were five Greek Revival columns. One of them had a plaque that said the columns had been retained from the façade of the Rhinelander Building, which had been on the site before the construction of the present building.

Pretending interest in the vertical shafts, capitals, and cornices, Worthington looked over at the driveway leading down into the underground garage and carefully noted the two brick guardhouses that flanked the driveway. Only one of them was manned. The policeman inside the booth seemed to be preoccupied with some reading material because every time a car slowed in front of the guardhouse, the policeman inside would give the man behind the wheel a superficial glance and wave him down into the garage.

Worthington watched him do this three times, and knew he had discovered the weak link in the chain that he had been

searching for. Looking around him, he saw that Madison Street
was deserted. He gave a long, satisfied sigh. Dinny'O had already formed his plan for dealing with Vinda. All that was needed
was to lure him into the web. He looked at his watch: Thursday,
10:10 P.M.

Yes, early Monday morning would do nicely, very nicely.

The Versailles Room of Park Avenue's Royal Crescent Hotel
was an upscale piano bar with an upscale clientele.

Morty Hymowitz had stationed himself at the end of the marble bar so that he could take in everything that happened. A
tuxedoed black man was at the ivories, crooning Cole Porter.
Hymowitz was too preoccupied with the singer to notice the
businessman with stylishly layered hair who had just come over
and ordered a drink. Some minutes went by, and Hymowitz
listened as the velvety voice sang a succession of love songs. An
attractive woman strolled into the room and caught his attention.
She smiled at the piano player and ambled over to the bar,
discreetly sizing up the clientele.

The businessman watched as her eyes sought out the bartender. He saw the man behind the stick tilt his head toward
Hymowitz, and the woman's eyes flickered in acknowledgment
as she went over to Hymowitz and gracefully seated herself on
the vacant stool next to the theatrical agent.

The man with the expensive haircut took out his handkerchief, brushed it across his mouth, and said, "Our pigeon has a
hooker on his branch."

Brooklyn's 60th Precinct, a serene limestone cube with the chaos
of Coney Island flowing into and out of its doors, had extravagant
art moderne lanterns flanking its entrance. The station house
was located on West Eighth Street, and the precinct's boundaries included Brighton Beach, a middle-class Jewish neighborhood that had in recent years been transformed into Little
Odessa by thousands of Soviet emigrés. Russian-language news-

papers were sold in candy stores and on newsstands. Signs lettered in Cyrillic cluttered store windows, and Russian was spoken virtually everywhere.

It was late Thursday night when Vinda parked in front of the Six-oh. Getting out of the car, he went inside the station house and walked over to the sergeant enthroned behind the high desk. Showing the sergeant his shield, Vinda asked, "The Samovar Squad, Sarge?"

A poster of Lenin preaching to the masses and a blood red flag emblazoned with a crossed hammer and sickle decorated the walls of the second-floor office.

A man somewhere in his thirties, with broad shoulders and insolent eyes, sat behind a desk, spooning soup into his mouth. Vinda walked into the office and introduced himself.

"Jerry Petrovich, Lou," the man said, breaking off a chunk of black bread and asking, "Like some?"

"Is it borscht?"

"Naw. Borscht is beet soup. This is real Russian borscht; it's made with cow parsnips. Some friends in the precinct send it in to us."

Reaching to the side, Petrovich pulled out the bottom drawer of a file cabinet and took out eating utensils, including a bowl with a badly chipped rim. Picking up the plastic container from his desk, he poured borscht into the bowl.

Spooning up some soup, Vinda asked, "How many Russian-speaking cops are assigned to the Samovar Squad?"

"Five of us, Lou. We're sort of an anti-crime, community-relations, intelligence-gathering unit." Dunking bread into the yellow mash, he added, "The telephone message directed us to render all possible assistance. *Qué pasa*, Lou?"

"Are you familiar with the underground medical network the emigrés got going here?"

"The Russkies got themselves a thriving business. Word is they even have a hospital stashed someplace within the command."

Vinda took out the photograph of Frank Griffin and leaned it up against the base of the fluorescent desk lamp so that it faced Petrovich. "I have reason to believe that a Russian dentist made this guy a pair of razor-sharp fangs."

Petrovich glanced up at the photo, and went back to his soup. "The recent wave of homicides?"

"Yes. In January of '80 the guy in the photo borrowed ten large. Now that's a serious piece of change, and it makes me think that maybe in addition to his fangs he also had his appearance changed."

Petrovich tossed a chunk of sodden bread into his mouth. " 'At's eleven years ago. A lot of people have come and gone since then."

"Will you nose around, show the photograph to the right people?"

Petrovich took out two pleated paper cups and an unlabeled bottle of clear liquid. He poured some into each cup and handed one over to Vinda, saying, "Homemade pepper vodka."

"Friends in the precinct?"

"Of course."

Vinda sipped the drink. "Smooth stuff."

"Be careful with it. Two or three belts of this, and your balls start doing the bunny hop." He crumpled the cup and tossed it into the wastebasket. "I'll see what I can find out for you. But you have to understand that the people around here don't have much respect for our criminal justice system, so we don't have much leverage with them." The cop smiled as he leaned forward, caressing his forefinger with his thumb, gesturing money.

"How much?"

"Have to negotiate. But if you're in a hurry, it's the fastest way."

"Do whatever you gotta do, but get me that information."

TWENTY-EIGHT

WHEN VINDA RETURNED TO HIS OFFICE EARLY FRIday morning, he found the two detectives who had tailed Hymowitz to the Versailles Room waiting. Hanging up his coat, Vinda looked at the bleary-eyed detectives and asked, "How's our friend Vinny?"

The one with the designer hair said, "He left the bar 'round midnight with a hooker. We tailed him to a location in the West Village. They resurfaced around three, and we saw Vinny Boy put the hooker into a cab. We decided to go for the broad. She got out at Fifteenth and Fifth, and we scooped her up."

"Was the lady cooperative?" Vinda asked as he moved behind his desk and sat down.

The other detective, an older man with thinning gray hair and a vivid scar on his face, replied, "Most definitely. Especially after I explained to her my responsibility to report all violations

of the Federal Tax Code, and what the tax consequences of her
unreported income might be. According to the lady, our boy is a
regular, and he's into kinky in a big, big way."

After the SID detectives had gone, Vinda got on the phone to
Malcolm Webster and asked for some additional favors. "Whatever
you need," the dead girl's father promised.

Vinda made one more call after that, and then left for the
fourteenth floor.

"I'm going to need some money to buy information," he told
Sam Staypress. Leventhal was handling the case at the command
level, bypassing everyone in the chain of command. He
was keenly aware that the case that had made him PC could also
break him.

"How much?"

"I don't know."

"Go down to Audit and Accounts and get it out of the confidential
fund. Do whatever you have to do, but clear this damn
case."

Returning to his office, Vinda found Agueda and Hagstrom
typing reports while they had their morning coffee. He beckoned
the women outside, led them into the corridor, and, leaning
up against the brick wall, avoiding their prying eyes, told
them that he was going trick-or-treating with Hymowitz.

Keeping his voice low, Vinda laid out his plan. "I think this
guy has important information that he refuses to give up." His
eyes dropped to the floor, then came up, meeting Agueda's.
"It's distasteful, I know that, so it's strictly a volunteer job. You
can both pass and I'll get an undercover out of Narcotics."

"I'll do it," Agueda said, without a trace of hesitation.

"You sure?"

"Yes, Lieutenant, I'm sure."

Shortly before ten that morning, a portly man carrying a suitcase
came into the office and announced, "I'm Sid Williams,
Malcolm Webster's squib man. I'm looking for a Lieutenant
Vinda."

A little later, Inspector Acevedo came in with the Pizza Squad detectives Vinda had requested: Amandola and Bosco.

Looking over the detectives from the squad used to infiltrate criminal networks, Vinda thought, These guys really look the part.

With all the players present, Vinda introduced Williams and the Pizza Squad detectives to the other members of the cast, and proceeded to tell them what he had planned for Morty Hymowitz.

"I like it," Marsella said.

"I'll now turn it over to Sid," Vinda said.

The squib man looked at the two female detectives and asked, "Who's playing Scarlett?"

"I am," Agueda said.

Clicking open his suitcase, Williams said, "For this melodrama to play, split-second timing is an absolute."

He pulled a black negligee out of the suitcase and displayed it before them, adding, "The gown is lined on the inside with Kevlar body armor. Between the gown and the armor we insert little packets of animal blood and explosive squibs that will rupture the packets when we set them off with a radio signal."

Talking directly to Agueda, he explained, "Body squibs are torso-impacting, so when I set them off you are going to feel as though you've just taken a solid shot to the gut. Can you handle that?"

"I think so," Agueda said cautiously, then she asked, "How many rounds are you going to set off?"

"Probably only one," Williams said, sliding his eyes over her body and adding, "Don't let the pigeon's hands roam over you, because if he does, he'll feel the Kevlar and the packets."

"I understand," she said, looking directly at Vinda.

Williams reached into his suitcase and came out with two revolvers. Handing them to Bosco and Amandola, he said, "These are props that only fire blanks, so please don't get them confused with your own weapons. Now, I'll bust in with you, and if you play your roles right, the pigeon will be so scared that he won't even know I'm there."

Holding up his remote control, he went on to say, "When you fire, I'll fire. Remember, you're supposed to be pros, so don't go crazy and start shooting up the place. One round should do it—and remember, squibs hurt the person they go off on. Any questions?" he asked, darting his eyes from detective to detective. "Good. Since there are none, I'd like all the actors to adjourn with me to the set. I want to choreograph this playlet."

After they had gone, Moose handed Vinda the phone, saying, "For you, wouldn't give his name."

"Lieutenant Vinda?"

"Yes."

"I killed all those women."

Another space cadet, Vinda thought, saying, "Sure you did, pal."

The low voice had a brogue. "My name is Dinny'O."

Vinda sat up in his seat, straining to catch every word, motioning Moose and Marsella quiet. "If you're the man, prove it. We get a lot of crank calls."

"The Eternal One grows fangs in my mouth at the time of sacrifice, and He commands me to do those awful things."

Vinda could hear heavy breathing at the other end of the line. "What do you want?"

"Forgiveness. If I surrender, will I be forgiven?"

Vinda held the mouthpiece away from him, staring at the circle of pinholes. Space cadets don't surrender, he thought, but he put the phone to his ear and said, "Absolutely. I promise."

Worthington stepped away from the pay phone and was swallowed by Grand Central's crowd. He exited the station at Forty-second Street and hailed a taxi. Settling into the backseat, he directed the driver to take him to 60 Hudson Street.

•   •   •

Vinda hurried down the marble staircase into Grand Central's graceful rotunda, and, as he had been instructed by Dinny'O, walked over to the information booth.

Moose and Marsella entered a little later and encamped on stools in the open-air bar at the head of the staircase.

Standing in front of the booth, Vinda watched travelers dash over to the clerks, seeking train schedules. If this guy was serious about giving himself up, this was the perfect place for him to do it, he thought: crowded, plenty of exits and vantage points to see if it was a setup—and too many prying eyes to prevent the police from doing a dance on his head, or worse. He checked the time: 11:30. They had an hour to wait to see if Dinny'O was for real.

The taxi drove into Hudson Street, a boulevard of gloomy factories and warehouses, and stopped in front of number 60. Worthington paid the driver, got out, and went into the building's lobby. After consulting the directory, he took the elevator up to the fifth floor, then entered the door bearing the legend DEPART-MENT OF BUILDINGS, ARCHITECTURAL DRAWINGS.

Three years ago, Worthington had played the role of a detective in a movie thriller about a detective's search for an elusive killer. He had stolen his realistic-looking police credentials from the prop trailer. Now he flashed those bogus credentials at the clerk on the desk. "Morning, I'm with the police department's Engineering Bureau. I need to see the drawings for One Police Plaza."

The clerk looked at his identification, wrote his name down in the log along with the nature of his request, and looked up the file number of the drawings for police headquarters.

Sitting at a drafting table fifteen minutes later in an office in the building, Worthington took out several sheets of tracing paper and began to trace the blueprint page he had selected from the tray of drawings.

·   ·   ·

The suburban shopping rush gushed through Grand Central Station as Vinda looked at his watch: 1:30 P.M. Galled at being had, he shrugged haplessly up at Marsella and Moose, and walked away from the information booth. Going up the staircase with an uneasy feeling bubbling in his stomach, he asked himself, What is this space cadet up to? Why drag me here to wait for nothing to happen? I'll find out soon enough, I suppose. If this guy is Worthington, he's outthought me every step of the way.

TWENTY-NINE

MORTY HYMOWITZ ARRIVED AT THE VERSAILLES Room after ten. He slipped the headwaiter a palmed ten and followed him to a table near the dance floor.

Scanning the crowd, he decided that it was the usual Friday-night mix of assholes, tourists, and cheaters. He called over the waiter and ordered a VO whiskey in a pony glass. Hawthorn drank white wine; Vinny hated it. It tasted like horse piss to him, but it was an essential prop when he played his midtown show-business role.

A piano player crooned old Gershwin melodies, while the Latin trio that also played on weekends stood by ready to play the next set.

Vinny was sipping his drink when he spotted the woman in the black velvet slacks and bolero jacket standing alone near the entrance, watching the man at the ivories. She had black hair, a dark, beautiful face, and a truly great ass. Ogling her as he sipped his drink, he waited until the Latin trio was on, got up, edged his way over to her, and asked, "Would you like to dance?"

She gave him a brief smile and looked around for somewhere to put her pocketbook; finding none, she shrugged and said, "I'm sorry."

He gallantly took her bag. "May I?"

She released it to his care. He went over to the headwaiter and said, "Mind this for me, Charles." Vinny walked back over to her and asked, "Do you like Latin dances?"

"Very much."

"Good. So do I." Taking her into his arms, he glided her around the dance floor in time to the samba beat. "I'm Vinny."

"My name is Adriene. You're a great dancer, Vinny."

"Thank you," he said, grinding his hips close to hers.

The businessman with the carefully styled hair, standing at the bar, blew his nose and said into his handkerchief, "Bingo."

Hearing the transmission over his car radio, Vinda continued to stare out the windshield of the unmarked car. He was parked across the street from the hotel, sitting alone in the passenger seat. The thought of Adriene with the slimeball agent made his skin crawl. He was really annoyed at himself for allowing her to play the role she was playing now, but, he rationalized, cops do what they gotta do.

The television anchorman told his viewers that the fear that had gripped the city was now spreading to suburban areas. The cameras showed tracking shots of a newswoman interviewing suburbanites in shopping malls.

Worthington had just returned to his apartment from his rehearsal hall, where he had worked out for two hours. He was now in Valarie's room, dressed in his sweatsuit, watching television.

He looked over at the prie-dieu and said, "They're all so incredibly stupid, Val."

He got up from the bed and left the room. Walking down

the hall, he threw open the closet door. Reaching behind clothes, Worthington unfastened the hidden panel on the back wall. He dug out the square of wood, and leaned it up against the wall.

He smiled as he looked in at his abundant supply of death. Reaching inside, he took out grayish bars of plastic explosives and a box of detonators and timers, and went back into his wife's bedroom. Sitting down on the bed, he picked up the phone and dialed police headquarters.

"Central to Special One, K."

"Special One, standing by," Vinda transmitted.

"Special One, Central has a 'Dinny'O' on land line insisting to talk to you. Says it's urgent. Want us to pipe the call through to you, K?"

"Affirmative, Central."

After a series of electronic beeps, Dinny'O's brogue came through faintly to the police car. "You didn't come alone this afternoon as I told you to."

He's trying to con me, Vinda thought. "No one was with me."

"I saw other policemen there."

"If you did, they weren't my guys. And another thing, pally, I don't like being jerked around. If you want to surrender, good. But either way, you're mine."

"Don't you want to help me stop doing those awful things?"

"If you give yourself up, it will be a lot easier on you. And you will find true peace. I promise you."

"You and your men won't try to hurt me?"

"No, we won't."

A long silence formed a bridge between them. Finally the other voice said, "I don't trust you. I want to come in, but I can't believe you won't hurt me."

"You'll not be bothered, I promise you."

"Will you be in your office at eight o'clock Monday morning?"

"I'll be there."

"And I want you to have all your men there with you. I don't trust them not to be lying in ambush for me."

"They'll be there." Vinda was tempted to try something. What would happen if he addressed his caller by name? He dismissed the idea as quickly as it had come. Why let this lunatic know that his identity was no longer a great secret? And who the hell was he dealing with, anyhow, Worthington or Griffin? The voice was different from Worthington's. He decided to play it safe.

The man on the other end, his voice almost lost in a burst of interference, said abruptly, "I will telephone you Monday at precisely eight. It will be necessary for me to speak with each of your men. And don't play games with me. If I'm satisfied that they are all with you and not out in the street lying an ambush for me, I'll tell you where to come and meet me."

"Will it be someplace in the city?"

"It will be near police headquarters. Do we have a deal?"

"Yes."

Worthington slammed down the phone and rolled across the bed laughing, and gasped, "Oh, yes, Lieutenant, do we ever have a deal." He sat up and studied the drawings he had traced of police headquarters. Then he unwrapped a bar of Semtex and began molding the plastic explosive into isosceles triangles.

Hymowitz and Agueda dipped and swayed, pelvis to pelvis, hips rolling to the merengue beat. Agueda shimmied away, turned, and merengued back into his arms. "You're a great dancer, Vinny."

"So are you. I love the perfume you're wearing. What's the name of it?"

"Quartz." She turned, shimmied back to him, noticed Marsella and Hagstrom dancing nearby. She winked at them.

Hagstrom smiled back.

Morty pressed against her; she felt his hardness, smiled at

him, and thought, You scumbag. The quicker this thing plays, the quicker I'm rid of El Disgusto. She slithered back into his arms. "I'd like to leave."

"Me too."

A limousine double-parked in a line of other limousines pulled out and glided to a stop in front of them. Moose, wearing a chauffeur's cap, dashed around the front of the car to open the door.

When they were settled into the rear compartment, Hymowitz slid his hand onto her knee and said, "I have a place in the Village."

"I'd prefer my apartment. You'll like it—I promise you."

As the limousine slid away from the curb, Marsella and Hagstrom dashed out of the club and rushed across the street to their waiting department auto.

"It is now trick-or-treat time," Vinda radioed, as both cars made a fast U-turn to follow the limo.

"Ten-four," Bosco radioed back. The Pizza Squad detectives and Sid Williams were parked across the street from Webster's penthouse apartment. Amandola waved to Webster, who was standing in the lobby with the doorman. Webster acknowledged the signal and slipped the doorman a fifty-dollar bill, saying, "They're on their way."

Seven minutes later the doorman rushed out of the lobby to open the limousine's door. "Good evening, Miss Adriene."

"Good evening, Edward."

Stepping off the elevator into Webster's penthouse apartment, Hymowitz walked into the living room and over to the plate-glass wall that looked out on the terrace. He briefly admired the view, then turned, leering at Agueda.

She abruptly went into the bedroom. Following her inside, he came up behind her and pushed her down on the bed, throwing himself on top of her, his mouth seeking out her breasts as his hands groped between her legs.

She bucked him off and leaped up from the bed, saying, "I'll be right back." She went into the bathroom and locked the door. She undressed, carefully hanging her clothes on a hanger. Reaching behind herself, she unfastened her bra. Looking at her underpants, she decided there was no way she was taking them off.

She picked up the nightgown from the top of the vanity and slid it over her head. It felt heavy and uncomfortable, but looked sheer and sexy. The magic of Hollywood, she thought, going over to the towel niche. Reaching under the stack, Agueda slid out the portable radio she had placed there earlier. Making sure the volume control was on low, she switched it on, and pressed the transmit button three times.

The rest of the anxious cast were waiting in the lobby when the three squelches sounded over Vinda's portable radio. He looked grimly at Hagstrom and said, "She's going in."

Bosco and Amandola, along with Sid Williams, piled into the waiting elevator.

Aware of her racing heart, Agueda opened the bathroom door. Hymowitz was naked under the sheets, stroking himself. His eyes were wide with lust and his mouth agape. "I want to watch you play with your clit while I jerk off. We'll come together," he moaned.

A regular Don Juan, she thought, padding over to the bed, praying that they'd arrive soon. He was stroking himself faster and faster, and he was panting.

She silently prayed, Where are they?

"Open your legs, I wanna see your pussy," he ordered, tossing off his sheets.

"How ya doin', Vinny?" Bosco said, stepping into the room with Amandola and Williams lurking behind him.

Vinny cowered up against the headboard, the thing in his hand wilting like a dying violet.

Agueda looked over at the intruders, demanding, "Who the hell are you?"

"We're friends of Vinny's," Bosco said, scratching the side of his neck with the barrel of his gun. "We gotta have a business conversation with him, so why don't you go into da toilet and powder your nose?"

"How dare you force your way into my home!" Agueda said, standing up on cue and reaching for the telephone.

"Heeey, Vinny, tell your lady friend she's endangerin' her health," Amandola said.

Glaring her defiance at them, she dialed. Amandola leveled his gun at her. "Put it down, lady," Amandola warned.

"Fuck you."

Amandola fired once. A bullet hole exploded in the black lace, blood spurted down over her chest. She reeled backward, knocking over the night table and slamming into the wall. She looked down at Vinny with an expression of shocked disbelief, her lips moving as if she were about to say something, but before she could get the words out, she crumpled to the floor.

Marshall Hawthorn defecated.

His nose turning up from the smell, Bosco sat down on the bed and carefully spread the sheets over Hymowitz's stomach, covering the mess. "Tony No Chin heard you've been using his name for protection."

"No! I swear!" Hymowitz squirmed uncomfortably in the mess he'd made.

"We got word you used it the other day to a police lieutenant in the Grill Room of the Four Seasons," Amandola said.

Bosco added, "The cop checked to see if you had the right to use Chin's name." Caressing the scared man's face with his gun barrel, he added, "Chin got to wonderin' how a two-bit piece of shit like you got to be the agent for a movie star."

"Please don't hurt me," Hymowitz pleaded.

"Hurt you?" Bosco said. "The Chin don't hurt his business partners."

"Business partners?" Hymowitz asked, bewildered.

"Yeah," Amandola said, "sort of a life insurance partnership." He rammed the barrel into Hymowitz's flabby stomach. "Now that we're all friends, tell us what you got on the Merrill dame that got her to use you."

"Nothing. I swear."

Bosco leveled and cocked his gun at Hymowitz's head. The agent shut his eyes and blurted, "A porn flick she made for me."

"You produced it?"

"Yeah, yeah. I was going to distribute it. But that was when she landed that part in the soap. So I figured she might be on her way, and I held on to it, for myself, you know, if she ever got big."

"How many copies are there?" Amandola asked.

Hymowitz began to tremble. "One. It's in my apartment."

"Get cleaned up," Amandola ordered. "We're going to go get it."

Peeking over the side of the bed at the body, Hymowitz asked, "What about her?"

"What about her?" Bosco said.

Snow pelted Vinda as he walked into Jessica Merrill's West Seventy-ninth Street town house the next morning. Once in the living room, he handed her the rumpled bag he'd been holding. "Is this what's so important to get me up out of bed early on a Saturday?"

"An old movie of yours," he said, looking around the tastefully decorated room, "*Beauty and the Beast.*"

She raised her eyebrows, grinned wearily, and said, "I assume you have been talking to my agent." She brushed a tendril of hair from her forehead, and pried open the canister. Unwinding lengths of film up to the light, examining footage, she offered, "Bad lighting, bad directing, and bad acting." She dropped the canister, watching as it rolled across the floor, unraveling. "You must have gone to a lot of trouble to wrest that away from Vinny."

"I thought you might like to have it. A present, from me to you."

"How generous," she said, looking at him. " 'And what, pray tell, can I give you in return?' the damsel asked blushingly." She toyed with the gold chain around her neck as she glared at him.

"Frank Griffin. Where is he?"

Her brow wrinkled with contempt. "You went to a lot of trouble for nothing. I haven't seen or heard from Frank in years."

"I don't believe you."

"Frankly, my dear, I don't give a damn what you believe. Furthermore, let me tell you that that flick on the floor is valueless to you or to anyone else who might want to use it to blackmail me. I made that when I was a kid trying to claw my way up. My publicity people would have a field day with anyone who tried to hurt me with that. Young, starving actress, et cetera, et cetera. I'm sure you get the picture."

"Morty Hymowitz was blackmailing you with it."

"Wrong. Morty *thought* he was blackmailing me with it. He wasn't. The truth is, the poor jerk is a good agent. His insecurity, which is caused by his justified lack of self-esteem, makes him an aggressive businessman. Besides, I only pay him five percent, while most other agents get ten. So you can pick up your movie and march out of here with it."

"I have reason to believe that Griffin is responsible for several homicides in the city."

"Nonsense! Frank was one of the kindest, gentlest men I've ever known."

"Why did you help Michael Worthington get his start in the movies?"

"Please leave my home now."

"Griffin and Worthington are one and the same, aren't they?"

"Get out!"

"Griffin had his appearance changed by a Soviet emigré doctor. He would have needed someone familiar with that community to make the connection for him. Your real name is Ramenki. Do you speak Russian, Miss Merrill?"

"Leave my home immediately, or I'll call my lawyers and have you arrested."

"Hindering prosecution is a serious crime."

"Get out!" She ran from the room. Rushing upstairs, she plunged into her bedroom and locked the door behind her.

Wrapping herself in her arms, she leaned up against the wall and tried to stop shaking. She began retching. She cursed in Russian, sucked in a deep breath, and held it. The front door slammed, and she blew out her breath and ran over to the window.

When she heard Vinda's car start, she went over to the closet and took down her overnight bag. Going over to the dresser, she began throwing clothes into the bag, saying, "I'm not going to live my life in someone else's nightmare."

Michael Worthington folded Valarie's dry cleaning over the shopping cart's handlebar and pushed off down the aisle, selecting things off the shelf. Strolling around the corner, he pushed the cart over to the appetizer counter, and said hello to the clerk named Mary.

"Morning, Mr. Worthington," she said from the other side of the counter. "And how is Mrs. Worthington today?"

"She's pretty good today, Mary," he said, scanning the contents of the display case, asking, "How is everything at home?"

"Himself is still thinking about getting a job. He's considering his options." Mary looked around to make sure no one was nearby. Leaning over the counter, she whispered, "Detectives were in here the other day, asking a lot of questions about you and Mrs. Worthington."

T H I R T Y

T HE PETROGRAD RESTAURANT, LOCATED IN A
one-story brick building on the corner of
Coney Island Avenue and Neptune Avenue,
had heavy, deep red drapes across its plate-
glass windows.

Police Officer Petrovich, from the Six-oh's Samovar Squad,
was pacing outside when Vinda drove up to keep their hastily arranged Saturday-night appointment. The policemen exchanged quick handshakes.

Petrovich said, "I located the doctor who operated on the guy
in the picture. His name is Turgenev. He's willing to powwow
for two large."

"Can we get the price down?"

"He started at five."

Vinda shrugged with his hands. "You'll have the money Monday, around midday. I've received approval for the disburse-
ment, but didn't know how much to draw."

Jerking his thumb at the restaurant, Petrovich said, "This joint is a hundred percent Russkie, so when we go in, stick close, and let me do most of the talking."

Petrovich led him into the restaurant's narrow vestibule, where there was a short line. Two burly men were at the door, checking names off the reservations list. When the policemen reached them, Petrovich spoke in Russian to the men, and they both roared with laughter. One of them opened the door and shooed them inside.

"What did you say to them?" Vinda asked.

"I asked them if cops had to pay."

The banquet hall was heavily tainted by cigarette smoke. Long rows of collapsible tables stretched the full length of the hall, and were smothered with a conspicuous display of food. Only a few people were sitting at the tables; most of them stood around in the aisles, talking and drinking. A six-piece band played off-key jazz as corpulent men and women lurched clumsily around the dance floor.

"What kind of a restaurant is this?" Vinda asked.

"All you can eat and drink for forty bucks paid in advance. Reservations definitely necessary. They won't sit down to eat until after midnight; the entrees aren't served until around two in the morning, and it ain't Lean Cuisine."

"Not too good for the digestion."

"Tell me about it," Petrovich said, patting his budding stomach.

They went over and stood to the side of the bandstand, the Samovar cop scanning the room. "Lou, see the three guys across the hall talking, a little to the left of the fire exit?"

"I see them."

"They're the mailmen. If anyone wants to guarantee delivery of anything inside the Soviet Union, they go through one of them. Now look to the right of the mailmen. The baldheaded guy in the bad-fitting blue serge."

"I got him."

"He's Konstantin Turgenev. Used to be a top craniofacial

reconstruction surgeon until arthritis and Parkinson's disease bit him in the ass."

"Does he see us?"

"He's pretending we're not here, but he sees us all right. We'll wait here until he makes his move," Petrovich said, going over to the table and pouring two glasses of vodka.

Turgenev continued talking to the man he was with, seemingly unaware of the policemen's presence.

Petrovich sipped his drink. "Turgenev loves to talk about his medical talent, so give him his head and let him blab. Turn him off when you have to, or else he'll go on all night, but cut him a little slack."

The policemen waited, sipping their drinks. Petrovich poured himself another, and started singing something in Russian. Vinda was no linguist, but the cop in him figured the song to be reasonably obscene.

Vinda looked at him and muttered, "You better go slow with the firewater."

Turgenev laughed and headed for the front of the hall. He sat down at one of the empty tables with his back to the drapes, giving him a clear view of the entire room.

"Showtime," Petrovich whispered when Vinda jolted him. "I'll wait here."

Vinda picked up a bottle of vodka and two glasses and walked down the aisle, edging around and through clusters of people. Coming up to the surgeon, he scraped back a chair and sat. Turgenev wore a ghastly wolfish grin. "Do you speak Russian?"

"No," Vinda said, and poured two glasses of vodka, putting one of them down in front of the doctor.

Turgenev clamped the glass between his arthritically deformed hands, hands that used to lovingly clasp medical instruments, now crippled, uneven, useless fingers barely capable of working a doorknob. He brought the glass up to his mouth and drank.

Vinda watched him, saw him looking at him, and picked up

his glass and drank. Pushing platters of food aside, Vinda rested his elbows on the table. Then he leaned in close to Turgenev and said, "I understand you're a plastic surgeon."

He scoffed. "I was a god, that is what I was, until this." He held out a deformed hand. "Do you know what I used to do?"

Sipping vodka, Vinda said, "No, I don't."

"I used to create life. I used to take grotesque people, people who had spent their entire lives in hideous isolation, sexually repressed nomads who had never known the joys of another person's body. I would give them new faces and new lives. I was a god." He drank more vodka.

Vinda said, "Your patients must have been grateful."

"Grateful! They were more than grateful. I saved a woman from suicide. She had fibrous dysplasia, which is a bony deformity of the forehead and eyes. The bone becomes fibrous, and turns the features into that of a gargoyle. This woman had spent her entire life hiding from the world. She was twenty-six when she came to me." He held up his hands. "These, *these,* turned her into a beautiful woman, and gave her a new life. She became an unrelenting sexual dynamo. There was nothing that she would not do for me, nothing."

A skeptical smile crossed Vinda's mouth.

Turgenev saw, and said, "Yes, she and a lot of other women begged me to fuck them. They wanted to thank me with pleasure. But I never once fucked a patient. And do you know why? Not out of any sense of propriety or medical ethics, I assure you. I didn't do it to any of them because they all worshipped me, and it is far better to be a god than a moaning, grunting, sweaty human who loses his godliness when he ruts like an animal."

Vinda drank more vodka. He put his glass down, took out the picture of Griffin, and set it down on the table, propping it up against bottles, facing Turgenev. "Did you make him handsome?"

That grin again. "My money?"

"You'll have it Monday morning."

"Then come back Monday morning."

Vinda drank, put the glass down. "I need the information now. Our word is good, Doctor."

Turgenev looked across the hall at the Samovar Squad cop, Petrovich. He made a quick jerk of his head and said, "Yes, you have always lived up to your word." He put his hands down on his lap as if suddenly ashamed of them. "He was sent to me by the daughter of a friend who had to vouch for him."

"Jessica Ramenki?"

"Yes. He wanted me to make him a pair of real fangs." He saw Vinda's surprise and said, "I am also a dentist. Don't be surprised by that. Many plastic surgeons start out as dentists. Reconstructive surgery was invented by a dentist during World War One. Anyway, I told him that I could make them for him, but that his teeth were too badly bucked. He then asked me if I could change his appearance, and I told him that I could."

"Didn't you realize that those fangs were deadly weapons?"

"He told me he needed them for a theatrical production."

"A theatrical production, my ass."

The awful grin came over Turgenev's face. "Don't you want to know how I changed his face?"

"Sure, tell me."

"I did his ears first. After making an incision behind the ear, I opened up the helix and, with a burr, scooped out the excess cartilage. It is the cartilage that blocks the flow of blood, forming the cauliflower. After I unroofed the cartilage, I reshaped the ear and redraped the skin. I saved the excess and used it on his nose. I opened up his nose and reshaped the tip."

He drank more vodka. "Then I made an incision across his mouth and, using mini-plates and screws set into the bone, elevated his upper jaw, setting back the anterior segment of his teeth six millimeters. In the process he lost two of his teeth, but the net benefit was that he also lost his ugly smile.

"Now, with the upper jaw impacted superiorly, his lower jaw automatically came forward. I then had to make an incision behind his lower lip and cut away a piece of the small chin bone in such a way as to allow the smaller portion to be advanced one centimeter. And your friend had a new face."

Vinda looked at Turgenev with a mixture of awe and anger. He opened the folder he had brought with him, and took out several photographs. Holding them up so that Turgenev could see them, Vinda said, "Tell me when to stop," and began showing them to him, one at a time.

Excitement rushed through Vinda as the doctor pointed his deformed hand and said, "Stop. That is the man with my face."

Vinda felt a sense of anticlimax as the old man eagerly grabbed the publicity still of a smiling Michael Worthington.

The bells of Saint Andrews pealed out across Police Plaza as bent-over parishioners fought blustery wind to make Sunday morning's nine-fifteen mass.

On the fourteenth floor of police headquarters, a well-dressed but gaunt police commissioner looked out from behind his desk at Vinda, Inspector Acevedo, and the deputy commissioner of legal matters, Israel Sabba.

"We hit Worthington's apartment around one this morning," Vinda said. "He was gone. I have the building under surveillance on the chance he'll return."

The DCLM leaned over to Vinda. "You know, of course, Lieutenant, that you lacked reasonable cause to conduct a warrantless break-in of Worthington's home?"

Vinda glared at Sabba. "I was in close pursuit."

The DCLM countered, "Close pursuit, Lieutenant, is unrelenting continuous pursuit immediately after the commission of a crime or escape."

Vinda had an urge to yank out the clumps of nose hairs jutting from the DCLM's nostrils.

"I want this guy stopped, and I don't care what it takes to do it," Leventhal said. "Forget these legal hangups. We have a total maniac running around out there."

"Sir," Sabba said, "I was only trying to point out that if Worthington should be the subject of an illegal arrest, he'll walk in court."

Vinda said, "Bullshit! He's not going to walk anywhere except into a looney bin."

Acevedo asked, "Where do we now stand, John?"

"Worthington is among the missing, and we don't know if he went for a drive in the country or to visit friends, or if he knows we're looking for him," Vinda said. "He telephoned me Friday night and told me he's going to surrender Monday morning. The point is, I don't want to unnecessarily drive this guy underground."

"You're saying we don't go public, and wait," the PC said.

"Yes. Until tomorrow morning. I not only want him in custody, I also want his supply of explosives. I get very nervous when I think of how much Semtex and God knows what else he's got hidden somewhere in town."

"Have you applied for a search warrant for his apartment?" the PC asked.

"Not yet. I have the place staked out, but I don't want to panic him. I'll get the warrant tomorrow if he doesn't show in the morning," Vinda said.

"Let's all say a prayer he comes in Monday," Sam Leventhal said. The soft sound of a church bell crept into the tension-filled room. "But I don't believe he will," Leventhal said gloomily.

The Chelsea Bayou featured blackened redfish on its Sunday brunch menu. A Dixieland band was at full throttle when Vinda and Agueda entered the Seventh Avenue restaurant late Sunday afternoon. Vinda had cut the team loose around two, telling them, "I'll see you all in the ayem."

Agueda had loitered behind, doing busywork, mustering the courage to say, "If you're not doing anything this afternoon, I'll spring for brunch."

She caught him off guard; he still felt uncomfortable about the other afternoon, but he quickly decided that it would be better to clear the air between them. "That would be nice, Adriene, but the tab is mine."

During the drive to the restaurant they chatted amiably about the case, the latest scuttlebutt in the Job, both of them careful to avoid any mention of what was happening between them. Once seated, they both ordered Bloody Marys, and turned their attention to the music coming from the tiny bandstand.

Their drinks came; she began to stir hers with the celery stick jutting out of her glass; he kept his eyes fixed on the band. The silence between them grew until it hung over them like a gloomy sentence of death.

Minutes passed. Without looking at her, he said, "I'm sorry about the other day."

She took his head in her hands and turned his face to hers. "John, you're not an invalid. You need to have an emotional life. You need to make love to somebody. If not with me, then with somebody else."

"Every time I think about you, or we're together, I feel unfaithful. I can't help it, it's the way I am. Don't waste your time with me, Adriene, you could end up being the queen of leftovers."

She rankled. "Don't flatter yourself, John Vinda. I haven't been exactly waiting for you all these years."

"I'm sorry. That was not a nice thing to say. Toward the end, Jean used to tell me to live in the present when she was gone. I wish I could."

She squeezed his hand. "Let's order."

Late Sunday night, with most of police headquarters in darkness, and Madison Street deserted, a bus drove into Park Row. The policeman assigned to the guardhouse busied himself by studying flash cards for the forthcoming sergeant's examination.

Worthington sat behind the wheel of the rented black sedan he had parked under the Brooklyn Bridge's colonnade, with an unobstructed view of Madison Street and the guardhouse. He had been there for ninety minutes, and during that time not one car had driven down into the garage. He switched on the headlights and pulled out into Madison Street.

Slowing the car as he drove up onto the curb cut, he braked to a stop in front of the guardhouse, rolled down his window, and was about to hold up his bogus credentials when the policeman inside looked out at him, and waved him down into the garage.

Coming off the ramp, Worthington drove past the dispatcher's cage; the man inside was watching television. He drove into an empty space and parked. Consulting the drawing he had made on tracing paper in the Department of Buildings, he got out of the car, taking his knapsack with him. As he looked around at the sweep of cars, he heard the thunderous hooves of horses and a bugle sounding the charge coming from the dispatcher's office, but he saw no one, and headed for the steel door with the glowing Exit sign.

He hurried down the staircase, exiting into a long empty corridor lined on both sides by blue doors. Constantly consulting his drawing, he moved along the hall. When he came to the door he wanted, he tried the knob, found it unlocked, and quickly slipped inside.

Two boilers filled most of the room; a jumble of chalk-white pipes snaked across the ceiling, sharing the space with wide, shiny ducts. Large electrical switch cabinets were fixed to the walls. In the center of the cavity, spread out around the boilers, eight steel girders rose vertically up from the bedrock below and disappeared into the ceiling, part of the building's support system that ran through the entire structure. He heard the hiss of escaping steam.

After looking around and seeing no one, he went over to the first girder, removed a charge from his knapsack, and saddled it around the column, with triangles of Semtex fastened on both sides of the girder. He primed the detonator at the apex of the charge, and set the twenty-four-hour timer for 0800. Examining his handiwork, he smiled. Shaping the plastic explosive into isosceles triangles and priming them at the apex would direct the energy of the explosion inward, crushing the steel and causing the building to cave in on itself.

He took out the hand-painted sign he had made at home, and taped it around the column, hiding the charge. It read, DO NOT REMOVE. Policemen obey orders. Even to the death, he thought, walking over to the next girder.

THIRTY-ONE

A RAGTAG LINE OF MEN BEGAN ASSEMBLING OUT-side the Third Street Shelter shortly before seven o'clock Monday morning. The doors would open soon, and breakfast, consisting of coffee, American cheese on white bread, and oatmeal, would be served.

Across the street from the shelter, on the fourth floor of a five-story walk-up, Jessica Merrill rose up out of the bathtub and began toweling herself. Outside, in the apartment's minuscule kitchen, Laura Steward made breakfast.

Fifteen minutes later, Jessica, dressed in jeans and a sweater, came out of the bathroom. Laura was pouring coffee.

"Perfect timing," Laura said, and asked, "Must you leave?"

"Afraid so. I'm flying to Saint Barts this morning. I must get away. My life is closing in around me, suffocating me. I need to be alone, someplace where it's warm."

"I understand."

They sat at the tiny table next to the window, sipping coffee and staring down at the zombie-eyed men shuffling into the shelter.

"Pour souls," Jessica said.

"Sometimes I dream that I'm homeless, that I haven't worked in a year, and have to choose between becoming a hooker or scavenging garbage cans for food."

"And what do you choose?" Jessica asked, breaking off part of a croissant.

"The garbage cans."

Holding her cup up to her mouth, Laura asked, "Did you ever speak to your producer about that part for me?"

"He's agreed to test you."

"Oh, Jessica." Laura put her cup down and leaned over and gave Jessica a hug of gratitude. "Thank you, dear friend, thank you."

"When I get back, we'll start rehearsing you for the test. I'll get you ready."

"Why didn't you tell me last night?" Laura asked with a smile.

Jessica looked slyly around at the door to the bedroom. "You didn't give me time."

Vinda watched the second hand sweeping around the face of the wall clock. Hagstrom sipped tea. Moose was reading a copy of *Audubon* magazine, and Agueda was working the *New York Times* crossword puzzle, occasionally looking up to glance over at Vinda. Cleaning his nails with a silver penknife, Marsella announced, "I don't trust this hump to show. Why is this guy so insistent that we all be here at eight?"

"He wants to surrender," Moose said, "and he's afraid we'll whack 'im if we catch him out in the street."

"Bullshit. Psychos like him don't surrender. They go on doing their thing until we corner them, and even then they don't give up. They go out of the picture in a blaze of psychotic conflagration."

Everyone looked at Marsella. Agueda whistled; Hagstrom said, "Psychotic conflagration? Very good, Tony."

"You know what I mean," Marsella said, cleaning the blade on the edge of the desk.

At seven-thirty that morning, Andy Fowler walked into the boiler room of police headquarters and heard the familiar sounds of his domain. Entering his small office, he switched on the desktop radio to 1010 WINS to further reassure himself that all was as it should be in his world. He opened his locker and changed into his blue workshirt and trousers. Sitting at his cluttered desk, he paged through the morning paper to the sports section, and peeled the plastic lid off his coffee container. An announcement came over the building's loudspeaker system, breaking his concentration on the list of the day's races. Reaching up, he switched off the speaker and returned to the sports section. After making his selection, he picked up the telephone and called the building's bookmaker in the Printing Section.

Michael Worthington lay on his back, pressing the Nautilus's weights above his chest, his eyes fixed up at the banks of fluorescent light fixtures that hung down from the ceiling of his storefront rehearsal hall. His naked body glistened with sweat as his muscular arms strained to press the load.

The television on top of the bridge table was on. He listened as he strained. His bulging knapsack was on the floor; its reflection shone in the polyurethaned surface. On top of the table, next to the television, his saintly Valarie reposed in an open oversized suitcase.

A ribbon of weather reports rolled across the bottom of the screen just as the newscaster read off the latest London gold price. "The time is now 7:42 A.M.," the newscaster said. Grunting, his neck and chest straining, Worthington yanked the bar over his head and called out triumphantly, "Soon, Val, soon."

.   .   .

Sam Leventhal walked into the task force's office and slumped into a chair. "Any coffee?"

Moose reached into a soggy bag and pulled out a container. "I bought a few extra," he said, handing it to the police commissioner. "It seems it's always like this on the important ones, waiting, drinking coffee, bullshitting about the old days."

"That's the way it's always been, and that's the way it will always be, I guess," Vinda said, flipping through the case folder, looking for something he might have overlooked.

"Any word from our friend?" the PC asked.

Flipping through reports, Vinda said, "No."

Hagstrom looked over at Sam Staypress, a glimmer in her eye. "Commissioner, when you came on the Job, were you still able to flash the tin and get into the movies on the arm?"

Vinda rolled his eyes; all bets were off during periods of nostalgia attacks while waiting in the Job, but there were boundaries. He looked at the PC and saw amusement in his eyes.

Sam Staypress sipped his coffee, smiled at Hagstrom, and said, "We used the tin for everything in those days, didn't we, John?"

"I don't remember," Vinda said, going back to the folder.

"I wonder what the new kids in the Job call getting things on the arm?" Moose asked.

"Getting it on the Master Tin," Vinda said, laughing.

"The lingo might change, but it's still the same Job," Agueda said, looking at the Whip fondly.

Sam Staypress looked up at the clock, turned to Vinda, and asked, "John, do you remember Louie Corona?"

A broad smile spread across Vinda's face; he looked up from the case folder and at the blank faces of Agueda and Hagstrom, and explained, "Louie Corona was one of the first gay guys in the Job to come out of the closet." He glanced up at the clock.

"Louie was one tough cop, but when he came out, the bosses in the Job didn't know what the hell to do with him. The Job was top-heavy with crusty old-timers who believed in all that straight-arrow stuff, in public. Anyway, we were all assigned to

Brooklyn North Detectives, and the Borough was having its annual retirement party. Louie shows up with his lover. Well, let me tell you, the brass didn't know what to do. They all gathered at the bar, bitching about what nerve Louie had coming with his 'friend.' " Vinda looked up at the clock.

"Louie, who always had a lot of balls, prances over to the borough commander, a straitlaced old-timer by the name of Patrick O'Kelly, looks him in the eye, and says, 'Would you like to dance, Pat?' "

Everyone in the office laughed. Vinda looked up at the clock, went back to the case folder. The pages were open to the Fives on the bombing of The Women's Register meeting. Reading them over, he was reminded of what Dinny'O had told May Gold. He hated the police and he was going to destroy them.

He's going to destroy them, he said to himself over and over, quickly flipping to the Bomb Squad's reports on the plastic explosive, Semtex.

Something clicked inside him, and he thought, I've been a complete fool—he has us all gathered here like lambs waiting to be slaughtered. Jumping out of his chair, he stared up at the clock and shouted, "The bastard is going to blow up the building!"

As it had done every morning for the past ten years, the coffee kicked in eight minutes after Andy Fowler finished the container. He got up and walked into the small toilet in the back of his office and dropped his trousers. Sitting on the "throne," gazing out into his kingdom of boilers, steam pipes, and ducts, he listened to the joyful rush of steam and metallic scrapings that signaled the beginning of a new workweek. Then, during the middle of a grunt, he saw that there was something askew in his kingdom. Tied around one of the support columns was a sign that read, DO NOT REMOVE.

What the hell was that all about? he wondered. Nobody but nobody does anything down here without first coming to see me.

·   ·   ·

Vinda rushed out into the corridor and pushed the fire alarm. Bells and klaxons sounded throughout the building. He dashed back into his office, dialed 911. As soon as the operator came on the line, he said, "Code Red-One. No drill. My authority, Lieutenant Vinda."

"Bomb threat, no drill, your authority, Lieutenant," the operator confirmed.

"Yes."

"Code Red-One, Code Red-One" blared out over the loudspeaker system.

Leventhal grabbed Vinda's shoulder. "Are you sure?"

"No, I'm not sure," he said into the PC's face, "but I don't want to gamble with any more lives. I'm the idiot who gave this guy the perfect setup."

Throughout police headquarters, policemen and civilians stopped whatever they were doing, looked at the person next to them, and walked to the nearest exit. Floor wardens went to the elevator banks and directed people to use the stairs instead of the elevators. On the ground floor, members of Headquarters Security rushed to open all exit doors.

Communications Unit operators transmitted the following message to their divisions: "Communications Unit will be going off the air temporarily. Units on patrol will communicate through their own commands by land line and portable radio."

Auxiliary radio operators assigned to each borough command rushed from department buildings to waiting RMPs that would speed them to secret backup radio facilities scattered throughout the city.

Andy Fowler hitched up his trousers and went outside to investigate the sign around the column. Going over to the closest one, he yanked down the sign, and an expression of terror came over his face. Running to the next one, he ripped off the sign and exclaimed, "Oh God!"

He ran back into his office and dialed 911. When he heard the prerecorded message announcing that Communications was going off the air, he switched on the loudspeaker, heard the Red-One, and ran back outside.

Emergency Service and fire units cordoned off Police Plaza, as streams of people flowed from headquarters. A Bomb Squad station wagon squealed to a stop inside the frozen zone. The driver, Detective Ben Sirbo, and his partner, Detective Jack Hourigan, got out and began lugging out the black valises containing the tools of their trade. Hourigan, who was sliding out the last valise, stopped what he was doing and asked his partner, "If you wanted to take out the Big Building, how would you go about it?"

Sirbo pondered the question a second or two and said, "Saddle charges of plastic explosives around the main support columns. I'd plant the stuff Sunday night when the building is practically deserted, and set the timers for early Monday morning before anyone could find them."

They looked at each other and exclaimed in unison, "The basement!"

"All of you, out of here," Vinda ordered.

Agueda, her face twisted with concern, asked, "What about you?"

Vinda's face reflected the anger and shame he felt. "I brought this guy to our front door. Least I can do is make sure this floor is clear. Once I do that, I'm out of here."

"It could be too late then, John," Leventhal said.

"Look, Commissioner, I'm the Whip. Now out of here, all of you."

The detectives hesitated. The PC scowled at Vinda and told the detectives, "Out. All of you, now."

Moose and Hagstrom tugged Agueda out of the office.

"Now you, Sam," Vinda said. "They're going to need the PC on the ground."

The police commissioner had no sooner left when an Emergency Service cop and a fireman lugging an axe rushed in. "Get out of here!" the cop shouted. Vinda showed them his shield and said, "I gotta make sure this floor is clear." He refused to let anyone die because of his stupidity.

"This place might go any second, Lieutenant," the fireman said.

The Emergency Service cop went to say something to Vinda, but restrained himself and made a fatalistic shrug instead. He turned to the fireman, asking, "Can you take out that window?"

"Sure," the fireman said, and began to smash the window glass with his halligan tool.

The Emergency Service cop set his tool chest down on a desk and removed a length of soft braided nylon rope and a thick pair of work gloves. Paying out the rope, the cop said, "This is fast rope, Lou. The military use it to rappel cliffs and swoop down out of helicopters. A person who is good at it can travel fifty feet a second."

Securing one end of the rope to a desk, he continued, "We're on the eleventh floor, eight-foot ceilings, add another two feet for flooring, giving us ten feet a story, or a hundred and ten feet to the ground. We can be down in about two and a half seconds."

With the rope now secured, he tossed the other end out of the huge hole the fireman had made in the window and asked, "Wanna give it a shot?"

"I've seen fast rope used in training exercises at the range," Vinda said, shoving his hand into a glove.

Wind from the hole in the wall tunneled the room, tossing and swirling things about.

"Remember, Lou," the cop said, as he and the fireman looked around anxiously, "if you have to slide down, use your hands and legs as brakes, and don't go too fast or you'll lose control."

"I'll remember," Vinda said. "Come on, guys, let's make a fast check of the floor and then get out. We better use the rope. If my guess is right, we're not going to have time for the stairs."

·   ·   ·

"You look familiar, lady," the taxi driver said to his fare.

"I have that kind of face," Jessica Merrill said, wishing he would shut up. She abhorred garrulous New York cabdrivers, preferring to be left to the inventiveness of her own thoughts. How could the police believe that Michael was that awful killer? He's strange—no, he's very strange, I'll admit that—but a killer, no, no, no.

Looking out the window at the passing scene of upended garbage cans, dirty streets, clogged traffic, hawking peddlers arrayed along Canal Street, and drunken windshield cleaners staggering through traffic with filthy squeegees, she thought, Life in this town really sucks. Turning away from the window, she sat back and listened to the soft music playing on the taxi's radio.

Andy Fowler, kneeling, with sweat trickling down his armpits, gingerly gripped the tip of the detonator with his fingertips and began gently sliding it out of the Semtex.

Ben Sirbo threw open the boiler room door, causing Fowler to gasp. Sirbo plunged into the room, followed closely behind by his partner, Jack Hourigan.

"There are eight of them!" Fowler shouted to the detectives.

The telephone rang exactly at eight as Vinda and the other two men returned to Vinda's office. Vinda snapped it up. "Hello?"

"Morning, laddie."

"Where are you?"

"Are all your detectives there with you?"

"Yes, they are."

"Tell me, laddie, did you ever see the fright in a person's eyes as the life was throttled out of them?" The brogue was gone, replaced by Worthington's real voice. "You murdered my wife. We sinned against Him, but I received absolution because I gave him brides to serve Him in Valarie's place."

"Tell me where you are, Frank."

A cold silence on the other end. Then: "Frank is dead."

"Michael Worthington, then."

"I wish I could be there to see the terror in your eyes as you tumble into hell."

Sirbo and Hourigan ran from girder to girder, deactivating the charges. There were four left. They were running to them when the first explosion blew them off their feet. Fowler was hurled to the ground. Chunks of concrete and plaster rained down on them, causing a dust storm inside the confined space.

The second explosion hurled down slabs of mortar. "Get into my office!" Fowler screamed, tugging Sirbo and Hourigan by the arms, gagging from the choking dust.

Vinda heard the rumble in the bowels of the building. The floor and walls shook; the office's glass front shattered. Vinda forced himself up off the floor and stumbled over to the window. The Emergency Service cop and the fireman went first, both of them handling the rope with practiced ease.

Vinda leaned out for the seconds that seemed like hours that it took first one, then the other, to reach safety. Taking hold of the rope with his gloved hands, he backed out of the window, rappelling off the façade just as another explosion rocked the building, making him dangle helplessly. His legs frantically locked around the length of rope beneath him as the wind battered him against the brick façade of One Police Plaza.

The crowd in the street behind the police barricade let out a collective gasp at the sight of his desperate struggle. Agueda buried her face in her hands, unable to look. Hagstrom slid a comforting arm around her, as she watched Vinda fighting for his life.

Another explosion seemed to lift the building up off its foundation and slap it back down. The structure disappeared inside a whirl of smoke and debris; flames shot up out of the base of the cloud of dust and smoke.

Gusting winds quickly blew the smoke away; the building sagged inward. Vinda had been slammed repeatedly into the brick; he had a gash across his forehead, and blood streamed down over his face and clothes. Fighting not to lose consciousness, he brushed his eyes across his arms in order to clear his vision, took a deep breath, and swung his body into the rope, scissoring it between his legs. Inhaling deeply, he relaxed his grip slightly and plummeted down. He was going too fast; he jammed on the brakes just as another gust hit him, twirling him around and entangling him in the rope. Hog-tied, he fought to untangle himself. He was still far from the ground.

Firemen rushed to set up a huge air mattress under the dangling police lieutenant.

Emergency Service policemen armed with automatic weapons stood inside the frozen zone, helplessly watching Vinda's plight.

Agueda broke away from Hagstrom's embrace and ran over to them, demanding, "Shoot the rope, cut it so he'll fall into the bubble."

"We can't fire these weapons without the express orders of a captain or above," one of the cops told her.

"Nonsense!" Agueda shouted at him. "He'll die up there unless we get him down."

Moose and Marsella ran over to them. "They won't shoot him down!" Agueda told her partners.

Moose and Marsella drew their revolvers, took aim, and began firing single-action at the swaying rope. Agueda drew her weapon and joined the firing line.

Hagstrom ran up to the Emergency Service policemen, thrust an angry finger into one of their faces, and shouted, "He's one of ours, you assholes!"

Startled by the ferociousness of her challenge, the Emergency Service cops looked at each other, and one of them said, "The hell with it." He unslung his weapon and leveled it at the rope; the others followed suit.

Soon a fusillade of lead stitched across the façade above Vinda, shrapneling him with shards of brick. And suddenly the rope snapped, hurling him downward toward the air bubble.

"You're Shirley MacLaine," the taxi driver told his passenger, regarding her in the rearview mirror. "I rekernize ya from da movies."

"I'm not Shirley MacLaine. I'm just a woman about to miss her flight because of the awful traffic," she said, suddenly aware of the news bulletin interrupting the music: "Police headquarters in lower Manhattan has just been rocked by a series of explosions, believed to have been caused by bombs. As yet there are no reports on the number of casualties. Stay tuned for further reports."

Jessica fell back into her seat, her eyes falling to the Vuitton carryall wedged between the seats. Michael had given it to her as a birthday present one year. They had just finished their first film together. Michael and that Rambo friend of his, Otto Holman, were always talking about guns and explosives. They seemed to live for the shootout scenes.

Then another bulletin came over the radio concerning the explosion at police headquarters. Michael and his damn explosives, she thought impulsively, and a flash of horrific clarity caused her to bite her clenched fist. "It was Michael," she whispered.

With a burst of sudden determination, she opened her pocketbook, thrust a ten-dollar bill through the security grille to the driver, and said, "I'll get out here."

She shoved open the door, grabbing her carryall. Dodging through traffic and angry horns to the other side of Canal Street, she broke into a trot when she reached the sidewalk, abandoned her luggage, and ran toward police headquarters.

Michael Worthington leaped up off the Nautilus machine, his eyes riveted on the newscaster who had just interrupted the game show with a special bulletin. A remote camera at the scene

panned over the sagging building. Worthington clenched his
fists when he saw that the building was still standing. He listened intently.

"Emergency crews will not be able to search through the
rubble for survivors of this tragedy until a determination is made
if there is danger of immediate collapse. There are unconfirmed
reports of many dead and injured."

Worthington's back arched in delight as he broke into gales of
raucous laughter. He scooped Valarie up out of the suitcase and,
holding her in his arms, waltzed around the room, singing,
"Oh . . . how we danced . . . on the night . . . we were
wed. . . ."

Vinda tilted his head back so the ambulance attendant could
swab the gash on his forehead; he jumped from the sting of the
anti-infective solution.

The rest of the team were canvassing the spectators on the
chance that Worthington had come to inspect his handiwork.

Commissioner Leventhal climbed into the ambulance. "How
do you feel?"

"Like I just had a close encounter with a herd of buffaloes."

"You're going to the hospital, Lieutenant," the attendant said.
"We're going to need X-rays. And that gash needs suturing."

"Later," Vinda said. "Stick a Band-Aid on it for now." In-
clining his head toward the PC, he asked, "Any word on injuries?"

"Not yet. Thanks to your fast thinking, I don't expect there'll
be many. We've been receiving garbled transmissions from a
couple of Bomb Squad detectives trapped in the boiler room,
along with the chief engineer. Apparently they were in the process of deactivating the devices when the damn things blew.
Emergency crews are trying to get to them now."

"He suckered me, Sam."

"Sometimes we make a wrong turn in the Job, you know that.
We're only human, John. Don't start beating yourself."

A policeman climbed into the ambulance, saluted the police commissioner, and asked, "Lieutenant Vinda?"

"Yes."

"Jessica Merrill asked me to try and find you. She says she needs to talk to you," the cop said.

Pushing the attendant's hand away from his head and sitting up on the bunk, Vinda asked, "Where is she?"

"We have her stashed in our RMP inside City Hall Park."

Agueda and Hagstrom were circulating through the crowd gathered in front of the Municipal Building when Agueda saw Vinda and a policeman crossing Centre Street, heading toward City Hall Park. "I'll be right back," she told Hagstrom.

Jessica Merrill slumped in the rear of the police car. His face grimacing from pain, Vinda slid into the seat next to her. She looked at his bandaged head and his stained clothes and said, "I'm sorry. I just couldn't bring myself to believe that it was Michael."

"Why do you believe it now?" he asked, delicately touching the bandage over his head wound with his fingers.

"I heard the bulletin; then I remembered his obsession with explosives. He and Otto Holman were always talking about them. And then it came back to me. That awful day at Rue St. Jacques, he slipped something into my shopping bag. He told me he'd bought a present for a friend. But I hadn't seen him buy anything all day."

His clean suit, Vinda thought. He said, "Worthington and Griffin are the same man. You knew that, didn't you?"

"Yes."

"What hold does he have over you?"

"Valarie was my half-sister."

Vinda's surprise was real. "What?"

"My sister," she repeated. "Frank Griffin was a good man. And he was good to my sister, very loving, gentle. His world fell apart when she was killed. He disappeared for a while. Then one day he telephoned and asked to borrow money. I'd just gone through an expensive divorce and had a run-in with the IRS, and didn't have it to lend him. He got it from someplace, and then asked me to contact a plastic surgeon my parents had known from the other side."

"And so he had his face changed, right? And you helped him get parts when he became an actor, calling himself Michael Worthington," Vinda said. "But you never knew about the fangs he had made, right?"

"What are you talking about?"

Vinda ignored her question and asked angrily, "Weren't you aware of his delusions about Valarie being alive?"

"I knew. I couldn't tell anyone. He loved her so much that he wouldn't allow her to die."

Vinda thought fleetingly of Jean, wondering if he too could have let his grief turn into madness.

"I knew it was delusional, but what real harm did it do anyone, I asked myself. I felt responsible for him. He was the only real family I had left, the only person who really cared about me."

"Where is he now?"

"I'm not sure. A while back he rented a small storefront on Forty-seventh Street off First Avenue to use as a rehearsal studio. We used it together once."

"Do you know the address?"

"No, but I can point it out to you."

The car's door was jerked open. Agueda stuck her head inside, and said, "How ya feelin', Lieutenant?"

Knapsack slung over his left shoulder, the bulky suitcase clutched in his right hand, Worthington stood on the corner of First Avenue and Forty-seventh Street, sucking in the invigorating air. Their Calvary was over, their Trinity secured. Now he could get on with His work.

His eyes looked across the avenue and came to rest on the

large bronze sculpture on the grounds of the United Nations. Saint George on horseback, poised triumphantly above the wreckage of a Soviet SS-20 and an American Pershing II missile carved into the shape of a dragon. He had read about the piece in the newspapers; it was titled *Good Defeats Evil*. Good defeats evil, he said to himself over and over, convinced that it was a message from Him. Stepping off the curb, moving sideways around stalled automobiles and buses, he made his way to the other side of the street.

Agueda drove the RMP up onto the sidewalk, blocking the entrance to Worthington's rehearsal hall. Guns drawn, the detectives smashed open the door and charged inside. A fast search of the premises revealed no one there. The television was on.

They rushed back outside and found Jessica standing by the car pointing across First Avenue. "There," she said.

Agueda hit the accelerator and the RMP shot off the sidewalk into First Avenue, ricocheting off a car's fender. Heedless of the traffic, she forced her way across to the other side.

Hearing the commotion behind him, Worthington turned and saw the police car maneuvering his way. When he saw Vinda and Jessica together in the back, his eyes filled with hate. Hurriedly shrugging off his knapsack, he grabbed a grenade from it, pulled the pin, and lobbed the missile at the onrushing police car.

"Get down!" Agueda shrieked, cutting the wheel sharply to the right and diving under the dashboard.

Vinda shoved Jessica to the floor and covered her with his body. The RMP rammed into the side of a bus. The grenade exploded, piercing the body of the RMP with steel splinters. The main force of the explosion was taken by the engine block. It lifted the car up and blew out its tires and windshield.

"Adriene?" Vinda called frantically.

"I'm all right, I think," Agueda called back.

"Me too," Jessica said.

Vinda reached out and shoved the door open, crawling over Jessica into the roadway. "Adriene, get on the radio and get us some help. And stay here with Jessica. This guy might try to double back here to take her out.''

Crouched under the dashboard, Agueda snatched down the radio and transmitted, "Ten-thirteen, Four-seven and First."

Worthington had leaped over the railing and was running through the United Nations Park with his suitcase banging against his leg and his knapsack clutched in his other hand.

Vinda leaped over and ran after him. A burning anger filled him with resolve. This lunatic was not going to go meekly to the looney bin. This case would be marked closed by "Exceptional Clearance." Without warning, he found himself in the middle of a hail of bullets. He dived to the ground, rolled over on his side, and saw two United Nations policemen, with their guns drawn, running toward him. He quickly pulled out his credentials and, holding his shield above his head, screamed, "I'm a cop! I'm a cop!"

The United Nations policemen ran up to him. "What the hell is going on?" one of them demanded, just as the explosion of another grenade sent both policemen sprawling to the ground. One of them rolled over on his back, moaning, as blood spread across his chest.

Worthington darted along the esplanade that ran along the side of the General Assembly Building, heading toward the East River. Tourists scattered in panic. Vinda, in close pursuit, suddenly halted, took aim, decided he did not have a clear shot, lowered his weapon, and again ran after him.

Worthington ducked behind the Statue of Peace. Vinda dived to a prone position behind a bush, aiming his revolver at the statue. Worthington bolted, making for the graveled footpath. Vinda fired two rounds that missed, then popped up on his feet and ran after Worthington.

The gardens led down to a promenade deck that overhung the shoulder of the Franklin Delano Roosevelt Drive; below the highway the East River lapped at the stone embankment of the seawall.

Rushing up to the deck's railing, Worthington looked over his shoulder, saw Vinda, and climbed up on the railing. He pulled on his knapsack and, clutching his suitcase to his chest, jumped down onto the highway, oblivious to the mass of speeding cars.

Vinda saw him running north along the shoulder. He aimed, and fired one round. Worthington was hit in the leg; he fell and dropped his suitcase. Valarie flew out, falling to the ground. Vinda jumped down after him.

Worthington pulled himself up onto his feet. Grabbing the highway's railing, he limped away from his tormentor. Running behind a big reel of construction cable stored on the highway's shoulder, Vinda took careful aim and ordered, "Griffin, stop!"

Continuing to drag himself along the railing, Worthington took another grenade out of his knapsack and leaned over the railing, trying to catch his breath. "I hate all of you!" he shouted at Vinda. He pulled the pin and started to lob the grenade.

Vinda fired two rounds. Worthington sagged from the bullets' impact, dropping the grenade.

Vinda ducked behind the wheel of cable. The explosion hurled Worthington over the railing. Vinda rushed up to the barrier and saw him covered in blood, clinging to the rocks, with the water's hungry current tugging at his legs.

Worthington's dazed eyes sought Vinda's, his hand reaching up toward the policeman. "Valarie, Valarie," he pleaded weakly.

Vinda turned and saw the doll on the ground. He picked it up. For a second he considered tossing it down to the dying man; then he remembered all the young women the man on the rocks had killed so remorselessly and horribly. Young lives needlessly and cruelly snuffed out. He put the barrel of his gun to the head of the doll and fired.

"Valarie!" Worthington shrieked, as the current yanked him from the rocks and swallowed him.

Vinda hurled the deflating, ridiculous doll after him and watched it vanish below the black water, weighted down by its habit.

Vinda stood there, staring into the river, and then he heard the approaching sirens, and his name being shouted. He turned and looked up at the promenade and saw Adriene crying and waving down to him.

Vinda shakily waved back to her. He felt a rush of joy pour through him and a sense of profound release, as if some heavy burden had been lifted from him. He did not know how their future together would play out, but, as he called out her name, he knew that the past had been buried and he had finally returned to life.